CONVICTION

LESLEY JONES

EDITING—Swish Design & Editing

COVER DESIGN & INTERIOR FORMATTING—T.E. Black Designs;
http://www.teblackdesigns.com

PHOTOGRAPHER—Reggie Deanching @ RplusMphotography

COVER MODEL—Connor Smith

For my dad.
Everything I am, you raised me to be.
I hope so very much I've made you proud of the person I've become.

A NOTE FROM
FOR THE READER

THIS BOOK HAS BEEN WRITTEN using UK English and contains euphemisms and slang words that form part of the Australian spoken word, which is the basis of this book's writing style.

Please remember that the words are not misspelled, they are slang terms and form part of the every day, Australian/UK lifestyle. This book has been written using UK English.

If you would like further explanation, or to discuss the translation or meaning of a particular word, please do not hesitate to contact the author – contact details have been provided, for your convenience, at the end of this book.

I hope you enjoy a look into the Australian/UK way of life.

Bird - A female, woman.

Blown you out – Moved on. Dumped.

Crib – Dwelling or house.

Fag - A cigarette.

Minge –– Vagina.

Nobjockey - Homosexual male.

Numpty - A fool, idiot.

Old Bill –– Police.

Ponce - To beg or freeload.

Skint - Having no money, poor.

Toots - To smoke or inhale.

Weirdo - A person who is considered strange to other people, it's a derogatory term.

PROLOGUE

CONNER

DECEMBER 31ST 1999

I LEANT BACK ON MY brother's car and took a long draw on my cigarette, blowing out the smoke as I looked up at the sky. I wanted to be sick, my stomach was churning and my head was beginning to ache. I flicked the cigarette to the ground and watched as it rolled into a drain.

The car park at the supermarket was almost empty. The last of the shoppers had gone home. Home with their cases of beer, their sausage rolls and party poppers. Home to their families to start the celebrations that would see in the New Year, the new millennium and for me, what should've been a whole new life. But she's not there, she didn't come.

All of the planning, working long hours so we'd have enough money for a deposit on a flat or a room and she just didn't turn up. She was over an hour late. I'd called and called her mobile, left messages and sent texts but nothing, not a word.

My heart actually hurt, it was fucking painful just to breathe. After everything we'd been through to get to that point, I just couldn't believe she'd not turn up, without a single fucking word.

My brother pressed on the hooter of the car and I almost jumped out of my skin.

"What the fuck, Miles?" I shouted. He laughed as I glared. I wanted to cry, like a big fucking pussy, I actually wanted to cry.

"She ain't coming, Reed. Your posh bird's blown you out. Now come and get in the fucking motor, before you freeze your bollocks off."

I chewed on the inside of my lip as I tried to make up my mind what to do. I pulled my phone out of my back pocket and tried her number one more time. It once again went to answer phone.

"We're done Meebs, we're fucking done!" I ended the call and jumped into the passenger seat of the BMW my brother had just bought.

"You all right bro?" he asked. I hated it when Miles got all sensitive and caring; it made my throat tight and my eyes sting. I shrugged my shoulders and just kept staring ahead.

"She's a nice girl and she's fucking gorgeous, but she's from a different world. Her old man and that stuck up bitch of a mother of hers were never gonna let this happen, and don't get me started on that prick of a brother, he's a complete nobjockey."

We sat in silence for a few seconds. I couldn't disagree. Everything he said was true. She was out of my league, but she loved me regardless. I know she did.

We'd met at primary school. I was two years older and she was tiny, like a fairy or an angel. She had the palest skin, the blondest hair and the bluest eyes and my belly would do strange things every time I saw her.

She was the best friend of my friend Josh's sister. I would see her outside of school sometimes at their house and I think I knew even back then that I loved her, but I also knew even then that our worlds were different.

Her mum was some kind of councillor or government minister or something like that. Her dad was a police commissioner for the Met' Police. My dad was an alcoholic and former soldier. My mum was dead.

When I was eleven, I left the primary school that I loved and went to the local secondary school. Josh went to the posh Catholic boy's school a few miles away. He lasted two weeks before he was expelled and joined me and the rest of the commoners at our run-down establishment for education.

I didn't see her much for the next few years, the occasional glimpse from Josh's bedroom as she left or entered Sophie's room that was about it. They were young and giggly. We were at secondary school, where the girls had curves and tits. Some of the older girls would let us have a touch or would give us a flash around the back of the gym block when they wanted to ponce a fag from us. There were some nice girls at our school, the good girls, but there were also a lot of sluts, which came in handy over the years. Like my brothers told me, those were the girls you practised on and practise we did. Thinking back now, that might've been how it all started. That need for control, to push boundaries, to see just how far you could make someone step out of their comfort zone and what they were prepared to give, take or do to get what they wanted.

It all started innocently enough, I'd managed to get Carly Simpson into a bedroom at a party one night. We were at the house of some kid called Colin from our school. His parents were on holiday and he was staying with his Nan, but putting his parents' empty home to good use he had arranged a party. We were seventeen, but there were kids there much older, which meant plenty of alcohol and weed. So, I'd poured a shit load of Lambrini into Carly, given her a few toots on a joint and then convinced her to come upstairs with me, in the hope she'd let me come inside her, or over her, I wasn't fussed. I was seventeen, I just wanted to come and I'd prefer it if there was a girl involved and not just my right hand. I wasn't a virgin; that cherry had been well and truly popped a couple of years previous.

I'd kissed her senseless at first, got her all worked up nicely before I slid my hand over her ribs and up to her tits; brushing my hands over her nipples as they passed. I repeated the action until eventually, I brushed my thumbs backwards and forwards continuously. I was getting rougher and rougher each time until she was moaning into my mouth. Carly was eighteen and I knew a lot of boys had shagged her, two of my brothers included… at the same time.

"What d'ya want me to do to you, Carly? You wanna fuck?" She looked up at me with unfocused eyes whilst biting down on her bottom lip. "Can I fuck your mouth?" She nodded.

Quick as a flash I jumped up from the bed and got my dick out, just as I did, the door flew open and Josh was standing there. I looked him in the eye and then gestured slightly to where Carly was now sitting on the edge of the bed.

"Come in, shut the door." I looked down at Carly waiting for her to object, but fuck me if she wasn't smiling. I tilted her chin up so she was looking at me. "You want Josh to watch, or d'ya want us both?"

What?

I'd heard the rumours. She'd let Jed fuck her from behind while Miles face fucked her six months ago, so I knew she'd be up for it. I just wanted to see if I could push her a little bit further.

"You wanna fuck her cunt or her face, Josh?" I knew him well enough to know that he wasn't gonna be wanting to put his dick anywhere near whatever Carly had going on between her legs. Most of the men in our town under thirty had been there and so had a few of the women from what I'd heard, and I most definitely wasn't going there either.

"Face," Josh replied.

"Me too. Can you manage both of us, Carls?" She thought about it for a second, then shrugged her shoulders.

"Don't both come at once, else I'll choke.

My sex life came to a grinding halt just two weeks later when Josh and Sophie's parents threw a party on Christmas night. Josh was allowed to invite a mate and because I was at their house more than I was ever at my own shit tip, it was me that attended.

We'd been standing in the kitchen for about half an hour, admiring the wives of Joshua's dad's mates, when the girls walked in. They were just fifteen and were both now attending the all-girls Catholic school on the smart side of town. I'd never seen either of them in anything other than school uniform or casual clothes and when they walked into the kitchen to get a drink that night, I almost embarrassed myself like the teenage boy that I was and come in my pants.

"Fuck," I hissed out between my teeth. Josh turned to look at me and away from his cousin Amy's boyfriend he'd been talking to. He must've followed my stare because I heard, "fucking hell" from beside me.

Sophie had on a skin tight, gold, satin type dress and she looked about twenty. She was a pretty girl, tall, with long blondish hair, but she was Josh's sister and I'd known her since she was three. I just didn't view her as anything other than a little sister. Meebs, on the other hand, she had played a starring role in many of my wet dreams and right-hand encounters over the past few years, which, yeah, made me a complete perv but what can I say, the girl just did things to me, she always had. If I allowed thoughts of her into my head, she probably always would. That's why I've spent so many years blocking out the fact that she even exists. Blocking out the taste of her lips, the curve of her hips, and the scent of her hair. I shut it down and take control, always. Never again will I let a woman own me like she did, never afuckingain.

That Christmas night she had on a pair of skin-tight black

leather trousers and a red shiny top, which literally looked like a silk hanky hanging from her neck. It was held together at the back by a few chains crisscrossing her bare skin. She had tits now. They weren't big, but they were noticeable, and my dick had most definitely noticed them. She was still tiny. Five feet one or two at the very most, but she most certainly wasn't skinny anymore. Her waist was still small but fuck me, she had hips and the sexiest, roundest, little arse I'd ever seen.

"Reed!" Josh smacked me in the chest with the back of his hand.

"What?" I snapped back at him.

"Jailbait, mate. She's off limits till she's sixteen."

I let out a long sigh. "Yeah, yeah, I know. But I'm only human, you can't blame me for looking."

"Look all you like," he replied, "just keep your hands to your fucking self."

I didn't leave her side for the rest of the night. Fuck! I didn't leave her side for the next year. We were inseparable. For three whole months, we did nothing but hold hands and kiss when we were together. She was a good girl, not yet sixteen and as desperate as I was to change all of that, I already loved and respected her too much to force her into anything before she was ready.

Then one night in November, my brother Tyler asked if I would babysit my nephew, Ethan. Meebs took the night off work but lied to her parents and we actually got to spend our first night together. Our first time together. Her first time... ever. She was a virgin and she chose to give her beautiful self to me that night. We'd been seeing each other for almost a year and I swear to God I'd nearly died a million times over from the worst case of blue balls ever in those first few months. The muscles in my right arm were getting at least a twice daily workout and my hand permanently ached... but I loved her, she wasn't ready and I was prepared to wait. It had taken three fucking months before she let me even touch her tits, three months. Another three before I got my hand in her knickers and we were together a whole nine months before I'd finally convinced her that my dick didn't bite and I'd be more than happy if she would just give it a little stroke.

And then she did it, fuck me did she ever? With words of encouragement and instructions from me, I got my best wank ever. She was shaking and so nervous that she was doing it wrong, but as soon as she saw my reaction, the effect *she* had on *me*, the power it gave her over *me*... that was it. My blue-eyed angel was gone, replaced by a five foot nympho, who suddenly wanted me as much as I wanted her. Hands, mouths, tongues and teeth, we just couldn't get enough of each other, but the opportunity for actual sex just never happened.

Then that night at Tyler and Jenna's it did. It was soft and beautiful, it was slow and so fucking delicious. She was it for me, my everything. No other girl or woman existed on this planet the night she gave herself to me. If I'd had any doubts before, the moment that I finally slid my body inside of hers, our fingers laced together either side of her head and our eyes locked, they were gone and I was done, hers.

At that moment, when that first tear slid from her eye and rolled back toward the pillow and she whispered, "I love you Conner, I love you so much." I knew there and then that I loved her like no other and would love her forever. But now, all these years later, I try constantly *not* to think about that night. It's locked away with every other memory of her. Thoughts of her ruin me. I don't hate her, but I hate what she did, and I hate that she didn't turn up. I hate what happened because she didn't turn up and I hate that afterwards, when all the shit hit the fan, she never once tried to contact me. So yeah, fuck her! Fuck her and the ache she still has the ability to cause in my gut and my chest, on the rare occasions that thoughts and images of her manage to slip their way into my head. Fuck her for still having the ability to cause that lump in my throat and that squeezing sensation of my heart.

PROLOGUE

NINA

DECEMBER 31ST 1999

"OH, COME ON NEEN, WHAT'S wrong with you this morning?"

I rolled my eyes at Sophie. "Will you please stop asking me that? There's nothing wrong. I just don't have the money to spend on new clothes right now. We've just had Christmas and I'm skint." I wasn't. I'd hardly spent a penny on Christmas and had been saving religiously since September, but I couldn't tell Soph that. She was my best friend and I loved her like a sister. She knew each and every one of my hopes, dreams and desires, but she had no idea about my plans for that night. As far as she knew, we were meeting up and going to a friend's party to see in the new millennium. I felt bad for what I was going to do to my best friend, but I couldn't let her know. I didn't want to put her in a position where she'd have to lie on my behalf. So the less she knew, the better.

Despite the miserable expression on my face, I was buzzing inside. I couldn't wait to see Conner later, and I couldn't wait for us to set off on our new life together. If there was another way, then we wouldn't be doing this, but my parents just wouldn't see reason. They never did. They'd had my life all mapped out for me. Do well at school, go to college, then on to uni'. Then throw away all of that studying by marrying someone respectable, producing a couple of kids and staying at home and becoming a dutiful housewife, by being at my husband's beck and call. Supporting him at all times, while he made his way up the corporate ladder at whatever mind numbingly boring profession he might possibly have.

The problem was, most of those options weren't included in my life plan. Not that I really had a plan. Not for my life, not for anything. I wasn't much of a planner, much more of a free spirit and it drove my mother insane. She hated that I didn't feel the need to wear the latest designer label and that I didn't need the latest phone, handbag or accessory on the day they came out – or ever for that matter. I was a jeans, hoodie and Converse kind of girl back then. The biggest plan I'd ever made in my life was for that night. That plan would change everything. It would get me away from my stuck-up parents, arsehole of a brother and the stockbroker belt town that I'd spent the last sixteen years growing up in.

"Neen… Nina. Oh look, there's Conner."

"What, where?" I looked up at Sophie, then around the chaos of the Primark store that we were in.

"Well, that got your attention. What the fuck is wrong with you? I think you need coffee or an energy drink. Were you and Con up till late getting down and dirty again? How many times is that now?" Soph elbowed me in the ribs while I blushed.

We did get down and dirty that night. Well, as down and dirty as you can get in the back of a car in December, but we did all right. I shudder as I thought about his hands on me. He was my first, my one and only and I loved him like nothing on earth. Not only was Conner smoking hot to look at, but he was just so beautiful inside. He'd had a shit life, but despite the hand that was dealt him and the awful thing that he'd witnessed as a small child, he was a good person and we loved each other with such an intensity that I wanted to cry every time I looked at him.

Soph finally bought a half dozen pieces from the Primark sale and we headed back to the car. I didn't want a coffee or an energy drink. I wanted to get home and pack my bag. It was just after twelve, I was meeting Conner in our local Sainsbury's car park at six.

It was as we approached Sophie's car that I heard him call my name. Sophie and I turned at the same time to see my brother and his best friend Marcus walk toward us.

In the ten or so steps it took for my brother to reach us, the pain ripped through me. I was confused at first, I didn't know what had hit me. My breath and my step faltered as I walked toward my brother. The sharp pain eased, leaving me with a dull ache, down low in my belly.

"Where are you girls off to?" my brother asked.

I opened my mouth to answer and the pain hit again, this time much worse than before. My legs went from under me, spots appeared in front of my eyes and everything went black.

CHAPTER ONE

CONNER

I STAND ON THE EDGE of the stage, eyes closed, arms raised, caught in the draft of the giant fans sitting in the wings, my hair lifts off my neck and it feels good, so fucking good. I count the beats to the final drum roll of our last song for the night... for the tour in fact and wait for the roar of the crowd as I pull my earpiece out. I open my eyes and look out across the sea of faces, arms waving in the air as Jet throws his arm over my shoulder and kisses my cheek. He's wearing a white feather boa around his neck, black leather jeans and he's shirtless and barefoot. Gunner Vance and Dom Trip, our drummer and bass guitarist join us front and centre of the stage, and we all take a bow.

We're done. Eighteen months on the road is finally over. I'm going straight back to England tomorrow, and I won't have to look at the ugly fucking faces of my other three bandmates until sometime next year. Well, I'll probably see Gunner at some stage as we live not far from each other, but the other two are crazy Americans and unless we have any public appearances scheduled, then naaa, I'm done travelling for a while. I'm heading home, home to England, my house, my dogs, brothers, nieces and nephews and I can't fucking wait.

A pair of knickers land at my feet as a girl screams, "Reed, take me home, take me home and fuck me." I bend my knees and shield my eyes from the house lights that are starting to come on so I can get a better look at her.

Jet leans down and says in my ear, "Get her up here, just in case the rest don't show, man."

I look up at him. "Can you see her? What's she look like?"

He shakes his head and winks at me. "I don't give a fuck. She has holes, at least three that are of interest to me, get her up here and let's get back to the room to play."

I tap the security bloke on the shoulder and point to the girl that screamed out to be fucked. I'm not sure if they're her knickers Dom now has on his head or not, but I'm sure it's not gonna be long till we find out. The giant security guard lifts the girl up over the barriers and onto the stage. She turns around to the crowd and punches the air, earning herself a massive cheer and a few boos. Jet hooks his arm over her shoulder and steers her off stage while we all follow.

No nonsense tonight, no backstage meet and greets, no fake smiles, just straight in the cars and back to the hotel to play. Gunner and Dom are both married, their wives are backstage waiting for them as we head toward the corridor. People are hanging about everywhere, and as a beer gets shoved into my hand, I pause for a second and take a few swigs.

"Mr Reed, sorry to trouble you sir, but I wanted to give you these and wondered if you'd just take a look at them?" I lift up my sunglasses and look at the bloke standing next to me, he's more of a kid than a bloke, eighteen, nineteen at most. He has a few sheets of paper rolled up in his hand and he's holding them out to me.

"What are they?" I ask, gesturing with my chin at the paper.

"They're songs, sir. Songs that I've written. I've put my email address and cell number on the bottom. I just thought, well..." He blushes and looks down at the floor. "I'm good. What I write is good fucking shit and I just need a break. I just need someone to listen."

Fuck, I might be a prick a lot of the time, but I'm not a complete arsehole, especially when it comes to kids that need a break. That was me once, all I needed was a break and Jet happened to come along and hand it to me on a plate, *after* he'd tried unsuccessfully to get me to suck him off that is. But once we established that wasn't going to happen, he invited me to join the band anyway, and the rest, as they say... is fucking history.

"What's your name, mate?" I ask.

"Mitch, Mitchell White. It's all on there."

I give him a wink. "Okay, Mitch Mitchell White It's All On There. I'll take these back to England with me, I'll have a look at them. If there's anything I see with potential, I'll be in touch. How's that sound?"

His eyes widen. "Seriously, you're not just fucking with me?"

Jet appears at the kid's side and runs his hand over his chest. "Ohhh, pretty new toys. For me?"

"Fuck off Harrison, your toys are waiting back at the hotel."

He folds his arms across his chest and pouts like the diva he is. I hold my hand out for the song sheets, and the kid passes them to me. "Now fuck off out of here kid. There's nothing but freaky weirdo's hanging around backstage after our shows, and you're best staying well away from any of them." He nods and is gone in seconds. I turn Jet around and push him toward the exit and our limo that's waiting to take us back to the hotel with the lovely Lara, who we pulled out of the crowd earlier, already naked and sitting with her legs open on the back seat.

We climb in, close the doors, open the central console and find what we're looking for. A bottle of vodka and a nice big bag of Charlie, with six nice neat lines all ready for us on a little, mirrored silver platter.

Jet sits on the leather seat next to me and we both stare between Lara's legs at her bare pussy for a few seconds.

"Top or tail?" I ask him.

"Hmmm, I might have a little taste first, then tail." The girl doesn't say a word. Jet must've told her what we like, what we expect while I was talking to the kid. Quiet, compliant, no questions asked. Just do as you're told, speak when you're spoken to and don't ever expect a rerun. What you'll get in return will be a night to remember and some mind-blowing sex that will push all your boundaries and the best orgasms and drugs of your life.

Jet lifts the mirror up to his face and snorts a line up each nostril through the platinum straw that he always carries with him. He passes the mirror to me and I hoover up my two lines quickly.

I'm about to pass it across to Lara when Jet jumps in, "Na ah man, I wanna play." He crawls on his knees over to Lara and then reaches out to me for the mirror, which I pass back to him. He tips the whole lot onto the front of her pussy. Then he just leaves it sitting there. "Put your feet up on the seat sweetheart and open those legs just as wide as you can for me."

Without saying a word, she does as she's told. Jet leans forward and licks from her arse to her clit and I watch and enjoy as she shudders.

"You like that?" I ask. She looks down her body and across to me and nods.

"She tastes good Reed, you wanna try?"

Fuck that, I don't lick no chick's twat, especially one that's naked in the back of a limo ten minutes after meeting me. Ergh. Who knows who or what's been there before me? I like sex with randoms, but I have certain standards. I don't put my lips on their mouth, so there's no way I'd be putting my lips on their minge. If they want to put their lips on my dick, that's fine by me, their call. I don't make no one do anything they don't want to. I might coax, bribe or tempt but never force.

"Na, I'm good. You do what you gotta do first, dude." Without hesitation, he pushes two fingers inside her.

"Oh God," she moans as he begins to move them in and out.

Her eyes are closed, and her back and hips are arching off the seat. Jet looks over his shoulder and gestures for me to join him. He pulls his fingers from inside the girl and sucks on them. I think he's going back in, but instead, he dips his wet fingers into the coke and starts scooping it inside her, moving his two fingers in and out as she moans and arches her back, once again lifting her arse and hips off of the car seat.

My dick's hard now the coke's kicking in. My heart rate accelerates, and I want to get involved. I reach over to the centre console and find the condoms and throw one to Jet.

"Turn her around," I order him. I sit back up on the seat opposite and undo my jeans. I pull out my cock and start to stroke myself as Lara crawls on her knees toward me. I lift her chin so she's looking me in the eye. "Jet's gonna fuck you from behind. I want to fuck your mouth while he does that. Is that all good with you?"

She shrugs her shoulders. "Can I have another line of coke first?"

I nod. "Just one though, he's shoved at least two lines inside you, it'll absorb through your skin soon and you'll start to feel it hit you."

She winks. "I already can. One more line and I'll be good to go for the rest of the night. I know my limits." I pass her the mirror and she lines up and snorts another hit. She's on all fours on the floor of the limo. Jet's on his knees behind her.

"Can I fuck your arse?" he asks her. . . Always the gentleman our Jethro.

She looks over her shoulder at him. "Do you have lube?"

Jet looks up at me and gestures to the console that divides the seat in half. We use this limo company all the time, they know exactly what to provide and are always discreet. I search inside, find what I'm looking for and toss the tube to Jet. Then I pass him the big pink vibrator that I've also found in there.

"Wonderful." Jet winks.

Lara reaches out and takes my cock in her hand, she squeezes at the base and strokes up and down a couple of times before she flicks her tongue over my tip, pushing it into my slit as she does.

My hips buck forward, and my hand grips her hair. All the while, she takes me deeper down her throat. I tilt my head back on the car seat, enjoying the sensation of her hot mouth swallowing my cock as I watch Jet slide on a condom and lube up his fingers. I'm not gay or even bi for that matter. I'm not watching because I want to see or admire his dick. I'm watching so I can tell him what to do, not that he doesn't know, he's a fucking expert but he likes to be told, and I like to tell him. I have to tell him. Not just him, anyone that's involved has to be prepared for me to tell them exactly what to do. I have to be in control and I just love to push the boundaries, push people to their limits. Some are a bit resistant at first, especially if it goes against what they think is normal or right, but once you encourage them to give it a go, to just try it, they're soon lost in the moment and giving themselves over to doing all kinds of wrong.

I nod my head toward the vibrator lying on the back seat. "Turn that on and push it inside her, but I don't want her to come." Jet reaches behind him for the toy. I pull Lara's hair gently so she raises her eyes to once again meet mine. "Jet's got a toy back there with him. You happy to play?" She nods with my cock still in her mouth. "Good girl. Just yell *'shift'* if you want us to stop doing anything. You got that?" She nods again. "Suck my balls into your mouth and enjoy what we're about to give ya." I nod my head at Jet and feel Lara's mouth tighten around me as he pushes the toy inside her. "In and out slowly," I tell him. She moans and the sound vibrates around my balls, which have both now been sucked into her hot mouth. "Suck my cock back again Lara, take it as far down your throat as you can. Jet's lubed his fingers and he's gonna slide them in your arse. You want that?" She releases my balls from her mouth and I shudder as the cool air of the limo hits them.

"I want his cock in my arse, not just his fingers. I want your cock in my cunt, his cock in my arse, Reed. Can I have that?" I stroke my fingers down her cheek and over her jaw. I love women like Lara, no bullshit, no pretending that she's little miss innocent. She knows exactly what she wants, she knows exactly what makes her feel good, and she ain't too scared to ask for it.

"Not a lot of room to manoeuvre in here. Don't worry, we'll make you feel good, then when we get back to the hotel, there'll be more people to play with, and we can get you all filled up again. You can get every hole fucked if that's what you want. Would you like that?" I nod slightly to tell Jet to slide his fingers in her arse while I talk to her. Her back arches and I watch as she pushes back toward Jet.

"Oh God, yes, yes Reed, I'd like that. More Jet, I want more," her voice is ranging from high to low as Jet moves his fingers in and out of her arse.

"Suck my cock, Lara. Take it deep and then Jet will put that toy back inside you while he fucks your arse, but I want you to suck me first." I know once she comes she'll be good for nothing for a while and I'm not gonna be left hanging with a hard-on. Once I blow my load, they can blow theirs. She takes my cock back into her mouth and drags her teeth up and down the shaft. It's only just not painful, but I like it. I grip her hair and push her head down as I lift my hips. "Fuck her arse, Jet. Slide inside and make her feel good. Tell her what you're gonna do to her." I don't want to talk right now, I just want to lose myself in the sensation of Lara's hot, welcoming mouth on my body and blow down the back of her throat.

"I'm gonna fuck your arse now baby. I'm gonna fuck it hard and bury myself inside you, and while I do that, I'm gonna push this dildo deep inside your cunt. You're gonna feel so stretched and so full, they're gonna hear you come in Moscow with how loud I'm gonna make you scream. You ready for this baby?" She moans against my cock but doesn't answer him. I raise my hand to Jet, he knows exactly what that means and slaps Lara across her arse while I hold her head in place and push my hips into her face. "Answer me, Lara. You fuckin' ready for this?" I pull her by her hair and she releases my cock from her mouth with a pop.

Not breaking eye contact with me she says, "Yes, yes, Jet I'm ready." She keeps looking at me as she speaks and I just know what that look means. I'm clueless about women and emotions and how to read them in general. But when it comes to fucking and what they want, I can read every little sigh, whimper, moan or look, and I know precisely what Lara's look means right now. It's not really my thing, it triggers too many memories of what happened to my mum, but I don't mind obliging her just a little bit.

Just to be safe and to make sure I've got this absolutely right, I ask her to confirm for me first, "you like that, me pulling your hair, him slapping your arse?"

She bites down on her bottom lip and nods her head. "D'ya think I'm weird?" she asks.

Jet leans forward and grabs her hair, not harshly but enough to make her turn her head. "I think your fuckin' perfect, baby. Now you just relax while I get myself inside you and when I do, I'll slap that pretty ass of yours and I'll pull your hair just the way you like it. You can forget Moscow, they'll be hearing you in Melbourne with the way we'll make you scream. Now relax baby, just relax." She turns back around to look at me. Her hand's wrapped tightly around my cock as she strokes up and down. I don't want to be in her mouth until Jet's buried inside her, just in case it hurts and she bites down on my dick. Yeah, it's happened before. Just the once, but I'm not likely to forget it.

Jet strokes his fingertips down her spine with one hand and with the other he squeezes more lube onto the bottom of her back, then uses his fingers to drag it where he needs it. He squeezes more lube into his hand and rubs it over his condom covered cock, his eyes meet mine as he does. Unlike my fine self, Jet will fuck anything with a hole. He prefers women, but if there are none available, he'll happily fuck or be sucked off by a bloke. He's told me many, many times that he'd love to be fucked by me, and I've told him just as many times it ain't gonna happen. Jet lines his cock up with Lara's arse, and I watch her eyes flutter while he begins to push inside her.

"Relax baby. Relax so I can get inside you," Jet tells her.

"Open your eyes and tell me that feels good, Lara. We need to know you're okay. That feel good?" She opens her eyes, just as Jet must push in further, her back arches and she lets out the most animalistic moan. It's carnal, sensual, and so fucking erotic I almost come in her hand.

"So good Reed, it feels so fucking good. Please let me suck you. I want to taste you." I shake my head. "Just a few more seconds and you can, but let's get you on your way first."

Jet pushes all the way inside her as I speak. I watch as his hands hold onto her hips and he begins to pump slowly into her. His eyes are on me as he bites down on his bottom lip.

"She feels good Reed, good and tight but I wish she were you. I wish this was your arse I was fucking." He doesn't take his eyes from mine. I don't get scared when he says these things anymore. I know he means every one of them, but they don't terrify me like they used to. He's my mate, I love him like a mate, but that's all. I like kinky, weird, fucked up sex, but I don't want to fuck men. I don't fancy men. I've watched two men fucking. Actually, I've watched three and four men fucking, I've got off on it come in my hand, and all over a bird's face while I've watched a few times too, but it's because of the eroticism of the moment. It's watching them get off that's made me get off, it has nothing to do with the fact that they are men.

I slide my cock back into Lara's mouth and push my hips up as the momentum of Jet pushing into her arse moves her forward. She pushes on the underside of my cock with the flat of her tongue, forcing it up to the roof of her mouth. She swallows and gags slightly, and the sensation is almost too much. I pull on her hair and Jet takes that as a cue to slap her arse again, in turn making her moan around my cock.

"Push the toy back in, full speed, push it deep but be gentle," I tell him. Lara again groans around my cock with anticipation and I watch her face as Jet follows my instructions. My eyes move from hers to Jet's, both of them are staring right at me. Lara starts to moan continuously now and the vibration feels fucking spot on. I get that all too familiar tingle at the base of my spine as my balls begin to tighten. I wrap her hair tightly in my hand and hold her head still as I lift my hips and fuck her face.

"Yes, yes Reed. Harder, fuck her harder. Oh God, I can feel that vibrator against my cock. Fuck, I'm gonna come. Come Reed, let me see your face. Fuck Reed! Fuck, I want you. I love you Reed, I fucking love you."

I shut my eyes to try and shut out Jet's voice. I know he's a sensitive soul, but I don't do all that love shit. I feel it, I write it in my songs, but that's as far as it goes for me… since her. I don't say those words out loud to anyone except my family.

My arse cheeks clench almost as tight as my balls and my dick throbs painfully as I come inside Lara's mouth. I squeeze my eyes shut tight, but it doesn't help. It doesn't keep her away. Yeah, when it's good I see stars. I get that white flash of light when I blow my load, but in amongst it all, every time, there's always a pair of blue eyes, long blonde hair and the face of an angel. My angel, Amoeba. It's been fifteen years and a whole world of hurt and fucking heartache since I last saw her. Yet, she's still there, still here, in my head, my belly and my heart and I so wish to fuck that wasn't the case.

CHAPTER TWO

W E WALK TOWARD THE HOTEL lobby like we're kings of the fucking world. One because we can and two because, well basically, we are. Our album is at number one and has just gone platinum. We have four songs sitting inside the music download chart, and our eighteen-month world tour has been a complete and total sellout. On top of that, I've just come in the mouth of a bird we pulled out of the audience at our show while riding in the limo back to our hotel. *Who does that I ask ya?* Me, Conner fucking Reed, that's who does that.

Fuck her! Fuck her and her blue eyes and her blonde hair and those fuck-eyed freckles that are all over her nose after just ten minutes in the sun. Fuck her and the boring little life she's probably leading. Married to someone that Mummy and Daddy and that prick of a brother of hers actually approve of. Someone who didn't grow up on a council estate, whose dad wasn't an alchi and whose mum wasn't a junky, murdered by her dealer. I bet whoever he is, he's never gotten a blowjob in the back of a limo.

What if he has? What if he's gotten a blowjob from her? What if she loves it? What if she loves *him*? What if she's had his babies?

I don't care.

I do, I care too much.

Fuck!

I need to shut my brain down. This is why I try and stay away from coke, it makes me think. It makes me think far too much. I need a drink. I need to get up to our room, watch some randoms fuck when I tell them to, and I need to get drunk. I need to drink until my brain shuts the fuck up and I can go to sleep and not dream... not dream of any of them. Not her, not my mum and not Miles.

A few photographers are hanging about outside the hotel, and I take a couple of deep breaths and get my racing thoughts under control as we stop and pose, letting them earn their money. I need to shut her down. I need to shut down all thoughts of her and fuck them off out of my brain. It's been fifteen years... fifteen fucking years, and I seriously need to get a grip. I hate that she can still do this. I'm Conner Reed. I'm living the dream, and yet a single thought, a distant memory of a little blue-eyed, blonde-haired girl from Surrey can bring me to my knees.

Well. Fuck. Her.

Tonight, I'm not gonna let that happen. I'm gonna focus on the here and now and just how great my fucking life is. I'm buzzing from the coke, the last show of the tour and the fact that I've just blown my load in the back of the limo. I've had a good night so far, so let's pay it forward and give the paps the picture they need to pay their rent with this week. They're wankers most of them, but at the end of the day, it's their job, and I'm happy to help out anyone that's just trying to make a living.

The lovely Lara's still with us, and for some reason, which probably seems entirely logical in Jet's weird but beautiful mind, he's now carrying her monkey style toward the lifts that'll take us up to our penthouse, and the guests we invited to join us earlier. And then I see her, and my buzz and my good mood vanish in an instant.

Amanda Vale. Women like her are the reason I don't do return rides. I made the mistake of fucking her twice. She now assumes there's something between us, and that I just need to come to my senses and realise it. Yeah, right! What she needs to do is take the hint that I'm not interested, then fuck off and leave me alone. I don't do relationships. The problem is, she's a personal assistant to our manager, Lawson, and her dad's a significant shareholder in our record label, which all means she's around – a lot.

She's older than me, about forty I reckon. She's beautiful don't get me wrong. She's stunning and keeps herself in good shape, but none of that matters. Because *she's* not *her*. None of them are *her*, and that's why none of *them* matter.

"Oh dear, stalker alert at two o'clock," Jet says quietly from beside me as Lara sucks on his neck, her arms and legs wrapped around him as he continues to carry her like a baby monkey clinging to his chest.

"Yeah, I see. Don't make eye contact." We both keep looking straight ahead, aiming for the lift thats only destination is to our room.

"Reed," she calls out.

"Fuck," Jet and I both whisper together. We turn at the same time and face Amanda.

"Well, looky here, it's Miss Mandy. You coming up to play with us sweetie?" Jet asks her. She knows what he's asking. Amanda is aware of the kind of games we like to play, especially after a show. She's seen what goes on and knows how we operate, even joining us once. I watch as her eyes move from me to Jet, to Lara and back to Jet again.

"I actually wondered if you fancied going for something to eat, Reed." Her eyes move back to mine. Fuck, I don't want to be an arsehole, but there's no way I'm going anywhere with her.

"Sorry Amanda, I've already got plans," I tell her.

"But you're more than welcome to join us if you want," Jet adds.

"Will I have your undivided attention if I do, Reed?"

I shake my head before she's even finished speaking. "You know that's not how we operate, Amanda. Now if you don't mind, it's been a long tour, and now it's over I'm gonna go and have some fun before I fly home tomorrow." We turn and head back toward the lift and leave her standing there. I feel bad, but I shouldn't. We had a quick fuck in an office at the studios one drunken night and then she joined Jet and me for a foursome with some other girl, whose name I don't remember. Although technically, I just watched and directed the three of them in action, until the very last minute when I came in the mouth of the unnamed girl, pissing Amanda off big time. That was about three months ago, and despite me telling her from the start there was nothing more than sex between us, since then, she's continuously tried ways to be alone with me. She's invited me out for drinks, lunch, coffee, and dinner. She's tried them all. I've refused each and every offer, and yet here she is, still trying, still not giving up. She's persistent, I'll give her that.

I STEP OUT OF THE shower and grab a towel off the rack and wrap it around my hips. I grab another and rub my hair dry with it while wandering into the bedroom. I sit on the bed and stare down at the carpet, mentally preparing myself for tonight's events. We invited two couples and two girls back to join us. Plus, we've now added Lara to the mix.

The buzz from the coke I had earlier is wearing off and if the truth be told, I'd quite happily go straight to bed right now, but if I do that I'll start to think, and the first and probably the last thing I'll think about is *her*. I get the usual stab of pain in my gut and chest, the instant I allow her image to enter my head.

The night she didn't show up, my life changed forever. That night, changed the course I thought my life was set on. Her not showing resulted in my brother's death and me going to prison. Ultimately, all of those things had led me to Jet and the band, but I'd give it all up in a heartbeat if it meant I got my brother back and for the accident to never have happened. I look up toward the door as it rattles and Jet calls my name.

"Reed. Dude, hope you're not in there getting all depressed. Get out here and have some fun. Stop thinking and come join us."

I take a deep breath in and let it out slowly. It hurts. I don't know why but by keeping my breaths short and shallow, it helps keeps the pain away. When I breathe deep, it's like I let go of the tightness in my chest a little, which in turn, lets the ache and the pain out, or is it in? Either way, all these years later and it still hurts just as much.

"Reed, you hearing me?"

"Yeah man, I'll be out in a minute. Go get them warmed up and wet. Put on a porno or something. Yeah, put on some gay porn. I wanna see how the bloke with the muscles reacts. Let's see how far we can push him tonight."

"You're an evil, twisted genius, Conner Reed. I fucking love you. Don't be too long."

Twisted, now ain't that the truth. I'd moved on from my days of just liking to take charge in the bedroom.

I'd joined the band just as they'd made it big. I hadn't had to do the hard yards with the rest of them. Two months after Jet found me busking at Tottenham Court Road Tube Station and asked me to audition, we'd signed a recording deal. I'd gone from living on the streets and in homeless shelters, busking for a living, to staying at the best hotels around the world and having a lump sum of two hundred and fifty grand U.S paid into my newly opened bank account, with a weekly expense allowance of another three thousand added to that. I'd seriously died and gone to rock star heaven. That was peanuts compared to what I'm earning now. I pay more than that in tax a year.

What I discovered along with all of that is that women will do anything, and I do mean anything, just to be a small part of my world. But the biggest surprise came, when I found out it wasn't only women, it was blokes too. And being the twisted little freak that I am, I pushed and pushed, just to see how far people would go to get what they didn't know they wanted, and I soon discovered it was pretty much all the fucking way.

What resulted from that is what I'm about to do now. Mindless, dirty, filthy sex. It's the only kind of sex, the only kind of intimacy I can handle. I hate soft, gentle touches. I hate whispered words of love or terms of endearment. I want nothing personal about the whole experience. My attitude toward sex is skewed and fucked up, and as much as I know it's wrong, I like nothing better than taking a seemingly happy couple and destroying everything they thought they knew about themselves and each other, sexually. And being Conner Reed, lead guitarist and sometimes singer for Shift, I always manage to get people to do exactly what I want them to.

Yeah, I abuse my status in life, so fucking what. You want a job as a roadie? Sure, tell your girlfriend to suck me off while you watch, and the job's all yours. You girls want backstage passes and access to the after party? No problem, strap this on and fuck your mate from behind while she sucks me off and I'll get you backstage at any concert you want. My life is fucked, so I didn't see why theirs shouldn't be too.

CHAPTER THREE

I STEP OUT OF THE tranquillity and solitude of my bedroom and into what looks like a scene from a brothel or sex club. On the big plasma screen on the wall, one bloke's being spit roasted between two others. The sound is down and Alex Gaudino's 'Destination Calabria' is pulsing through the suite's sound system.

The girls from the two couples we invited are straddling their boyfriend's laps, doing nothing more than kissing them. Oh dear, that just won't do. The two girls we asked to join us at the sound check earlier, are obviously a little more adventurous. One is sitting naked, except for a bra, on Jet's face, the other is sucking his cock. Lara, the girl from the limo, is cutting a line of coke on the granite bench top in the kitchen area. *The girl seriously has a problem!*

The room is dimly lit by a giant fish tank built into the wall. The whole area is bathed in a beautiful blue glow, only altering when the threesome on the telly changes position and the picture flickers.

I sit in the wing-backed chair facing the huge sofa everyone is occupying and wait for them to realise I'm here.

The girl sitting on Jet's face notices me first. She climbs off of him and walks toward me still wearing nothing but a bra, from which one of her tits is hanging out. Her makeup is smudged under her eyes, and she looks anything but attractive or sexy. I shake my head as she reaches toward my cock.

I'm wearing jeans and a T-shirt. I still haven't decided yet if I'm going to take part, but if they all look as rough as the woman standing in front of me right now, I'm likely to go with a no. I'll just take care of myself as I watch all of them carry out my orders. I get off on the power trip. Watching other people fuck, suck and lick because I've told them to, turns me on, or maybe, I'm just a perv who likes to watch other people having sex. Who knows? I've never discussed it with a professional, and I never intend to. It works for me, and that's all I really care about.

Jet sits up and pulls the head of the girl sucking his cock out of his lap by her hair. She wipes the back of her hand across her mouth. The two couples are now all sitting side by side on the sofa, the girls on the inside, wedged between the blokes. One couple are grunger types, both have tats and piercings. The other two look like a pair of fitness freaks, all toned and tanned. She's blonde with massive fake tits that are far too big for her skinny frame. He looks like Johnny Bravo from the cartoon show.

"What're your name's girls?" I watch Johnny straighten up. He doesn't like me talking to his girl. Hmmm, interesting.

"Shayla," the little punk princess says first. I look across to Jet, who's sitting cross-legged on the floor smoking a joint. She's just his type, but then again so is her boyfriend. Jet winks at me, he knows what I'm thinking, and he gives a little nod.

"Lacy," the Barbie Doll adds while twirling her hair around her finger. She's about twenty-five, not five. Does she seriously think that acting all cute and coy is gonna do things for me?

"You ever kissed a girl, Lacy?" She stops twirling her hair. Johnny shifts next to her and clears his throat, I think he likes that idea.

She nods her head. "Yeah, a few, back when I was in college." She tilts her chin defiantly at me.

"I didn't know that," Johnny says from beside her.

"You've never asked," Barbie replies.

"Did you like it?"

Oh, he really likes this idea, I'm gonna have some fun with these two.

She nods her head and smiles first at him, then at me. "It was different, much softer than with a guy."

"Did you just kiss, or did you do more?" Johnny asks her. She looks around the room at everyone. The two girls Jet was enjoying earlier are sitting either side of him now, and Lara's sitting next to them.

"Well, a couple of times we sort of made out."

"What's *made out* mean, Lacy? I'm English, it's not a term we use, so you'll have to explain."

She squirms a little bit, tilts her head to the side and says, "We fucked, okay? It happened more than once, and it's happened a few times since we left college. And yes Kale, before you ask, I liked it. I fucking loved it. It's different, girls know, they just know what to do, where to touch, how to touch another girl."

"Sheesh," Johnny says and runs his hands through his hair.

I turn my gaze to Shayla, who has a big grin on her face and before I can ask her, she says, "Fuck yeah. I'm bi, we love a three-way, don't we baby?" The boyfriend smiles, nods and takes a long draw on the joint Jet's just passed him.

"I love a three-way, and I love to watch Shay with another girl."

Johnny's now staring at Shayla wide-eyed and chewing his gum really fast. Jet turns, looks up at me and winks again. He knows my plan.

"Kiss Lacy, Shayla," I order. Johnny's jaw is now on fast forward, and I'm actually worried it's going to dislocate as he chews his gum at warp speed. Lacy pushes both hands through her hair and turns to Shayla.

They look at each other for a few seconds before Johnny says, "Do it baby, kiss her." Lacy straddles Shayla's lap and goes straight in for a kiss. It starts soft and gentle then they start pulling at each other's hair and rocking their hips into each other.

"Shit," Johnny hisses through his teeth.

"Fuck Shay, that's hot, baby," the boyfriend says.

"What's your name mate?" I ask the boyfriend.

"Dylan," he replies.

"Join them, Dylan." He doesn't hesitate and is in the middle of their kiss in seconds. Johnny sits forward and looks like he's about to object when Dylan yanks Lacy's hair and kisses her hard on the mouth. Instead, his mouth falls open and he stares.

"Take your tops off, girls," I give out my next order. Dylan pulls Shayla's over her head. Lacy does her own, and when she sees that Shayla's wearing nothing underneath, she takes her bra off too.

Shayla is tiny, with small perky tits. Lacy is long and lean, with huge fake tits. The contrast between them is striking, but I don't feel a thing, neither of them turns me on. What's getting me hard, is their unquestioning reactions to my orders. They've done exactly what I've told them to so far, and their boyfriends have gone right along with it. It's the power, the control. I know it's fucked, but it's just the way I am.

Johnny can't stay in his seat anymore and has decided to make a move, but it's Shayla he kisses first, then Lacy. Now I'm really gonna push things.

"Clothes off, all of you." Lacy, Shayla and Dylan don't hesitate. Johnny just sits back and watches them for a few seconds, he rubs his hand over his big square jaw. His eyes flick to mine, then down to Jet, who when I look, is now getting a synchronised wank from the two girls he was with when I walked in. The one on his left is having her cunt licked out by Lara, and I watch as she throws her head back and moans.

Johnny chews on his gum, slowly now, he watches as Shayla and Dylan suck on each of Lacy's tits. This seems to spur him into action, and within seconds he's naked. I notice Dylan stops and looks him over. He's ripped, but not in a natural way. I'd say that looking at his less than average dick size, his square and prominent jaw and his huge muscles, that he's overdone the steroids during his life. Still, Dylan seems to like the look of him.

"You like men, Dyl?"

He shrugs. "I don't mind."

I look at Johnny, who instantly starts to shake his head. "No dude, no way."

"No?" I ask him. "That's a shame, looks like Lacy's having fun, but if the answers no then you'll have to leave."

Lacy turns toward him. "Have another line of coke baby and let's just have some fun." Lara's instantly at his side with a mirror, four lines and a rolled up fifty dollar note. He looks around the room at everyone else, and as Pharrell and Daft Punk sing about getting lucky over the sound system, he takes the note from Lara and snorts a line up each nostril. He leans across the girls, grabs Dylan around the neck and slams his mouth against his.

Well, that was easy!

The girls join in the kiss and my heart rate speeds up, but I'm still not hard.

"Touch each other," I bark out, "I want to see your hands on and in each other, mouths too." I watch as Shayla smiles at Dylan. He adjusts his position on the sofa and leans forward. He takes Johnnie's cock in his hand and starts to stroke it. He slides down onto the floor and takes him into his mouth. They all move around. Johnnie's sitting back on the sofa, his legs wide open as Dylan sucks on his cock. The girls are kneeling either side of him. They lean across and kiss each other, and I watch as he slides a hand up each of their legs and pushes his fingers inside them as they alternate between kissing him and sucking on each other's tits.

Jet stands up, and I watch as he approaches Dylan. He's naked, with his skinny arse in the air and it's obviously too much for Jet to resist. I start to undo my zip. My dick has finally sprung to life and is now pressing painfully against the waistband of my jeans.

And then in an instant, my world changes.

The screech of tyres, the sensation of spinning, rolling, blue lights flashing, glass smashing, and above it all, above everything else is… this song. When everything went quiet and I looked across at my brother, his eyes were wide but seeing nothing. All I could hear was the voice of Anthony Kiedis, singing the Chili Peppers 'Scar Tissue' and it's all around me now. That song, those sounds and images, are surrounding me.

I try to get up out of the chair, but the room spins. I need to get to my room… get away. I need to get away from this song and these people. I don't do this song. I avoid this song at all costs, and now it's here, playing loud, surrounding me and making me remember.

Her – that night.

The night she didn't show.

We ended up places we shouldn't have been, wouldn't have been. And it's all because of *her*.

I head as quickly as I can back to my hotel bedroom. I'm vaguely aware of Jet screaming for someone to, "Turn the fucking song off." I just make it to my bathroom in time to throw up down the toilet. I can barely breathe as I fall to my knees. I struggle to get air into my lungs and feel like I'm about to choke on my own vomit, making the panic worse. I cling onto the sides of the cold toilet bowl, my arms shake as they hold my weight. This hasn't happened for a long time, a long fucking time, but I still hate when it does. It makes me feel weak, like a failure.

I'm Conner Reed, rock fucking God!

I have men and women around the world worship me. I'm the son of completely fucked up parents. I've watched my brother die in front of me and spent three months in prison for being in the stolen car my brother died in, but despite all of that, I've achieved cult status in my life.

Women want me, men want to be me and yet, one song, just one fucking song, can bring me to my knees. I can't believe that I still react like this. That song takes me right back to it like it's actually happening. I know I should see someone. I know I should talk about it, sit down with a professional, but I can't. I don't talk about my feelings. Instead, I write songs that sort of explain how I feel and I engage in mindless group sex, the kind where I remain detached and in complete control. Other people were in control that night, other people's actions controlled the direction my life went that fateful night and I'll never let that happen again.

Jet bursts through the bathroom door, his eyes are wide as he looks me over. I look up at him from where I'm on my knees in front of the toilet.

"You okay, dude?" I nod. I'm still breathing deeply and unable to speak. "I've shut the music down and sent them all home." He smiles his wonky smile at me and his blue eyes sparkle like the naughty kid that's usually lurking just below the surface of Jet's persona. He's too pretty for his own good. Women can't decide if they want to mother or fuck him, and blokes want to either fuck him or fuck him over, but he's a lot tougher than he looks. He's been a good mate to me and I love him like a brother. "Everyone except Lara, she's waiting in my bed."

I smile and shake my head. "Sorry, if I spoilt your night man. I've got this now, go back and have some fun." His eyes look me over as I stand up straight.

"I can send her away and stay with you if you want." I shake my head no as I walk past him and grab a bottle of water from the fridge in the bedroom.

"I'm just gonna watch some telly and try and get some sleep." He turns around to face me but remains standing in the doorway to the en-suite bathroom, his arms spread apart as he holds onto each side of the door frame.

"Reed, you know I'd send her home in a heartbeat and stay in here with you if you need me to." I keep my back to him as I walk over to the window and look out at the city lights below me.

"Jet, let's not do this, please mate, not tonight."

"I just wish you'd give us a try, Reed."

"Jet, I love you like a brother man, but that's it that's as far as it goes. I don't fancy men, I'm not gay. I'm not even bi."

"I'm not gay either. I... I don't know how to explain it, but if I were with you, there'd be no one else, man or woman. I love you Reed. I want to be with you. I want us to be a couple and to make a life together. I'd happily give up all of this. We could just fuck off, disappear somewhere and live our lives in peace and quiet." I've heard this so many times. I feel bad because I don't want to hurt him, but I just don't feel what he does. I turn away from the window and face him.

"Jet, I can't force myself to be something I'm not. You're my mate, my best mate, but I don't find you sexually attractive. I don't have any desire to fuck you or any other bloke. I like women, I like to fuck women."

He takes a step toward me, his arm out. He's wearing nothing but a pair of jeans that hang loosely from his skinny frame. His dark curly hair's a mess and hangs over one eye. He looks like a mixture of Jim Morrison and Michael Hutchence, and if I were gay, if I did have a thing for men, I'm sure I'd find him attractive but I'm not, and I don't.

"But you don't even do that, do you Reed?" He puts his hands on his hips, and that's when I know this is going to end in an argument. I'm mentally and physically drained. All I want to do is crawl into my lonely bed and dream about *her*. The only time I get peace, absolute peace, is when I dream of her. The sensation of her lips, her taste, the feel of her small hands on me, her smell. When I dream, it's all so real and that's where I want to be right now. Not standing here, having this argument with Jet, *again*.

Every time we're due to spend time apart he does this. Whenever we end a tour or have a break from recording and I'm heading back to England, he asks me again. Every time I say no, and it ends in an argument.

"You *don't* fuck them though do you? Not really. Not their bodies at least. You just like to fuck with their heads, same way you like to fuck with mine."

That comment right there pisses me off. "When have I ever fucked with your head? I've never been anything but up front and honest with my feelings for you. Never have I. . ."

Jet's lost it now, not even listening to what I'm saying as he talks over me. . .

"You sit back and watch, while you dish out your orders and touch yourself, but you hardly ever let them touch *you*. You never let *me* touch *you*. And even with everyone else, it's usually their mouth you fuck, or you jack yourself off all over them. Why can't *they* touch you? Why can't I touch you? Why can't anyone touch you? What are you so fucking scared of Reed?"

I take a swig from the bottle of water in my hand and breathe deeply through my nose. I have to loosen my jaw before I can even speak to him, he's got me wound up so tight.

"Jet, fuck off back to your own room. I'm not getting into this with you right now. My answer's the same as it is every other fucking time you start with this shit. No. Are you listening? No, I don't wanna ride off into the sunset with you, you're *not* my knight in shining armour, *not* my fairy-tale ending. I'm sorry, but that's just the way it is. Now fuck off and leave me in peace." He takes another step closer. "Just a chance, Reed, just one chance? I know we could be so good together. I just want a chance."

"No," I shout, "No, my answer's no now, and it'll always be no. I'll walk away, Jet. If you keep this up, I'll walk away from it all, you, the band, all of it. I'm not working with this hanging over us. You either get your head around the fact that it's never gonna happen or I'm fucking off for good, and I mean it this time. My life's fucked up enough. I don't need your shit adding to it." His shoulders slump as he stands in front of me. I feel bad, but I'm still pissed off, and I mean what I've said. I'm thirty-three-years-old, and I'm so sick of this life that I'm leading. I love the band and the music, but every-thing outside of that is seriously fucked. The sex, the women, the parties, all of it means nothing. It's all superficial bullshit, and I hate *it*, and the people that are part of *it*. I just want to go home to my family and step away from all of it, and the last thing I need is Jet and his 'let's have a relationship' drama going on while I'm at home. I don't need his phone calls and texts, begging me to just let us try. I want to sleep, and I want to dream, and right now, I just need him to go.

"One day, one day you'll understand," he says through gritted teeth. "You'll love someone so fucking much that it's painful and then you'll get it."

"No, no I won't. Not again, I won't. See, I've been there. I know what a lying, spiteful, deceitful little cunt love is and I won't ever go there again. So you just need to make up your mind, you either stop with all this bollocks and we come back in September, or we leave tomorrow and announce the end of the band, 'cause I'm done this time. I'm seriously done."

"But I love you, I fucking love you, Reed."

I'm done, I can't do this anymore. "Get out! Get out of my room and stay out of my life. I'll sort out a separate flight back to London tomorrow. I don't want you to call, text or email me. I want no contact with you, whatsoever. I'm done Jet, I just want some peace. Now, get out of my room and stay out of my fucking life."

He looks at me for a few seconds, and I have no idea what the look in his eyes means. He starts to nod his head. "Your call Reed, just remember that this was your call." He turns and leaves the room without looking back. I screw the cap on the water bottle and launch it at the door as he shuts it behind him. Fucking drama queen. I love him, but he does my fucking head in sometimes. I lock the bedroom door, pick up my bottle of water and climb into bed. I turn on the telly with the remote control and flick through the channels. Notting Hill is playing on one of the film channels, and that's all it takes for my mind to drift to *her*.

We went to see this film together. I moaned, but she reminded me that I'd promised to go with her and she would come with me to see the Green Mile. I didn't end up hating Notting Hill quite as much as I thought I would, but we never did get to watch the Green Mile together when it came out the following year. I leave the film on, I don't usually, any other night it'd be off... gone. I go out of my way to avoid anything, music, films, places, anything and anywhere that might remind me of her, or take me back to that night. But after everything else that's happened tonight so far, it seems a bit pointless.

I pile my pillows on top of each other, turn off the lights, lay back and attempt to watch the film. It takes all of twenty seconds before my mind starts to wander back to *her*. December the thirtieth, nineteen ninety-nine was the last time I'd seen her in person. I left her at the end of her drive. We'd spent the night making love in the back of my brother's car. We had a spot in the local woods where we'd park, climb into the back seat and worship each other's bodies the best we could through our clothes. I loved the rare occasions that we were able to share a bed, and I could get her completely naked. Five times, that's all it had happened. I've worshipped and fantasised about this girl for most of my life and I'd only seen her completely naked five times. I'd only gotten to fall asleep and wake up with her in my arms twice, and yet all these years on, I was still desperate to have that experience again. Despite what she did, despite what her actions caused, I was still in love with her.

Her family had categorically forbidden her from seeing me. According to them, I was from a rough and undesirable family. The fact we lived on the local council estate didn't meet with their approval either. So we'd spent a year sneaking around, seeing each other behind their backs. My brothers were good, Ty and Jordan both had their own places and let us borrow a bedroom for a few hours, and we even stayed over at Ty's twice, but it wasn't enough. We wanted more. We wanted to be together all the time, every day, so we set our plan in motion. I was at college studying music, but we needed to get some money together so we could try to get away. Tyler gave me a job as a labourer with his building firm, and I played the local pubs and bars in the evenings and on a Sunday afternoon. Meebs was still at school but was already sixteen. We wouldn't be breaking the law, but we knew they'd come after us just the same. She had a part-time job in a clothing shop at the local shopping centre, where she worked two evenings and every weekend. We both saved every penny we earned.

The plan was for Miles to drop us at Guildford Station that night and we were going to get the train to Cornwall from there. We chose Cornwall as we'd both always wanted to learn to surf. We loved the beach, and we thought, hoped, that it'd be the last place her parents and arsehole of a brother would ever think to look for us. She was going to leave a note, telling them that we'd gone to London. We planned to lie low in Cornwall for a while, see if we could pick up some work and then once the fuss had died down, we could head over to Europe and backpack our way around. Meebs would do bar work, I'd do whatever I could pick up, but was hoping that music would be a part of whatever I did.

We made love in the car that last night, we were both so excited and so in fucking love, that I still can't understand why she didn't show. I kissed her at the end of her drive and she told me she'd go to the ends of the earth with me, and that she couldn't wait for us to spend the rest of our lives travelling and just being together. She kissed me one last time and walked up the drive to that big, fuck off mansion she lived in with her mum, dad and Pearce, her prick of a brother. By the time I'd walked to the end of her street and gotten back in Miles' car she'd texted me and told me again how much she loved me. She texted me a good morning the next day and told me she was going shopping with Sophie, and then nothing. I didn't hear another thing. She didn't show, she just didn't show. I called *her, and* I called Sophie but got nothing. I finally got a hold of my best mate Josh, who was Sophie's brother and he told me that his mum had rushed off to meet up with them and they were going to some millennium party at a fancy hotel that night.

I have no idea what happened that day to make her change her mind, but it must've been something big because she never showed and I never heard from her again.

Miles could see I was devastated. He knew how much I loved her and how hard I'd worked to pull our plan together. So, he took me to the pub, and we had a few drinks. It was the last night of the millennium, and the place was mobbed, so at around nine, we left the pub and went to a party at his mate's house. But that was rammed too, people everywhere. The place stunk of weed and as soon as midnight was done with, I wanted to get home. I was tired, pissed off and had a banging headache. I wanted to go home, charge my phone that was now dead and hopefully wake up in the morning to a million missed calls and messages from Meebs telling me we were still on and this had all been one great big fucking balls up. I never made it home, not that night, not any night since.

We were about halfway across town when I noticed the blue light flash behind us. "The old Bill's up your arse Miles, will you be over the limit?" I'd seen him drinking at various times during the night, surely they would've all topped up in his system and he'd be over the limit by now.

"Fuck," he said out loud and banged his palm down onto the steering wheel. I looked at him, he was completely freaking out.

"What's wrong, did you have a toot on that joint earlier as well?"

He shook his head before looking at me. "It's a cut and shut Reed, the car's fucking dodgy. If they pull me over, I'm looking at doing time." His eyes were back on the road, and his foot was now back down on the pedal as we roared forward.

"What the fuck, Miles. Why? Why the fuck are you driving around in a cut and shut?"

"Because Reed, because for once I wanted something nice around me. For once, I wanted something that everybody else was jealous of. I didn't want to be that poor kid whose mum got murdered by her drug dealer. I didn't want to be Miles, you know, his dad's the piss head that used to be in the SAS," he grips the wheel tighter as he shouts. We're travelling down country lanes, and as I look down at the speedo, I can see that we're hitting tops of one hundred and twenty, one thirty miles an hour. The blue flashing lights of the police car are still following in the distance behind us.

"Slow down Miles, slow the fuck down."

"No, no Reed, I can't. I can't get caught. Don't you see, if I get caught, I'll get nicked. I'll probably go to prison, and all those arse-holes that talk about us, the people that look down their noses and think they're better than us, that think we're scum, like your girlfriend's mum and dad, I'll just be making them right. I'll just be making things worse for you."

Then everything seemed to happen in slow motion. A car came toward us, I think Miles tried to swerve, and we ended up going down an embankment. That's when the car split in two. The back end of the car rolled and pulled the front with it. A branch came through the window, and I ducked down in my seat, Miles didn't, and snap, his neck was broken. We came to a stop with the car on its roof. I could still hear the sirens for a while, then people shouting. While I hung upside down, trapped by my seatbelt, staring into the eyes of my dead brother, and all I could hear above everything else was the Chili Peppers sing about their lonely view.

Physically, I walked away unscathed. I had some bruising, some scratches and the nylon of the seat belt caused a friction burn across my neck and chest but other than that, I was fine.

The car was the result of two insurance write-offs being salvaged and welded together to make one car. Miles was well aware of what he was purchasing, but he didn't care. He was driving around in a thirty thousand pound car that he'd paid five thousand for, and that's all that had mattered to him. His safety, the safety of his passengers or anyone else on the road was inconsequential to him. He'd given Tyler's wife Jenna, a lift in that car when she was pregnant with their little boy Ethan.

As well as the details about the car, the coroner's report also concluded that he was three times over the legal blood alcohol limit and traces of cannabis and MDMA, otherwise known as ecstasy were found in his system. There was also a small amount of cocaine found in his pocket. It turned out, I didn't know my brother at all.

And because I'd been in a bit of trouble with the police when I was fourteen and fifteen, I spent three months locked up on remand before the courts decided there was nothing they could charge me with. I had no idea the car was illegal and no idea that my brother was over the limit. Well, maybe regarding the drink I had a clue, but I had no idea he'd smoked weed and had popped a pill. I knew he was no angel, none of us were. We were of the generation, and from an area where doing a line of charlie and popping a few pills on a Saturday night, was as standard as going for a few beers and a curry was to others. It's just how it was. I smoked my first joint when I was about thirteen, which was old compared to a lot of the kids at my school. What we didn't do though was get in a car and drive once we were stoned or high… ever. Apparently, my brother didn't live by that rule and that, combined with the condition of the car we were in, cost him his life.

My heart is pounding hard as I relive all of those events. I never usually let any of those thoughts or memories come to the surface but sometimes, sometimes, I'm just too tired to keep them away, and that's exactly how I feel right now. Exhausted. I want to get back to England, spend time with my brothers, their wives and their kids. I want to walk my dogs, play golf and sometimes, spend whole days doing absolutely nothing.

I close my eyes and drift off to sleep.

CHAPTER FOUR

I PULL THE PILLOW OVER my head to try and block out the screams. I can't remember what it was I was actually dreaming, but the girl screaming in my dream was beginning to piss me off. There's banging at my bedroom door, and I assume I've been shouting in my sleep and Jet's come to check if I'm okay. I've suffered from nightmares since the accident, I even walk as well as talk in my sleep.

My eyes open instantly as I hear a girl scream my name from outside my bedroom door, the same scream I thought I was dreaming a few minutes ago.

I jump up and unlock the door, its Lara, she's naked and sobbing. *What the fuck has Jet done to her?* Sometimes he goes too fucking far with his freaky sex shit. I'm weird, but he blows anything my twisted brain can come up with right out of the water. It's bad enough when it's in a group, but when it's just him and a girl together, they tend to get a little freaked out. Handcuffs, blindfold, ball gag and whips can be a bit too much all at once for a girl that's never tried it, especially one you've only met the night before.

Lara throws herself at me, and I can feel her shake. "Reed," she sobs and points to Jet's room across the other side of the suite while shaking her head. I start to walk over to where she's pointing when she says from behind me, "Don't Reed. Don't go in there." I turn and look at her with a frown, then carry on making my way into Jet's bedroom, calling his name as I do. He's not in his bed, so I walk through to his bathroom. His room's a replica of mine, with a huge sunken Roman bath in the centre of the en-suite, a walk-in shower on one side, toilet on the other. I don't see him in the bathroom, then as I turn to walk back through to the bedroom, I realise that the floor is wet. The bath is filled to the top with water, and some has spilt over the sides.

But it's red.

The water in the bath, the water on the tiles, is red.

Jet's lying face up at the bottom, eyes wide, staring blankly at nothing.

"No, no, no." I climb in and lift him up, screaming at Lara to call for help. Call for an ambulance, the paramedics, the police, any fucker that might be able to help me. I call his name and slap his face. "What have you done? What the fuck have you done?" He's cut his wrists, but he's not bleeding. *Perhaps he didn't cut deep enough? Perhaps the water's just red from where he's broken the skin?* I notice that he's blue around his mouth, so I hold his nose and start blowing in it. I don't know first aid, but I've seen it done.

I blow into his mouth.

I pump his chest.

I slap his face.

I pump his chest.

I scream at him.

I shake him.

I hold him.

I rock him in my arms, and I hold him tight.

I've no idea how long I've been sitting there when I hear a commotion and a policeman walks into the room, followed by two paramedics and another policeman. I don't say a word as they take him from me and get to work. But I know. I'm not an expert, and I have no idea what's the correct way to find a pulse, but I know he doesn't have one. I know he isn't breathing and they don't need to waste their time doing all the shit they're doing.

He's dead.

Jet's gone.

He's dead.

The next few hours were a blur. Lawson arrived in our room, then Dom and Gunner. The police wouldn't let me see anyone at first then Laws got a lawyer from somewhere, and he sat with me while the police asked me questions. I might've been in shock, but I wasn't stupid. I told them that I knew nothing; that we came back here after last night's show, there were a few people hanging around, but I wasn't in the mood to party, so I went to bed. The next thing I know, Lara's screaming and banging on my door. I assume Lara's giving her statement somewhere and hopefully she's saying something along the lines of what I am. Otherwise, we're both fucked.

Finally, Jet's body's removed. The forensic team pack up their stuff, and the police leave. I'm eventually allowed out of Jet's bedroom, where I've been held since the police arrived. Swabs and prints have been taken from under my nails, and from my fingertips. I'm still only wearing my boxers, and I'm freezing. I walk past Lawson and the boys, straight to my room and pull a hoodie and a pair of joggers from my case. I put them on while the boys all stand and watch.

Everybody's silent.

Jet's dead!

He swallowed a bottle of around thirty Valium, washed them down with a bottle of Grey Goose and then just in case that didn't work, he cut his wrists. As the Valium sent him off to a sleep that he'd never wake up from, he bled out around a quarter of the blood in his body until his heart just stopped. That's what the forensic team are assuming, but they won't know for sure until an autopsy is done. I'm amazed at how much info I took in from the paramedic's conversation with the police. A conversation that I'm probably never likely to forget.

I look at Lawson, Dom and Gunner. "Jet's dead," I tell them. "He washed thirty Valium down with a bottle of vodka and then just to make sure that the job was done, he slit his wrists. He's dead! I found him at the bottom of his bath. He's dead, Jet's dead!" They're all staring at me blankly, still not saying a word. "Do you hear what I'm saying, are any of you even listening to me? He's dead, he's fucking dead." I can hear myself getting louder and louder.

Gunner steps forward and wraps his arms around me. "Shit Reed, this is fucked. I'm so sorry you had to see all that mate." I'm not a big fan of human contact. I usually try to avoid it. When we're on stage or working it's different, I can deal with it, but once emotions become involved, I don't like it. I'm always worried that I'll lose control and start to feel, and I hate it when I feel. I'm feeling now, and it hurts, it hurts so fucking much.

I don't know where it comes from, but Dom's suddenly putting a whisky tumbler in my hand. I take it and go and sit on the edge of the bed and knock back the drink. It calms me down and warms my belly instantly.

"Sorry," I say, looking up at each of them in turn. "I'm sorry boys. Fuck! What a morning. What time is it?" I don't know how to act. I don't know what to say. There's always four of us, now there's only three. I don't know how to be three. I scratch at my stubbly chin and rake my hand through my hair, trying to get my thoughts in order and make sense of what's happened.

Laws sits down next to me. He's our manager, but he's only a couple of years older than me. He's usually composed, he's usually wearing a suit, and he's usually got the answer to each and every problem we might encounter. Lawson and I get on well, he's English, which is a start and he's single. We've spent a few wild nights together in the company of a few willing women. Lawson has the look of a well-educated English gentleman, but I happen to know that he's from Essex and a bit rough around the edges. Although he did go to university, so he's better educated than me.

"It's just gone one. What the fuck happened, Reed?"

Dom takes the glass from my hand as I stare down at the carpet.

I rub both hands over the stubble on my jaw again and look at Lawson.

"It's my fault. He did this because I told him I was leaving the band."

Lawson frowns. "What? Why? Why would you tell him that?"

Gunner sits down on a chair that he's brought in from the living area of the suite and sits on it. Dom comes back with a bottle of bourbon and four clean glasses. I watch as he sets them down on the unit below the television, fills them with pours than a double shot from the bottle, then passes one to each of us, before sitting his arse on the unit and stretching his long legs out in front of him, facing Lawson and me. My heart's still racing, and I watch my hand shake as I grip the glass.

Jet's dead.

My best mate's dead, and it's all my fault.

He killed himself because of what I'd said to him.

I drain what's in my glass and hold it out to Dom for a top up. My throat burns from the alcohol, but I like it. The sensation distracts me from the thoughts crashing through my brain.

"You know what, all these years I've blamed her. I thought it was her fault for not turning up, that my brother died." Dom passes me my refilled glass, and I take a sip. "But it wasn't her. It was me. First my mum, then Miles, now Jet. They're all dead because of me. It's me, not her."

"Reed, calm the fuck down mate and just tell us what happened," Lawson asks again.

I wipe my nose with the back of my hand and look at my band-mates. They all know my story, they know my mum was murdered and that my brother was killed, the whole fucking world knows that story. Every newspaper and magazine ran with it when we first made it big. They all jumped on the bad boy, Conner Reed bandwagon. 'Con the Con' being their favourite headline when they found out I'd been banged up. All the money they made reporting on other people's misery, and yet they couldn't come up with a better headline than that? Fucktards, the fucking lot of them. It had snowballed from there. Once they found out how my brother was killed and that I was in the car with him, the sympathy lasted for all of twenty seconds before they started reporting on the fact that I was locked up while the accident was investigated. Then the fuckers found out I'd been in trouble as a kid and that's when the 'Conner the Convicted' and 'Con the Con', headlines began.

It was the local corner shop. Me and two mates found the back doors to the local corner shop open one night, and we nicked some cigarettes and some bars of fucking Galaxy. We were kids, we had the opportunity to nick some fags and make some money; it wasn't an armed robbery. We didn't hurt anyone. We didn't realise we'd been caught on CCTV, and it didn't take long for the shopkeeper to recognise us and for the police to come knocking on our door. I was fourteen, I'd never been in trouble with the police before, so they gave me a caution, and my dad gave me a black eye and a split lip. I think he cracked a few of my ribs too, but I wasn't allowed to go to the hospital to find out. My only other offence was a caution I got for fighting. Once those stories were reported, some nosey young journalist decided to dig even deeper into my past and found out the details of my mum's murder. Then everything changed again, and I was 'Poor Reed' or 'Broken Bad Boy Conner Reed's Heart Breaking Past Revealed.' Or some other bullshit, piss poor headline.

But right now, right at this moment, it all becomes clear. They all died because of me. I was four-years-old when I unknowingly opened the front door to my mum's drug dealer. He choked her to death. Strangled her while I hid between the sofa and the wall. My brothers came home from school and found her dead and me still hiding. We were all sent back to live with my dad after that.

My mum had left him and moved us off of the army base six months before. But being back in London, back to the estate she grew up on, she'd soon fallen into all her old habits from her single days, one of which was heroin. Within weeks she was hooked and selling herself to pay for her hits. She was just out of rehab when my dad met her and had stayed clean for ten years, but as soon as she returned to London and her old friends, that all changed.

My dad had just left the army when we all moved back in with him. He'd gone back to Surrey and was living in a bedsit. Because of the circumstances and the fact that he now had four boys to raise, the council re-housed him and moved us all into a three bedroomed house. We lived in the rougher part of a nice area, and for a few years, despite not having a mum, we had an idyllic childhood. The trauma that had affected our young lives, mostly forgotten. My dad was fundamentally a good, hardworking man who loved his boys. He worked nights as both a nightclub bouncer and a supermarket security guard so he could be there for us during the day. But he'd never gotten over my mum leaving him and he'd never recovered from her death. He'd always drunk heavily, it was the reason she left him, but gradually, by the time I was about eight or nine, he was drunk all the time. He lost his jobs, which just gave him more time to drink. My two eldest brothers got out as soon as they turned sixteen and were working. Miles didn't actually mind living at home, my dad ignored him for the most part, but me, he'd take a swing at me every time I walked past him. I've no idea what I'd done to suddenly make him hate me so much. If I could have afforded it, I'd have moved out as soon as I turned sixteen too. But I wanted to go to college so I could study music, and I did for a while, but then once Meebs and me had come up with our plan to run away, I'd packed in college, started working and saved every penny that I could. I spent as little time as possible at home, and as my dad was usually at the pub or unconscious on the sofa, we rarely came into contact with each other.

I was seen by countless counsellors after my mum's death, but I didn't have anything to tell them. I couldn't remember a thing. I dreamt about her often. I dreamt about the scruffy man with the tattoos, how he pulled up her nightshirt, held on to her hair and laid down on her back as he moved his hips backwards and forwards. His jeans were pulled down slightly, and in my dream, she'd scream silently. He'd put his hand over her mouth and pull her hair harder.

She kept her eyes open and just stared at me the whole time, putting her finger to her lips, warning me to be quiet. I'd squashed myself into a space between the wall and the end of the sofa. I often dream of the same man sitting on my mum's chest, he smacks her around the face a few times, blood running from the corner of her mouth, but she just keeps her eyes on me. It's almost as if in this dream, I remember the other dream, I remember that she warned me to stay quiet. So, I remained in my hiding spot, and I kept quiet as I watched him wrap his hands around her throat and squeeze until she stopped moving, her eyes bulging out of her head, looking right at me. I have no idea if I dreamed what I'd actually witnessed or if it's what my brain has invented, but it never changes, it's the same two dreams all the time, and sometimes both scenes become part of one dream. The so-called 'experts' had no idea if I'd just blanked it all out, or if I genuinely didn't see anything. The dreams and occasional flashbacks told me that I'd probably seen it all, but I remained silent, keeping it to myself. I didn't want anyone else poking around inside my head, and I didn't want my brothers to have to know what I saw that day, so I just stayed quiet, kept it locked away.

They'd caught the man responsible the very same day. I picked his picture out of a book and told the nice lady that gave me Fruit Pastilles and Smarties that he was the man that came to our house that morning. He was the man that I opened the door to, but that was all I told her about that day. My evidence, combined with the DNA they'd removed from the scene and my mum's body, was enough to convict him. He's dead now. Died in prison but I still keep it all locked away.

Lawson's voice breaks into the horrors of my past and drags me into the nightmare of my present.

"Why did you tell him you were leaving the band, Reed? I don't understand why you would say that to him?" I knock back the drink in my shaking hand as he repeats his question.

"Did he start with the relationship shit again, Reed?" Gunner asks. He was the only one I'd ever confided in about Jet's propositions. We'd caught up in England a couple of years ago while the band were on a break and I'd told him all about it after Jet had bombarded me with a series of texts, declaring his undying love.

I nod my head. I struggle to swallow the lump in my throat, but I don't cry. I learnt not to cry after the first few beatings my dad gave me.

"What relationship shit?" Lawson asks.

I take a deep breath and try to speak without my voice wobbling, "Jet, he wanted... He had this idea that me and him should be together."

"What the fuck? What, you mean like together, together?" Dom asks. I nod my head, which is now pounding with a headache. Lawson's phone rings and he heads out into the living area of the suite, talking to someone about a press release and waiting until family members have been notified.

Dom's phone rings next, and he looks across at me as he speaks, "No baby, it's Jet. Reed's fine. Well, not fine, he found him, but he's safe." He covers his eyes with his hand and starts to cry as he explains to Jade, his wife, what's happened. He stands and walks into the bathroom as he talks. Gunner and I stare at each other in silence for a few seconds.

"Someone needs to let his dad know," I say.

"I think that's what Laws is arranging."

"You told Chelsea?" I ask him.

He nods. "I told her while you were still in with the old Bill. Her mum and dad are flying over to look after the kids while we get this all sorted out."

Fuck, we were supposed to fly home today. I can't go anywhere until I go to the police station and they take a full statement, they've already told me that. Then there'll be the funeral.

"The press are gonna be a nightmare with all this happening. I wanted to send the kids home, but Chels wants them close." His eyes come up to meet mine. "You okay, have you called home to let anyone know? Chels said social media is going off about what's happened. Most are reporting that it's you or Jet. You should let your brothers and your dad know."

Fuck. Yeah, my dad, Tyler and Jordan will be freaking out. I look around the bedroom trying to think where I last had my phone. I pick my jeans up from last night and find it in the pocket. It's on silent, and I have dozens of missed calls. I text both my brothers and tell them I'm fine and ask them to call my dad. Then I call Tyler first.

"What the fuck's going on, Reed? Jenna and Ethan are fucking beside themselves here, and Sandra's trying to stop Dad from getting on a plane over there."

My headache increases tenfold at the thought of what they've all been going through. "I'm sorry, the police wouldn't let me talk to anyone." I take a few deep breaths. "Ty?"

"What mate, what's happened? Just tell me you're okay? Ethan's in meltdown. It came up on his Twitter feed that you were dead, then all his mates started texting and Facebooking him. Dad's here, he couldn't sit at home waiting for news, and Sandra wouldn't let him catch a flight to you, so he came here. What the fuck's happened?" I can hear the panic in his voice.

"I'm okay Ty, its Jet..." I pause for a few seconds, "It's Jet, he killed himself. I found him in the bath and…" I trail off. I don't want to be doing this. I don't want to be explaining this again. "Ty, tell dad, Jen and the kids I love them, and I'm sorry. I had to give a statement, and I couldn't make any calls till it was done." Again, my thoughts are a scrambled mess. I just want to go home now. Go home and be with my family. "Tell Ethan not to repeat any of that. Let them all know that I'm okay, but they can't post anything online till Jet's dad has been told."

I hear him sigh into the phone. "So I take it you won't be home tonight?"

"No, no I won't. I've gotta go to the police station and make a formal statement, and then there'll be the funeral. It's pointless coming home just to fly back, and the press will be up my arse everywhere I go anyway." I look around and realise everyone's on their phones. Dom's still in my bathroom, Lawson's out in the living area, and Gun's still sitting in the chair he was in earlier. I'm not sure who he's talking to, but he is wiping tears from under his eyes. He's a big bloke, always working out. His arms are bigger than my legs, and he's probably taller than me by a couple of inches. Watching him cry is just breaking my heart right now, but I still manage to keep a hold of my own tears.

"You gonna be all right on your own with all of that, Reed? I can fly over if you want?" Now I really want to cry.

"I'm all right Ty, honestly. You stay there with Dad, Jenna and the kids. If you have any trouble with the press, ring Sharee at the label on the number I gave you before."

"Have you rung, Jord?"

"No. Can you do it now? I'll talk to him and Dad tomorrow. I just ain't up to explaining it all again."

"Yeah, no problem mate, I can do that."

"Cheers."

"Reed?" I hold my breath, waiting for my brother's words to come, hoping that they won't break me.

"I love you, bro."

"I know you do Ty. I know you do."

"You stay safe, yeah, and if you need Jordy or me to fly over just shout."

"I will, I will. I'll speak to you over the next coupla days and let you know when I'll be home."

"I'm so sorry, Reed. I'm so sorry about, Jet." I end our call.

I leave Dom and Gunner to their conversations and head out to the kitchen in search of some painkillers, just as the buzzer on the door goes. Lawson's still talking and gestures with his head for me to get it. I make sure the security latch is on before I open the door, just in case it's a crazy fan. It's worse, much worse. Amanda's standing in front of me as I look through the gap. I swing the door open and walk away leaving her standing there. She's so not who I want to see at this moment. I sit on the sofa, reach for the remote control and then change my mind, not wanting to watch the bullshit that's likely on the telly right now.

"I've booked a room and organised a press conference for three o'clock. Marty Goldman from the label is with Jet's dad now. I've cancelled everybody's travel arrangements and arranged first-class tickets for Gunner's in-laws. They should be here in the morning. I've organised extra security and the hotel has agreed to supply some of their own." I listen to Amanda's clear, clipped English accent coming from behind me as she informs Lawson of what she has arranged.

"Do you want someone from the funeral home to make contact with Mr Harrison or should I leave him to make his own arrangements?"

"No, send someone over. Marty's telling him that we'll take care of the arrangements. Can you organise some food to be sent up? Reed, what d'ya fancy?" I look over my shoulder and can't help but notice the way Amanda's eyes are on me.

"I'm good mate, I really couldn't face food right now."

He shakes his head at me. "Dom, Gunner, get out here," he orders. The other boys walk out, and we all stand and wait to hear what Lawson has to say. "I've called a press conference for three. I want you to get some food inside you, have a shower and try and look like you're doing okay." He looks each of us in the eye, and I think for a few seconds he's going to cry. "This is fucking horrible, and it's only gonna get worse over the next few days. Let's face the press together and then come back to my room and get totally fucked up. Let *me* answer any questions about *how* Jet died and about the band's future. Reed, it's all gonna be aimed at you, as the word already seems to be out that you were the one who found him. Just answer what you feel is appropriate and leave the rest to me." He looks at all of us again and lets out a long sigh. "How's everyone doing, honestly? How's Chelsea and Jade?" he asks Dom and Gun. "We've put extra security in place throughout the hotel and booked out all the rooms on this floor. I think it'll be best if the kids all stay here or fly home when we go to New York for the funeral, assuming that's where his dad wants it held."

"What about what Jet wanted?" Dom asks.

"What?" Lawson frowns in confusion.

"Jet wanted his funeral to take place at his house in Santa Monica. Then he wants to be cremated and his ashes scattered in the Pacific, in front of the house. He's talked about it a few times. He said it was written in his will."

We've all heard Jet say this. I don't know why Laws isn't remembering it.

"Shit! Yeah, he did. I remember him talking about it now." Lawson's face suddenly crumbles, and he starts to cry. Amanda reaches out her hand to him and pats him on the shoulder. It's a cold disingenuous move, and for the first time in a long time, I feel the need to actually want to give someone a cuddle, or is it that I'm suddenly overcome with the need to be cuddled, to be held. This life we lead is so fucking shallow and superficial. Until Gunner put his arms around me earlier, I actually don't remember the last time someone put their arms around me in a gesture of pure love and affection, because they just wanted to reassure me everything would be all right. It was probably the last time I left England, which is now over a year ago. Don't get me wrong, I've been touched. The boys, Dom, Jet and Gun, we all go in for the manly back slap kind of cuddle, and then there are the photos with the fans, they usually put their arms around me. But the last time, I had a real full on cuddle was probably from my niece, Evie.

She's my brother Jordan's little girl, and for some unknown reason, the kid loves me. All my nieces and nephews love me, but especially Evie. When I last left England, she'd clung to my neck and cried when I was leaving for the airport. She begged me not to go and asked to come with me. My brother had to uncurl her little fat fingers from around my neck to prize her hands away. I hate being away so much. Every chance I get I go back to England, but the kids always seem to have changed so much in the time I've been away. I

Skype and FaceTime them as much as possible, especially Ethan, he's my only nephew. We talk every Sunday afternoon, after his football match. We talk football, music and now that he's turned sixteen, we talk girls too if his mum, dad and sister aren't about.

I reach up and drag both my hands through my hair. I feel like my insides are on fire. I stand up from the chair I've sat down on at some stage, but my legs don't want to move, so I sit down again. My skin feels clammy, my heart's pounding and I suddenly feel sick. I want to go home. I want to be with my brothers and my dad. I want to be a million miles away from all this bullshit, and I don't want any of it to be true.

CHAPTER FIVE

J UST OVER AN HOUR LATER, we're all sitting in a row behind a table, the world's press piled into the hotel's conference room. A collection of reporters, television cameras, photographers and boom mics, along with a sea of faces sit, crouch and stand before us.

Lawson puts his hand up to silence everyone. The lawyer that was with me earlier sits to Lawson's left, I sit to his right. Next to me is Dom, then Gunner. The room slowly becomes quiet as Lawson clears his throat.

"I'm gonna read a short statement, and then I'll take a few of your questions."

He clears his throat again. "At ten forty-seven a.m. today, Jethro Matthias Harrison was discovered in his hotel room at the Ritz Carlton. Jet was found to be unconscious and unresponsive. EMT's were called to the scene, and despite numerous attempts to revive him, he was declared dead at eleven-eighteen. The cause of death is yet to be established, but the police are not treating it as suspicious and are not looking for anyone else at this time. Obviously, our first thoughts are with Jet's family. His dad and next of kin have been notified, and we hope that you'll be respectful and give them the space and privacy they'll need to grieve."

Dom lets out a sob from beside me and gets up and leaves the table. This is going to be so hard for him. They had been lifelong friends, gone through high school and college together. Jet was best man at Dom's wedding and godfather to his firstborn. Gunner moves up a seat and drapes his arm across my back and over my shoulder.

Lawson continues, "Jet was an exceptionally talented musician, intelligent, witty and loyal. He was a true friend, loved by his bandmates and adored by his fans. Millions across the world will be mourning with us at his untimely passing." He looks along to where Gun and I are sitting and swallows a few times and then back out at the sea of faces. "I'll answer just a couple of your questions. Please keep them brief and don't waste my time asking things that are disrespectful, or that you know full well I won't answer."

The cameras have been flashing the whole time we've been seated, but they quiet for a minute as the journalists call out their questions. The shouting is so loud that I can't make out a word any of them are saying, it's just noise, flashing lights and more noise. My head is pounding, and I want to get the fuck out of here.

Lawson points to a female reporter whose face is familiar. I think that she's interviewed us before. The room quiets marginally as she looks to me and says, "This question's for Reed." Lawson looks at me and nods. I nod back letting him know I'm okay with it.

She's short and slim with long fair hair. She's almost swallowed up by all the other reporters, cameras and boom mics surrounding her. I remember her now, her name's Brittany or Whitney or one of those all American kind of names. Her eyes are blue, and she gives me a small smile before she asks her question. I remember now why I liked her before, she saw us as humans when she's interviewed us in the past. We weren't just a commodity, she seemed genuinely interested. The photographer that was with her that day was a tall skinny girl, covered in tattoos and she introduced her to us as her wife, Charlotte or Charlie, something like that. I've no idea why I'm sitting here thinking all of this right now. Maybe it's better than thinking about anything else.

"Reed, just wanted to say to you and the rest of the boys from

Shift how sorry I am for your loss." I nod my head and try to say thank you, but my mouth is so dry that my lips move, but no sound comes out. "Is it true that it was you that found Jet this morning and that he took his own life?" The image of Jet lying at the bottom of his blood-filled bath suddenly flashes into my head, and I can't breathe. His eyes were open wide and staring right at me, just like my mum, just like Miles. I look at Gunner, then at Lawson, but I can't get any words out. I push back on my chair but stand too soon, and the table tilts as my knees hit it. I still can't breathe. I can breathe out, I just can't get a breath in. A jug of water and the glasses start sliding to the floor. Cameras start flashing, and the noise, the shouting and the questions start again. I just need to get away from all of it.

Lawson and Gun are at my sides and guide me out of the conference room and straight into the lift. I can hear them talking and asking if I'm okay, but the sound is muffled like I'm underwater. I bend over and stare at the floor, trying to focus on getting some air into my lungs.

"Fuck," I manage to say as I stand up straight.

The lift door opens, and I hear Lawson say, "I've had all your stuff moved to my room, Reed. I didn't think you'd want to stay in there." He gestures with his chin toward my old room. I both shake and nod my head, as I'm unsure of what the appropriate answer is. He opens the door to his suite with the key card, and I rush through to the bathroom and hurl into the toilet. The bourbon I drank earlier burns my throat on its way back up. My stomach now feels as empty as my chest and my heart. I splash my face with water and rinse my mouth.

As I step back out into the suite, Gunner, Lawson, Dom, Amanda, Chelsea and Jade are all in the room. Dom passes me a shot glass full of vodka, I knock it back. That's the last thing I really remember until my feet touchdown in England a week later.

CHAPTER SIX

NINA

MY FORK IS IN FRONT of my face with a small piece of salmon and rocket sitting on it. I'm not sure if my mouth is open, but it most certainly should be as I stare in disbelief at my husband. I can't believe the complete and utter bullshit he's spewing to a potential client right now.

"We've thought about it on and off over the last few years." He turns to me. "Haven't we darling?" I look at him blankly and place my knife and fork down. The little appetite I had, gone in an instant. "But to be perfectly honest," Marcus continues, "we like our life the way it is. We have a nice home, we enjoy our jobs and like to be able to take off for a holiday any time we want. Starting a family would change all of that."

I look down at my plate and swallow past the lump that's just appeared in my throat for some reason. Actually, the bullshitting virus my husband permanently seems to be suffering from must be spreading, because that's a big fat lie I just told myself. I know full well why the lump has appeared in my throat. It appears every time a conversation starts up around the topic of having children. The instant the words family, children, baby or pregnant are mentioned around me, it appears, that lump, that tightening in my chest and then it starts. It's like my blood turns to ice but not liquid ice. No, no, more like little jagged crystals of ice, sharp and pointy. Scratching their way through my veins. It starts at my toes and works its way through my body until the sharp, cold, pointy pieces push through the chambers of my heart. All the while, images of him... of us... of that afternoon and night flash through my mind. Images of when he left me all alone with my fear, my pain and the blood, so much blood. *Who would've thought that there'd be so much blood?*

"So what is it you do for work, Nina?" Charlotte Walters asks me. I pick up my napkin and dab at my mouth and above my top lip, which is probably displaying beads of sweat after my freak out of a few seconds ago. I look up at Charlotte, and her brown eyes meet mine, she gives me a slight smile, and I have the distinct feeling that she knows that I was just now on the verge of a psychological break-down... I seem to always be on the edge of some kind of breakdown when I'm around my husband or brother, or parents.

"I have a chain of four, hair, beauty and day spa salons." Her eyebrows raise with a look of surprise, but before she can speak, Marcus interrupts us, "Keeps her busy and out of trouble, doesn't it sweets?" I don't even look at him. I know I'll be in trouble later. I know he'll throw a little hissy fit about the fact that the conversation has steered to the topic of my career and hasn't been all about him. My husband is an egomaniacal arsehole sometimes, but I know how to calm him down, I'm an expert at stroking his ego.

"JUST ONE NIGHT, JUST FOR one fucking night, could the conver-sation not have ended up being all about you?"

I stare out of the window of the taxi, not bothering to face him as I reply, "Charlotte asked what I did, so I answered. Besides, it was you that mentioned how much we both *love* our careers." I use air quotes and finally turn around and face him.

"Well, it doesn't set a good impression telling them the truth. I know Andre Walters, he would see it as a sign of weakness. I want his business, and the last thing I need him to be thinking is that I'm weak." It's Marcus's turn to stare out of the window now.

"Just tell them it's me. Tell anyone that you need to that *I'm* the one with the fertility problem, *I'm* the one that can't conceive."

"Well, let's face it Nina, there's a bloody good chance that *is* the case." He remains staring out the window, oblivious to the effect his words have on me. I wipe the tears from under my eyes and stay silent for the rest of the journey home.

CHAPTER SEVEN

I TAKE OFF MY MAKEUP and clean my teeth. I've kept my bra, knickers and hold-up stockings on and hopefully, this will provide enough incentive for my husband to show me some attention. It's been almost three weeks… three whole weeks since we last made love. Since we had any kind of sexual contact really, apart from the odd kiss on the cheek. Marcus has never been particularly affectionate, but now, now I feel more like his sister than his wife and lover.

I climb into bed and press myself into him from behind. Sliding my stockinged toes, up and down his leg and my hand around his hip trying to reach into his boxers. He grabs my hand, takes it in both of his and brings it up to his mouth and kisses the back of it.

"Go to sleep, Nina. It's late, I'm tired. I'll sort you out in the morning before I go to golf."

My heart sinks and tears once again sting my eyes from his words… 'He'll sort me out in the morning?' Like he was doing me some kind of massive favour? Like being a thirty-one-year-old woman and wanting to have sex with your thirty-five-year-old husband, after a night out together was a ridiculous notion. What was wrong with me? What was it he found so repugnant, that despite the fact that I was lying here next to him, wearing my black, lacy, Victoria's Secret underwear and stockings, my husband wasn't even interested in turning around and looking at me, let alone giving me a goodnight kiss, or heaven forbid, fucking me?

Fuck.

Fucking.

Marcus and I have never fucked, that wasn't his style. Actually, he didn't really have a style, or rhythm for that matter. In the eight years we'd been married, he'd never once given me an orgasm. I managed them often enough on my own. Either by touching myself or by using my super duper, thrusting butterfly vibrator. But I wanted my husband to make me come. I wanted my husband to take his time, to lick and suck and fuck me to an earth-shattering, leg shaking, clit twitching orgasm. Instead, all I usually got was three thrusts, a squeeze of my tit and a grunt to let me know it was all over.

I know that sex isn't everything. But if he just paid me *some* kind of attention, if he could only *notice* me as a person, just once, it might help me not to feel so alone and so lonely. All I wanted was to feel loved and desired by my husband. He told me he loved me every day. He told me I was beautiful all the time, but he never showed it, he never made me feel it. He'd chased me for so long before we were together, almost begging me to go out with him and yet, when I finally said yes, it was like all the fight and passion he displayed while trying to convince me to go for a drink or to dinner with him, just vanished.

I should never have married him! It was my own fault, I knew what I was in for. Our sex life was passionless from the very first awkward attempt, and I didn't love him, not then, and I'm not really sure that I do now. But then my brother stepped in, bringing up my past indiscretion, threatening to take my story to the papers. Knowing full well the damage that might possibly do to my newly flourishing business and my mother's political career. Then he pulled his trump card. He'd loaned me sixty thousand pounds when I set up the first salon with Sophie, and if I didn't marry Marcus, he wanted it back, in full.

MUCH TO MY PARENT'S ABSOLUTE disgust, instead of staying in school until I was eighteen and taking my A levels, I'd left at just sixteen and found myself a job at a local hair salon. I'd never had any desire to be a hairdresser. After the way my life had changed on that New Year's Eve, and Conner had made the choices he had, never attempting to contact me again despite the letters I'd sent to him, I'd become a little lost and rebellious. I wasn't really sure what direction to take with my life, I just knew I needed to be on a path that I had a lot more control over. A path where I didn't need to rely too much on other people.

I was desperately hurt and heartbroken inside, but curling up into a ball and crying all day wasn't going to change anything. So I left school and took the first job that was offered to me. I did a three-month trial and discovered that hairdressing was what I was born to do. I finished my apprenticeship, did a further two years as a stylist, and then went into partnership with Sophie buying our own salon. Soph's parents were great. They lent her the money she needed for her share of the setup. My parents quite literally laughed in my face, and the bank did something very similar. My brother then stepped in and offered to lend me the money… as long as I agreed to go on a date with Marcus. Little did I know I was selling my soul to the devil.

Pearce and Marcus worked together at Marcus's dad's law firm. When Marcus's dad retired, Marcus would be put in charge, and Pearce was hoping to be made partner. Me dating the boss's son would be doing him a massive favour apparently. What I wasn't expecting was for Marcus to propose just six months later. I was twenty-two at the time, and I didn't want to get married.

All of my energy was spent on building my business. I explained all of this to him, and at the time, seemed to take it well enough and respected my decision. I didn't want to hurt him, but I just didn't love him. It was that simple. I was still numb inside from everything that had gone down with Conner and to make it worse, he was starting to make it big with his band 'Shift' and as happy as I was for him, it hurt, it hurt so fucking much.

I'd see his face on the cover of the magazines that we had in the salon, and I'd feel so much pride in the fact that he'd turned his life around and done so well, but I was also a little bitter. We had such plans. I'd really believed that we were so in love, but he just left me lying in that hospital, and despite all of the phone calls that were made, he chose to go out and sell drugs with his brother and had almost gotten himself killed. I don't know all of the exact details of what went on that night, I was high on the morphine that'd been pumped through my system. When I heard he'd been arrested and then remanded, I sent a couple of letters off to him, just asking for an explanation as to why he'd chosen to do that and to not be with me. He never replied. So I took that as a blatant knockback and decided to move on with my life. I deleted his number from my phone, buried the hurt, the sense of loss and betrayal deep down inside of me and carved out a new life for myself.

They say you never forget your first, and I'm sure that's probably true, but when your first becomes a singer and guitarist in one of the world's biggest bands, whose is heard continuously on the radio, and whose gorgeous face is continuously plastered all over every magazine, and permanently on TV, it's pretty much impossible.

For a few years, I fantasised that he would come back for me, hold me in his arms and tell me it's all been a big misunderstanding. But as the band's popularity grew and I heard the rumours and saw the images of him with a different woman every week, I knew that any thoughts or feelings Conner had for me were long gone and forgotten.

I'd managed to ward off any more proposals from Marcus for three whole months after his original offer of marriage and then a few things happened at once. Marcus's dad dropped dead on the golf course, and Marcus was put in charge of Newman and Associates law firm. Marcus, once again proposed marriage, but this time he'd told my brother what he was going to do and my brother informed me in no uncertain terms if I didn't accept, he would be pulling his money out of my business, with immediate effect.

We were just, only just, starting to break even and there was absolutely no way I could afford to pay my brother back, but I also didn't want to marry Marcus. He was a nice enough person, well off and successful and he was actually really good looking, in a very 'law-erish' kind of way, but I didn't want to spend the rest of my life with him. I told my brother that I would go to the bank and see if they would loan me the money. My brother promptly told me that if I didn't say yes and accept Marcus's proposal, then he would go to the papers and tell them everything about my relationship with Conner Reed, including what happened on that final night of the last millennium.

I didn't know what kind of effect that would have on my business or on my mother's career. She was now the local MP for our area and minister for something to do with things that went on overseas. I've never been sure of her exact title. But, I also didn't know what kind of effect the news might have on Conner's blossoming career. The press had already gone to town on the fact that he'd been to prison and that his mother had been murdered. Whatever our history was, I didn't want his name splashed all over the papers for the wrong reasons again.

So, I accepted. I thought I might grow to love Marcus and we would be okay. I tried, I really did try. I'm still trying, but nights like tonight just leave me numb and lonely. They leave me sad and regretful of my choices. They leave me feeling nothing but anger toward my brother and the way he manipulated me, but most of all they leave me feeling empty.

I let my silent tears roll from my eyes, into my ears and around the back of my neck before I eventually curl up into the foetal position and drift off to sleep. Knowing that I have no one but myself to blame for the way my life has turned out. I should've been stronger, I should've stood up to my brother and not let him coerce me into my sham of a marriage, and as much as I wanted to do something about it, I knew that I wouldn't. I would remain the dutiful wife, daughter and sister. I would remain a coward and accept my fate.

CHAPTER EIGHT

I WAKE TO A COLD, empty space on my husband's side of the bed. I wasn't a particularly heavy sleeper, so it always amazed me how he was able to slip out of bed and get ready for golf without waking me.

I stare up at the white ceiling of my bedroom and let out a long breath while contemplating the day ahead. After spending so many years working Saturdays, Soph and I had decided that the business was doing well enough that we could now afford to take the weekends off. We would still go in if there were something big like a wedding happening, but other than that we stayed away from the salons on Saturdays.

Despite me now being home, Marcus had never diverted from his usual plans and still spent most of his weekends on the golf course. This left me to my own devices most Saturdays and quite often on a Sunday too. I didn't mind. It didn't matter if my husband was home or not, I felt lonely regardless.

I look across at the clock and am surprised to see it's already after nine. I sit up and prop my back against the pillows and check my phone. Scrolling through my Facebook, Twitter and Instagram accounts, I check my personal and business emails. There's nothing particularly exciting happening in my online world, so I climb out of bed and head to the kitchen, almost falling over my dog Duchess as I step out of my bedroom door.

"What are you doing up here, Duch?" I bend down and scratch behind her ears. I love my dog, but I don't love my house smelling of dog, so the rule is that she's only allowed as far as the kitchen. She's outside most of the day so this isn't a problem, but she sleeps in the kitchen/dining area at night so the doors are always kept shut to stop her from wandering all over the house. Marcus obviously forgot to close the doors behind him this morning.

Duchess looks up at me with her big brown eyes. She's a super-intelligent dog, and I'm pretty sure she knows full well that she shouldn't be up here.

"Come on then, let's get you some breakfast." She wags her tail as she follows me downstairs. I open the back doors to a bright sunny morning and fill her bowl with a couple of scoops of dry food. Shutting the door behind me, I head back to the kitchen and make a coffee.

After I've had my caffeine fix and a muesli bar, I throw on my workout gear and take Duchess with me for a brisk walk around the park. It's after twelve once we get home. I shower, pull on a pair of shorts and a bikini top, pour myself a large glass of wine and lay out on a sun lounger in the garden. It's late May and a beautiful, early summer's day. I switch between reading a book on my Kindle, throwing the ball for Duchess to fetch and snoozing. Only getting up to top up my wine glass and to find a bag of crisps to munch on. I should really make myself something a little bit more substantial to eat, but I'm feeling lazy, and my liquid lunch has made me feel sleepy. I jump when my phone vibrates and chimes with a text message from Sophie.

Watchya doooooin????

I smile down at my phone as I read her message. Not that it's funny, it's just that it's from Soph and I can't help but smile when I think of her. She's my best friend and business partner, and I love the bones of the girl. She was spending the day shopping with her mum today. She'd invited me to join them, but the idea of trawling around a shopping centre on my day off held absolutely no appeal to me, so I declined. Enjoying a day to myself in the sunshine instead.

Me: *Well, I was enjoying a snooze in the sunshine, but some inconsiderate arsehole sent me a text and woke me up :(Why what you dooooooin???*

Sophie: *Well, that sucks sweaty balls, you shoulda gave them a bollocking!*

Me: *Pointless, they're too ignorant to care!*

Sophie: *Oh, harsh.*

Me: *Yeah, but totally necessary.*

I await her further response but get nothing for a few minutes, so I close my eyes and nod back off to sleep. I almost take off, God only knows how much time later when my phone actually rings.

It's Soph, but before I can complain about her waking me up again she asks, "Babe, do you have the telly on?"

I sit up on my lounger, goose bumps breaking out on my skin despite the late afternoon sun still beating down on me.

"No, I'm still in the garden, I've not even had my music on today."

She doesn't reply, and in those few beats of silence, my stomach rolls over and in on itself. I've absolutely no idea why, but my heart starts to pound in my chest so hard that I can feel my blood pumping strongly through the veins in my neck.

"Soph?" If my screen weren't telling me that the call was still active, I would've thought she'd hung up.

"Babe, I'm on my way over. I'll be there in literally five minutes. Just stay where you are. Stay in the garden."

"Soph, you're freaking me the fuck out. What's wrong?" I get up and head inside, going straight into the lounge and switching on the television. It turns on tuned to the weather channel. Typical Marcus, checking to see the forecast, making sure his day of golf won't be spoilt by rain.

"I've put the telly on. What am I looking for?"

"Neen… please… turn it off and just wait for me to get there. Please Neen, I'm not fucking about. Turn off the telly. I'm just rounding the corner into your street. I'm less than a minute away."

I turn the telly off and go and open the front door, but head straight back to the lounge. As soon as I hear Sophie come through the door, I turn the television back on and switch it to a news channel. A reporter's talking into a camera from in front of a hotel. I've no idea where in the world it is as I look more at the picture, not really listening to what's being reported.

Sophie's suddenly beside me. She takes the remote out of my hand and must press mute, just as an image of Conner, then Jet Harrison appear on the screen. Sophie takes my hand and tries to lead me over to my sofa, but I snatch my hand away. The room, or is it me, is swaying and I can feel the sweat on my top lip despite the fact that I suddenly feel freezing cold.

I look at Sophie and shake my head, terrified of what she's about to tell me. My mouth is hanging open, my eyes fixed, but not focused on her and I have the sensation of pins and needles all over my body. I'm trying desperately to make sense of what I see on the screen.

Conner.

Something's happened.

Something's happened, to my Conner.

All that's going through my head over and over is…

No.

Oh God.

Please no.

Not Conner.

I don't want this to be true.

I don't know what it is, but I don't want it to be bad.

Oh God.

Oh God.

"What? What is it Soph? What's happened? I don't... Soph, please tell me what's happened?"

"Neen, they're reporting that a body has been found in a hotel room shared by Conner and Jet. Nothing at all has been confirmed yet, but that's what's being reported."

I shake my head at her. I know it's been fifteen years, but I'd know. Don't ask me how, but I just know that if anything were to happen to him, I'd know, I'd feel it. I continue shaking my head, my mouth opening and closing, but no words coming out.

"Where? Where is this? Where are they?" I point at the television screen. The huge, enormous sixty inch, curved television screen is Marcus's pride and joy. His newest toy, but right now, I want to put my fist through the fucking thing. If the images stop, if I can't see the pictures or hear the reporters then it won't be true. It can't be true!

"Chicago babe. Shift's tour ended there last night." I shiver involuntarily. I'm freezing now, icy cold.

"Sit down, Neen. I'm gonna run up and get you a hoodie or something. Then I'll pour us a wine." I stare at her and give my head a small shake again, or is it a nod? I don't know, I can't think straight. I don't sit down, I remain standing in the middle of the room, staring at the television.

I hear Sophie's footsteps as she runs back down the stairs. Her phone rings at the same time as she passes me my hoodie. I pull it over my head and actually feel colder for the first few seconds that I'm wearing it, and I'm not sure if it's a shiver or an uncontrollable shake that rattles through me.

"Yeah, we're watching now," I hear Sophie saying into her phone from the kitchen, where she's gone to pour us a wine.

"Nina, I'm at her house now... hang on a sec."

She walks back into my lounge carrying a bottle of wine and two glasses. I watch her intently, anything but look back at that bloody television screen.

"Neen, please sit down, hun. You're standing there like a weirdo." She steers me over to the sofa and forces me to sit. I keep staring at her while she sits down and continues with her phone call.

"Do you know any more than what they're saying on the telly?" I don't know who she's talking to, but I'm hoping it's her brother Josh. Maybe with his connections, he might know something more than what's being reported.

"Oh, really? Fuck Josh." Her eyes come up to meet mine, but they give me nothing.

Josh runs his own events management company. He organises global tours for some of the world's biggest bands and artists. His company organises various events and promotions at club openings, film premiere after parties and all sorts of other occasions where a celebration might be needed. He'd done really well for himself, rubbing shoulders with the world's rich and famous and I knew that he'd kept in contact with Conner over the years. They used to be really close. Josh was away on a skiing trip that New Year when everything fell apart and Conner was sent to prison. I know that he used to visit him every couple of weeks, but when I didn't hear anything back after pouring my heart out in the two letters I'd asked Josh to pass on to him, I just stayed away from Sophie's house for a while. I stayed away from everyone and everything really. I became a bit of a recluse… sat at home, stayed in my room, ate crap and piled on the weight. Once I made the decision to leave school and get a job, I came back to life a little bit. Working in the hairdressers and dealing with the public was good for me and especially good for my self-confidence, which had been hovering around level zero after Conner had left me. Added to that was my mother always telling me I needed to lose some weight. My brother also joined in that chant, making snide comments whenever he was visiting my parents' house.

All of which caused me to retreat to my bedroom and just eat more crap.

"Yeah, I will do. Call me as soon as you hear anything. Love your face too. Bye."

My eyelids suddenly felt heavy, the adrenalin had slowed, and now I just wanted to sleep.

Sophie pours us both a glass of wine and slumps back into the sofa opposite me.

I watch her, really not sure if I want her to tell me what Josh has said or if I just want to leave this room, go up to bed and sleep soundly for a few hours, waking up to find that this has all been a bad dream.

"The only thing he knows for sure is that it's a band member, and the body was found in Jet and Conner's room."

I take a sip of my wine. "It's not him, I know it's not him." Sophie tilts her head to the side and nods at me slowly. "Don't look at me like that, Soph. I know we were young, I know it was a long time ago, and I know he did what he did." I take another gulp of my wine, my mouth feeling incredibly dry. "And just like I know all of that to be true, I know that Conner's not dead. I would know." I nod in an attempt to reaffirm my words.

She studies me for a bit, sipping on her wine. "Have you ever spoken to him since that night? I know we've never really spoken about it, but have you ever had any contact with him whatsoever?"

I shake my head, my eyes stinging with tears. Even after all these years, the hurt and rejection I felt back then is still painful. I've just never understood why he did what he did. Perhaps if I'd been given an explanation, some answers, I would've been able to move on.

"No, the last time I spoke to him was when I got to your house that morning and called to tell him I was going shopping with you." I chew on the inside of my cheek. "Pearce said he tried calling him a few times from the hospital, but he never answered."

Sophie takes a large gulp of her wine. I shrug, my nose stinging at the tears that desperately want to escape. "I wrote him a couple of letters and gave them to Josh to give to him while he was inside, but I never heard a word back, not a single word." I make a little noise as I speak and try not to cry. A tear finally wins the battle that I've been fighting to fall and plops from my eye onto my left cheek. I swipe it away, angry at myself for getting upset about something that happened so long ago. Angry that I'm so upset that something bad may have happened to someone that probably hasn't given me a second thought these past fifteen years, who has probably forgotten that I even exist.

"Josh never told me, that you'd given him letters I mean."

I lean toward our wine glasses with the bottle in my hand and top them up. They're big glasses, meant for red really, but we use them for white, something that continuously pisses my husband off, like the world will end because I've used the wrong glass.

I drain the bottle into the glasses, take another gulp and say, "Yeah, I gave them to him but we never really spoke about it afterwards. I couldn't face Josh back then. Couldn't face him telling me anything about Conner, well, him not telling me anything was really the problem. Every time I saw your brother, I was so hopeful, desperate in fact, that he might have a message for me, that in the end, it was a lot less painful to just avoid him. So, yeah, anyway, I never heard back from him, and I've never tried to make contact since."

We sit in silence for a few minutes and sip on our wine. The television is still muted and the scenes being shown are fans of Shift standing in front of the hotel they're staying at. They are holding onto each other and crying. Sophie's phone chimes as it receives a text message and my stomach has another little dance party inside my belly. I keep my eyes on the telly and notice that the banner along the bottom of the screen is displaying a message that states that the band and their management will be holding a press conference at three p.m., Chicago time. I instantly reach for my phone on the coffee table to work out what time that will be in the UK.

"They're holding a press conference at about eight o'clock tonight our time," Sophie states.

I put my phone back down and let out a long breath.

"You doing all right, Neen, honestly?"

I'm closer to Sophie than I am any of my family members. As ashamed as I should be, but I'm actually not, of the fact that I love her more than my parents or brother.

We work together five days a week, and we have dinner together at least once a week. I visit *her* mum more than I visit my own, but she has no idea about the world of hurt I've lived with these past fifteen years. She has no idea about the deal I did with my brother to get the loan to buy our first salon, and she has no idea how desperately I was trying to make my marriage work. I burst into tears, and she's at my side in an instant.

"Oh Nina, come on babe. Let's not get too upset till we know what's going on."

I shake my head while wiping my eyes with the back of my hand.

"I don't know why I care, Soph. I really wish I didn't give a shit. He left me… he left me at the worst possible moment in my life. After everything we'd planned, after everything he'd promised me, he just left me." I gulp on my drink and almost choke on my words, my sobs and my wine. "He left me lying in that hospital bed and went out to sell drugs with his brother. I just wish I knew why Soph? I just wish I knew what happened between me speaking to him that morning and him doing what he did that night…" I pause for a few seconds and try and draw a breath. The wine has hit me already, and I'm feeling light-headed and emotional.

"Has Josh never said anything? Never mentioned that Conner had told him how he ended up with Miles that night?" She tucks her legs underneath her and sits back into the corner of the sofa.

"The only thing he ever asked was where we were that night. My mum had already told me that she'd told him, we all went to a function at some hotel, so I just stuck with that story."

Sophie's mum, Jen, had come to the hospital that night and held me while I cried myself to sleep. I'd never even told my own mother about my stay in the hospital and I probably never would.

"Have you ever told him the truth since?"

She shakes her head. "No hun, that's not my secret to tell. As far as I know, the only people that know are me, you, your brother, Marcus and my mum. I don't think my dad ever even knew for sure what happened, and he certainly never mentioned it if he did work it out."

My phone alerts me of a text message, it's Marcus. I swipe it open to read.

Lunch ran over. Still have another 4 holes to play. I'll get dinner out with the boys so it'll probs be a late one. Don't wait up. xox

I roll my eyes. Fucking golf! It bores me senseless. Bit like my husband, and if I'm being honest—which the wine tends to make me do—exactly like my marriage.

"It's Marcus, telling me not to wait up."

"How're things going between you two?"

Sophie's aware that we've been trying for a baby and that things have been a little bit tense between us.

"They're okay, mostly."

"Mostly?" she asks with raised eyebrows. Sophie's not a fan of Marcus, she thinks he's too stuck up and full of himself. She's probably right, he can be, but he's not like it *all* the time just *most* of the time.

"He's still refusing to go and have any tests done. Reckons that we need to give it another six months."

"And are you happy with that?"

I shake my head. "No, I've made an appointment to see my doctor on Tuesday. I need to know if there's a problem. Marcus is pretty convinced that if there is, it'll be with me, so I just need to prepare myself. I need to know one way or another."

"Neen, I'm sorry, but your husband can be such a prick some-times. Who the fuck tells their wife that if they fail to conceive, then it's probably their fault?" I open my mouth to speak, but she puts her hand out to stop me. "No, let me just say this. He should be supporting and reassuring you right now. He should be telling you that everything is gonna be fine and that it'll all work out. Not disap-pearing every weekend to play fucking golf, and definitely not telling you that it's your fault you've failed so far in getting knocked up."

I smile at her. "I'm actually glad he's at golf most weekends. It means I don't have to deal with him," I admit.

"If you feel like that, why the fuck are you trying for a baby with him? Why the fuck did you marry him in the first place for that matter?" I look at her for a few seconds, debating whether I should tell her the truth. Before I can answer, she surprises me by asking, "Do you love him, Neen? Can you see yourself raising a family and growing old with him?" My eyes meet hers for a long moment. "I've seen Nina Matthews in love. I remember how you used to look at Conner and I've seen the way you look at Marcus, and it don't compare, babe."

"Soph, I was fifteen and stupid."

"No Nina, you were fifteen and in love. Now you're thirty-one and most definitely not in love." She drains her glass. "D'ya have more wine? Please tell me you have more wine?" I nod and go to get up. "Nah, you stay here, I'll fetch it. Stay here and think about your answer. I've wondered for years why you married Marcus Newman. I was shocked that you ever even agreed to go out with him, let alone decided to marry him. I'm your best friend Neen, I'm sick of being bullshitted to. I want you to be honest with me." She's standing in front of me now with her hands on her hips. "Now, where's the wine?"

"Fridge in the utility room." I flick my wrist and point my finger in the general direction of where the wine can be found.

I look over at the television, the banner along the bottom is just repeating the facts that they know. *"Body found in hotel room being shared by Conner Reed and Jet Harrison. Press conference to be held at three p.m. local time."*

It's just gone six-thirty here. In less than two hours, I could quite possibly be facing the fact that the man I've thought about on a daily basis since I just turned fifteen might be dead. World famous rock star, Conner Reed, the boy I gave my virginity to, might actually be dead.

"So, come on. No bullshitting me." Sophie passes the glass of wine she's just poured me. We both curl our legs underneath us and sit in the corners of the sofa, facing each other.

"Neen, I know, I was there that day, but we've never really spoken about it over the years. I've always assumed it was just too painful for you, so I've left well alone." She looks over my face, and I can see her eyes shine with unshed tears.

"Please be honest with me. I'm your bestie. We're supposed to share shit, but I've always felt like I was missing something about that night… about you marrying Marcus. There's some part of the story I don't know about."

I hear Duchess whine from outside the patio doors and turn to see her sitting there, her sad eyes watching us through the glass.

"I need to feed, Duch."

"No you don't." Sophie stares at me, unwavering.

"Yeah, I do, and when I come back, I'll tell you everything."

I SETTLE MYSELF BACK DOWN into my corner of the sofa, wine in hand. I take a sip, despite the fact that I already feel quite pissed and know that I should really stop.

Sophie has turned the sound back up on the television, but it's just going over the earlier reports and showing the room where the press conference will be held. I feel sick to my stomach. I know I shouldn't, I'm a married woman, and it was all a very long time ago, but for me, Conner Reed was it. He was the one, but I rarely let myself admit that.

Soph mutes the telly and turns her gaze back to me.

"Are you still in love with Conner Reed?"

Well, I wasn't expecting that. Despite the wine I've consumed, my mouth is unnaturally dry again, and I run my tongue over my teeth before I speak.

"That night, that New Year's Eve, Conner and I were leaving." She frowns and tilts her head to one side.

"Leaving?" I sip my wine and nod my head. "Leaving where?"

"Here, leaving town," I reply.

Her shoulders slump, and she looks all over my face for a few seconds.

"You mean like, running away?" she shakes her head as she speaks. Like that couldn't possibly be what I meant.

"Exactly like running away," I tell her, not breaking eye contact as I speak. Her face crumbles as she looks down into her wine glass.

"And you didn't tell me? You weren't going to tell me, were you? You were just going to leave and not say a word."

My heart pounds hard in my chest, and my face burns at my admission. "We were going to contact you later, once all the fuss had died down."

We're both quiet for a few seconds. I need to explain this adequately so that she understands.

"We didn't want to put you and Josh in a position where you would've had to lie for us, so we didn't tell either of you."

Sophie has a tear on her cheek as she looks up at me.

"So what happened then? Why didn't he turn up? Why didn't he come to the hospital? Pearce called and called him."

Now it's my turn to cry. The ache in my chest travels up through my throat and escapes through my mouth as a sob. "I don't know… I don't know, Soph. All these years and I still don't know why he didn't come, why he just left me there?"

Her phone goes off, and I lean forward and grab a couple of tissues from the box on the coffee table and wipe my eyes while she's reading her message.

"It's Josh. The press conference is about to start."

She comes and sits next to me and turns the sound back up on the television with the remote. The cameras are all pointed at a table that's empty, apart from some drinking glasses and a jug of water. Suddenly the flashes start going off, and there's movement in the corner of the screen. A man walks out and sits down behind the table, I've no idea who he is. He has some pieces of A4 paper in his hand which he shuffles a couple of times before laying them down flat and staring at them. I'm so focused on him and his actions that I don't at first notice Lawson Knight, Shift's manager, appear and then take a seat.

And then he's there.

He's there.

Alive.

He's alive!

The noise that escapes me is like nothing I've ever heard a human make before. I laugh, cry, sob, choke and try not to vomit all at once. My tears are instant, but I don't care. In that split-second, the whole world can go fuck itself.

He's alive.

Conner Reed is alive!

I'm almost overwhelmed by the relief that I feel. Sophie has her arm around my shoulder, our heads are pressed together, and we both cry. We listen as Lawson makes a statement, announcing the death of Jet Harrison, but my eyes are unmoving, focused solely on

Conner's face until Dominic Trip, the band guitarist, lets out a loud sob then stands and leaves the table. He's a big man, but his shoulders shake as he loses control and quietly cries unashamedly while trying to escape the glare of the world's press.

Lawson carries on speaking. I hear his voice, but I don't take in the actual words that he's saying. Then I hear a woman's voice. She's asking a question, and I think it's aimed at Conner. My heart breaks into tiny pieces and freefalls when I watch the sheer anguish and pain, then panic wash over his beautiful face. He looks from Lawson to Gunner Vance, the band's drummer and then tries to stand, but staggers backward as his knees lift the table. The table, along with the jug of water and the glasses all go flying. Everyone gets up and leaves. The journalists and their cameras are eerily still and silent for a few seconds before the news cuts from the press conference back to the studio.

Sophie mutes the television again, and we both sit for a few long minutes in our own silence. I feel exhausted. Emotionally and mentally drained and my heart is aching for Conner. Who's going to hold him tonight? Who's going to let him cry and then be there to kiss away his tears?

"That's just so awful," Sophie whispers, her voice thick and rough from crying. I nod my head.

"All I can think though Soph, is that at least it wasn't Conner. What kind of person am I to think that?"

She leans forward and grabs the box of tissues and puts them on the sofa between us. We both take a couple and blow our noses and wipe at our faces.

"It makes you a normal person, Neen. A normal human being." I raise my eyes to meet hers as she continues, "You don't think that Dom and Gunner's family are sitting at home thinking thank fuck their boys are safe? Of course, they are. You love Conner, of course you want him to be safe over and above everyone else. That's what love is."

Even though my eyes are already sore and stinging, I rub at them with the back of my hand.

"Stop saying that I love him. I used to love him. I haven't seen or heard from him in fifteen years. I care about him, yeah and I'm happy that he's safe, but I don't love him. In fact, I'm still pretty pissed off at how he treated me all that time ago."

I swallow the last of the wine in my glass. It's gotten a little warm, and I shudder as it goes down. Warm white wine is so not pleasant.

"If you weren't still in love with him, you would've moved on from what happened fifteen years ago. You still love him! It was written all over your face while you watched all that unfold. You felt every bit of pain he did because you love him."

"Fuck off," I tell her.

"No, I won't fuck off. Now tell me the truth. Tell me why you married Marcus the prick, and admit to me that you're still in love with Conner Reed."

I top up both our glasses and begin telling her the story of how I came to marry Marcus Newman.

CHAPTER NINE

SOPHIE SITS FORWARD ON THE edge of the sofa, her elbows resting on her knees, her fingers steepled in front of her lips. She hasn't said a word as I told her what my brother had done and how unhappy I was in my marriage.

"At the end of the day Soph, I allowed this to happen. I paid Pearce back a couple of years ago, but I've remained married to Marcus because it's safe. I don't have to feel, and I don't have to worry about the risk of being hurt, because I know that what I feel for him is nothing like I felt for Conner. Marcus could never hurt me like Conner did, I don't think anyone could."

She moves back to the corner of the sofa and faces me, crossed legged.

"Do you know how fucking angry I am with you right now?"

My eyebrows shoot up in surprise. "Why are you angry with me?"

She gives a small laugh and shakes her head. "Why, Neen? Why the fuck d'ya think?" Her eyes are wide and look all over my face. "I just can't believe you kept this from me. Why didn't you tell me? Why didn't you ask for my help? Apart from the fact that you married someone you didn't really want to, you put our partnership, our business and ultimately, our friendship at risk. My mum and dad would've lent you the money or acted as guarantors for a bank loan."

She shakes her head and rakes her hand through her long blonde hair. "I love you. I love working with you, and I'm so fucking proud of what we've achieved, but fuck Neen, I'd give it all up in a heartbeat to see you happily married and in love with a husband that you actually chose to be with, not someone you were blackmailed into marrying."

I give a nervous laugh. "I wasn't blackmailed into marrying him."

She shakes her head some more, then looks up at the ceiling for effect before looking back at me. "No? Well, what would you call it then, Neen? Your brother threatened to pull his money out of your business, *our* business, if you don't say yes to his boss's marriage proposal. What is that, if it's not fucking blackmail?"

Anger rises up from somewhere within me. I'm not sure if it's because Sophie's got it all wrong, or because I know that I have.

"It's a marriage of convenience, Soph. It suits both of us."

Tears run down her face as she continues to shake her head at me. "You can't honestly believe that, babe? You're such a beautiful person, Nina, inside and out. You deserve so much more than a marriage of convenience. So much more."

I don't know if it's the wine we've consumed, the drama of the events that we've watched play out on the television today, or just two lifelong best friends being totally honest with each other, but we both cry.

"God, I need a cigarette," Sophie states.

"No, you don't," I tell her. Sophie quit smoking three years ago. She'd gone from an occasional social smoker to a twenty-a-day girl when her marriage started to fall apart.

Her marriage to a crazy Italian chef had been a disaster from day dot. They married just two weeks after meeting, and just three months later she caught him shagging one of the waitresses from his restaurant. Luckily my brother had represented her, and she didn't have to give up any of the business as part of the divorce settlement, despite him trying to lay claim to half. What she did give up though, was about twenty pounds in weight and in return gained an addiction to nicotine. It eventually took a client asking Soph to go and find a mint or some gum to chew, because she couldn't bear the smell of tobacco breath in her face as Sophie cut her fringe, to convince her that she needed to quit the habit.

"No, you're right. I need something stronger, like a joint. Have you got any weed in the house?"

I roll my eyes at her. "Soph, my husband has a law firm. Of course, I don't keep weed in the house."

"Well, that's just another reason why you shouldn't be with him." She stands from the sofa on wobbly legs. "I'm gonna find another bottle of wine then. I'm staying here tonight, by the way. I'm far too drunk to drive."

"That's fine," I call to her back as she staggers off in search of more wine.

I hear her talking to Duchess as she makes her way through the kitchen. I switch the television to a music channel, sick of seeing Shift's press conference being played over and over again on the news. Of course, it's a Shift song playing. I look at Conner on the screen as the camera zooms in on him. The film clip is of a live performance of 'What If?' It's one of their earlier songs. Conner has long hair, much longer than it was the last time I'd seen him in person, and much longer than it was when I saw him today. He stares right into the camera as he sings and plays guitar as I study his face. There's no denying how beautiful he is. He has dirty blond, almost bronze coloured hair and olive skin. His lips are full, his bottom lip being much plumper than his top and they've been on me, those beautiful lips have been all over my body. My heart rate picks up, and my skin heats at the thought. But it's Conner's eyes that I always found so appealing. They are the strangest colour and look different according to the lighting around him or his mood. They're a stunning combination of blue-green and grey. Mostly a bluey-greeny colour, but when he was pissed off, that's when you would notice the grey. He's gorgeous, there really is no other way to describe him, and even though he's a man, he really is beautiful.

"So, you didn't answer my question earlier." I look up at Sophie as she flops down on the sofa, cold bottle of wine in hand. I'm actually surprised she can remember that she even asked me a question but in saying that, I don't remember her asking me a question.

"Anyway, it doesn't matter, I already know the answer." I watch her as she tries to pour the wine without unscrewing and removing the cap. We both realise at the same time that the lid's still on and collapse back on the sofa in fits of laughter.

We eventually make it to bed around three a.m., both of us curl up in my vast, king-sized bed. Despite the day's traumatic events, after the wine we've consumed, two hours of me whooping Sophie's arse on Sing Star and two hours of us dancing around my living room to 'Ultimate Party Hits' being played on the music channel, I crash as soon as my head hits the pillow.

Marcus doesn't arrive home until midday Sunday. He stayed at a friends after drinking too much, but couldn't phone and tell me as his battery was dead. I realise as he explains that I don't really give a shit where he was, what he was doing, or who he was doing it with. I just don't care.

MONDAY IS BUSY WITH WORK, and I take a trip to see my doctor on Tuesday. She arranges for me to have some blood tests and an ultrasound. Once she's sure that there's no obvious problem as to my failure to conceive, despite not taking any precautions for the past eight months, we'll sit down and work out a plan. She doesn't seem overly concerned and has told me that it takes some couples a month to fall pregnant, some, a couple of years. That's just the way things went. Marcus has a different doctor to me, but at the same surgery and Trish, my doctor has recommended that he makes an appointment to get himself checked out the same way I have. As I'm leaving her consulting room, I bump into Jay, Marcus's doctor. I've never really spoken to him before, and I'm surprised when he says hello.

"Hey Nina, how's Marcus feeling now?" he asks with a friendly smile. I look at him with a frown. I don't remember the last time Marcus was sick, let alone came to see his doctor. I watch a flicker of something cross over his face as he sees my reaction to his question.

"Marcus is fine, I wasn't aware he'd been sick." He laughs nervously as I stop walking and look at him.

"Well, you know, not sick exactly..." He opens his mouth a couple of times as if to say more, but nothing comes out.

I've worked with the public now for almost half my life. I'm not naturally an outgoing person, which tends to make me a good watcher and listener, which in turn, has meant that I've gotten really good at reading people. Hairdressers are almost like therapists for some of our clients. They sit in our chairs, they get served a beverage of their choice, including wine or champagne, and while they sip their drinks and get their scalp massaged, they open up. They vent about the things that have pissed them off and they quite often spill secrets or gossip that they've been hanging on to. Some of the gossip is the absolute truth, some complete and utter bullshit. I've learnt over the years to spot the bullshit and the bullshitters. I've learnt to spot when someone is about to cry, when someone needs your opinion and when someone needs you to just nod, smile and let them spill their guts. What I'm witnessing now from Doctor Jayer Patel, right in front of me, is a man panicking, which in turn is making me panic. *Why has Marcus been to see him and why do I not know about it? Is he sick, ill, and not telling me?*

"Shit!" he half-huffs, and half says. "Sorry, I was out of line." I open my mouth to speak, when he continues, "Give him my regards." He moves off into his consulting room and shuts the door behind him. I stand alone out in the corridor for a few seconds, gathering my thoughts and debating whether or not to knock on his door and demand an explanation, but I never was the type to seek out confrontation. So I leave it and head back to my car, then to the supermarket to grab something for dinner.

Marcus texts, just as I get home.

Sorry babe, I'm in court tomorrow. Need to work late. Don't wait up. Love you, M x

I feel him slide into bed and open one eye to look at the clock. It's eighteen minutes past one. I turn and spoon myself into his back and kiss his shoulder.

"Hey," I whisper.

"Sorry, I woke you, babe. I should've gone to the spare room."

"No, that's fine. You're very late."

"Unexpected fraud case was landed on us. We have to be in court at nine tomorrow morning, and I wanted to make sure we were prepared. There was a lot to go over."

"Did you eat?" I ask as I reach around and run my hands over his belly. I feel his stomach muscles tense as I touch him.

"Yeah, we had takeaway delivered to the office. Go to sleep, I'll talk to you in the morning."

I desperately want him to turn around, to wrap his arms around me and to kiss my neck. To just have one night where I could fall asleep feeling loved, desired and wanted. Instead, I swallow back my tears and go to sleep pressed into his back as tightly as I can, feeling lonelier than ever.

CONNER

I<small>T TAKES ME A FEW</small> seconds to work out what's just happened. I'm wet, someone just threw water over me, and I'm now soaking wet.

Fuckers!

My head aches but not nearly as much as it should, considering the alcohol and drugs I've consumed since my feet landed on British soil. I've no idea how long it's been? How long since Jet's death... since the funeral? I've no idea about anything anymore, only that I'm thinking and I hate thinking. Thinking leads to remembering and I hate remembering. Remembering leads to feeling and I don't want to feel – I *really don't* want to feel.

"Time's up Reed. Get your arse out of bed and into that shower before I drag you out." I open one eye, and the light shining into the room from the open curtains hits me like a laser beam.

"*Fuck!*" I complain. "Shut the fucking curtains and get out," I say loudly. I want to shout, but shouting will require effort, and I simply don't have the energy for anything that requires effort.

"Move your fucking arse boy. I won't warn you again." I don't need to open my eyes again to know who's talking to me. It's my dad, and he sounds thoroughly pissed off.

My dad and I had done a lot of bridge building over the last ten years or so. Once I had the money, I'd gotten him into a rehab program, where it was discovered he was suffering from a form of Post-Traumatic Stress Disorder, otherwise known as PTSD.

I'd been a baby when he had gone off to fight in the Falklands war. He was part of the Special Forces that landed at San Carlos, otherwise known as Bomb Ally. His squad had been key in securing the beachhead, allowing the safe landing of further troops to fight in the conflict. His unit had come under fire numerous times, and he'd witnessed things a young man in his twenties should never have to. Added to this were operations in the Gazza Strip and Northern Ireland. The toll of which had been massive on his mental well-being.

He'd come home on leave, to his wife and four little boys and just couldn't handle the normality of it all. He turned to drink, which led him to become violent toward my mum. She eventually left him and went back to her old life—which my dad knew nothing about—as a junkie. Whoring herself out to pay for her next fix. This ultimately led to her death, something else that severely affected my dad's already less than healthy mental state. He spent the next fifteen or so years drinking himself into oblivion. As soon as the band signed their first deal, I gave my brothers the money to get him some help. Once he'd dried out and had seen a psychologist for well over a year, he finally started to get his shit together. He asked to see me, and we sat down and had a long overdue heart to heart.

His problem with me as I was growing up, it turned out, was merely that I looked like my mum. My brothers look more like him, brownish hair, blue eyes but my hair was more of a dirty blond, and I had the bluey, green coloured eyes that my mum had. And that trait is what had caused him to take a swing at me every opportunity he got. We sorted out our shit, and now he lives in a bungalow on the grounds of my house, with his new wife, Sandra. Sandra works as my housekeeper and cleaner, my dad as my groundsman and they take care of the place and my dogs while I'm away on tour or doing stuff with the band.

None of the shit my dad went through as a soldier gives him the excuse to behave the way he did, but once he was given the help that he needed, he admitted and accepted that he'd been in the wrong. He's not had a drink in years and was once again playing a major part in the lives of myself and my brothers and their families. Our relationship would never be perfect but he's my dad, and I love him. I'd lost too much in my life to hold grudges.

"Dad, draw the curtains and fuck off."

"He's going nowhere. We're going nowhere. You're going to the shower."

Who the fuck's voice was that? I open one eye again and through the bleariness, can see what looks like about a half dozen people standing in my bedroom doorway.

What the actual fuck?

I shut my eye again and huff.

"I don't know who you are, or what you want, but I'm telling you all now, I'm not getting up. So you can all go get fucked."

I turn my head in the opposite direction, just to let them know I'm not moving.

"Oi… Reed, I've flown twelve thousand miles to come and see you. I'm not talking to you from your bedroom doorway, and I'm not coming in because I'm scared of what I might catch. I'd rather take my chances with Ebola than step foot in there and face whatever's causing that smell. It's rank."

For fuck's sake! They're not gonna leave me alone are they?

I roll over onto my back and slowly sit. Opening my eyes, I take in the people standing in my bedroom door. There's my dad, with a bucket in his hand, Lawson, looking thoroughly pissed off, Tyler, standing with his arms folded and trying hard but failing not to grin and the biggest surprise of all, Josh Gardner, my life-long best friend. I can't help but smile as soon as our eyes meet and then it hits me.

Everything I've held inside for the past few weeks, every thought, feeling and emotion that I've drunk myself into unconsciousness to forget, come rushing to the surface. I rest my back against the head-board, bring up my knees, drop my head between them and cry, like a fucking pussy... I cry.

My dad is the first one there. He stands at the edge of my bed, pulls my head into his chest and holds me, and it feels so fucking good. Something as simple as human contact, being held by someone that genuinely cares, you can't put a price on that. I wrap my arms around his waist, press the side of my face into his chest and hold on tight while I just let the tears come. My shoulders shake and my chest and throat hurt with the force that they leave my body. My dad just keeps holding me, gently rubbing the back of my head.

"Let it out, son, let it all out. You shoulda done this weeks ago." I feel him take a deep breath in and then let it out slowly. "Take it from someone who knows, locking yourself away from the people that love ya and drowning your sorrows in a bottle, never helped anyone."

Somewhere in the distance, I hear my dad's wife Sandra, telling everyone to get out and go and wait downstairs.

"We love ya, Con. We're all worried about ya, mate. Now get yourself in the shower and put on some clean clothes. Sandra's gonna make some breakfast and strip this bed."

I look up into my dad's blue eyes, but he kneels down so we're at eye level and rests his hands on each of my shoulders. "None of it's your fault," he shakes his head as he talks. "None of the horrible things that's happened to you are your fault. You're a good man, Conner. You could've grown up to be a complete arsehole, blaming the world for all the things that were out of your control, but you didn't. You turned it all around, and I'm so very proud of you son, so very, very proud of the man you've become."

I take in a shaky breath, stunned at my dad's words.

"In saying all of that, you stink boy, so do us all a favour and go and get in that shower."

I wipe my nose on the back of my hand and give him a small smile.

"Thanks, Dad."

"Anytime mate, anytime." He pats my back a couple more times then leaves.

I MAKE MY WAY DOWN to my kitchen, feeling like shit but looking and smelling a whole lot better than I have for the last few weeks, or however long it's been since I got back from the States.

As I reach the bottom of the stairs, I can hear talking and laughter coming from the kitchen. For some reason, the sounds mixed with the smell of bacon makes my chest and my throat tighten again. Tears sting my eyes as I hear my brother laugh. I'm suddenly overwhelmed by the loneliness I've felt since Jet's death. I know it's my own fault. I know I've handled things badly by shutting myself away from the people that wanted to help me, but I felt like everything was out of my control. What Jet did, my thoughts, feelings and emotions, the fans reactions and grief, they were all things that were out of my control. So I stepped away. If I couldn't control the situation, then I'd remove myself and find something I could control. I locked myself away with a case of Wild Turkey Pure Honey and drank myself into beautiful oblivion. But I know now is the time to sort my shit out and face the world. It was time to take back control of my life.

Everyone except Sandra is sitting around my large dining table. I love this room, it's the reason I'd bought the house. It is one big open space that contains a large kitchen and breakfast bar, a huge dining table that seats fourteen, a couple of big leather sofas, that face a massive open fire and my big, fuck off television. There are timber bi-fold doors that go around three sides of the room and open out onto the patio, pool and gardens of the property. I smile to myself as I look around at everyone sitting at the table. If they knew how proud I was of this room they'd all take the piss out of me, but if you'd had the upbringing I'd had and lived in some of the places I did, you'd get where I was coming from. This home is mine. I own it outright. No mortgage and no loan. It was in serious need of renovation and modernisation when I'd bought it, and I worked side by side with my dad and my brothers to make it what it is today.

Damn, fucking straight I'm proud.

My eyes meet Josh's, and he gives me a small smile and a head nod.

"What the fuck you doing here, Gardner? You're looking sharp man… looking sharp."

He stands up from the table and doesn't hesitate to take the three steps toward me and pulls me in for a blokey cuddle and a few slaps on the back.

"Good to see ya, mate. So sorry about Jet. I did leave you a few messages, but from what I hear things have been messy for the last few weeks. You doing okay?"

I let out a deep breath. "I've been a total mess, to be honest with ya Josh, but I know I need to get my shit together. There's nothing I can do to bring him back." I look him square in the eye as I speak. I have no secrets from Josh, we've known each other since infant school and although we don't get to catch up with each other too often these days, I still love him like a brother.

"You look really well, Josh. It's good to see ya."

"Thanks, I just had a week away with Soph."

My stomach lurches and my chest tightens at the mention of Josh's sister, Sophie. It's not that I don't like the girl, I do. Growing up, she was like a little sister to me, but she's Meebs' best mate, so we usually don't mention her. It's sort of an unwritten rule between us. We're blokes for fuck's sake, we don't do all that feelings bollocks. He knows I hurt, but he also knows that I don't want to talk about it.

"How is she?" I ask. He nods his head slowly. He also knows what I'm asking, without actually saying the words.

"She's good. She's good…" I can hear the but coming. He hesitates before going on.

Do I want to know?

Do I care how Meebs is?

I know nothing about her life except that she and Sophie are in business together and have a chain of hair salons. I only know this much, because Tyler's wife Jenna goes to their salon in Esher and she mentioned it to me.

On the rare occasions Josh mentions his sister, he usually just nods and says, "She's good, they're both good." My heart is banging in my chest so hard, that it's forcing the blood through the veins in my throat so fast, it's actually painful.

I fucking hate this. Hate that she still has the ability to affect me like this. She's a hairdresser from a small town in Surrey. I'm the lead guitarist for one of the world's biggest bands. I've face fucked actresses, supermodels and even royalty but none of them, not one, has helped me move on from the girl that didn't show. The girl that left me when she was just sixteen.

I look away from Josh for a split second, planning on leaving it at that. My brain has a rush of thoughts as it tries to convince me that I don't care… that I don't give a fuck whether she's okay or not. Why should I? But my fucker of a heart takes charge of my movements and my head swings back, my eyes meet his, and my eyebrows raise, letting Josh know that I want him to continue with whatever he was about to say. He gives a subtle nod. This is what makes men such uncomplicated creatures, we've had an entire conversation without a single word being said. No thoughts, feelings or emotional bullshit required.

"She's okay," he shrugs his shoulders as he talks.

She's okay? Well, what the fuck is that supposed to mean?

I don't care. I don't want to know.

I do care. I do want to know. I want to know everything.

Does she ever think about me, talk about me? Does she miss me? Does she listen to my music? Is she proud that she once knew me? That once upon a time, she loved me, that I loved her? Does she know that some of my best songs are about her? But most of all, what I want to know more than anything, is why? Why the fuck didn't she show up?

Sandra shoves a plate with a couple of bacon rolls on it, into my hand and I walk toward the table without looking back at Josh. I sit down and she places a cup of tea in front of me too. As much as the food smells good, I'm not sure if my stomach can handle it. I ran out of bourbon two days ago and I've slept pretty much continuously since then. No food, just water.

"You look like shit," my brother points out.

"Yeah, he smelt like it earlier too," my dad says, winking at me at the same time.

"I didn't come down here to get insulted. You can all fuck right off if that's all you're here for," I tell them.

Sandra ruffles my hair. "Ignore them Con, you smell lovely now... Although, I will be wearing gloves when I change those sheets. You had any women up there?" I raise my eyes to meet Lawson's. It's his turn to wink at me now. Shit! Amanda! What the fuck was I thinking?

Lawson had turned up with Amanda in tow, a couple of days after we got back from America. Amanda, a case of bourbon and a very large bag of blow. There was only one way that evening was gonna go and it did. We all ended up, shitfaced. Lawson fucking Amanda in the arse while I fucked her face.

I woke the next morning to her trying to climb on top of me. I pushed her off onto the bed, straddled her chest and wanked myself into her mouth, by which time, Lawson was awake and started eating her for breakfast. I came all over her face, then left them to it. Going back to my own room, locking the door before showering and crawling into bed.

I've never had sex in my bed, I have another room where that kind of action takes place. My bedroom is strictly out of bounds.

"Nah, not in my room. But you might wanna wear a Hazchem suit when you do the round room," I tell Sandra, in answer to her question.

"Jesus Reed, what kind of women are you bringing back here?" Josh asks.

"Oi, don't put this on me. Lawson brought her here," I try to defend myself.

Lawson folds his arms across his chest defensively. "I brought her here for you, Reed."

"Yeah, then took her to the round room and fucked her brains out," I argue.

"Right," Sandra shouts over the top of us. "I'm gonna tackle these dirty sheets, rather than listen about your filthy exploits." We all laugh as she heads off wearing rubber gloves, a plastic apron, a disposable mask and carrying a pair of stainless steel tongs.

I take a bite out of my roll and chew slowly, swigging on my tea to help it on its way down my throat. As soon as Sandra's out of the room, Lawson says, "Don't make out you're all sweet and innocent in front of Sandra. You and I both know what happened with Amanda."

Seriously, did he have to in front of my dad?

"I don't think I wanna hear this," my dad says.

"We do," Tyler and Josh both say at the same time. I shake my head at the pair of them.

"Glad to see you're still a fan of the three-way, Reed. Would hate to hear that your sex life has gone to shit, as well as your looks."

"Fuck you," I tell Josh. "Why you here anyway?" He looks across to Lawson. I lean back in my chair and lace the fingers of each hand together behind my head, stretching back and giving my stomach room to accommodate the roll I've just eaten. I've managed one, I definitely can't manage the other though. I push my plate away and

Tyler leans across and grabs the roll in an instant. I take a sip of my tea and look between Lawson and Josh.

"I came here specifically to see you today," Josh begins, "but I'm in the country for The Triple M event next month." My heart rate picks up as I wait to hear what he's going to say next. Triple M is a charity event that takes place every year at venues all around the world. Shift took part in the first ever event back in 2001. We were one of the first bands on stage. Nobody had really heard of us back then. It was, in fact, one of my very first live appearances. We'd played at the event a few more times since then, but as one of the headline acts. It was for a great cause. The charities involved helped kids getting back on their feet after rehab, getting them off the streets. There was a charity that helped aspiring bands and musicians, giving them free access to instruments and a recording studio. These were all things I cared passionately about.

Joshua's business 'Dig It Events' had been the organisers and promoters of the event for the last five years. Shift hadn't been able to take part the last three years though, because of tour and recording commitments.

"I've just finished getting everything organised for the Australian show, and now I'm back here getting things organised for the UK," he continues, "and we'd really like you to be a part of it." It's not a question, it's just a statement of what he'd like.

My mouth suddenly feels dry, my lips sticking to my teeth. I sit up straight in my chair and let out a long breath, then breathe in deeply. I can feel the beginnings of an anxiety attack happening and focus on my breathing for a few seconds to ward it off. I haven't had one since the first day that I got back here. I walked in the house and my dogs, Duke and Kaizer, came bounding toward me. I don't really understand what happened next. As I rubbed around their throats and ears, I was suddenly overcome with complete and utter panic, and for a few minutes, I really thought I was having a heart attack. My dad and Sandra were there, and my dad's military training kicked in. He got me to focus on him and my breathing, and eventually calmed me down. I'd felt the beginnings of one a couple of times since, but by using the techniques my dad had taught me, I'd managed to shake off the feeling. I breathe in deeply through my nose now and concentrate on letting my breaths out slowly. My dad reaches across and pats my shoulder.

"You all right boy?" he asks. I nod my head but don't speak for a few seconds.

"I don't think I can. I don't think I'm ready," I tell them both. Josh nods slowly.

"All right mate, I totally understand."

"Sorry." I shrug in apology.

"Na, it's all right. I just thought I'd ask. One of the charities that's being headlined this year helps young people suffering from anxiety and depression and who have either attempted or considered suicide."

Shit, now I feel bad.

Fuck!

"We just thought, you know, with what happened to Jet that it might be something you want to be involved in."

I go to take another gulp of my tea but the mug's empty. My thoughts are bouncing around my head in a million different directions.

I need to stop being such a pussy.

I need to do this.

I need to give back.

"I don't think I can do it. I want to. I really want to, but I just don't think I can get up on that stage on my own."

"No, no, no," Lawson jumps in, "you wouldn't be on your own." He looks across at Josh before continuing, "Gunners in. I've spoken to him this morning and he's up for it. Dom's away on a family holiday and he's promised Jade that he's taking a complete break for the next two months, so he can't make it… but…" He looks at Josh. Josh looks at me. "Marley Layton will front for you."

Tyler spits tea across the table.

Whoa.

What the actual fuck!

"What we thought was, you could rehearse for the next two weeks and work on a mix of Shift and Carnage songs, sort of a tribute to both bands. It's sort of fitting, don't ya think?"

"Fuck, I don't know what to say," I tell him.

"You've gotta do it, Reed. Fucking hell! Marley Layton, he's the reason you wanted to learn to play guitar." I look across to Tyler, unable to help the smile as I think about how Miles and I used to sing and play air guitar to Carnage songs and I know in an instant that I've got to do it. Not just for Jet, but for Miles too.

As if reading my mind, Tyler says, "Fuck, can you imagine if Miles was here? You'd have no choice, you'd have to do it." Tyler wipes a tear from under his eye as he talks.

I feel my dad's hand rest gently in the middle of my back as he says from next to me, "You do what's right for you, son. Don't feel pressured. I know it's a good cause and everything, but you need to be sure this is right for you. That you're ready to get back up there so soon."

I nod my head at my dad. "Yeah, I know Dad, I know what I need to do."

I look between Lawson and Josh. "What day is it?"

"Monday," they both say together.

"How long till the gig?" I ask.

"It's next Saturday, so less than two weeks," Josh replies.

"Fuck!" My palms are actually sweating. I look at my brother, then at my manager. "D'ya think I can do these songs justice?"

"Of course, you can," Tyler states.

"Fuck yeah," Josh adds.

"Do you really need to ask?" Lawson asks.

"When can I start rehearsing?" Not sure if it's Josh or Lawson that'll know the answer.

"Tomorrow," they both reply together.

"Fuck!" I say again.

CHAPTER ELEVEN

NINA

I've had the shittiest month since shitty months were invented. I've barely seen Marcus. The fraud case that was landed on him last minute has turned out to be a lot more complicated than the company first thought and the court case is still dragging on.

I had though, managed to find a moment to approach him about why he'd needed to see the doctor. He told me he'd popped in to see him about a sore wrist. He was due to play in a golf tournament and wanted to know the best way to strap it up so it didn't hurt throughout the day. I didn't believe a word of it and I actually believe that he knew full well that I knew, he was lying. He wasn't happy that I knew he'd been to the surgery and wanted to know how I knew. I was totally honest, I told him I'd been there to see my doctor and why I had seen her. He seemed fine at first, but then I informed him that she'd suggested he see his own doctor and maybe arrange to get his sperm count checked. That's when he became pissed off and stormed out of the house to walk the dog, which is something he never did. He's not a big fan of dogs and has never shown any patience or affection toward Duchess. When he came back, he sat me down and told me that he'd really been to see Dr Jay to get himself the kind of check-up that I'd had with my doctor, and that the results had come back showing everything was fine with him and like he'd thought all along, the problem was with me. Apparently, he hadn't told me sooner because he knew how upset I'd be.

I was beyond upset, I was devastated. I knew that I had polycystic ovaries, but unlike some women, I had very few symptoms other than irregular periods. I'd gained a serious amount of weight and become anxious and depressed after Conner left me, but I've always put that down more to the split than my condition. I'd managed to get my weight back under control with exercise, a reasonably healthy diet and a lot of encouragement from my husband and mother. The period irregularity had been brought under control by going on the pill. My only real concern was that since I'd stopped taking it, almost a year ago now, I'd only had four periods.

After a stressful couple of weeks waiting on my results, all my tests came through from my doctor, and they were actually better than I'd been expecting. My bloods were all good, hormone levels fine and the ultrasound showed that I only had a couple of very small cysts and they were both on the same ovary. My other ovary was perfectly healthy, and as far as she was concerned, there was no reason why I couldn't conceive naturally. She told me to go away, keep practising and to come back in six months if I still wasn't pregnant.

I'd researched online and was secretly charting my temperature and worked out that based on the very heavy period I'd had in May, my next most fertile few days would be in the middle of June, so I booked Marcus and I a weekend away in York, just for two nights. We would leave Friday and head back on Sunday so he couldn't complain about having to take time off from work. I planned on doing nothing but having sex with my husband. I'd booked us into the honeymoon suite of a four-hundred-year-old hotel, inside the city's walls. Four poster bed, claw-footed slipper bath, the works.

I wasn't a quitter. I was determined to give my marriage and our attempts at parenthood my all, but I knew as I planned our little getaway, that this was it. If this weekend didn't ignite some kind of spark, it was probably time to admit defeat, lick my wounds and end my marriage.

The court case Marcus was working on was due to wind up on the Tuesday, with a verdict delivered by Thursday at the latest. I'd booked the Friday as well as the weekend off of work and was really looking forward to it.

Marcus and I had been averaging sex, less than once a week for the best part of a year, sometimes only once a fortnight and right now, it had been eight whole weeks. This wasn't unusual when he worked on a big case so I wasn't too worried and I planned on making up for it on our weekend away.

Sophie had just come back from a week in Greece with her brother, who'd arrived back in the country after three months' work in Australia. Today was her first day back at the salon but she only had two clients booked in so she'd gotten the apprentice to put a conditioning treatment on her hair, then wash and blow dry it into big bouncy curls. Now that was done, she was bored and hanging around the reception area, going through our bookings.

I finished with my client, let the receptionist take her money and waved her goodbye.

"I see you've already booked the weekend of the twenty-first off?" she asks with a smile. I raise my eyebrows in surprise. I hadn't told Sophie about my plans for a dirty weekend away yet as I hadn't seen her.

"What d'ya mean? Yeah, I've booked it off, I'm going away that weekend. I've booked the Friday off too." Her face falls.

"You're going away? Shit, where you going?"

"I've booked a dirty weekend away in York with Marcus."

Her face screws up. "Ewww. TMI, Neen, TMI."

"Well, you asked."

"Yeah, sadly, I did."

She looks over my face for a few seconds. "How are things?"

I shrug my shoulders. I have no idea, how things are. Lonely and sexless mainly.

"I want the truth. How are things really, Neen?"

I let out a long sigh. She's my best friend, if I can't tell her, then I really am alone in this world. I motion with my head, saying, "Office."

We make our way to our office at the back of the salon, where we have a pair of leather sofas and a large coffee table. We have the usual office furniture too, but we have the sofas so we can escape and relax for five minutes on busy days. The staff have their own break room, but this is somewhere for just Soph and me to retreat to. We have a coffee machine, a microwave and a fridge so we're pretty much self-contained.

Sophie goes straight to the fridge and pours us both a large glass of wine.

"Come on then Matthews, spill. What's your prick of a husband done now?"

I roll my eyes as I take a sip of my wine and sit back into the sofa. "He actually hasn't done anything."

"So why'd you hesitate when I asked you how things were?"

I let out a long breath and pick at an imaginary piece of fluff on my black trousers. My eyes sting as I fight the tears. Sophie was only away a week, but it's suddenly hitting me how much I missed her.

It's Thursday. Marcus hasn't been home until after I've gone to bed for over two weeks, and we haven't had sex for fifty-six days. Apart from my clients and the people that I work with, I'd barely spoken a word to anyone for almost eight days.

"I missed you," I tell her. Sophie's face lights up with a real, genuine smile that shines in her eyes.

"I missed you too baby chick. I wish you'd have come with us."

"How's Josh?"

"He's great. Really busy, but great. We clubbed all night and lounged around the pool all day. He asked how you were doing."

I smiled as I thought of Josh. We used to be really close, but he was too close to Conner, and it was just too painful to be around him, so I distanced myself. Then he'd moved to London to work, so I didn't see him about too often. Since he'd set up his own business, I'd hardly seen him at all. He was always travelling around the world, organising functions and events, or just enjoying life.

"Anyway, back to you. What's going on? You look sad."

Shit! Tears sting my eyes again. I take a few deep breaths and swallow them down.

"I just feel like I'm the only one in this marriage right now."

"Pfft. What d'ya mean, right now? From what I've seen, it's been like that from day dot."

"Don't Soph, I need your support right now, not your opinion of my husband."

"Neen, I'll support you in most things. I've always had your back and you know that. But, him… staying married to him? No, I'm sorry, he's not right for you. You get more miserable every day. I feel like the longer you're with him, the more of you I lose. You're fading away in front of me, Neen."

My bottom lip suddenly has a mind of its own and I lose all ability to stop it trembling.

"I think it's over. I think, I mean… I don't know. I just don't know what I can do anymore, Soph. I can't make him want me. I can't force him to fuck me." I've never confessed to Sophie about my lack of sex life, but now I've told her the truth about why I married Marcus, she might as well know the whole story. Plus, the glass of wine I've just gulped down into my empty stomach has gone straight to my head.

"What? Wait a minute? You're not having sex? Since when? How long and why do I not know this?"

"No. Since forever. The whole time we've been together and you don't know, because I didn't want to give you another reason to hate him. I didn't want to have to come up with another reason to justify staying with him."

"Fuck Neen… or not, in your case."

I give her a small smile.

"I've told myself that this weekend away is to try and get pregnant."

Her perfectly shaped eyebrows shoot up to her hairline. "Neen, you're not still seriously considering…"

I shake my head. "No, let me finish," I tell her. "I've kidded myself that this weekend away is all about making a baby, but I know…" I lose it and start to cry. "I know in my heart, it's really my last attempt at saving my marriage, Soph."

She moves from sitting opposite to sitting beside me.

"Neen, I'm sorry. I'm really sorry. I shouldn't say the things I do about Marcus. I'm your friend and I should be more supportive of your choices, but fuck babe, the bloke's a complete prick and if he's not up to scratch in the bedroom, then what's the point? Why are you even trying to make it work?" She brushes my hair from my face and tucks it behind my ears.

"I don't know. I just didn't want to give up without one last try. I think I was hoping that things might change if I got pregnant. If we had a baby together, I thought it might bring us closer."

She shakes her head. "And what if it doesn't? What if things are just as bad? He's a lawyer Neen, d'ya seriously think he'll let you walk away with his kid?"

Shit, I hadn't even thought about that. I let out a long breath and look up at the ceiling.

"What am I gonna do?" I turn to look at her again. "Do I just walk away?"

"Well," she says, with a smile on her face, "instead of going away with him next weekend, you could come with me. Josh has given me VIP tickets to this year's Triple M, event."

"Shit, I forgot that was next weekend."

We had attended this event a few times over the years but only when Shift *weren't* playing. They'd been absent since Josh's firm had taken over the organisation of the event, so we'd gone VIP the last few years and had made a significant donation to the charity by way of a thank you. We were massive Carnage fans back in the day and had seen them live a few times. Conner had worshipped Marley Layton and always aspired to play and sing as well as he did. I suddenly wondered how he was doing. Whether the band would carry on without Jet? There'd been all sorts of speculation in the press, but no official word from the band.

"Has Josh spoken to Conner, d'ya know? Did he say how he was doing?" I ask without thinking.

Sophie looks at me with a shit-eating grin spread right across her face.

"What?" I ask her, with a frown.

"See that… that right there. What you just said right then is the reason you need to walk away."

"Why? What did I say?"

"Babe, we're sitting here discussing the demise of your eight-year marriage and whether it's worth fighting for and you've just asked about Conner. Your head's already moved on. Your heart just hasn't caught up yet, but that's because it's a good heart and wants to do the right thing, but your head, your head is wise and has already packed its bags and moved the fuck on."

She throws herself back on the sofa, wearing a self-satisfied smile.

ON FRIDAY, MARCUS WINS HIS case. He falls through the front door, blind drunk, at three in the morning, making so much noise that Duchess must think we have a burglar and she starts barking, waking me up. I go downstairs and find him sitting on the bottom step with his head in his hands.

"You okay?" I ask from the top of the stairs, looking down at him. He turns his head slowly and tries to focus on me.

"I'm sorry," he says so quietly that I can hardly hear him.

"That's okay. Congratulations."

He shakes his head, still trying to focus on me. "No, I'm sorry. I'm so sorry, Nina."

I move down the stairs toward him. The lamp on the hall table is on, and I can see how glazed over his light blue eyes look.

"You coming to bed?"

He closes his eyes for a long moment, then holds his hand out to me. I move further down the stairs and take it. He pulls me into his lap and kisses me with more passion than he's ever shown in our entire marriage. My body responds instantly. My nipples harden, and I moan into his mouth while my hands rake through his hair. He pulls away and looks down at me.

"I do love you, Nina." I've waited so long to hear him say those words like he means them and I want so desperately for my belly to do backflips and my heart rate to increase. I want my heart and my insides to react the same way that my body does. But what my body wants is sex. It would react this way to anyone that kissed me the way he just did. What my heart and my soul want, need, is so much more.

"That's good to hear," is all I can manage to say. He tries to stand up while still holding on to me, but he's too drunk. I slide to the floor and walk up behind him, worried in case he might fall backwards. Not that I could do a lot if he did. He's almost six feet tall, and I'm only just five.

When we get to our room, he flops down onto the edge of the bed, and I take his shoes and socks off for him. I pull his shirt over his head, then push him back so I can undo his suit trousers. I pull them down and over his hips. I go to reach for his boxers, but he grabs my wrist.

"Come here," he says. I straddle him as his legs hang over the side of the bed, feet planted firmly on the floor. He pulls my vest up and takes my nipple in his mouth and bites it, hard, too hard.

"Oww," I protest. His hand has wrapped around my hair, and he pulls at it roughly while flipping me over onto my back. He grabs my face between his thumb and fingers and forces me to look at him.

"Don't make out. You like it rough. I know you like it rough."

What the fuck? He's never said things like this to me before, and he's never behaved like this either. He lets go of my hair and my face. Despite his drunken state, he manages to free himself from his boxers and pull my knickers to one side. Without any kind of foreplay, he tries to push inside me. He's not fully hard, and because I'm not wet, it's painful, and I let out a little yelp.

"Don't Nina, just don't. I know you like it rough. I know it," he says through gritted teeth. He grabs my face again and stares angrily into my eyes.

"Is this how he fucked you? Is it?"

I don't know this person, I've never seen Marcus like this. My heart is racing now, but for all the wrong reasons. His mouth smashes against mine, and he bites down on my bottom lip. I start to panic and dig my heels into the mattress, trying to push myself off his lap and away from the bed, trying to escape. He grabs me by the throat and squeezes, hard. He's bigger, stronger than I am, and I don't stand a chance when he pushes me to my back and forces his hips between my legs.

"Don't you fucking dare, don't you ever try and run away from me. You fucking stay here and you take it. You take what I'm giving you, you little slut."

I pull at his hair, claw at his back, but it just seems to spur him on. He captures my wrists and roughly holds my hands against my sides and restrains them there.

He's fully hard now and has no trouble forcing himself inside me. I cry out in pain at the stinging and burning sensation. Marcus isn't that big, but my muscles are clenched tight and the intrusion unwelcome. I start to cry. I'm angry more than anything but also humiliated.

"Marcus, please, what are…? Why are you doing this?"

"Don't Nina. Just stop pretending you don't love this. Is this how he fucked you? Is this how you got fucked by your rock star bit of rough?"

"Oh my God, why are you saying this? What the fuck is wrong with you, Marcus?"

"Shut up! Shut up! Just shut the fuck up and take it," he shouts. Spit is frothing at the corners of his mouth and hanging from the middle of his lip. He frees my wrists, and I try desperately to get away from him, but start to see dots in front of my eyes as he squeezes my throat tighter this time. I'm gripped by panic for a few seconds, but then adrenaline kicks in and I make one last-ditch attempt to buck him off me and push him away. I give it everything, pulling at his hair, trying to claw at his face. He grips my wrists in his hands again, holding them at the side of my head. I try to roll from side to side. Panic, hurt and anger build inside me all at once. This isn't happening, my husband wouldn't do this to me. I lean forward and bite down on his shoulder. He stops his brutal thrusts, that drive him deeper inside of me, and I think it's all over until his fist comes down viciously and he punches me in the jaw.

My head spins, but I don't pass out. I do stop fighting though and lay utterly still. He thrusts a few more times, grunts then stills.

I can taste blood in my mouth where I must've bitten my tongue or my cheek. I remain motionless for a few more moments, trying to gather my thoughts. I open my eyes when I hear Marcus start to snore, his weight pressing down on me. I move my hand to cover my mouth before a sob can escape and wake him.

It takes a few attempts, but I eventually manage to manoeuvre myself out from underneath him. On shaky legs, I leave him snoring, face down on the bed and head for the bathroom down the hallway. I don't even make it to the toilet. Instead, I throw up in the shower, then turn it on, rinse away the mess that I've made and step inside and cry like I've never cried before. I cry not for what's just happened, but for every day I've spent wasting away in this miserable marriage.

My mind is racing. I just can't make sense of what's just taken place. In my own home. My own bed. With my own husband. What would force him to behave like that? What could've triggered that kind of behaviour? Whatever it was, nothing justifies him treating me like that.

Nothing.

He hit me.

He fucking hit me.

I start to cry again, the full realisation of what my husband just did, suddenly overwhelming me.

I stay in the shower for ages, letting my tears flow while I scrub the smell and all traces of him from my body. I try to think straight. What should I do? Should I leave? Now, or in the morning? Should I give him a chance to explain, to apologise? What if he wakes up and does it again?

I suddenly panic that the sound of the shower might wake him up. I jump out and wrap myself in a towel, still shaking uncontrollably. I go down to the laundry and pull out a hoodie and my hammer style yoga pants from the dryer. I head back upstairs and get my phone from beside the bed. Marcus is still face down snoring. I stand and watch him for a few seconds. He looks like an angel in his sleep. His blond curls need cutting, He never usually lets it get this long, but he's been in court every weekday and on the golf course most weekends.

I wipe my tears away on the back of my hand and walk out of the room. I call Duchess from the kitchen and grab my keys. I jump in my car and drive straight to Sophie's.

I SIT IN MY PARKED car, outside Sophie's flat and attempt to organise my thoughts. I don't remember the drive here. I don't remember getting dressed, collecting Duchess, or picking up my keys.

I look down at my dog, curled up in the footwell on the passenger side.

"What just happened, Duch? Why did he do that?" I wrap my arms around myself and try to stop shaking. My throat and chest ache as sobs wrack through me. Duchess puts her head up on the seat and looks up at me with her brown puppy dog eyes.

"What did I do? What could've happened to make him do that to me, hey girl?"

I sit in my car for a few more minutes trying to calm myself down. I have a key to Sophie's place. I actually used to live here with her before I moved in with Marcus. It's above our very first salon we opened together. I look up at the windows and considering the time, I'm not surprised that there are no lights on.

Sophie and I had been out to a wine bar after work tonight. I'd only had a couple of glasses as I had to drive home. Sophie had polished off a second bottle because she just had to walk across the street to get home. She'd probably passed out cold as soon as she got in, so I didn't want to let myself in and startle her.

I give Duchess a rub around her neck and ears and take a few calming breaths before pressing call against Sophie's name on my phone. It rings out three times before she finally picks up on my fourth attempt.

"Neen?" she croaks out in her sleepy voice.

I cry.

I try not to, but I can't seem to control myself.

"Neen… What the fuck? What's wrong? Nina, fucking talk to me."

I can't. I can't get the words out. I can barely get a breath in or out, so words have no chance.

I start to panic. I'm scared that I'll drop my phone and pass out. A million different ridiculous scenarios run through my head, but no words come out of my mouth. Then suddenly, something inside my dysfunctional brain kicks in, and I hit the horn as hard as I can. I keep pressing it. Someone, somewhere, has got to hear that and come and help me.

Duchess starts barking. I undo my car door, trying to drag air into my lungs and suddenly she's there. Sophie, in a pair of sleep shorts and nothing else, and she's screaming at me while trying to cover her boobs.

"What the fuck, Nina. What's going on?" She's bending down with her head in the car, Duchess keeps barking, while I keep crying.

"Fucking tell me, Nina? Are you hurt? What happened, just tell me what happened. Shush Duch, shush."

I start to feel calmer, the sensation of my blood whooshing through my ears stops, and I manage to breathe.

"Inside," I whisper to her, "I need to get inside."

She looks all over my face and body. Her brows pulled down in concern.

"Of course, of course," is all that she says.

WITHOUT ME EVEN NOTICING MY feet had touched the ground, I move from my car, up a flight of stairs and into Sophie's flat. Where I'm now curled into the corner of her sofa, with a blanket over me.

Sophie disappears for a few seconds, then reappears with a hoodie on over her shorts. She goes into the kitchen and pulls a bottle of wine from the fridge and two glasses from the cupboard, setting them down on the coffee table in front of us. Without saying a word, she pours us both a large glass, then pulls a packet of cigarettes from a drawer in the coffee table and lights one. She passes me my wine. I'm not sure if I want to drink straight from the bottle or throw the contents of my stomach up again into the nearest receptacle.

Sophie takes a long draw on her cigarette, then a swig of her wine. Her eyes on me the whole while.

"You gonna tell me what the fuck is going on? Coz you're scaring the fuck outta me right now."

I cry, again. I'm not overcome with the great heaving wracking sobs like I was earlier. This time I just cry silently. Duchess puts her head on my leg, I stroke it and meet Sophie's concerned gaze.

"He hit me."

Her face screws up in confusion. "What? Who?"

I suck in my bottom lip to try and stop it from trembling.

"Marcus," I whisper.

"What? Marcus hit you?" she shrieks. I nod my head. Sophie shakes hers. Her mouth opening and closing, but no words coming out. She suddenly jumps up and puts the overhead light on, instead of just the lamp and looks at me.

Her face crumbles.

She starts to cry.

"Oh my fucking God Neen, look at your face. He fucking hit you. That fucker actually hit you."

I nod my head continuously, we both cry while clinging onto each other. After a few moments, she asks, "D'ya wanna tell me what happened?"

She moves to the other end of the sofa, and we take simultaneous swigs on our wine. The sun is coming up, the birds are singing, and Sophie and I are drinking wine.

"I don't know what happened. He won the fraud case and came home around three, blind drunk." I wipe my eyes and nose on the sleeve of my hoodie and continue, "He must've fallen into the hall table or up the stairs or something because I heard a noise, then Duchess started barking." My dog's ears twitch at the mention of her name, she opens one eye then closes it again, her head still in my lap.

"I got up and went to the top of the stairs, and he was just sitting at the bottom, his head in his hands… he looked, I don't know... He turned around and looked at me, he could barely focus, but he looked at me and told me he was sorry."

"Sorry for what?" Sophie asks, frowning in confusion.

"I don't know. He said he was sorry and held his hand out to me."

"Hang on, hang on a sec. Let me get you some ice, your face is swelling up as you're talking. Looks like you're hiding a roast potato in your cheek and it's not attractive, babe."

"Cheers Soph," I reply sarcastically. She rolls her eyes at me and then heads to the kitchen to pull an ice pack from the freezer. She wraps it in a tea towel and hands it to me, before sitting back at the opposite end of the sofa.

"He held out his hand, and I went to him," I continue, shuddering as I put the ice pack to my jaw. "He pulled me into his lap and told me that he loves me." I look across at my best friend... my best friend, whom I should be able to tell everything to, but suddenly, I feel ashamed. I feel so ashamed of what my husband did to me. Ashamed that I didn't fight harder. Ashamed that I haven't left him sooner.

"What, Neen? What happened then?" My mouth is watering, and for a few seconds, I worry that I'm going to vomit again. I shake my head at Sophie, trying to find the words. I'm struggling to explain what happened next because, in all honesty, I have no fucking idea.

"I don't know, Soph. I don't understand what happened. He was fine. He was all over me. We went upstairs, and he collapsed on the bed, and I started to undress him."

I know I'm pulling an ugly cry face as I lose control of my emotions and, to be honest, I don't really care. "He lost it Soph, he just lost it, and he went for me."

"I don't understand, babe. What d'ya mean he went for you? He just hit you? What? What d'ya mean?"

"No, no, no." I let go of a loud sob. "No, he threw me onto my back. He called me a slut and a whore. He said... he said he knew I liked it rough. He told me not to make out. He pulled my hair and squeezed my face in his hand really hard." She's shaking her head in disbelief as I explain what happened. "He was saying things like, '*Is this how he fucked you,*' '*Did your rough rock star, fuck you like this?*' He was spitting and frothing at the mouth. I told him to stop. I screamed Soph. I screamed, and I cried, and I clawed, but he was too strong and I just couldn't... I just couldn't get away from him. I tried so hard," my voice is high pitched as I recall the panic that I felt, the disbelief that I still feel.

Sophie has moved up the sofa and is sitting next to me, holding my hand in both of hers. She's crying as hard as I am.

"I bit him. I bit him, Soph. I bit his shoulder."

"Good, the fucker, I hope you bit a lump out of him. Fuck! That fucker. I'm gonna kill him when I see him. What the fuck is wrong with him? Why the..."

"That was when he punched me," I interrupt her. "He punched me almost unconscious, and then he fucked me."

"Oh my God, Nina. Oh my fucking God. That's rape! He fucking raped you. Your husband that cunt you married, fucking raped you?"

"No, he didn't, it wasn't... We were about to have sex anyway, and he just flipped out. It's not the same." I know what Marcus did was wrong, but it wasn't rape.

"Stop Nina. Stop fucking defending him," Sophie shouts, and I flinch away from her. "I'm sorry, but just stop. Stop and think about it. He forced himself on you. You asked him to stop. You said, '*no.*' You tried to fight him off, and *he hit you*, Neen. When you said '*no,*' when you struggled and fought back, he *fucking hit you* and took what he wanted. If you were a total stranger, that would be classed as rape. Why should the fact that you're his wife make any difference?"

"Nobody's ever hit me before," was all that I could think of to say.

"You should go to the police."

"What? No. No fucking way. He'll lose his job. Get struck off, even. No."

We sit in silence for a few minutes or seconds. It could actually be hours, I don't really know. My thoughts are racing, and my head is pounding. I need time to process all of this. I'm not stupid. I'm fully aware of the fact that many people would be revolted by what my husband had done to me. Many wouldn't have hesitated in running to the police, but I was pretty sure that wasn't the path I wanted to go down.

"Will you at least do one thing, Neen?" Sophie's voice interrupts the maelstrom of thoughts occurring inside my now wine-addled brain.

I raise my eyebrows as I ask, "What?"

"Will you let me take a couple of photos of your face?"

"Why?"

She lets out a long breath and shrugs her shoulders. "Insurance... evidence. I don't know. What if he comes here? What if he tries something again?"

"I don't think he will. He's never done anything like this before. He's never even mentioned my relationship with Conner before."

"I wonder what triggered him to do something like that tonight then."

"I've no idea."

"Well, if you've no idea, how do you know it won't happen again?"

I nod, then shake my head, feeling totally confused. "I don't."

"So, can I? I don't trust him Neen, and that's got nothing to do with me not liking him. I just don't trust him. He's a lawyer, he knows every trick in the book. Even if you went to the police right now, which I think is absolutely the right thing to do, by the way, even if you went to the police and accused him of rape and assault, I bet he'd know how to wriggle out of it. He'd know of some technicality that would get him off, and if he didn't, I bet he'd have a contact or a colleague who would."

I keep my eyes on her while I try to remain focused as the realisation of the enormity of the situation washes over me. Nodding my head, I tell her, "Take the photos. Take them on your phone and email them to me, yourself and the business email."

My husband might generally be mild-mannered and gentle around me, but I'm fully aware of how ruthless he is in business. His law firm hadn't expanded so rapidly since he took over because he didn't know his shit. He knew it, and he executed his dealings with finite precision.

"D'ya think I should seek legal representation, Soph?"

"I don't know, babe. Where are you going with this? What's your next move?"

I tilt my head back and look up at ceiling. Tears escape from each corner of my eyes and roll down my face and neck.

"I've no fucking idea."

"Is this the end d'ya think? Is it over for you?"

I nod without hesitation. "Yeah, I think it is. I think my marriage is over."

"Then I think we need to get these photos taken and then find you the best lawyer we can on Monday morning."

Despite the increase in my heart rate, I suddenly feel a sense of complete and utter calm wash over me. I've tried my best. I really have tried, but there's just not enough there to make me want to stay and fight anymore, especially after tonight.

"Okay, get your phone. Let's get some pictures and then I need to sleep."

CHAPTER TWELVE

I'M WOKEN BY THE SOUND of Clean Bandits 'Rather Be', this week's ringtone of choice, playing over and over again. I struggle to open my eyes and then to get my bearings.

I'm on the wrong side of the bed to where I usually sleep, and someone is spooning me from behind. Marcus doesn't spoon. A doorbell rings. Then my phone starts again.

Marcus.

Shit, Marcus!

Last night.

I sit up, my head spins, then pounds.

Sophie mumbles something and then turns to face the other way and carries on sleeping. You could put a rocket up that girl's arse, and it wouldn't wake her. I've never known anyone to sleep as soundly as Soph.

I grab my phone off the bedside table and head out to the open plan kitchen and living area where Duchess is wagging her tail. I'm amazed that she's not standing with her legs crossed when I look at the clock and realise it's almost eleven o'clock.

My phone shows that I have over twenty missed calls from Marcus as well as eight text messages.

I slide down the kitchen cabinet and sit on the tiled floor as I give Duch some attention.

"Well girl, this is the first day of the rest of our lives, and as soon as I've had a wee I'll take you down for one." She tilts her head from side to side as I talk and she listens.

I put a handful of dry food in a bowl I take from the cupboard. Soph always keeps a supply of Duchess's favourites here, for the odd occasions when she's looked after her for me.

As I head off to the bathroom, the intercom buzzes and someone bangs on the front door, just as my phone rings again. It's Marcus on the phone, and my guess is, it's also him who's downstairs at the front door.

I totally expected him to be here looking for me this morning, and surprisingly, I feel rather calm. I go to the bathroom and then to the bedroom and pull on the clothes I was wearing last night. Sophie's sitting up rubbing at her face.

"What's happening? What time is it?"

"It's almost eleven, and Marcus is downstairs."

"Fuck. I don't want that crazy fucker up here, Neen. He can fuck right off."

"I need to talk to him. He won't go away until I do and I have to let Duchess out anyway."

"Wait, I'll come with you. We'll walk her over to the park. I don't want him in here, Neen, I'm serious."

"Well, hurry up then before Duchess disgraces herself over your kitchen floor."

I go back to the bathroom and splash my face with water and clean my teeth, noting in the mirror the lovely purple bruise I have spreading from the side of my mouth to the edge of my jaw. I consider covering it with makeup but then think, *fuck it, let him see the damage he's done.*

I send Marcus a text telling him I'll be down in a minute while I wait for Sophie to pull on some clothes and do whatever she needs to do in the bathroom. She doesn't need to do a lot to look ready, her eyeliner is tattooed on, her eyelashes are extended, and her eyebrows are waxed, tinted and sculpted into a perfect arch. She looks like she's made up her face to go and do battle with my husband without wearing any makeup at all.

"You okay?" she asks as we head down the stairs, toward the front door, toward Marcus.

"Surprisingly, yeah, I am."

"Good." She nods.

"Let's go deal with the fucker."

She opens the front door, and Duchess pulls me straight through it, and he's there, leaning against the railings between the path and the road. He's wearing jeans and a white Ralph Lauren Polo with the collar up. It's a look I hate. Sophie told him once that all polo shirts should have '*I look like a cunt*' embroidered underneath the collar, to try and stop men standing them up, but he took no notice, perhaps because he is a cunt. As if reading my mind, Soph whispers in my ear, "Whoop, whoop, cunt alert." And despite how much it hurts, I can't help but smile.

He lifts his mirrored aviators onto his head and steps toward me.

"Nina, baby, I'm so, so sorry."

Sophie steps in front of me. "Stay the fuck away from her."

"Stay out of this, Soph. It's got fuck all to do with you. Why are you even here?" he asks, gritting his teeth as he speaks to her.

"Don't talk to her like that. She's here because I want her here. Sophie stays, or I go. Make up your mind," I tell him.

We're standing on the street, right outside one of our salons, in full view of my staff and clients. Without saying a word, I cross over the road and into the park opposite and onto the sectioned off area where I can let Duchess of her lead. Luckily, I brought a couple of carrier bags down with me because the first thing Duch does is take a crap.

"Charming," I hear Marcus say from beside me. I look around for Sophie and find her sitting on a bench a few feet away.

"We all need to crap, Marcus, it's a perfectly natural bodily function. What do you want anyway? Spit it out, I need to get back home and take a shower."

"Nina, we need to talk. I... I don't know what to say. I don't know what happened."

I turn and look at him. Straight into his pale blue eyes and feel... nothing, absolutely nothing. Not fear, not loathing. Nothing. He could be a stranger to me. With a steady voice that actually amazes me, I say, "You're here saying sorry, and yet you claim that you've no idea what happened. If that's the case, what is it you're actually saying sorry for?"

He lets out a long sigh, or a huff or just a breath, I'm not sure which, and I don't really care.

"I just know... I remember, things got a bit rough. I may have said some things—"

I hear a "Pfft, d'ya think arsehole? Like fuck you can't remember," from Sophie.

I turn and meet his gaze. "You called me a slut and a whore. You told me that you knew that I liked it rough and to take what you were gonna give me—"

He steps toward me shaking his head. "Nina, baby. I'm so sorry—"

I step back away from him and held my hand out, letting him know to stay back.

"You pulled my hair, and you squeezed my face and then when I fought back, when I tried to get away from you, you *punched* me in the face." My lips tremble as I speak, but it's anger that's bringing on the tears. Anger at what he did to me, anger at the memory of how fucking helpless I felt last night. "You pinned me down and fucked me," I tell him through gritted teeth. His mouth's hanging open, his hand rakes through his hair and he shakes his head.

"No, no Nina. I wouldn't, I would never—"

I tilt my head toward him so he can get a good look at me and his handy work.

"Look at my face, Marcus. Look at my fucking face," I snarl at him. "I want you to stay away. Don't call me, in fact, don't contact me at all. I'll be around in the next few days to collect my stuff. I'm moving out."

"What? Wait, no. No, Nina. Fuck no. You've not even given me a chance to explain or say sorry."

"I don't care Marcus. I'm done! It's over."

He steps toward me again, I step away, *again*. Making the distance between us even further this time.

"Don't come near me," I warn.

This time Sophie stands up too.

"I'm not doing this, Nina, I'm not standing in the middle of a shitty dog park discussing our marriage. Now come home, and we can sort all of this out."

"No Marcus. I'm not going anywhere with you. Like I just said, we're done. I'll come and collect some stuff tomorrow, and I'll arrange to collect everything else in the week."

The coldness returns to his eyes. "Fuck you, Nina, fuck you!"

"If only you would've Marcus. If there wasn't eight-week gaps between each shag, I might've been prepared to listen to your bullshit excuses, but we haven't even got that as a foundation to work on."

"Eight weeks? Jeeezusss and I thought I was in a drought," I hear Sophie say and again, I try not to smile.

Marcus swings around and glares at her. "You best stay the fuck out of my business, Gardner. I bet you've been filling her head with bullshit all night. I bet this has all come from you."

Sophie steps toward him, showing absolutely no fear. "Actually, I think you'll find this all comes from the fact that you're not man enough to make love to your wife once in a while, and then when you do, you punch her into unconsciousness and fuck her against her will… Yeah, I have a feeling that's definitely where all this comes from, you prick."

He glares between us, his hands opening and closing into fists. "Fuck the pair of you. You fucking pair of dykes."

"Oh, very mature, Marcus. At least I can get it up more than once every two months."

He swings for her, he actually pulls his arm back and starts to swing a punch toward Sophie. And while people stop and stare, I just stand there frozen to the spot.

"Do it," Sophie screams at him, "Fucking do it, you coward. I'll have the police on you in an instant, lawyer boy. Just you fucking watch if I don't."

He spits on the ground between us and turns and walks away.

SATURDAY NIGHT, SOPHIE AND I GO clubbing. We dance until it feels like my feet are bleeding and we get absolutely hammered; falling through her front door at around five in the morning.

We spend most of Sunday in bed recovering. There's a spare room at Sophie's place with a perfectly functioning queen sized bed, but for some reason, Soph seems reluctant to let me out of her sight. I actually don't mind. It reminds me of the old days, back when my life was a little less complicated.

We wandered drunkenly over to the park with Duchess, after returning home and I take her out again at ten. Sophie must hear her crying at around noon and takes her out once more, and I finally crawl out of bed around four, shower and take her for a long walk, letting her run free around the dog park for an hour, while feeling incredibly guilty for keeping her so couped up.

There's a bit of a garden up on the roof that Soph and I had landscaped when we first bought the place, but there's no shelter up there as yet. I'll go and buy Duchess a kennel tomorrow, at least then she can spend the day outside until I decide what I'm going to do with the rest of my life.

At around seven, Sophie emerges from the bedroom, freshly showered and looking like a model. We order a Chinese takeaway to be delivered and discuss my plan of action for the next few days.

We Google divorce lawyers and decide not to use anyone too local, just to reduce the risk of them being an acquaintance of Marcus's and there being a possible conflict of interest. Sophie comes up with a couple of possibilities both based in central London. We store the numbers and will call them first thing Monday morning.

I decide to take a few days off from work just so I can have a bit of time to decide what I'm going to do with the rest of my life. I'm hoping that a divorce should be pretty straightforward. We have no children, and I'm financially independent. Marcus earns a lot of money these days, but I don't expect him to share any of it with me. The house is in joint names, but if he decides to make things difficult, I'll walk away and let him keep it. It's not that I'm soft, stupid or a pushover, it's just that now I've come to the decision to end my marriage, I want it done. I want to draw a line under this part of my life. I'm thirty-two later this year and more than happy to be single.

I'm not looking for love or any other kind of relationship right now. I'm just going to enjoy being single for a while. Like Sophie said, I'd become lost over the last few years. I've lost a sense of who I am and allowed myself to become who Marcus wanted me to be. I'm not blaming him, I take full responsibility for allowing it to happen. I could've fought harder, I could've refused to marry him when my brother insisted, but I didn't. Marcus was a safe option. I knew that I would never love him the way I'd loved Conner Reed. Therefore, he would never be able to hurt me the way Conner had. I didn't realise though that the loneliness and indifference from my husband that I felt during my marriage hurt almost as much as Conner leaving me the way he had.

DUE TO SOPHIE'S PERSISTENCE, WE get an appointment with Attwood, Chalmers and Co, for Tuesday morning. They have come highly recommended and have handled a few relatively high profile divorces and achieved excellent results for their clients. I wasn't too fussed about a great result, I just wanted a divorce. Sophie, on the other hand, insisted that we use the best divorce lawyers out there, as in her words, *"Marcus was a slippery little fucker, who couldn't be trusted as far as his dick could rise while watching me fuck myself with a twelve-inch dildo. Which, from what she'd heard, wasn't very far!"*

I spat my coffee, she shrugged and just said, "What? You know, it's true."

Late Monday morning I received a call from my brother. He was beyond pissed off with me, even more so when I told him something that I should've told him years ago… to go fuck himself. It was my life, and I would live it however I see fit. I gave him a brief synopsis of what took place between Marcus and myself on Friday night, and he told me that I probably just pushed him too far, and I should've been more compliant after the very stressful month Marcus had just had. I hung up the phone.

My mother was the next to call. I was surprised to hear from her. I'd grown used to her indifference to my life, my entire existence in fact. Really, I should've been expecting her to be in touch once she'd heard the news. Marrying Marcus was the only positive thing I'd done with my life, according to her. My career choice being the biggest negative. Not that that stopped her from using my salons for a free wash and blow dry twice a week, free haircut every four weeks or discounted facials, massages and just about every other treatment she could claim from the girls that ran our spa rooms. She'd even tried to garner discounted Botox from the doctor that rented a room from us once a month. No, my mother was all about getting what she could from my business, all while telling me how disappointed she was that her daughter was a hairdresser.

Once I'd made it clear to my mother on the phone that my mind was made and I wouldn't be giving Marcus a second chance, she ended the call, but only after telling me that I've never failed to disappoint her.

The meeting with the lawyer goes well. He's rather looking forward to going up against another lawyer, and I wonder whether Marcus will use someone from his own practise to represent him. Personally, I wouldn't be surprised if it was my own brother. I can only assume that because they specialise in corporate law that it won't be.

Nathaniel Attwood is charming, amusing, and intelligent, he is also very well versed in all things pertaining to the laws of divorce. He also happens to be around thirty-five and smoking hot. Sophie and I spend the first fifteen minutes of the meeting with our mouths hanging open and imagining lots of things involving him, us and his big wooden desk, instead of listening too much of what he was actually saying.

"Mrs Newman?"

Shit, I'm looking right at him, but entirely oblivious to a word he's just said to me. He tilts his head to one side and smiles. He has a sparkle in his blue eyes as he rolls his pen between his thumb and index finger.

I've answered the usual stuff, like name, age, occupation and address while on auto-pilot. I must've then zoned out as thoughts of sex with Nathaniel Attwood, preferably on or over his desk enter my head. I don't know why my thoughts have turned in such a sexual direction, I'm not usually like that. I've only ever slept with two men in my life, and they both let me down massively.

"I'm sorry Mr Attwood. It's been a stressful couple of days, I zoned out a bit there for a minute." I can feel a blush creep up my neck and over my cheeks as his eyes don't leave mine. I hear Sophie clear her throat from beside me as I realise we're just staring at each other in silence.

"I totally understand. Would you both like some coffee?"

"Coffee would be great," I tell him.

He lets out a long sigh, still not taking his eyes from mine and presses the intercom on his desk and asks someone to bring in coffee for the three of us.

"So, Mrs Newman—"

"Please, Mr Attwood, can you not call me that? My name's Nina, Nina Matthews. I stopped being Mrs Newman in the early hours of Saturday morning when my husband punched me in the face."

His smile and the sparkle in his pretty blue eyes is gone in an instant.

"Your husband hit you?"

I nod my head, yes.

"Did you report this to the police?"

I shake my head, no.

"I took photos of her face," Sophie adds, "but she refused to get the police involved." She turns toward me. "You need to tell him the rest. You need to tell him what happened Friday night and you need to tell him what happened at the park on Saturday."

The secretary knocks on the door at that moment and comes in with the coffee. She sets the tray down and leaves.

"Ms Gardner is right. You need to tell me everything, Nina, even if you don't want us to use it, we still need to know."

We sit quietly for a few seconds while sipping on our coffee. Nathaniel puts his cup back in its saucer and says, "This interview is just meant to be a preliminary meeting where we take down your basic details and decide if we can work together." He tilts his head from side to side. "I think we'll get along just fine, Nina. But ultimately, it's your call on whether you want to retain us to represent you." I look over at Sophie, and she nods. Nathaniel continues, "This shouldn't really be about anything personal, on my part at least, so I'm going to remain as impartial as possible. But given what you've just revealed Nina, I *want* to represent you, and I really want to kick this fucker's arse and achieve the best outcome that we can for you."

"Fuck yeah," Sophie says from beside me.

"I would also like to achieve this as quickly as possible." He looks at me, eyebrows raised, expecting an answer.

I take a deep breath. "I just want to be able to draw a line under this and not be married to him anymore. If he wants to be an arsehole about things, then let him get on with it. I just want a divorce, and I want it as quickly as legally possible."

He keeps staring at me, blinks a couple of times and asks, "Do you have time to go through all of the paperwork now, or shall we make another appointment and get things finalised then?"

Nathaniel cancels his next appointment, and we spend the following hour going through everything I need to be able to submit my divorce petition to the courts. If Marcus agrees and doesn't contest anything, I could be divorced within the next eight weeks.

Nathaniel is confident that he can lodge the papers within the next couple of days so, hopefully, a copy of the petition and something called The Acknowledgement of Service should be with Marcus by the beginning of next week. I leave his offices feeling a little less stressed about the whole thing and confident in his ability to push my divorce through quickly. I was worried beforehand that because of what Marcus does for a living, no one would want to represent me, but Nathaniel seems to see Marcus as a challenge. I like him, under different circumstances, we could probably have been friends.

We leave the offices of Attwood, Chalmers and Co and head for the nearest pub. Discussing the various ways we had imagined Nate with the big nob, as Sophie has christened him, could take us in his office. Against the wall and over his desk being the two most preferred methods. We end up on the last train back to Surrey, a little worse for wear after the three bottles of wine we consumed.

Sophie has a client booked in at ten-thirty on Wednesday. Actually, it was originally my client, but Soph offered to cover me for all of this week, allowing me to take some time off. I can hear her cursing me as she crawls out of bed on Wednesday morning though.

I have a local builder coming at midday to put a shade sale and kennel up on the roof garden. The parapet wall is about six feet high, so I don't have to worry about Duchess escaping, and as the space isn't shared with anyone else, I don't have to worry about where she craps.

By Friday, having heard nothing from the solicitors, Marcus or my family, I'm feeling upbeat. My divorce is underway, the salons are all doing well, Duchess has had no problem adjusting to her new home and considering it's been less than a week since my life swerved off course, I'm feeling happier about myself than I have in a long time.

On Friday night, Sophie, myself, Donna and Maria, a couple of our salon managers, head across the road to the wine bar opposite our flat. It's a beautiful summer's evening, and we buy a couple of bottles of wine and find a table outside in the courtyard. We sit in the late evening sun, talk shit and generally chill out. Until my phone rings, at the same time as my husband and brother arrive.

I watch them at the bar from my chair in the courtyard while answering my phone. I can see from the display that it's Nathaniel Attwood and my stomach churns – I think I can guess what he's about to tell me.

"Hey Nina, sorry for calling you so late on a Friday, but I've been in court all day."

'Not a problem, what can I do for you?"

"You in the pub?" he asks.

"Wine bar actually."

"Lucky thing, could do with a drink myself. Hope it's somewhere nice?"

"Yeah, it's not bad. Just a little place across from where we live."

"Well, enjoy. Just wanted you to know that Mr Newman should receive the divorce petition either today or by Monday morning. The court sent the papers out last night, directly to his office address as per your instructions."

My eyes are on Marcus, he knocks back the drink he's just ordered, turns around and looks right at me.

"Shit," I say into the phone.

"Nina? Is there a problem? Please don't tell me you've changed your—"

"No, no. He's here! He's just walked in. He never comes here."

"Fuck. Are you with someone? Nina? Are you safe? If he starts any trouble, call the police."

Marcus takes about four steps toward me, his face expressionless, his glare icy cold. He then diverts and heads toward the men's toilets.

"Nina, answer me for fuck's sake."

"I… he… he ignored me. He looked at me but didn't acknowledge me."

"Who are you with?"

"I'm with Sophie and a couple of our salon managers."

"Right, listen to me. If he's received the petition and now turning up where you drink, I would consider that intimidation. If he tries to talk to you, make sure you have witnesses. Don't let him get you anywhere alone."

"Okay?"

"I wish I were nearer, I'd call in for a drink myself."

"It's all good, the girls won't let anything happen to me."

I look around the table as Sophie is telling a story about a blowjob she gave a bloke who's just walked in, he blew all over her tits and ruined her Chanel blouse. I've heard the story a dozen times, but everyone else is listening intently, and they're all oblivious to the fact that my husband is here, accompanied by my brother.

"Have a good weekend, Nina. Stay safe, and I'll be in touch next week."

"You too, Nate."

Nate? Shit, where the fuck did that come from? Sophie's head swings around as she catches on to who I'm talking to. She makes an O shape with her mouth and picks up a wine bottle, pretending to suck it off. I know Nathaniel can't see any of this, but my cheeks are on fire, regardless.

"Oh, and Nina?"

"Yeah?"

"If that little prick causes you any problems, don't hesitate to call me, you hear?"

"Thanks, I won't."

"You won't?"

"I will."

Shit!

"I mean, I won't hesitate. I *will* call."

"Good... and Nina."

"Yeah?"

"I like you calling me, Nate... a lot."

Holy fucking shit. Is my solicitor, lawyer, legal representative trying to chat me up? Is that even allowed?

"Enjoy your weekend, Nate," is all I can manage, before ending the call.

Everyone at the table is looking at me, but my eyes are drawn to Marcus walking back toward the bar. He joins my brother, and they both turn and stare *at* me, but right through me at the same time. Like they don't see me. As if I don't exist. A frisson of fear travels through me, and I shudder.

"Well? What did Nate and his nob want?" Sophie asks.

I shake my head. "Right, please don't all turn your heads ladies, but Marcus and my brother are standing at the bar. Nathaniel, my lawyer, seems to think that Marcus may have received the divorce petition today."

"That fucker," Sophie says while keeping a smile on her face.

"Did you tell your lawyer that he's here?" Maria asks.

"Yeah, he said I'm not to be alone with him and if he starts anything to call the police immediately."

"Would he start anything though, in such a public place?" Donna asks.

Under Nathaniel's advice, I've informed all my staff that Marcus and I are divorcing, but I've also advised our managers that things are a little tense and that they are to call either one of us if he ever turns up at any of the salons causing trouble. Despite his actions toward me, then toward Sophie in the park, I'm actually not expecting any problems from him. He's a highly sought-after corporate lawyer, there's no way he would risk his career just to make my life difficult. In the eight years we've been married, Marcus has never behaved like he did last Friday night and I'm really not expecting him to again.

"No, I don't think he would, but it doesn't hurt to be careful."

We order some food and try to enjoy the rest of our evening. I move my chair, so I'm no longer directly facing the bar and try my best to ignore the fact that my soon to be ex is here.

Sophie is doing *her* best to convince me to go with her to the Triple M event tomorrow, but I'm not sure if I fancy it. I was expecting to be spending this weekend in York, trying to get pregnant. I shake my head at that thought. Just a week ago, I was considering having a child with Marcus. Today, the idea of his hands anywhere near me, makes the hairs on my neck stand on end and my stomach roil. Unconsciously, I turn my head toward the bar and see that he and my brother are talking to two women. I quickly look away, not because the thought of him with another woman bothers me, because it honestly doesn't, but because I just don't want to give him the pleasure of thinking that I care, which he will if he catches me staring.

"Just ignore them, Neen. He's doing it to try and piss you off. He's a fucking child."

"I'm fine. I pity the poor girl, to be honest." It hurts a little bit, but I won't tell anyone that.

Over the next couple of hours, Marcus and my brother totally ignore me while Sophie convinces me that I most definitely, will indeed, be going to tomorrow's Triple M event.

The four of us leave together. Despite the fact that we only live across the road, Maria and Donna refuse to let us walk alone.

As we pass my brother and Marcus at the bar, Pearce steps in front of my path, in a well-executed move that everyone except Sophie, because our arms are linked, would fail to notice.

Marcus says into my ear, "If you seriously think this is over, that I'll just walk away without a fight, then you're sorely mistaken. I thought you knew me better than that Nina, but then you always were a stupid little cunt. We're not over until I say we are. You'd do well to remember that."

I don't flinch at his words. I should, he's never called me a name like that before. Right now, all I feel is justified in seeking a divorce. Fuelled by the conviction of my actions, I look from him to my brother.

"Not capable of confronting me on your own, Marcus? Feel the need to bring a sidekick to bully me? Well, sorry, you don't scare me. You know why? Because I've got Sophie and she's got bigger balls than either of you two. Now fuck off out of my way. Oh, and you'll be hearing from my lawyer about this. He's already been in touch with the manager of this place and asked him to keep his cameras on you all night. You know, just in case you decided to once again behave like a prick. Marcus, it really is boring just how predictable you are."

I have no idea where the words come from, but there they are. It just so happens that we do know Mike the owner really well and he does just happen to be standing at the bar looking over at Soph and me. I smile my best smile at him, just as Marcus turns his head to follow my gaze. Mike winks and nods his head. Marcus steps a little closer to me, I step back.

"Get the fuck away from her, knob-jockey, else I'll call the police," Sophie says through gritted teeth.

"Marcus, what's going on?" the girl that's been hanging off my husband all night asks.

She's tall and lean with sharp features, nothing like me whatso-ever. I wonder for a moment if she's more his type? If perhaps *this* is the type of woman he should've married? If this is the type of woman he might want to have sex with more than once every couple of months *because* she's the complete opposite of me?

"Hey," I say cheerily, "My name's Nina. I'm Pearce's sister. He blackmailed me into marrying Marcus here about eight years ago. Sadly, for a number of reasons, one of them being that Marcus can't get it up more than once every three months, he was served with divorce papers today, so all being well, he'll be all yours in about eight weeks. Good luck with that."

She stands looking at me, mouth hanging open until Sophie steps forward and using her index and middle fingers, lifts the woman's bottom jaw up to meet her top.

"And might I suggest," Sophie says sweetly, "you either stock up on Viagra or invest in a fucking good vibrator because if you're relying on lil' ol' limp dick here, you're gonna be left severely frustrated. Just like my girl Neen has been for the last eight years." She winks at the girl, looks down at my brother, who's a good five inches shorter than her and says, "Fuck off outta my way and get back to the Shire, ya Hobbit."

Sophie yanks on my arm, we step around my brother, Marcus, and their party and collapse giggling into each other as we walk toward the door.

CONNER

I'VE SPENT THE LAST TEN days in musical heaven. Marley Layton is a genius and a legend. Added to all of that, he's a fucking nice bloke. He's had Gunner and me in tears of laughter, and he also had us in tears as he shared with us what he's been through with his band and his family.

He has a state of the art studio built on the grounds of the estate his house sits on and Gunner and I have rehearsed there every day since last Tuesday. I've stayed over a couple of nights. I think he could tell how down I felt so he invited us to join him and his family for dinner. Gunner declined the invite because he had Chelsea and the kids waiting for him at home, whereas all I had were my dogs, who were probably already in bed with my dad and Sandra by that time.

We'd sat out on his back deck, smoked some great weed and talked shit about every possible subject you could imagine. He told me stories about a three-way he had in a toilette at the White House. How he and his wife Ashley had had a quickie in a cupboard at Buckingham Palace, of meeting presidents, prime ministers and royalty and it had all happened because of his music. You name it, he'd done it, and he'd done it with his wife at his side and while raising three kids.

I don't mind admitting, I was jealous. When I watched him and Ashley together, the way they'd shared so many experiences, I wanted what they have. They asked me about women, if there was anyone special and for the first time, in a long time, I told them the story of Meebs and me. From going to infant school together to me being her first. Our plans to run away and her not showing, and about all the songs I'd written about her over the years.

"Did you write, 'Where I Are' for her?" Ashley asked the second time I stayed over. We'd drunk a litre of Grey Goose and smoked a lot of weed. I was feeling chilled, but a little bit sad for some reason. It was the Saturday before the concert. One week to go and I think my nerves were starting to get to me. I'd had a terrible night's sleep the night before, and I'd felt off all day. I'd fucked up nearly every song we'd practised, and I'm amazed Marley hadn't kicked my arse and called the whole thing off.

We haven't made it public knowledge that we're performing together. The event is already a sellout, so it's not going to increase ticket sales. Live recordings from each act will be made though so there may be an increase in the album sales.

If the truth be told, the main reason I don't want any publicity is in case I bottle it. I'm absolutely crapping myself at the thought of getting up on that stage without Jet. If our performance is made public knowledge, I'm worried that I'll crumble under the pressure. I've managed to keep the anxiety attacks under control, but they're still about. I still feel a bubbling in my toes and my belly if I let my mind wander. The weird thing is, thinking and talking about Meebs calms me down. Thinking about her blue eyes, her soft skin and her round little arse chills me the fuck out and still has the ability to make me horny. Fuck, I really need a shag. Well, when I say shag, I mean I need to blow down someone's throat, over their tits or their face, I'm really not fussed at this stage. The problem is, there needs to be more than just the two of us. I can't handle the intimacy of just me and a woman. I can't handle even the *thought* of being buried balls deep inside a woman and have her look into my eyes. My skin heated and my heart rate speeds up as the early sensations of a panic attack start to bubble in my belly.

I must've fidgeted and looked uncomfortable as I heard Marley say from beside me, "It's all right, Reed, you don't have to talk about it if it makes you uncomfortable."

I sat up straighter in the chair I was slouched in. Marley passed me a joint and I took a long draw before passing it to Ashley.

"Nah, honestly, I'm fine. I'm good." I smiled at both of them.

"Yeah, 'Where I Are' is about her," I continued while running my hands through my hair as I think about that song. "I wanted to call it, 'Gravy On Your Roast' but the label were worried that people would think it was a euphemism for some kind of a kinky sex act or drug-related."

They both laughed.

"The label police are such wankers. The crap they come out with," Marley said.

"How are you fixed?" Ashley asked, "Contract wise I mean? If the rest of the boys wanna call it a day, can you carry on by yourself or is your contract void because of Jet's death?"

"D'ya know what Ash, I have no idea. I'll have to ask Lawson to look into that tomorrow."

Marley looked across the table to me. "Well, if you wanna carry on by yourself and you want a bit more artistic freedom than the big labels give ya, come and sign for us."

My belly did a backflip and landed somewhere near my balls.

Fuck!

I was about to get a hard-on over a record deal.

"Babe, that joint was meant to share," Marley leant around me and spoke to his wife.

"Yeah babe, I know, but it's gone out, and you've got the lighter."

He threw it to her.

"Love ya," he said and blew her a kiss. She caught the lighter with one hand.

"You better love me, ya fucker."

I felt like a complete fucking sap. Watching the two of them, the way they interacted and bounced off of each other. The way one told a story, and the other remembered the names of the other people there or added their memory of the story. It made my heart feel warm, my belly feel all fluttery, and my throat feel tight. I was turning into a little bitch. A thirteen-year-old girl had bigger balls than I had at that moment.

Ashley lit the joint and passed it back to me. I took a draw and passed it on.

"Talk to Lawson tomorrow," Marley said, "Find out what the go is and if you're interested, sit down and have a chat with Len and me."

I nodded. "I'm definitely interested. If it's doable, I'm in."

"Good," he replied.

"Well, that's his career sorted. I'm gonna have a scroll through my phone tomorrow and see if I can find him a good woman."

I smiled and scratched at the stubble on my chin, while my chest felt like it was being squeezed.

"Thanks all the same Ash, but I'm happy being single for now."

Why the fuck did saying that cause such a lump in my throat?

WE HAD A REHEARSAL AT the venue on Friday morning, and sound checked Saturday morning before the TV crews arrived.

Up until this point, we've managed to keep our performance together a secret from the press. I'm nervous but feeling much better about getting up on stage. It's been good catching up with Gunner, and Marley has been a massive support. I would even go as far as saying that I'm feeling the buzz like I used to right now.

And then Lawson arrives, with Amanda in tow. I've not seen her since Lawson turned up at my house with her a few weeks back, I'd left her with a mouthful of my spunk and then headed off to my bedroom. She's messaged me nearly every day since then, and I've ignored her each time.

I'm not an arsehole, I'm never rude or disrespectful to the women I fuck, but I always make it clear that all they will get from me is sex. I have no more to give.

THERE ARE DRESSING ROOMS AND a bar upstairs at the venue, and I've spent the rest of the morning hiding out up there away from the press, with Gunner. As one of the organisers, Marley has been running around like his arse is on fire, making sure everything is in order. It's his manager and brother, Lennon that I'm talking to at the bar when Lawson and Amanda arrive.

"Reed, how you feeling? You ready for this? It's filling up downstairs."

Lawson leans in, shakes my hand and gives me a pat on the back. I shrug.

"Bit nervous," I tell him honestly.

Amanda smiles and moves in to try and kiss my cheek.

Why? Why would she do that?

I dodge the kiss, nod my head and smile, "Amanda." She glares but still runs her hand up and down my arm. I watch Lennon, watching our exchange. His eyes meet mine, he gives a smile, rolls his eyes and shakes his head slightly. He and Marley must be approaching fifty by now and have been in this business a long time. I'm sure they've dealt with *a lot* of Amanda's over the years.

"Not sure if you've met before? Lawson, this is Lennon Layton. He runs Carnage Creations with Marley."

I notice Amanda's head swing around at the mention of Lennon's name. Lawson and Lennon start chatting, and I stand back and watch as Amanda ingratiates herself into the conversation by telling Lennon how she's followed his career for years.

Yeah, right!

"That fucking woman makes my skin crawl," Gunner whispers in my ear, while passing me another beer. "She always looks at blokes like she wants to eat them. Chels reckons she's got a thing for you. Didn't you fuck her once, at the studio?"

I turn sideways to face him so that our conversation can't be heard.

"Yeah, and I made the mistake of going back for a blowjob a coupla times since. She's text me nonstop for the last few weeks."

"Silly boy, Reed, silly boy." He shoulder bumps me.

Lawson says my name from over my shoulder, and we spend the next ten minutes discussing the legalities of me leaving our current label and signing with CC, the Layton's label. I can't help but notice the way Amanda moves until she's virtually pressed into Lennon's side. She throws her head back and laughs exaggeratedly at something he says, then turns and says something into his ear.

Lawson watches her, his eyes then meet mine. I shake my head, letting him know that I'm not happy that she's here.

A hand suddenly appears from nowhere and grabs Amanda's hair. We all step back, as a stunning looking woman with dark skin and long dark hair shoves Amanda out of the way.

"Have some respect for yourself love. That's *my* husband, and *he* is in *no way* interested in *you*."

"Fuck, bitch fight," Gun says from beside me, and we clink our bottles together.

"I'm sorry, I wasn't... I mean, I don't know..." Amanda tries to speak.

"Fuck off," the other woman says, "Now," she orders when Amanda fails to move.

"We'll see you down at the VIP bar in a while," Lawson says to Gun and me, then turning to Lennon, he holds out his hand, and they shake.

"Good talking to you, Lennon. I'll be in touch once I get our contracts lawyer to go through the paperwork we signed with the label."

Len nods. "Sweet, look forward to it... but Lawson... "

"Yeah?"

"Don't ever bring her near me again." He gestures with his head to Amanda's retreating form.

"Yeah, I'll have words. I'm really sorry about that," he looks between Lennon, and who I assume is Len's wife, as he speaks.

I feel sorry for him, but hope he's learnt his lesson where Amanda is concerned. As I keep telling him, the woman has no boundaries and refuses to take no for an answer.

He walks away and has only gone a few steps when the woman that yanked Amanda by the hair says to Lennon, "What the fuck, babe? What was ya doing standing there, letting her get all in your space?"

Lennon shakes his head. "Jim, seriously? She was like a fucking rash, came out of nowhere and was suddenly all over me. These boys'll tell ya."

She turns to look between myself and Gun. I hold out my hand, "Conner Reed." I lay on the charm and give her my full megawatt, posing for the camera smile, trying to diffuse the domestic Amanda has potentially caused.

"And this is Gunner Vance."

She shakes both our hands. "The boys from Shift, I know who you are. I'm really sorry for your loss. Jet was a great bloke. I've met him a few times over the years. Our kids are big fans. I'm Jimmie

Layton, Lennon's wife." Her brown eyes look right into mine, and I know that she means what she says. You meet so many shallow, insincere people in this industry, in this job, that it's so gratifying when you meet people that actually mean what they say.

"Thanks," Gun and I both say at the same time and clink our bottles at our unison.

We stand and chat with them for a while. The fact that I'm going to perform alongside Marley later has even been kept secret from her we discover as we talk, and I appreciate the fact that despite being family, Marley and Ash have stuck to their word.

We eventually make our way down to the VIP area to wait for our performance. We still have a couple of hours, but it's water only from here on out. Today is not the day to appear on stage off my chops as I've done so many times in the past.

CHAPTER FOURTEEN

NINA

I STAND AT THE CORNER of the bar and people watch while Sophie talks with some makeup artist that's here as a guest of one of the bands at the Triple M event.

I watch a group that are standing to the side of the bar. There's six of them, all in their early twenties. Three boys, three girls. Life's beautiful people. I think at first they must all be models, but as I study them closer, I wonder if they might be all one family because they actually look alike. There's one girl, aged about twentyish, who is just stunning. She's taller than the other girls, with long brown hair, olive skin and the most amazing blue eyes.

I watch as a blonde woman, aged about forty approaches the group. She looks vaguely familiar for some reason. She gives them all a kiss and a cuddle before getting herself a drink from the bar. She's beautiful too, tall and blonde, with big brown eyes and an even bigger smile. She nudges one of the girls as she whispers something in her ear.

"Mum that is wrong, so wrong. He's gotta be ten years younger than you," the girl says, and they all laugh.

I suddenly have a pang of something shoot through me, jealousy?

Loneliness? I'm not sure. I've never had that kind of relationship with my mum, not with any of my family. We've never been close, and I've never felt like I belonged with them.

I knock back my third very large vodka, then take a glass of champagne from the tray of a passing waiter.

"You aiming to get completely smashed?" Sophie shoulder bumps and asks from beside me.

"Yep," I reply, "I think this week calls for it, don't you?."

She grabs two shots from the tray of the next waiter that passes. "Amen to that, sister." She hands me a shot, we clink our glasses together, then down them in one.

"Fuck!" we say in unison.

"What was that?" I splutter through the burn in my throat and chest.

"Lighter fuel I reckon," Sophie coughs.

"Showing your age now, Soph. Do they even still make lighters that require fuel?"

"No, but they obviously still have excess amounts of the shit left, so they sell it in fancy stainless steel bottles with a name like Triple Z and sell it to idiots like us."

I tilt my champagne glass toward her. "Here's to idiots like us." She taps her beer bottle, gently against my glass.

"Love ya, baby chick." I smile at her use of the nickname her brother had given me a long, long time ago. I was about eight years old and had stayed over at their house one night. When I went down to the kitchen the next morning wearing a pair of yellow pyjamas and with my blonde hair sticking up all over the show, Josh had greeted me with, "Good morning, baby chick." And the nickname had stuck with the pair of them.

"Did you talk to your brother yet?" I ask, she shakes her head.

"Na, I text to tell him I'm here, but I've not heard back. He'll be busy as fuck I reckon."

I was secretly glad that Josh hadn't come over and spoken to us yet. I always felt so awkward around him. He knew my secret. He knew how desperate I'd been for Conner to get in touch with me all those years ago, and he knew that Conner had rejected me.

The makeup artist Sophie had been talking to earlier was joined by her hairdresser husband. I smiled as I was introduced but then zoned out and went back to people watching. Hoping that imagining the exciting lives of the people around me would push away the thoughts of the dickhead that had abandoned me so long ago.

I turn back and start watching the beautiful people standing to the side of me again when I notice a huge bald man come walking through the now crowded VIP area. People move out of his way, or he moves them as he makes his way through. He's followed by a tall, dark-haired man. He looks about fifty, and he's gorgeous. If I were ever going to go for an older man, he would be it. He's wearing jeans and a long-sleeved T-shirt, his dark hair is longish and pushed back from his face, a mixture of grey and black stubble covers his chin. There's just something about him that says, 'I like sex' written all over his face.

I've apparently gone without for far too long, apart, that is, the shitty experience I'd had with my husband last Friday, which had offered me no release whatsoever.

I never usually look at men and think about what it would be like to get down and dirty with them, but my thoughts have been in the gutter a few times this week. First with naughty Nate the lawyer and now with this unknown random. Perhaps a shag with a complete stranger is exactly what I need. *I wonder if I could live with myself after mindless sex with a stranger though?* I finish my drink and grab another, thinking to myself, *well there's only one way to find out!*

I watch as the DILF is followed by three children who are so very obviously his. Two boys and a girl aged about fourteen. The boys are the absolute image of their dad. The girl is tall, slim, with long dark hair and big brown eyes. They head toward the original group of BP's, my new nickname for the crowd of genetically blessed human beings congregating to the side of the bar.

I watch as the DILF turns and watches a woman approach with a teenage girl. Again the woman is stunning, tall, slim, long brown hair and the bluest eyes I think I've ever seen on an olive-skinned person. She too looks vaguely familiar, but I've far too much alcohol buzzing through my veins to try and think too hard about who she is. I'm sure it'll come to me later. She stops right in front of me and says to the girl, who has her arms folded across her chest, "Stop sulking, Lula, I really don't need this today."

The girl turns toward her with a frown. "Let me stay downstairs then. Harley's down there."

The woman tilts her head and closes her eyes for a moment. She lets out a long breath.

"Harley is eighteen, you're eleven. You are not going downstairs. You'll stay up here with the rest of us, and you *will* stop wearing a face that looks like a smacked arse. Do I make myself clear?"

Shit, eleven. I would've put her at fourteen or maybe even sixteen, easily. I was the opposite, thirty-one and still looked about twelve.

The girl stares at, who I assume is her mum through narrowed eyes but says nothing. Then flips her hair over her shoulder and heads toward the rest of the group. The DILF grabs the girl's arm and says something into her ear. She shakes her head then nods. He says something else, and she smiles the biggest smile, stands on her tiptoes and kisses him on the cheek and walks over to the rest of their party.

I'm entranced, sipping on my champagne as I watch all of their interactions. Emboldened by my alcohol consumption, I continue watching, unashamedly.

The woman approaches the man. "How did you do that? What did you promise to make her smile like that?"

The DILF smiles the sexiest, lopsided smile I think I've ever seen as he looks at the woman. If I believed everything that I was taught during my Catholic education, I'd swear to God and all that is holy, that my ovaries just exploded watching him smile at her like that. He pulls her into him and whispers into her ear, all the while, he has one hand cupping the back of her head, the other has a handful of her arse cheek. He bends his knees slightly so that he can look into the woman's eyes and my heart melts.

I want that! What they have. The way he looks at her. I want a man to want me like that. She leans in and kisses him on the mouth and grinds herself against him.

Oh. My. Fucking. God.

She's in a public place. A room packed with celebrities and her children present, and she doesn't care. I want to be her. I want to be as brave as her. I want to love someone so much that I would be brave enough to not give a fuck about who might be watching me behave like that.

My heart hurts, and I can't help but feel a little bit angry and resentful. *Why can't that be me?* I just want to feel loved, cherished and wanted. I want someone to look at me like nothing else in the world exists. I want someone to want me, to need me like they need air. I just want to be loved.

I wipe the tears, that I've just become aware have fallen, from my cheeks and try to compose myself, when I hear Sophie say from beside me, "Oh *fuck*! *Fucking hell*. Shit." I turn and look at her but she's not looking at me, she's staring straight ahead. I follow her gaze and my heart slams into my rib cage and stops. Dead.

CONNER

W HEN WE GET DOWNSTAIRS TO the VIP bar, we're met with a few stares. This is the first time any of the members of Shift has been seen in public since Jet's death. Marley has assured us that the area would be strictly off limits to fans, with passes being allocated to industry insiders and direct family members of the artists performing only.

The first few bands have already played. There's a comedian on stage now, and a lot of people are watching the big screens, listening to his performance.

As we approach Lawson, I'm disappointed to see that Amanda is still here.

"What the fuck, Laws? Why didn't you send her home?" I ask him when we get to the small round table he's standing next to.

"Chelsea will be here in a little while, she'll do her fucking nut when she sees her," Gunner says.

Lawson looks down into the glass of bourbon that he's holding and swirls the amber liquid around and over the crushed ice, sitting at the bottom. "I can't fucking get rid of her," he states, turning his back on Amanda and toward us while he speaks.

"She's done a coupla lines, and she started really playing up and getting loud when I asked her to go."

Gunner's phone rings, playing 'Where I Are.' My heart rate accelerates, the way it always does for that split second as I allow thoughts of *her* to flood my brain. He answers the call.

"Fuck, Chels is here," Gunner says to me. I've entirely missed him actually having that conversation while trying to *not* think about Meebs.

"I've warned her Amanda's here. She reckons she'll swing for her if she lays one of her bony hands on me or you today. I told her that she'll have to join the queue. I thought Lennon's wife was gonna put her on her arse earlier."

I shake my head and say as quietly as I can, "I tell you what, if she puts her hands on Marley and his missus catches her, she'll cut her fucking throat. She's a lovely girl Ashley, but I wouldn't wanna fuck with her."

"Oh, but I thought you didn't want to fuck with anyone, Conner? Didn't think you were actually up to it," Amanda says from beside me.

How the fuck she got there without me realising I have no idea?

"Amanda, darling. I'm up to fucking *anything* with a pulse. I just happen to be very particular whose cunt I put my cock inside."

She stands with one hand on her hip, her other tilts her glass back as she finishes her drink. Her eyes never leaving mine. I look over her face and think that it's sad really, how desperate she is for attention. She's a gorgeous looking woman.

I actually feel sorry for her for a few moments, until I hear Chelsea say, "Hey babe," from beside me.

"Talking of cunts," Amanda says, clearly loud enough for everyone to hear.

"That's enough," I tell her. "Get her the fuck out of here, Laws. I don't want her around me or any of my dealings again. You either get rid of her or I'll find myself a new manager."

Lawson grabs her arm. "I warned you, didn't I? I fucking warned you." Lawson moves, steering Amanda with him.

"See ya," Chelsea waves and smiles cheerily as they pass her by. She turns to me with a grin. "Reed, please try and be a little bit more choosy whose mouth you stick your dick in, in future, because she's a fucking nut job and liable to bite it off one of these days."

"Sorry Chels. I'll run my next conquest past you first before I blow down their throats, shall I?'

"No, but I'll happily try them out first for you if you like," Gunner adds. Chelsea backhands him, right in the solar plexus and he caves in like an old man.

We all laugh, and I turn around and look away as my friends start to suck face.

My eye catches a short blonde girl standing at the bar. She's wearing light blue skinny jeans and fuck me, *is she wearing them*. I tilt my head to the side, looking at her perfectly round arse. My cock twitches and I close my eyes for a few seconds. That simple male reaction of looking at a woman momentarily floors me. I've spent so many years hiding behind filthy, dirty, gratuitous, controlling sex that I rarely allow myself an unexpected hard-on. It's a little reminder to myself that somewhere in that twisted heart of mine lurks a human being. A man capable of feeling emotions – loving, needing, wanting.

I rake my hand through my hair and let out a long breath. I need a shag! Not a blowjob, not a threesome, I think I actually need to connect with someone, skin on skin, eye to eye.

I watch as the girl with the perfect arse lifts her long blonde hair up off the back of her neck and lets the air get to it. She has a tattoo hidden there, and for some reason, I have an almost uncontrollable urge to go take a look at what it says.

My eyes are drawn to the tall blonde standing next to her at the bar. Perfect arse is wearing a pair of green, killer heels and it strikes me that they are almost the exact same colour as my favourite custom-made guitar. They have a heel about four inches high on them, but she's still about five inches shorter than the girl standing next to her. The thought of a straightforward fuck no longer feels like such a good idea, not as good as a threesome with these two, anyway. Especially if perfect arse keeps those heels on.

The tall blonde flicks her hair over her shoulder and turns and faces the room just as a waiter offers me something to eat from a tray loaded with little bits of toast with brown or pink stuff on them. I shake my head and politely decline his offer. My eyes travelling instantly back to the girls at the bar. The tall blonde is looking right at me, wearing an almost horrified expression.

Everything starts to slow down – sounds, my heart, my very existence. She says a couple of words to her friend who turns and follows her gaze until her eyes land on me. My heart crashes into my sternum, shatters into a gazillion tiny pieces, and falls and falls and falls… eventually landing somewhere deep down in the pit of my stomach.

I watch as her hand actually rushes to her chest like she's been shot or has pain there. It's almost a theatrical move. Her other hand reaches out for the bar, and I instinctively step forward when it looks like her legs might give way. I watch her mouth open and close, and I feel myself sway in rhythm with the rise and fall of her chest.

Without taking her eyes from mine, she steps toward me. I want to move toward her, go to her, but my legs refuse to cooperate.

And then suddenly, she's there, right there in front of me.

My hand has a mind of its own and starts to reach for her, I ball it into a fist and force it back down to my side.

She's just how I remember her.

She's beautiful.

So, fucking beautiful.

"Meebs," I thought I was saying it in my head, but somehow my lips move, and the sound comes out of my mouth.

Her face crumbles, and she lets out a sob. Her hand goes to her mouth and covers it. She shakes her head while tears run down her cheeks. I don't know if the room is actually silent or if I just can't focus on anything but her.

"Don't. Don't call me that. I'm not your Amoeba," she says.

"You'll always be my Amoeba. Nina Amoeba."

"I stopped being your anything when you left me in that hospital all on my own," she almost hisses the words through her gritted teeth.

"What? What hospital room?"

Her shoulders slump, and I watch as she completely deflates in front of me. Her eyes meet mine, and she looks so sad, so fucking sad and broken.

"You didn't come, after all the things you said, all the promises you made and when I needed you the most, you didn't come for me. You left me, Conner. You left me."

Sophie's there, and without warning flies at me. "What did you say? What the fuck did you say to her?"

I look between the two of them. My mouth opens, then closes, but I can't seem to make a sound. I start to feel the first bubbling of a panic attack in my toes and my belly. I close my eyes and concentrate on nothing but getting one breath in and then slowly let one breath out.

I can hear Lawson asking what's going on. Then Tyler's voice is in my ear.

Where the fuck did he come from?

"Breathe Conner, just breathe through it. Do it the way Dad showed you."

I open my eyes and look into my brother's worried face.

"You got this?"

I nod. Feeling calmer.

"I got this. You called me, Conner. You never call me, Conner."

He smiles. My dad's Conner or Con, and somehow I'd ended up being known as Reed to save confusion. My brothers called me Reed, so when I went to school, everyone else called me Reed. It just stuck.

Everything slowly comes back into focus, sound and smell. The room stops spinning and starts coming back into view.

"Fuck," is the only other thing I can think of saying.

Tyler passes me a bottle of water, and I unscrew the cap and take a few big gulps.

"Where'd she go?" I look from side to side around the room, but she's nowhere to be seen.

"Where'd she go, Ty? Where the fuck did she go?"

Fuck, I need to get a grip.

"She's here. Someone took her to the office so she could sit down. Sophie and Jenna went with her." He looks over my face with his eyebrows drawn together.

"What happened? Why's she here?" he asks.

"I don't know... She's with Sophie. Josh probably got them tickets," I tell him.

"Well, a heads up from Josh would've been handy."

"Tell me about it," I reply.

Lawson reappears, walking down a corridor from beside the bar. A lot of the top bands are making their appearances now, and the crowd has thinned out. The majority of people choosing to watch from the balcony that runs all around the upper level, rather than on the big screens in the VIP bar.

"What the fuck was that all about? Who's she?" Laws asks.

"She's my..." I struggle to find a word to use to describe what Meebs is to me.

"She's the gravy on his roast," Tyler tells Lawson. His mouth drops open.

"That's her? That's... Whatever that name is that he calls her?" he asks Ty like I'm not even here.

"Amoeba," we both say together.

"What the fuck sort of name is Amoeba?" Lawson asks.

I can't help but smile as I remember how it came about.

"I've known her for years, we went to the same infant and primary school. She's always been really tiny. Little, with blonde hair and blue eyes. Everyone was always calling her titch and shorty, things like that. When me and Josh went up to secondary school, we were in biology, and there was a drawing on the chalkboard. It sort of looked like a fried egg, but with a blue middle, instead of yellow. Written above it, it said, 'Amoeba – small, single-celled organism.' Josh and I looked at each other and at the same time said, 'Nina'." I look between them both and shrug my shoulders. "And that was it, Nina Amoeba. We were about thirteen and a complete pair of arse-holes. We couldn't wait to get to his house and terrorise the shit out of her. She would've been about eleven at the time, and I thought she was the most beautiful girl I'd ever seen." I take another swig of my water, totally aware of the fact that I must sound like a complete cunt. "We thought the new nickname would piss her off. Instead, she smiled and said, 'I love it. In fact, when I grow up and have a daughter, I might actually call her Amoeba, I like it so much'."

Lawson shakes his head as he pats me on the shoulder. "Conner Reed, what a fucking pussy."

CHAPTER SIXTEEN

NINA

I CAN'T BELIEVE HE'S HERE.

I can't believe, after all these years I reacted like that.

I wanted to slap him.

I wanted to claw at his face.

I wanted him to pull me into his arms and never let me go.

I wanted him to love me again, just like he used to.

I think I might be a little bit drunk.

I look up from where I'm sitting on a chair, in an office at the club. Conner's brother's wife Jenna is leaning against a desk next to Sophie looking at me, wearing a frown.

She passes me the bottle of water she's holding. I take a deep breath and then take a sip from the bottle.

Sophie's texting on her phone but looks up at me. "I'm so sorry, Neen. I swear to God, I had no idea he was gonna be here."

My bottom lip trembles. I just can't believe it all still hurts so much.

Jenna steps forward and passes me a tissue.

"Thank you," I say very quietly.

I lost my virginity to Conner at her house. *I wonder if she knows that.* I give her a small smile.

"Good to see you, Jenna." She gives me what's hopefully, a genuine smile back.

"And you Nina, it's been a while."

"Fifteen years. Ethan was just a baby," I tell her.

"Wow, a lifetime ago. He's sixteen now."

I nod as I try to wrap my head around that fact.

"How you feeling baby chick? You lost it there for a bit," Sophie asks.

"I'm feeling better. Sorry about that. I was just so shocked to see him after all this time. I don't know what happened."

"I can't believe my brother never told me he was gonna be here. You just wait till I see him."

"It's not your brother's fault, Soph. It's just one of those things. I'm surprised it's not happened sooner. Not that Conner and I have mixed in the same circles the last fifteen years," I say with a shrug.

"What d'ya wanna do?" Sophie asks. "Stay and watch the show or leave?"

"Drink myself into oblivion?" I ask her with another shrug of my shoulders.

Can I be out there? Where he is?

In the same building? The same room?

Breathing the same air?

"I'm gonna go and find Ty. I don't wanna miss Reed's performance."

My heart stutters.

"Conner's performing? Here?" I ask. My eyes land on Sophie. I really should capture this moment. Her mouth is wide open, but no words are coming out. This is something that rarely happens unless, of course, there's a sex act involved. In which case, I make a point of not being around to witness such deeds.

"Yeah, it's all been kept hush hush. He's been really nervous."

She gives me a big smile. "You should stay and watch, I know you'll love the performance."

My eyes move to Sophie. "Your call, babe. I'm happy to do whatever you wanna do," she tells me.

I stand from the chair, and my head spins a bit. I've sobered considerably, and I don't like it. I want to get so drunk that I can't remember my name. I don't want to be able to feel by the end of the night. I want to be numb to the ache in my chest, and oblivious to every single memory I have of Conner Reed.

Jenna unexpectedly wraps her arms around me. "Stay Nina. Tyler would love to see you. I've no idea what went on between you and Reed, but it's been too long since we've seen anything of you."

"Okay, we'll stay. I'll come and find you both," I tell her

AFTER I USE SOME OF the makeup that Sophie never leaves home without, and fix myself up in the bathroom adjoining the office, we head back outside to where the concert is in full swing. Sophie grabs us a couple of drinks from a passing waiter and captures my hand as we make our way out to the balcony that overlooks the stage.

We watch a couple of bands, and then listen as a well-known TV presenter appears on stage, giving a running total of what the day has raised so far and tells us that we're in for a surprise with the next act that's about to perform.

My stomach churns, and I knock back the third glass of champagne I've had since leaving the office we were in.

The whole place falls silent. The lights go out, leaving only the emergency exit signs glowing. The curtain is still covering the stage when the very first notes of a song I know so well starts to play. The whole place erupts as the curtain lifts to the band hidden behind it playing, 'With You,' an old hit of one of my all-time favourite bands, Carnage.

Sophie and I scream like we used to as school girls when we heard this song. We lose ourselves in the music for a few seconds. I dance with my eyes closed and my arms in the air. I know every single word and sing at the top of my voice, letting thoughts of the fucked up mess I've made of my life disappear.

And then the crowd roars even louder, and I swear, I actually feel the building shake.

I open my eyes to see what everyone is reacting to and for the second time in a matter of hours, my heart comes to an abrupt halt.

He's there.

On stage.

The boy I loved so very long ago is now a man.

A God.

A rock God.

"Conner Reed and Marley Layton both on stage together. My heart can't take it," the girl standing next to me, says to no one in particular.

"Oh my God, Neen, look at him." For some reason, I feel a pang of jealousy in my chest at the thought of these women watching him, wanting him. Thinking that they know him.

"Don't look at me like you wanna punch me. I meant Marley Layton, not fucking Reed. Although... I've gotta say, Neen, watching the pair of them on stage has given me a bit of a clit-on."

I stare at her blankly for a few seconds. It's not so much the inappropriateness of my friend's words, it's that I have so many emotions swimming through me, along with a fair amount of alcohol that I can't seem to form a sentence.

"He's still got it. He's still fucking hot. I'd totally do him, even if he is fifty." I smile and shake my head at Sophie as she moves to the music. "Reed looks good too though, you've gotta admit it, Neen."

I look back down on the stage. He does look good. He looks like he's doing what he was born to do and an immense feeling of pride washes through me.

No wonder he was feeling nervous about performing. Marley Layton was his absolute hero when we were younger, and Carnage, the band Marley was in, was our favourite. We'd been to see them together a couple of times, and now, here he was, living his dream up on stage with his idol.

My heart's racing as the song comes to an end. The crowd quiets as Marley addresses them, thanking everyone for coming and all that had been involved in making the event happen. He then thanks, Conner and Gunner Vance, Shift's drummer for performing with him and then he moves to Conner's spot, while Conner moves to the front of the stage.

"People," he shouts into the mic. The crowd goes wild.

"This is a little song that I think you all might know. This is a song I wrote about someone very special to me." My stomach break-dances around my belly, and my heart feels like a hand has punched through my chest and is squeezing it tight. I can't stand here and listen to this. If he's going to dedicate a song to his girlfriend, I have to leave, I *need* to leave. But I don't. I stand gripping the ledge that travels along the edge of the balcony and wait for his words to flay me.

"This is for you, Nina, and no matter what, you'll always be my Amoeba."

"Fuck. Me." Sophie says from beside me.

The crowd erupts again as the band rocks out to, 'Where I Are.'

"Holy fucking shit," are the words that come out of my mouth, while my brain digests the lyrics of the song being sung by the man that has owned my heart for so very, very, long.

It's moments like these when I stare at the stars, when I look at the moon and wonder where you are.
Do you like the same things, and do you ever think of me?
Do you ever think of me, and wonder what could've been?

Do you ever look at the stars and think of me?
Do you ever think of me, and wonder where I are?
Where I are.
You hated tomato sauce on your chips and marmite on your toast.
You didn't like your feet tucked in bed, but loved extra gravy on your roast.
I knew you inside out, but would I know you now. Would I know you know?
Would you pass me in the street like none of it mattered?
Would you just walk by, like what we had wasn't real?
Please tell me it mattered, I need to know that it mattered.
I can sometimes go for days but then a smell, a sound, or the words of
a song.
It brings it all back, reminds me that it all went wrong.
You hated marmite on your toast.
Loved gravy on your roast.
Do you have moments like these when you stare up at the stars?
Do you ever think of me, and wonder where I are?
Do you ever think of me, and wonder where I are?
I wanna know you again,
I wanna stare into your eyes.
I wanna watch you while you sleep.
I wanna kiss away your pain.
But until that day,
I'll look up at the stars, and wonder where you are?
And hope that you're looking at them too.
And wondering, where I are?
Please tell me.
Please, please tell me.
That you wonder,
Where I are?

Sophie has her arm around my shoulder, and I grip her hand with both of mine. I've heard this song hundreds of times, but I've never really listened to the words. To be honest, I usually turn the radio down when a Shift song gets played, and Marcus just turns it off if they even get mentioned.

The song ends, and I feel almost bereft. I want it to go on. I want to hear Conner say that he wrote it for me again. I want to feel the words and his voice wrap around me, to make my world good again.

"Why didn't he show, Soph? Why'd he leave me like that? If the words in that song are true, why did he never come for me?"

"I don't know, babe, I really don't know."

She wipes a tear from under my eye with a napkin. "But ya know what? The only way to find out is to ask him, and we want that pretty face of yours looking perfect when you do."

"What? No. No way. I'm a mess Soph, and anyway, there's no way I'll be able to get near him after that performance." He'll be surrounded by groupies and supermodels. Why would he want to talk to me, the girl he left behind?

Sophie says no more. We turn back to the stage and watch the rest of the set. Just as the boys are taking a bow, someone puts their hand on my shoulder. I turn and come face to face with Tyler Reed.

"Nina, how are you? You're looking well." He leans in and kisses my cheek. I don't know why, but I get a lump in my throat when I look at him.

I thought he was going to be a part of my life.

I thought I was going to be a part of his family.

"I'm good Ty. A little bit drunk, but I'm good."

"Jenna's just gone over to the bar, d'ya wanna come and have a drink with us?"

I fumble around my fuzzy brain, trying to find the words I need to use, to make a sentence that will explain why I couldn't possibly join him and Jenna at the bar for a drink, when Sophie says from over my shoulder, "We'd love to. Lead the way."

CHAPTER
SEVENTEEN

CONNER

"**F**UCK YEAH!" GUNNER THROWS HIS sticks into the crowd and then pulls me into his nine-foot-wide chest.

I'm not usually so emotional, my nieces and nephews are normally the only ones that get to me, but this last month or so has been hard. There have been times since losing Jet that I've wondered if I'd ever be able to do this again. I've doubted my ability to be able to perform, to sing, to play guitar. I've thought that without Jet by my side, it would be too hard, but today has blown all of my self-doubts out the window. I'm fucking buzzing. My blood feels like it has electricity charging through it.

"Yeah. Come on," Marley roars as we head off stage. "You fucking rocked it, Reed. You fucking slayed them."

I will never, till my dying day admit to anyone what his words have just made me feel. Marley Layton is God to me. My heart is hammering so hard, I wouldn't be surprised if I've broken a rib or two. I can't wipe the smile off of my face, but at the same time I can't swallow down the lump in my throat. I want to jump for fucking joy, skip like a six-year-old girl, slide down a rainbow and kiss a unicorn. Fuck cloud nine, I'm up around seven hundred and eighty-seven.

But still, still I know there's something missing, and I feel it deep down in my gut when Gunner walks straight into Chelsea's arms while we head to our dressing room.

Marley throws his arm over my shoulder. "I know it's hard mate, but you've done the right thing getting up there so soon. I know it hurts and you feel like a part of you is missing but believe me, it's the best fucking therapy."

Ashley is waiting in the dressing room and pops the cork on a bottle of Cristal as we come through the doors.

"Well done boys, you were brilliant." She wraps her arms around Marley's neck and licks the sweat off of his throat.

"Babe," he complains, "You know playing live makes me hard. I'm gonna have to fuck ya now."

She pulls back, looking at him like she'd happily get naked right here, arches her eyebrow and says, "Come on then rock star."

Marley grabs the bottle of champagne with one hand and his wife with the other and drags her out the door. "I'll see you at the bar, boys. I need to be inside my wife for a bit."

"Bit of what?" Gunner asks, passing Marley on his way in the door. His arm slung over Chelsea's shoulder.

Fuck!

I feel lonely.

Lonely and horny.

Not a good combination.

I wonder if Meebs is still here. I asked Tyler to try and keep her hanging around after we finished our set. I need to talk to her. I have no idea what exactly I'm going to say, I just can't let her leave without finding out that she's okay. That she's happy with the life that she chose instead of me, and I need to know what her little melt-down earlier was all about. The thought of standing next to her, being that close makes me lightheaded. Lawson, the prick, was bang on with what he'd said earlier.

"Conner Reed, what a pussy."

I head straight for the shower with a raging hard-on.

I WALK PAST THE SECURITY blokes at the top of the stairs, giving them a nod and a smile. There's another lot at the bottom, making it pretty impossible for anyone to sneak past and get up to the dressing rooms where all of the day's performers are either getting ready or chilling after their acts.

I can't believe that Josh has gone to all this trouble, but didn't bother to warn me that Meebs would be here with his sister. I'll be having words with the fucker when I eventually catch up with him.

I've sent a text to Tyler, asking him if he's seen Meebs and if she's still here, but he hasn't replied. I'm more nervous as I approach the VIP bar than I was before going on stage earlier. The adrenaline from performing and my unexpected reunion with the girl that's fucked with my head all these years is still buzzing through my veins.

My chest feels tight, my palms sweaty and my legs wobbly. I shake hands with various people, virtually ignore the pats on the back and words of congratulations and condolence that I receive from celebrities, sports stars, actors and musicians. None of them getting more than a nod and maybe a smile. I can't focus on anything other the conversation I'm practising in my head. If she's there, at the bar, what am I going to say?

I try to force down the anger that bubbles up when I think about the way she just left me hanging that night. But fuck it! I'm pissed off, and I want some answers. I need some closure, I deserve at least that much from her.

I take a few steadying breaths and enter the bar. Clearer in my head now what I want to say. If Meebs is still the same girl I used to know inside out, then going in aggressive with all guns blazing is *not* the way to go. She used to hate confrontation. She was bullied a bit at school, being picked on for being so tiny, she learnt to walk away at a very young age. Don't get me wrong, she wasn't scared of anyone, she always stood up for herself, but she would do it with words, only all too aware that she wouldn't beat them physically.

I decide to go for the indifferent approach. *If* she's still here, I'm gonna act casual, buy her a drink and ask her how she's doing. Eventually leading up to what happened that night and the one question that's gone around in my fucking head for fifteen years... *Why?*

If I know the answer to that, I'll be okay. I'll be able to move on. I've fucked models, actresses, pop princess, *shit*, even a couple of real princesses, but none of them have ever come close to making me feel anything like what I felt for Nina Matthews, and I need to draw a line under that shit tonight.

And then I see her.

She's at the bar with Sophie, my brother and sister-in-law and Lawson. Fucking Lawson and he has his hand on the small of her back, just above her arse. That perfect, peachy round arse, covered by those painted on jeans and those shoes on her feet. Fuck me, those shoes.

Everything that I'd just convinced myself I was going to say, the way I was going to act, goes right out the window the instant I see Lawson's hand on her.

"Who's my driver?" I ask Lawson. He turns with a smile on his face, blue eyes sparkling. It takes every ounce of control I have not to knock his teeth down the back of his throat.

"Ah, the man himself. We were just talking about you. Fantastic performance, Reed. How's it feel to be back up there?" he asks.

Now I want to punch him even more. We're at a charity event that's trying to raise money for kids coming out of rehab, and he's obviously buzzing on more than beer.

"Fucking great. Now, who's my driver and where's my car?" I ask.

He knows I'm serious. I'm not a diva, I never pull the rock star card, but he's fucked me off big time today. First by bringing Amanda along, now by being off his chops, but mostly what's really fucking got to me is the fact that he's touched *her*. He had his hands on *her*. The girl I've dreamt about touching for so fucking long, he's touched *her*, and I want to snap each and every one of his fingers and ram them down his throat or up his arse. I don't care where, as long as it causes him pain.

He sends a text and looks at me, nerves making his eye twitch. Good, I'm glad I make him nervous. He's my mate as well as my manager, but he does *not*... touch... *her*... ever.

"Chill Reed. Your driver's Matty. He'll be at the doors that you came in. Down the back stairs and out the emergency exit. Have a beer and chill for a few, and he should be here."

"I don't want a fucking beer, thank you very much."

Tyler is watching me as he throws pistachios into his mouth. My eyes meet his.

"You good bro?" he asks.

"I'm good."

Sophie and Jenna are both staring at me, not sure what's going on. I haven't looked at Meebs, I can't. I know it'll hurt.

"Matt's outside," Lawson announces.

Without giving myself chance to over think it, I grab Nina's hand. I force my eyes to meet hers, they're wide with shock. Good, I'm fucking glad I've shocked her.

"We need to talk. Say goodbye to everyone, Meebs, you're coming with me," I tell her.

"What? I..." she stutters.

I expect Sophie to start shouting and screaming. Instead, she fist pumps the air and shouts, "Fuck yeah."

I don't say another word to anyone. I keep a tight grip on Nina's hand and pull her through the crowd and along the corridor toward the emergency exit doors. We head down the stairs in silence and out through another emergency exit. There's security at all of them.

Matt, my usual driver when I'm in England, is waiting outside leaning against a Land Cruiser. He nods his head and without a word, opens the back door of the car. I stand aside to let Nina in, but she stops dead in her tracks and folds her arms across her chest.

"Get in the car, Meebs. I'll take you home, but we need to talk first."

Her eyes meet mine, her chin tilts in defiance, but her eyes are shining like they're filled with tears. "I'm not going anywhere with you."

"Meebs, get in the fucking car. The very least you can do is give me an explanation."

A tear rolls down her cheek, and she swipes it away angrily.

"The very least *I* can do? The very fucking least *I* can do. You've got some nerve, Conner Reed. After everything *you* put *me* through, the very least I can do is give *you* an explanation? Get fucked."

I pick her up by her waist and lift her into the car, evoking a scream. Climbing in after her, Matty shuts the door behind us.

Matty has been my driver and close protection since the band first made it big. Over the years, he's become a mate, and he knows me well enough now to wait outside the car and give me a minute to talk to Nina.

Nina. I don't know why I'm now calling her Nina in my head. She's Meebs, always will be, whether she fucking likes it or not.

I tilt my head back and stare up at the roof interior of the car.

What the fuck am I thinking?

There's probably a hundred paps surrounding the venue, and if any of them have one of those big fuck off zoom lenses they like to use, they've probably just gotten a dozen shots of what looks like me kidnapping a tiny blonde.

Fuck! I have kidnapped a tiny blonde.

I turn to look at her. She's pushed as far into the opposite corner of the car as she can get, as far away from me as she can possibly be.

Her bottom lip is quivering, and she wipes away a tear with the back of her hand.

"I'm sorry, Meebs. I'm so sorry. Please don't cry."

She wraps both her arms around herself, and I feel like a complete cunt for making her cry.

"I just wanna talk. I just wanna know what happened."

She turns to look at me. "Now you wanna talk, Con? Now, after all these years?"

I nod my head.

She's beautiful.

So fucking beautiful.

I'm fucked.

Totally fucked.

"Well, I'll talk. I'll tell you what happened. You broke my fucking heart that's what happened," she shouts.

I rake my hand through my hair. I don't know how I broke *her* heart when *she's* the one that didn't show.

The driver's door opens, and Matt sticks his head in. "I've gotta move the car, boss. We're causing chaos."

I nod at him, then turn to Meebs. "Will you come back to my place with me? Just so we can talk?"

She glares at me for a few seconds, then nods, saying very quietly, "Just to talk."

Good, because I have no intention of letting her go anyway, not until we have talked at least.

"Take us to mine please, Matt."

He doesn't reply, just nods and pulls off along the narrow road behind the club. There's security stopping anyone unauthorised getting to the back of the building, but beyond that, I spot at least twenty paps waiting at the end of the street.

I reach out along the seat and hold my palm up and watch Meebs for her response. Silently begging her to reach out to me. She stares at my hand for a few seconds, but instead of putting her hand in mine like I'm hoping, she slides across the space between us and straight into my lap. Without saying a single word, she wraps her arms around my neck, buries her head into my chest and sobs.

It's the best feeling in the world.

Ever.

I don't care that she's crying. I don't care that she's sobbing so hard her body is shaking. I just care that she's here, with me. That I'm the one that's holding her and I know as sure as shit that I don't ever want to let her go.

It feels like a lifetime since I allowed myself to be this intimate with another human being. There's been plenty of sex over the years. Dirty, filthy, fucked up sex, but none of that compares to what I'm feeling right now. There's nothing sexual about the way I'm holding her. We're both fully clothed and haven't even so much as kissed, but this is the closest I've allowed anyone to me in a long time. Probably since the last night I spent with Meebs.

I wrap the seat belt around both of us and duck my head, burying it in her hair as we drive through the fans and photographers.

"Fucking psychos," I hear Matt mumble as flashes go off all around us and people bang on the car. This is the reason I'm driven about in a vehicle the size of a tank, to keep *me* safe and the *crazies* out. Don't get me wrong, I love our fans. Love meeting them and finding out about them, but I don't love it when they throw themselves in front of a moving car that I'm travelling in. That shit scares the fuck out of me.

Eventually, we make our way through the crowds and into the Saturday night London traffic.

Meebs sobs have stopped, and her breathing has steadied. I tilt her head back slightly and can see she's fallen asleep. I brush her hair out of her face and just stare at her. Yeah, creepy I know, but fuck it. She stinks of booze, so I'm assuming she's pretty drunk and not about to wake up from her inebriated snooze anytime soon, so from East London to my house in Surrey I take in every inch of her gorgeous face as she sleeps. I watch her eyelids flutter and her little, wet, pink tongue, flick out and over her lips every now and then. I watch her throat move as she swallows and I watch her tits move up and down as she breathes. I try not to think about how she looks naked. I try not to think about the fact that she's much curvier than she was when she was sixteen. I try not to think about the fact that I've been inside her and that I've come inside her cunt, her mouth and in her hand, over her tits and her belly. I try not to think about any of that, and I *really* try not to get a hard-on.

I fail miserably.

I want to kiss her on those perfect lips. I want to kiss her pale cheeks with their light dusting of freckles. I want to kiss her nose and her eyelids. But I don't. I manage to keep my shit together and manage to keep my lips to myself, all the way home.

When we pull up on the drive outside my house, she's still sleeping, and in all honesty, I'm more than happy to spend the night in the back of the car rather than let her go.

I can't resist any longer and gently press my lips to her forehead. My heart skips a few beats, and my head spins as my mouth makes contact with her skin. So long, so fucking long I've waited for this.

It's official, take my dick and replace it with a vagina, I've seriously become the world's biggest pussy. And I don't give a fuck who knows it.

"Meebs," I whisper softly, "We're here, baby. Time to wake up."

Matt pulls to a stop and comes around to the back of the car and opens the door.

She doesn't stir.

"Meebs, baby. Wake up." She rolls her head in a circle, stretching her neck.

"Nooo. Let me sleep, Soph. I was dreaming of Conner."

I can't help the shit-eating grin that spreads from ear to ear, across my face. I look at Matty like I'm expecting a pat on the back.

He frowns at me, a total look of confusion on his face. He doesn't get it. He doesn't understand how happy, how fucking elated I am to hear that she wants to keep sleeping so she can dream some more about me.

"Get the front door Matt, I'll carry her in."

He looks from me to her with a frown. "She all right is she, Reed? Not on anything?"

"She's fine, Matt. Just too much to drink. Get the door and punch the alarm code in before that goes off and sets my dad and the dogs off."

He looks at me for a few seconds more.

"What the fuck, Matt, she's pissed. I haven't drugged her, and I'm not gonna touch her. Her name's Nina, and I've known her years."

Why the fuck am I explaining myself?

"It's just that she didn't seem too keen to get in the car with you, boss."

"Matt, I'm not a fucking rapist. Now open the front door."

I actually admire the fact that he's worried about her safety but hate the fact he thinks I'm capable of something like that.

He heads toward the big front doors of my house and unlocks them. My dad and Sandra are about somewhere, but probably over at their own place. I'm assuming the dogs are inside with them seeing as they've not come charging over yet.

I slide out of the car with Meebs in my arms. She wraps her arms around my neck and cuddles in closer and the urge to kiss her, hard, almost stops me in my tracks. I walk with her through the house to the kitchen and living room and lay her down on one of the big leather sofas. I'm surprised when I look up and see Matty standing watching me.

"This must be her phone, it was on the back seat." He passes me a phone in a shiny pink case.

"Cheers." He doesn't move.

"Her name's Nina Matthews. She's thirty-one and owns a chain of hair salons called Amicus with her business partner Sophie Gardner. If she's on the news tomorrow because she's missing, then you know where to send the old Bill."

He swallows and nods.

Fuck me. Do I actually look like a rapist or sex offender?

Yeah, don't answer that.

CHAPTER EIGHTEEN

NINA

W AVES OF CONSCIOUSNESS SLOWLY START to lap against, first my mind and then my body. I try to cling to my dream for a few moments longer. I can't remember what it was about, but Conner was involved. I could feel him, smell him. . . Then boom, out of nowhere, a big fat tidal wave of reality comes crashing down on me. My eyes fly open.

He was here.

Right here.

Sitting in an enormous leather bean bag.

Watching me.

"I fell asleep." Yeah, when in doubt, state the obvious.

"You did," he smiles as he speaks, and my heart and my belly perform a synchronised jig.

He's so fucking beautiful.

I know he's a man, but there's just no other way to describe him. He has a beautiful face. Full plump lips, possibly the most kissable lips I've ever seen in my life. A strong jaw, which right now, is covered in stubble. I shudder just thinking about how that would feel against my skin, trying so hard to remember how it *had* felt against my skin.

I'd kissed those lips. Reed, the world-famous rock star was, once upon a time, Conner Reed, my boyfriend.

I push myself up to a more seated position and look around the room that's being lit by just a couple of lamps. There's a huge flat screen television, a big open fireplace and an enormous leather sofa, identical to the one that I'm lying on.

"I'm in your house?" It's a question, not a statement this time, as I'm not really sure where I am.

"You are," again, he smiles as he speaks. His blue-green eyes sparkling in the lamplight.

I'm actually a little surprised. I'd imagined him living in a penthouse apartment, filled with black leather and chrome furniture. This, this is beautiful. It's a home, a real home.

"It's beautiful," I tell him.

"Thank you. It needed a lot of work when I bought it. My dad and my brothers helped me fix it up."

My eyebrows shoot up at the mention of his dad. They never got along when he was younger. Well, it wasn't so much that they never got along, it was more that his dad was always drunk and angry.

"Well, you all did a great job. I really like it."

"I'm glad." He smiles. It's not his 'rock star' smile, it's almost a shy smile. The smile of the eighteen-year-old boy he used to be, that I used to know. The boy that I loved so very much. The boy that I was so sure loved me.

I will not cry.

"I've imagined you here so many times, Meebs."

I cry.

He gets up from the bean bag, but I put my hand out to stop him from coming closer. So instead, he just sits forward, resting his elbows on his knees, rubbing his hands together.

It's not that I don't want him closer, I do, almost more than my next breath. But first, I need answers.

"What happened, Con? What happened that night? What happened to us?"

He rakes his fingers through his hair.

"You didn't come, Meebs. After all the plans we made, you didn't fucking show."

"I was in the hospital, I couldn't just leave. I thought you would've come to me."

He frowns, looking totally confused. Shaking his head, he says, "You said that earlier, about the hospital, I don't understand. What hospital? Who was in the hospital?"

He's lying, he's got to be lying. I press my fingertips into my temples to try and stop the headache that's building inside. Conner passes me a glass of water and two headache tablets. I throw both the tablets to the back of my throat and swallow them down with the entire contents of the glass. With how much alcohol I've consumed the last couple of days, I'm surprised I don't feel much worse.

Conner takes the glass and passes me a box of tissues. I must look a complete mess with all the crying I've done tonight.

"D'you want a cup of tea?" he asks, and I can't help but smile. Conner and his tea. It was such a part of the boy I knew, I'm so glad that hasn't changed.

"You still need twenty cups a day to function?" I ask. He shrugs and gives me that same shy smile as earlier.

"Thirty when I'm in the studio."

He holds his hand out to me. "Let's have a cup of tea and some toast, then you can tell me what happened that night and why you were at the hospital."

I stand and take his hand, realising then that I'm barefoot. My shoes are sitting neatly at the edge of his sofa. He notices me looking at them.

"I like your shoes, the colour matches my favourite guitar," he says, sounding almost nervous.

"Thank you, we obviously share great taste in colour," I tell him. I want to be angry with him and say something bitchy, but I just haven't got it in me and, I might possibly still be a little drunk and unable to think clearly.

"We always did like similar things," he takes my hand as he speaks and I let him lead me to the kitchen. My thoughts a jumbled mess in my head. *How can he not know why I was at the hospital that night?* Sophie called him, my brother called him. They both left messages, letting him know what was going on.

TEN MINUTES LATER WE'RE SITTING at his kitchen bench, drinking tea and eating hot, buttery toast. We've not really said much, but as Conner gets up to make himself another cup of tea, he says, "So come on then, Meebs, what happened? Tell me why you never turned up that night?"

I take a sip from my cup, grateful that I have some food in my belly and not just alcohol. It's four in the morning, but I now feel wide awake. Adrenaline is pulsing through my veins.

Fifteen years I've waited to have this conversation with him and now finally, the opportunity that I never thought I'd have, is here.

He leans back against the kitchen worktop, his arms crossed over his chest, mug of tea in his hand. Conner was always a bit on the skinny side, and he's still pretty slim now, but he has muscles, and I can't help but cast my eyes over his forearms and his biceps and notice the definition he has going on. His chest is much broader than I remember and he may even be a little taller.

He's wearing a pair of light blue jeans, a three-quarter sleeved black T-shirt, with a white T or vest underneath. He looks like a model, a rock star, but most of all, he looks like Conner Reed, and I feel just like I did back when we were younger… inadequate.

"Do you really not know?" I ask him. "Please don't lie to spare my feelings. I'd much rather you were honest."

He looks up at the ceiling like he's debating telling me something. "Meebs, I stood in that carpark, freezing my bollocks off for an hour waiting for you to show up. I called your phone over and over. I swear to you, I had no idea that you were at the hospital. Now please, will you tell me why? Why you were there?"

He's telling the truth. Despite the years apart, I know he's telling the truth. What reason does he have to lie? He's Conner Reed, he has zero reasons to lie, my feelings are irrelevant to him.

"I lost our baby."

He stares at me blankly for a few seconds, then frowns. "What?"

He really didn't know. I start to feel nauseous.

How does he not know?

"I spent the afternoon and all night in the hospital losing our baby."

He shakes his head, his eyes never leaving mine. "No. Meebs… no." He puts down his drink. Both hands rake through and then grip at his hair.

"Why didn't you call me? What… I can't…" I watch as he paces in front of me, still gripping his hair.

"Why? Why the fuck didn't you ring and tell me what was going on?" he shouts.

"Why? Why? Because I was in the middle of a miscarriage, Con, that's why. I was in pain, I was bleeding. Sophie rang you, Pearce rang you. All I got was a 'fuck you, we're done' message left on my phone in return."

"No," he shouts. "No fucking way. I got nothing. I called your phone, I called Sophie's. I got nothing. Meebs, I swear, I swear to you." His eyes are wide as he begs me to believe him. "I didn't have a clue. No one called, no one left a message. I only left you that message when I didn't hear from you. When you didn't show."

I feel strange. Like I'm floating. My skin prickles, like little shards of ice are settling all over it, but my insides, my belly and my chest, they feel too hot. Almost like everything is bubbling and boiling inside me. My head feels like a snow globe that's just been shaken, my thoughts, the little white flecks churning around inside. I really don't know what to think or feel about what he's telling me. It doesn't make sense, and I have no idea where to try and start working out what could've happened that night. How things could've gone so wrong for us.

He leans forward, toward me. His hands gripping the edge of the marble worktop. His beautiful eyes are looking all over my face, and it suddenly strikes me, this is real. We're really here. After all these years, we're finally here, together, discussing what happened that night.

We stare at each other in silence for a moment. The churning in my belly and of my thoughts eases mildly as I look into his beautiful blue-green eyes, which are looking more like a grey kind of colour right now. They're shining like he's about to cry.

"You know what hurts the most, Meebs? You know what hurt me more than anything?"

I shake my head, my mouth opens to say no, but nothing comes out. So I just shake my head, not breaking his stare.

"After... after the accident, when they locked me up, you were the one person..." His jaw trembles and I ache to reach out to him. "You were the one person I thought I could rely on. I was so sure that you'd get in touch. That even if you'd changed your mind about us running away together, that you loved me enough to reach out, to visit or write me a letter at least. My brother was killed, and I was remanded, locked up." The expression on his face changes, his tone becomes harsh. "You abandoned me, Meebs. You did exactly what everyone warned me you'd do. You proved that I wasn't good enough, that I was just your bit of rough. You stayed away," he sobs out the last few words and tears run down his face. He wipes his nose with the back of his hand and storms out through the timber doors and onto a decked area, which seems to run around the ground floor of the house.

"I thought you'd left me in the hospital, Con. I thought you didn't care. I stayed away because it's what I thought you wanted," I shout after him. I sit motionless for a few moments, then move my hands to grip my head. If I press down hard enough, it might hold my thoughts still.

None of this makes any sense. Sophie's my best friend, she wouldn't lie to me about calling Conner that day. Josh was Reed's best friend. I gave him the letter I wrote to take to the prison and give to Conner when he went to visit. Josh promised that he would. *Why would they lie? Why would either of them want to lie to us?*

I get up from the stool and go in search of a bathroom. I seriously need to wee and maybe vomit, I've not decided yet, and I most definitely need to splash my face with some cold water.

The guest bathroom isn't hard to find, and once I'm done, I wash my hands and splash my face with cold water, I no longer feel the need to be sick. I wipe the makeup from under my eyes and head back out to Conner. Determined to get to the bottom of whatever went on, all those years ago.

CONNER IS LEANING WITH ONE elbow resting on the wooden handrail that runs around the deck. He's smoking a cigarette while looking out over a large pool below. He doesn't look at me as I lean my back against the handrail and watch him.

"I wrote to you," I tell him, eventually.

He turns toward me with a frown on his face.

"I wrote you a letter. Asking, *begging* you, to just explain why? *Why* you chose to drive about, selling drugs with your brother and not come to the hospital. I wanted to know why you didn't want to be with me when I'd just lost our baby? I wanted to know what had happened to change so much about the boy who left me at the bottom of my parents drive. The boy I loved and was so sure loved me. I wanted an explanation as to what could've happened to change all of that in just a few hours."

He reaches behind him and puts his cigarette out in an ashtray, then turns his attention back to me.

"I wanted you to know," I swallow hard and try to continue without crying. It doesn't work. "I wanted you to know that I forgave you, Con. That no matter what, I knew we were strong enough to work it out. I knew we loved each other enough to get through whatever shit had happened that night. I wanted you to know that *no matter what*, I would always love you." I don't even attempt to fight the tears now, I just let them flow.

"So why didn't you send it to me?" He asks. I close my eyes, letting the reality slice through me like a knife. He really didn't get the letter.

"I did," I whisper, "I gave it to Josh and he promised he would get it to you."

I watch him blink rapidly as he tries to make sense of what I've just told him. He shakes his head, tilts it to the side, licks his lips and closes his eyes for just a few seconds. This is Conner processing. Trying to make sense of what I've just told him. I know this because, despite the years, I still know Conner.

"But why? I don't understand. He's a mate. Josh wouldn't do that."

I shrug and shake my head.

"I don't know Con, but I swear to you, I asked Soph to call you from the hospital, and I gave Josh a letter to take to the remand centre to give to you."

He rakes his hand through his hair. "I don't get it, Meebs. They're our mates. They wouldn't. Why would they lie to us? Why would they want to keep us apart?"

My throat can no longer contain the sob it's been fighting to hold back, and it bursts out as I answer him. "I don't know... I don't know, but I swear, I swear to you, I asked her to call, and I wrote you a letter. I loved you, Con. I loved you so much. My heart broke. I was so confused, so hurt and angry." I'm struggling for breath now. My sobs have escalated into full-on heaving, snot bubble, ugly crying.

He turns and pulls me into his arms and holds me tight. He sways us from side to side, running his hands over my head, up and down my arms and back.

"I've missed you so fucking much, Meebs, so fucking much."

This just makes me cry harder.

"Please don't cry baby. Please, I hate seeing you this upset."

He called me baby. He just called me baby, and the word is like a drug, a sedative. I suddenly feel like I can't stand up anymore, that I need to go to sleep, right now.

"I'm getting to the bottom of this. I want some fucking answers." He grabs my hand and pulls me, stumbling, back through the house and to the sofa. He reaches for his phone, which is sitting next to mine on the coffee table and makes a call.

I can hear someone answer, but Conner doesn't greet them.

"I don't care where you are or who you are with. You find your sister, and you get to my house now."

I'm assuming it's Josh and although I can't hear the words, I can hear from his tone that he's protesting.

"Don't," Conner roars, making me jump. "Don't fuck with me, Gardner. Get in a cab if you've been drinking. Get your sister from wherever she ended up and get to my house, now."

CONNER

I SPEND THE NEXT HOUR sitting on the opposite end of the sofa to Meebs. She tells me exactly what went on that New Year's Eve and I explain to her what happened when she didn't show up. For the first time in a long time, I talk about the accident and how it all unfolded. I tell her about the court refusing me bail because of a stupid conviction for shoplifting when I was a kid and a few other minor run-ins I'd had with the police. I tell her about busking in London, my chance meeting with Jet and joining the band.

"That was one of the worse few hours of my life," she says very quietly. Her light blue eyes are wide, and as the sun is now coming up, I can see them shining with unshed tears. She looks so young, small and fragile, all curled up in the corner of my sofa.

"What was?" I ask. Not sure what she's talking about.

"When the news first started to come out about Jet's death. The first reports were unclear who it. . . if it was. . . They didn't know which. . ." Her hand goes to her mouth, and she touches her lips with the tips of her fingers, and I'm instantly hard. She blinks, and a tear rolls down her cheek. Despite her tears, I'm still hard.

"I thought at first you were dead. I thought, I thought. . ."

I can't leave her to cry like this anymore. I move to where she's sitting and pull her into my lap. I brush the hair from her face, and I kiss away the tears. For a few delicious moments, she lets me, but then she stops and pulls back.

"Con," I can feel her breath on my mouth as she whispers my name. I breathe in the citrusy scent of her skin and the minty smell of her hair. My dick twitches and my balls pull tight. I lean in to start kissing along her jaw…

"Con, I'm married."

No.

My breath and my words stick in my throat while my brain fights to process this news.

She's married. To someone else.

"I'm in the process of getting a divorce but, yeah, technically, I'm still married."

Yesssss.

Thank you. Thank you. Thank you.

Thank fuck!

Thank fucking fuck!

I actually have to mentally restrain myself from fist pumping the air above our heads.

"That's… I'm sorry that you're going through that."

I'm lying.

Totally lying.

"It's all good. He's a dick. I never should've married him."

Nope.

No, you shouldn't.

I nod my head, agreeing with everything that she's just said.

"Why are you nodding your head?" she asks.

Busted!

"I, I was just…"

"Con, are you trying not to smile?" she accuses.

"No, I, of course not…"

She leans back, taking in all of my face with those big blue eyes.

"Conner Reed, I've known you since I was five-years-old. I may not have been in your life for the last fifteen years, but I still remember how the corner of your lips twitch when you're trying not to smile, and I remember how you could never look me in the eye when you lie."

She remembers all of that about me? All these years and she still remembers. I don't know why, but I can't think of a single word to say. The fact that she knows me so well and still remembers those small details, it's fucking with my brain's ability to think straight.

We sit in silence for a few seconds. Both of us trying to wrap our heads around the fact that we're here, together. The revelations, the unanswered questions. There's just so much to take in.

Her tongue flicks out and swipes across her bottom lip before she sucks it in and drags her teeth over it.

"Meebs," I close my eyes as I say her name. "Fuck, baby girl. I just, I can't even. Can you believe this? That we're really here, together like this?"

She gives her head a small shake and smiles. "Did you ever…" she cuts off and looks down at her fingers, which are laced together in her lap.

"Did you ever think about me, Con? Once the band made it big. Did I ever cross your mind?"

I close my eyes, and for the first time ever, I willingly allow the pain I've held down for so very long to wash over me. I don't fight it. I let my heart beat free of the fist that's gripped it for so long. I exhale that very last bit of air from my lungs, the one that I've always held on to, afraid, that if I were to let it out, all the hurt would escape with it. I feel a spike of adrenaline course through my veins and the beginnings of a panic attack. I rake both of my hands through my hair and take in a deep breath, before opening my eyes and looking at her.

"You've no fucking idea, Meebs. It hurt so much though. To the point where it was physical. I fought it. Every day I pushed it down, kept it locked away." I run the backs of my knuckles over her cheek and along her jaw, suddenly overwhelmed with the need to touch her. She's sitting in my lap, but I need to feel her warm, soft skin. "Every day. No matter how hard I tried to fight it, every day there would be a sight, a sound, smells, words, songs. There were so many triggers. Most of the time it would only cause a short, sharp stab of pain," I look right into her eyes as I speak. No matter what becomes of us, no matter what happens after today, I need to lay it all out there. Tyler's the only one I've admitted any of this to. The band knew that she hurt me, they knew she was my muse for most of my songs, but they had no idea to what degree that hurt still affected my every waking moment and still haunted my dreams.

"But some days," I continue, "some days it floored me."

Two large tears roll down her cheeks. I slide one hand around the back of her neck, the other around her waist and angle her face and body toward me. I can't wait any more. I need to feel her mouth on mine.

CHAPTER TWENTY

NINA

MY HEAD SPINS AS I scramble out of his lap. I can't let him kiss me. I've barely hung on these last fifteen years. If I go there now, it'll be game over for me. It's fine for him, he's Reed, he can have anyone he wants, but for me, the realisation has hit me tonight. For me, there *is only* him. There has only ever been him, and that makes me feel pretty shitty. I must've been such a terrible wife. I stayed married to a man I didn't love for eight years. I used him because he was safe, and I'm wondering now if Marcus always knew this. If he *always* felt second best. *I wonder if that's what his little outburst was all about the night he attacked me?*

I need some air, some space between us. He's every girl's dream, every woman's fantasy and it would be so easy to get swept away by him and the memories of what we once had. But we live in two different worlds now. He's a rock star, worshipped by millions around the world, and I'm a hairdresser in the middle of what might possibly be about to become a very messy divorce.

I head past the kitchen table and through the timber doors that Conner went through earlier. I lean at the same spot he did and draw in a shaky breath. The sun is almost up, and the birds are singing. It's the beginning of a new day. Just another day for most of the rest of the world, while mine feels like it's been flipped on its head.

Within a few seconds, he's here at my side, but he doesn't say anything. We stand in silence. I can feel his eyes on me, but I remain staring ahead, looking out across the swimming pool and tennis courts. Beyond that is a beautiful, chocolate box looking cottage. Other than that, there's not another house in sight. Just miles of rolling countryside.

"Why'd you run Meebs?"

You know that thing that always gets written in books, about not letting out the breath you didn't know you were holding? Well, I actually do that. I let it out long and slow. Feeling my heart beat rapidly in my chest and throat.

"I've spent fifteen years trying to get over you, Con. Eight of them married to a man that I didn't love, just because he was a safe option. If I didn't love him, then he couldn't hurt me like you did." I finally turn and look at him. He's leaning back on the handrail, his arms crossed and folded over his chest. I let my eyes roam over his handsome face and down to the hollow of his throat where a few wispy chest hairs stick out from the V of his T-shirt.

It's too much. He's too fucking hot. Too sexy. What I'm feeling, what he's stirred inside of me, it's all too much.

I close my eyes and look away before continuing, "It wouldn't matter if he left me like you did."

"That's not fair, Meebs. I never fucking left you."

I turn and once again look into those stunning eyes of his. *Fuck!* I wish he were ugly and a complete arsehole. This would all be so much easier.

"I know that now."

He reaches out and pulls me to stand between his legs. Leaning his head down, he kisses my forehead.

"I loved you so much, Meebs, I would never have left you. I hate that you thought for a moment that I did."

Hearing him say that after all these years should bring me peace, but I actually feel anger bubbling away in my belly.

His hand travels to the back of my neck, he lifts my hair up and runs his fingers along my spine, to my hairline. I shiver.

"What does your ink say?" How the fuck does he know I have a tattoo there? Even my parents don't know. "How'd you know about my tatt?"

He pulls away so that he can look me in the eye and I get the shy smile of *my* Conner again.

"When you were standing up at the bar with Sophie earlier, I was… I noticed you. I mean, I didn't know it was you, but I was—"

"Looking at my arse."

He gives me possibly the sexiest smile that's ever been bestowed upon a woman, in the history of mankind or womankind. I sway slightly on my feet but manage to keep my eyes open just so I don't miss a second of it.

"Yeah, how'd you know?"

I shrug. "You've always had a thing for my arse." He turns up the volume on the smile and any resolve I have left dissolves, puddles, right at my feet and then just evaporates like it never existed at all.

"I've always had a thing for you, period."

"Have you?" I want to smile and not a little smile either. A big fat cheesy grin kind of smile.

"Since you were five-years-old. Since the very first day you set foot on the playground of St. Mary's Catholic Primary School. I thought you were an angel or a fairy."

Warmth spreads from my heart, my cheeks and my toes until my whole body feels like it's glowing. I can't help but smile up at him now, my cheeks ache too much from trying to hold it at bay. This all feels too easy. It feels natural… right.

"What's it say, the ink?"

My smile fades. "It's just a date."

"A date?"

I nod my head.

"What date?" he asks.

I look up at the sky and then back into his eyes. "It's the date of the worst day of my life." My nose stings and I fight to keep my lip from trembling. "It's the date that I lost our baby and the date that I lost you."

He brushes a tear away from my cheek with his thumb, and I don't even flinch. The familiarity of his touch overwhelms me. So many emotions jumble together, fighting their way to the surface. Between them and the lack of sleep, my legs start to buckle and I sway.

Conner pulls me toward him, his arms wrap tightly around my back, and he kisses my neck. There's no space between our bodies. He brings his mouth level with mine. His eyes are open and searching my face as his lips meet mine. They're unfamiliar for just a split second, then almost instantly it's like a spark to a fuse that ignites a memory.

Home.

His touch.

His smell.

His taste.

It's what's been missing from my life for so long, and now, finally, I feel like I'm home.

CONNER

HUMAN CONTACT. IT'S SUCH A simple thing. Something that so many people take for granted and it's not until you've been without it for an extended period of time that you realise how much you've missed it.

I felt like I was melting. My insides were a hot molten mess, dissolving me from the inside out. I actually don't remember the last time I'd kissed a woman full on the mouth. A lightning bolt of guilt shoots through my chest as I think about the way I'd conducted my life over the years. Threesomes, orgies, anything to make it less personal and none of it, not a single one of those weird, kinky, fucked up situations I'd been in before, could touch this moment.

I've watched an Australian supermodel getting eaten out by a Russian Princess while the Princess got fucked up the arse by Jet and I fucked the mouth of the model. It was the sort of situation many would pay money to watch, let alone be involved in, but it'd left me cold. I'd shot my load down the model's throat and left the room feeling nothing but a sense of release from the need to come. But this, this moment right now, where I have Meebs' small body crushed against mine, both of us fully clothed, my mouth gently caressing hers, my tongue slowly probing, seeking access, this is a moment I want to last forever. Right now, I would give back every sordid, sexual encounter of my life, in exchange for a moment like this every day.

She moves her hands from my shoulders and up into my hair, pulling my mouth down harder on hers as she opens and finally allows my tongue access.

I can't hold back now. I move my hands to her arse, lift her up, turn and sit her on the handrail. Her legs are wrapped around my hips, and I grind into the heat between her legs, gyrating my hips around and around, in between rocking into her. She breaks our kiss and throws her head back.

"Oh fuck, shit, God," she moans. My dick feels like it's going to split the seam of my jeans and hers. I make use of the way her head is tilted back and lick from the hollow of her throat, up her neck to just below her ear. Then kiss along her jaw all the way back to her mouth.

"Come to bed with me?" I speak while my lips are still on hers.

"No," she pants.

"Why? I want you so fucking much."

"You don't know me."

"Oh, I know you. I know you from the inside out, Nina Amoeba." I drag my teeth along her jaw. "Every inch." I lick from her throat, across her collarbone. "Every freckle." I kiss her nose. "Every sigh." I rock my hips into hers as I bite down on her earlobe.

She pulls back and meets my gaze. Her lids look heavy like she's struggling to keep them open. I'm not sure if it's tiredness or lust that's causing this, but judging by the way her cheeks are so beautifully flushed, I'll go with the latter.

"I don't know you. I know Conner, but I don't know Reed."

I kiss her gently on the mouth, just because I can, and because I need to.

"Reed's gone. Reed stopped existing the second my lips touched yours."

"You're full of shit," she almost moans as I drag my teeth over her lobe again and bite down on the curve between her neck and her shoulder. She shudders, and I swear to God, I've just shot a load off in my boxers.

I pull away so I can look into her eyes as I speak, "No bullshit, Meebs, not with you, not ever." I push her blonde hair back from her face and run my thumb along her tattoo on the back of her neck.

"We made a baby together. You had my baby in your belly and my heart in your hands. I don't know what happened, Meebs. I can't even begin to get my head around what could've gone on. How we ended up apart that night." I rest my forehead against hers. "One kiss, my lips brushing against yours and it's all there, and I don't think it's a case of it all coming rushing back. What we had, it never went away. It's always been there. It's stayed with both of us. We've carried it around all this time, and all it would've taken was for one of us to reach out. One of us to make contact." When I look down, I can see tears hanging from her lashes.

"It's so unfair, Con. All these years, we could've been making a life together. We should've been together, not apart, miserable and lonely."

I kiss the tears from each of her eyes. "Please don't cry. I hate seeing you cry."

"I know, I'm sorry, but I'm so fucking angry Con. Like, raging angry. To the point where I want to cause somebody harm."

I smile at that thought. I don't think I've ever met anyone as gentle as Meebs.

"Don't look at me like that. I go to boxercise now, have done for years. I can throw a blinding right hook," she says in all seriousness. I try not to laugh.

"I'd like to see that some time."

The buzzer sounds for the intercom at the gate.

"That must be Josh and Sophie," I tell her.

"Perhaps you'll get to see my right hook sooner than you think," she comments while following me into the house.

I PRESS THE BUTTON THAT activates the electronic gates and then go and open the front door, leaning against the frame while watching a black cab wind its way up my drive. The wheels haven't even stopped turning before Sophie jumps out.

"What's going on, Reed? Where the fuck's Nina? I've been ringing and ringing her phone. If you've hurt or upset her, you fucker." Sophie's long-legged stride bounds up the steps to my front door.

"She's in the family room." I gesture with my head, in the general direction she needs to go.

After paying the cabbie, Josh turns to face me. He and Sophie must've gone home to change at some stage as they're both wearing T's and jogging bottoms.

"This better be fucking good, Reed," he says as he reaches my front door.

I don't reply and remain silent all the way back to where Meebs is standing in my kitchen. The kettle is on, and the coffee machine is pushing water through a pod and into a glass coffee cup. Sophie is sitting on a stool at the worktop, watching her.

"Tea?" I ask Josh. Assuming that Meebs already has Sophie's drink in hand.

"I'll have a coffee please," Josh replies.

There's an awkward silence while the drinks are made and all that seems to go through my mind on a loop, is that Meebs is in my kitchen.

She's here.

Right here.

Right now.

In my kitchen.

When everyone has a drink, I lean back against the granite

worktop next to Meebs. Just as I'm about to speak, Amoeba beats me to it.

"What did you do with the letter I gave you to give to Conner when he was locked up?" she directs the question at Josh, who looks from her to me.

"What?" he asks her.

"What's this all about?" Sophie joins in. Meebs gives her a death stare, which instantly shuts Sophie up and makes me think of the Shakespeare quote, *'Though she be but little, she is fierce'* and I instantly feel my dick twitch. Not because I have a thing for The Bard, but because watching Meebs stick up for herself is as sexy as fuck. Actually, whatever she does, she's as sexy as fuck.

"When Conner was locked up, I gave you a letter to take to him. It was one envelope, but there were two letters inside. I asked you to take them to Conner next time you were going to see him. I told you…" She stops and covers her mouth with her hand for a few seconds and looks at me, before looking back at Josh. She's struggling not to cry, and as much as it hurts my heart to watch her, I let her get the question out there. I let her feel that she's got control here. I think she needs it. "I told you that if he still didn't want to see me after he'd read them that I didn't want to know, for you to just not tell me anything," Josh is nodding as she speaks.

"Yeah, yeah, I remember. I tried to convince you to go and see him for yourself, but you wouldn't."

Meebs nods this time and turns her blue eyes to me. "I was too scared, Con. I didn't know the system. My brother said I needed permission or something from you. I was so scared you'd say, no." She looks down at the tiles on the floor, and I follow her gaze, noticing the pink polish on her toenails. Her feet and her toes are so tiny and sexy…

I'm fucked.

So totally fucked.

She's been back in my life for about twelve hours, and right now, if it were to become necessary in the next few minutes, I would be quite prepared to lay down my life for her.

"I should've been braver," she says very quietly.

"What? No, no, this isn't your fault." I pull her into me, hold the sides of her face in each of my palms and tilt it so she has to look up at me.

"This isn't your fault." I kiss her gently on the mouth. "This isn't *your* fault," I repeat.

"I gave them to your brother," Josh says.

She stiffens instantly in my arms, her eyebrows pulled into a frown as she turns around to face Josh.

"What did you say?" Sophie asks before either of us do.

Josh looks at me while letting out a long sigh.

"I saw him in the pub one night, and I asked how Nina was doing. He said she was doing great and moving on with her life." He switches his gaze to Meebs.

"I told him that you'd given me a couple of letters for Reed, but I hadn't had a chance to get to see him." He shrugs his shoulders. "*Fuck!* I fucked up." He scratches the back of his head as realisation dawns on him.

"He told me he would talk to you and see if you still wanted the letters delivered. He text me the next day and said that you didn't. Then he came around and collected them... he never, I never..." His eyes dart from mine to Meebs, and I know he's feeling almost as gutted as we are right now. "I'm so sorry. I gave him the letters and never gave them a second thought. He never told you, did he?"

She stands rigid in my arms, staring ahead at nothing. Her fists opening and closing. She turns to Sophie.

"When I was in the hospital, and I asked you to call Conner—" Sophie starts to shake her head almost immediately.

"Holy fuck, Neen," Sophie whispers.

"Why were you in the hospital? When?" Josh asks. Meebs ignores him.

"Why Soph, how? I asked you to call him. My phone was in your car, you had your phone on you. All you had to do was call him."

"He offered Neen. He told me to stay with you. He said you needed me with you more than him. He said he called and called him. He even took my car keys and went and got your phone from the car and told me that he called from your phone, in case Reed didn't recognise the number."

I'm frozen to the spot, even my chest is barely moving as I take short breaths in and out. My arms and legs feel like lead weights and my skin prickles and tingles in the weirdest way.

Meebs turns and looks at me, her eyes wide with disbelief. The flush she wore on her beautiful face earlier is gone. Her skin is now so pale, it almost looks see through. She swallows hard.

"My brother... I, you don't... I haven't told you what he did."

My world tilts. It spins off its axis, and I feel like I'm freefalling.

What did he do?

I'm going to kill him.

At that moment, there's no hesitation in my mind, not a single doubt. If she tells me that he laid a hand on her, if he touched her or even thought about touching her.

I. Will. Fucking. Kill. Him.

"What'd he do, Meebs?" I don't mean to sound harsh, that's just the way it comes out. Her face crumbles and never, for as long as I live will I forget the pain that's etched across her features right now.

"He stole my life. My brother. He stole us." She slides to the floor as she sobs. My reflexes are slow, but I manage to catch her before she hits the tiles.

I get on the floor with her and hold her while she cries. I'm still not entirely sure what exactly has gone on, but it obviously involves that little prick of a brother of hers, Pearce. Pearce *fucking* Matthews. My heart actually hurts the walls of my chest, it's pounding so hard when I think about what he might've done.

We all sit in silence for a few moments. Each of us trying to get our heads around all of the information that's just been shared.

"I still don't understand. When was Nina in the hospital?" Josh asks again.

Nobody answers.

Sophie wipes tears from under her eyes, then gets up and starts opening cupboards.

"I need a drink, Reed. What ya got? Nice crib, by the way. Totally not what I was expecting."

I'm still struggling to form words. I open my mouth, but nothing comes out.

"Will someone fucking answer me?"

Sophie and I both look at Josh. Meebs lets out a deep sigh but doesn't look up or say anything.

"Let me make us all a coffee, with a dash of something stronger in it, and I'll tell you all I know," Sophie says

"What did he do, Soph? Did he touch her?" Something flickers across her face for a split second.

"Who?" she asks me with a frown.

"Her prick of a brother, did he touch her?"

Meebs looks up from where her face has been curled into my chest and shoulder. She's a blotchy, tear-stained mess. The most beautiful mess I've ever seen.

"He didn't touch me. It's not what you're thinking."

Sophie shakes a bottle of bourbon above our heads.

"Will you pair of lovebirds please get up off the floor and show me how this coffee machine works? I need a drink, and if I need a drink, fuck knows what you two must need."

Meebs wipes her face on the back of her arm and gives me a small smile.

Pearce Matthews.

Pearce Matthews.

Pearce Matthews.

It's the only thing I can think of right now, that's going to stop me from getting a hard-on.

"The coffee machine is the same as the one at the salon in Reading," Meebs says.

"Ahh, right. Gotchya," Sophie replies.

I stand and pull Meebs up with me.

"Can I go and have a quick shower and borrow some clothes. I feel gross," she asks.

Fucking hell!

She's about to get naked... in *my* house.

I look between Sophie and Josh.

"Stop thinking those thoughts, Conner Reed. I just want a quick shower so I can feel clean," Meebs tells me.

"Yeah, and don't look at us like that either, coz we're not leaving," Sophie adds.

I take Amoeba up to my bedroom, show her how the shower works and pull an old Shift T-shirt out of my wardrobe.

"Is that it?" she asks.

"Is that, what?" I ask her, genuinely confused.

"Is that all you've got for me to wear? Are there no bottom halves?"

"I don't know how tall you think you are babe, but I think you'll find that'll come down to your ankles," I gesture with my chin toward the T.

"Fuck off. I'm not that short and I still want something on underneath." I chew on the inside of my lip as I think about her wearing nothing but my T-shirt.

"Stop looking at me like that, Con. I need to shower. Then we need to talk."

My belly churns at her words. I know that I'm not going to like whatever it is she has to tell me.

"Go shower. I'll leave you some clean bottoms on the bed."

CHAPTER TWENTY-TWO

NINA

As soon as I hear the bedroom door close, I strip off my day old clothes and step under the multiple jets of the shower.

I slide down onto the floor.

And I cry.

I cry for my lost baby.

My lost life.

My lost chance at loving Conner.

For all the years Conner could've spent loving me.

But they're not tears of pity. I'm not feeling sorry for myself, I'm way beyond that. I'm angry, so fucking angry. Rage like I've never known bubbles inside me to the point where it actually makes me want to vomit.

Our life together was stolen, our choices taken away. My entire adult life has been controlled by someone else's decisions, and I'm so fucking pissed off at the way I've been manipulated that I'm shaking from the inside out.

When I finally feel a little more in control, I wash myself quickly, turn off the amazing shower and step out into the bathroom. The space is beautiful. As well as the massive walk-in shower with the body jets, there are two sinks and a huge timber bath. I've never seen a bath made of wood, but this looks stunning against the natural stone coloured tiling.

Conner's home has really surprised me. For some reason, I imagined him living in a penthouse apartment, somewhere in central London. The décor brash and glitzy. Black, white and red leather, with lots of glass and chrome involved.

I don't know why I thought that? Con was never flash or a show off when we were younger. I've always considered him to be drop-dead gorgeous, but he was never up himself. He was just… Conner.

I wander out of the en-suite and sit on the edge of his enormous bed and look around the room. The bed and the bedside tables are made out of bleached timber, which contrasts beautifully with the gold, chocolate brown and red bedding that covers it.

On the wall facing the bed is a giant flat screen television and to the left of that is an open fire, with a huge wooden mantel that matches the timber on the floor and the frames of the floor to ceiling bay windows. In the space in front of the windows is what I can only assume to be a custom-made leather sofa in a rich chocolate brown, similar to the ones downstairs. The sofa is curved and follows the shape of the bay windows perfectly. To the right of the windows is a door and when I open it to take a peek inside, it reveals an 'only in your dreams' sized walk-in wardrobe. The space is probably three times the size of my bedroom that I'm currently sleeping in at Sophie's place. Everything's in order, jeans, shirts, suits, jackets. There are shoes on racks, undies, socks, ties and T's in drawers.

I close the door and step back out to the bedroom. I've used Conner's shower gel, shampoo, conditioner, deodorant and face cream. I cleaned my teeth with his toothbrush and paste, and now I'm pulling on a pair of his boxers and his T-shirt. I sit back down on the bed, which looks so inviting right now. I'm so incredibly tired. Both, physically and mentally exhausted. I'm beyond pissed off with my brother's spiteful actions and overwhelmed by the rush of emotions that being near Conner is evoking in me.

I don't know what this is? What it means for us, for him and me? Whatever we had in the past has stayed with both of us, but I'm having trouble believing that he's missed me as much as he's saying he has. He's lived the single, party life of a rock star. I've seen the photos, read and listened to the gossip in the magazines and on the celebrity gossip shows. I sort of tried to avoid them. The pictures of him with a different woman every week, the rumours about the wild sexploits that he and Jet, allegedly got up to. But, at the end of the day, I'm only human and a human woman at that, and as a woman, I've done what most women in my shoes would do… I googled and researched the shit out of those bitches that were captured hanging off his arm at various events. I know I was married to someone else, but I was jealous of those women regardless. I wasn't jealous of their long legs and flawless features. I was jealous of the fact that they were with *him*. He was meant to have been mine, and there they were spending time with and getting to know him. I often looked at the pictures and wondered if they knew him like I did? If they knew about his mum and how she died. About his nightmares. I wondered if any of them knew that he liked meat pie and HP sauce sandwiches, and endless cups of tea?

So much has been said last night and this morning, I'm wondering if this is just a knee-jerk reaction to being back in each other's company. Could we really just pick up where we left off fifteen years ago? We're two entirely different people now, we've each lived a life. How could we be sure that we'd have anything in common, or that we'd even get along?

In saying all of that, when he kisses me, when his arms are around me, I feel safe, secure and like I'm exactly where I'm meant to be. In those moments, it feels as though we've never been apart. I only hope it's not all just wishful thinking. That we're just clinging on to a stupid teenage dream. I'm finding it hard to believe that he'd give up his apparently wild ways to be with me. I'm just a hairdresser from Surrey and him, well he's Conner Reed.

I WALK INTO THE KITCHEN to find Conner, Soph and Josh all sitting around the huge dining table.

Conner was right about the T-shirt, it comes down to just above my knees, but I can't help but pull it down when his eyes roam from mine to look up and down my body.

"Fuck. Me." He mouths from where he's sitting and then gives me another one of those perfect smiles. The ones that give me a mini orgasm. A smilegasm. My lips twitch as I attempt not to smile at the self-diagnosis and name that I've given to my condition.

"Feel better?" he asks.

"Much," I reply, my cheeks flaming from the thoughts running through my dirty mind.

Conner pulls me a chair out, and I sit down next to him at the table.

"Sophie's just been telling me what happened that night. Why you were at the hospital," Josh looks across to me as he speaks.

"I'm so sorry, baby chick. I had no idea."

"It's not your fault, Josh," I tell him.

"I spoke to my mum that night, she told me that you were all going off to a hotel to celebrate. If she'd told me the truth, I would've told Reed, and this could've all been sorted out years ago. I feel so fucking bad. Like I've played a huge roll in you two being apart all these years."

Conner reaches out and takes my hand and gives it a squeeze while Josh talks, and once again, the move just seems so right, so natural and it doesn't go unnoticed by Soph. She gives me a smile as our eyes meet. I smile back, a feeling of contentment settles over me for some reason I'm not quite sure of yet.

"Honestly Josh. I don't blame you, Soph or your mum, she lied to protect me. I didn't want anyone to know. Even my own parents don't know."

They'd probably have thrown a party in celebration if they had found out. Conner was most definitely not the type of boy they wanted a daughter of theirs to be associated with, let alone knocked up by at just sixteen. Now though… now he's a rich and world famous rock star, my parents would be throwing me at his feet.

We all fall silent until Sophie speaks, "I didn't tell them about your brother and the money yet."

My belly does a few backflips, and my mouth instantly feels dry when I start to think about how stupid and naïve I was to let Pearce manipulate me in the way that he did.

I cover my face with my hands for a few seconds, then look up at the ceiling. Well, there's nothing I can do to change things, so I might as well just admit to how I allowed myself to be taken advantage of.

"Like most of the choices I've made in my life, my parents didn't approve of me becoming a hairdresser." I look between Josh and Conner, leaving my eyes to rest on Con's.

"When I lost you and the baby, I…" I struggle for a few seconds, trying to think of the right words to use, "I wasn't in a good place, mentally. I dropped out of school and off the face of the planet. I cut everyone, including Soph out of my life. I stayed home, locked in my room. I piled on a heap of weight and just, I don't know what… Anyway, I saw a job advertised in a local salon as I was walking by one day and went in and applied. Turns out, hairdressing was my thing, and I was good at it. I got my shit together, stopped the comfort eating, lost some weight, and got healthier both mentally and physically. I started seeing Sophie again, and ended up getting her a Saturday job at the salon." I smile across at her, remembering those days and the laughs we used to have. "We both completed our apprenticeships, then worked a few more years to gain experience, before deciding to set up on our own.

"We found a shop for sale in town. A great location, right across from the park and a wine bar, so lots of passing traffic and a two-bedroomed flat above it. The bank wouldn't even entertain the idea of lending me money and neither would my parents, so I asked my brother. He had some loan documents drawn up, and he lent me a hundred and thirty grand. I paid him back a small amount each month, and we agreed that the balance would be paid once the business was showing a profit and the bank would lend me the money."

I let my wet hair out of the scrunchy that's holding it in place, rewind it into a messy bun again and secure it. It didn't need touching, it's just a nervous move as I try to think how to tell Conner what I'm about to say next.

"Pearce was working with Marcus Newman at his dad's law firm and doing well. Over the next few years, Marcus asked me out a few times. I always said no. I threw myself into work and didn't really date anyone. That aside, I just didn't want to go out with him." I swallow a few times and run my tongue over my teeth. "My brother and Marcus started coming to the salon for haircuts and would turn up wherever I was out at the weekends and, of course, Marcus continued to ask me out. Eventually, I said, yes. There was nothing there, it was just…" I shrug my, acutely aware of Con's eyes on me. "I didn't feel anything for him. So there was no chance he could hurt me in the way I'd been hurt before." Conner squeezes my hand. "Then he drops a bombshell and asks me to marry him. I tell him no, I'm too young, too busy, just not ready." Talking about this, telling the story to others makes me even more aware of what an idiot I was. "We still kept seeing each other, and he tells my brother that he's going to ask me again. My brother… my loyal, trusting big brother, tells me that his career is riding on my response. If I don't say yes to Marcus's marriage proposal, he threatened to go to the press with a story about how Conner Reed had sex with an underage girl and got her pregnant, then abandoned her to go out and sell drugs, leaving her alone in the hospital after she miscarried their baby."

I watch Conner rake the fingers of his left hand through his hair. His right hand, never leaves mine.

"What a wanker. What a complete and utter wanker," Josh says.

"Oh, but it gets better," Sophie adds.

"Then he tells me, he wants all the money back that he loaned me. At that stage, it was still about sixty thousand. The business was doing well, but we were just about to open our second or third salon, I can't remember which."

I look Conner in the eye. "So I did it. When Marcus asked, I said, yes."

His stare gives nothing away. "You married Marcus Newman?" he asks. I nod.

Josh and Conner know Marcus. We all went to primary school together so they would've seen him around town with my brother over the years.

"And that's who you're divorcing? Who you've been married to for the last eight years?"

I nod again. "He was safe, Con. I wouldn't survive having my heart broken again, and there was no possibility he would be able to do that. I didn't love him, so I was safe. That doesn't mean that I didn't try. I did. I tried to be the perfect wife for him. I gave myself over to him. I let him, my brother and my parents mould me into what they wanted me to be." I don't want to cry, so I decide to end the story there.

"So why the divorce? What happened to you being the perfect wife and daughter?" Conner asks.

I let out a long sigh and look over at Soph, who gives me a small nod, encouraging me to go on. "I was so lonely. After all the begging and pleading Marcus had done to get me to go out with him and to be his wife, once he had me, he wasn't the slightest bit interested. We have nothing in common. He's away most weekends playing golf. We only really go out together if it's a work function for him, or some political event my mother insists we attend. But because I'm this stupid naïve woman, I'd convinced myself that we could make it work. That if we had a child together, it'd make everything right between us. But I can't even get that right." A tear drips from my lash and rolls down my cheek.

"Meebs," Conner says very quietly, shaking his head. I put my hand up, I need him to know what he's in for if we're going to give a relationship a go.

"When I miscarried, they found out I was suffering from poly-cystic ovaries. It doesn't mean that I can't have kids, but it could mean that it's more difficult for me to conceive and carry a child to full term, but yeah anyway, it's irrelevant now. We tried for a while to have a baby but it never happened, and now, with hindsight, that's probably for the best."

"The bloke's unstable. I know you want kids Neen, but you were lucky not to fall pregnant with him."

Conner's eyes flick from Sophie to me. "Why's he unstable?"

I let out another one of those breaths that they write about in books. "He came home drunk one night, and for no reason he attacked me."

"What the fuck, Meebs?" Conner pulls his hand from mine, laces his fingers together behind his head and glares at me. His brows drawn down into a deep frown. "Did you press charges?" he asks.

"He's a lawyer, Con, he'd lose his job. Be struck off even."

He pushes up from his chair loudly and stands. "So fucking what, it'd serve the fucker right. He put his hands on you Meebs. He should've been nicked for it."

I close my eyes and rub my fingertips over my temples. "All I want is a divorce, Con. If I press charges, he'll make it difficult. I just want to draw a line under the biggest fuck up of my life and be left alone to move on."

He's pacing the floor as he talks, "He should pay for what he did… What did he do, did he hurt you?" He leans on the back of the chair toward me.

"Yeah, he hurt her. I tried to get her to go to the police, but she wouldn't," I shoot Sophie a look as she tells Conner this.

He shakes his head at me. "If he comes near you again, I'll kill him. Him and your prick of a brother. I'll kill the fucking pair of them."

I have nothing left to say, no argument left in me. I'm so tired, so ready for sleep.

"I need to get going, Con. I've got a shit load to do today, and I've had no sleep," Josh says, standing up from the table.

"I'll come with you," Sophie adds, standing up too.

"Well, I might as well come with you two," I add.

"You can sit the fuck down, you're going nowhere," Conner says to me.

"Don't tell me what to do." I put my hands on my hips and look at him.

"Meebs, please. Will you stay? We need to talk."

I fold my arms across my chest and sit back in my chair, way too tired to put up a fight. I ask Sophie to make sure Duch is doing all right up on the roof terrace and to make sure she's fed and has water.

She gives me a cuddle. "Give him a chance, Neen. You two are so good together and still bang in love. This is like a real-life fairy tale. This is your chance at a happy ending, princess. I love you."

"I love you, too," I tell her.

Conner has called his driver to give them a lift home, and ten minutes later we're standing at his front door, waving them off.

As soon as Con shuts the door, he grabs my hand and pulls me up the stairs and into his bedroom.

"Get in bed, I'm gonna take a shower," he orders.

"Bossy much?" I mumble but climb into his bed anyway.

"You've seen nothing yet, baby." He winks, then heads into the bathroom.

'Winkgasm' being the last thought I remember running through my brain.

CONNER

I TURN THE BODY JETS in my shower to full blast and enjoy the sting as the water makes contact with my skin. I roll my neck and shoulders a few times, trying to release some of the tension and rage I've been holding in.

I'm angry at Pearce Matthews. He's a lying, deceitful little shit and I'm going to do what I can to bring that fucker down. Actually, it's more than anger I feel toward him right now. He's caused something dark to bubble inside of me, and I don't like it.

I'm so far beyond pissed off with Marcus Newman that I can barely see straight when I think about what he's done. Marcus *fucking* Newman. The bloke's a wanker. A stuck up prick and she went and married the fucker. I can't even allow myself to think about him putting his hands on her, but worse than the thought of him fucking her is the thought of him hurting her. *He hurt her.* How? *Why* would anyone want to hurt *her?* Especially her fucking husband. I can't even go there right now. I need to lock that one away and deal with it once I've got my head around what her brother did to her… *to us.*

I'm also angry with Meebs. I know she's been used as a means to an end, but why the fuck did she let it happen? She's not stupid, far from it. So why the fuck did she let her brother manipulate her the way he did? She has no problem standing up to me, so why the fuck didn't she stand up to that little dickhead?

I grip my hair and try and keep the rage buried deep down inside me. Turning the hot water up, I stand and endure the sting and burn as it hits my body. My usual routine when I feel like this would be to go to my place in the Kings Road and call up a few people for a night of sex. Horrible, nasty, humiliating sex. I'd watch and shout orders. I'd get off on others doing things that they ordinarily would never do. Wouldn't even consider, but because I'm involved, because I just have this way to somehow convince people that they do want to watch that woman suck their boyfriend's dick, while they fuck him up the arse with a strap-on, they do it. There might be a slight hesitation, but they always end up doing what I order, and you know what? They always end up enjoying it. The trick is, knowing just how far to push people.

I place my palm flat against the tiles as I fist my cock in my other hand. I need to come. It's the only way I can calm myself the fuck down.

I have Meebs waiting for me in my bed. My beautiful Meebs. *What would she think if she knew the truth about the things I've done, the things I've made others do?*

"Fuck!" I stop what I'm doing, lean my back against the tiles and slide down the wall.

What the fuck am I doing? Why did I make her stay here with me? I'm the last thing she needs in her life right now. I'm a fucked up mess, but I want her so fucking much. She fits. When I wrap my arms around her, when her little body is pulled against mine, she fits and all is right with my world.

I rub my hands over my face and stand back up and wash myself. I've no idea where I'm going with this. I don't know if I have it in me to have a healthy relationship. I want it. I yearn for it so fucking much, and I want it with her, but I don't know if I'm capable. I've spent so long running from relationships and intimacy, I don't know if I would even know *how* to be with someone.

Feeling as frustrated as fuck, I step out of the shower, wrap a towel around my waist and clean my teeth. My toothbrush is lying on the side of the sink and not in the holder where I usually keep it, and the thought that Meebs has had it in her mouth makes my dick twitch. I grab another towel and walk into my bedroom rubbing my hair dry with it and stop dead in my tracks.

She's lying in the foetal position, in the middle of my bed. She has on my T-shirt, and it's pulled over her knees, just her feet sticking out of the bottom. She's tiny, so fucking small and beautiful and perfect. This girl, this woman, has consumed my thoughts for most of my life. I've dreamt about her. I've written songs about her, and now here she is, in my home and in my bed. I consider myself to have a pretty vivid imagination but fuck me, the reality of her being here far outweighs anything my brain could've come up with.

Her hands are curled into fists and tucked under her chin. Her damp blonde hair is splayed out over the duvet cover. I move in closer, sitting on the edge of the bed so I can get a better view. Her fair lashes fan out across her cheeks, which are covered with a light dusting of freckles that spread across her nose. Her pale pink lips are in a perfect pout as she sleeps. Watching her like this brings order to my thoughts. The anger and aggression I was feeling earlier has dissolved. Looking at her flawless skin and natural beauty calms my raging mind, and I don't doubt for a moment what the feeling is that has settled in my chest.

Love.

I love her.

I've never stopped loving her, and it scares the shit out of me.

I want this. I want her, but I'm terrified I'll fuck it all up somehow.

If she were to know the truth about the way I've conducted my sex life all these years would she be repulsed, hate me, pity me?

Feeling overwhelmed I go into my wardrobe and pull on a pair of boxers and then go and lay on the bed. I wrap my arm around Meebs and pull her back into my front. I breathe her in and the realisation that she smells of me almost makes my heart beat out of my throat. I loved her before, back when we were kids, but this is on another level. I'm not sure if it's because I now know what it's like not to have her in my life, but what I'm feeling now… *fuck*… I don't know. I'm a songwriter, but I don't have words right now to describe this. I pull her in tighter and kiss right below her ear.

She lets out a little moan and turns around in my arms to face me. Her hand comes up and touches my cheek, as she mumbles, "I love you, Conner Reed. I love you so fucking much." Her lips find mine, and she kisses me gently, then continues sleeping.

Fuck, multiplatinum-selling albums.

Fuck, The Grammy's and The Brit Awards.

Fuck, the millions in the bank, the cars, horses and properties.

Fuck it all!

She loves me. This girl loves me, and I swear to each and every God that might be listening, I will sort my shit out, and I *will* be what she needs in her life. I will do *everything* and anything necessary to become worthy of her love.

Does that make me a pussy? Probably but I really don't give a fuck.

I WAKE TO THE SENSATION of a hot little hand wrapped around my hip. I open my eyes and realise that it's Meebs hair tickling my nose that's woken me. I kiss the top of her head, which causes her to stir. She moves her hand, and it comes to rests right on my dick.

Pearce Matthews.

Pearce Matthews.

Pearce Matthews.

Shit! Even thinking about her dickwad brother is doing nothing to lessen my hard-on.

Suddenly a pair of big blue eyes are looking up at me. She starts to smile, then her fingers move, and she frowns. Pulling her hand away from my crotch, she blushes and buries her face in my chest.

"Please tell me I didn't sleep all this time hanging on to your dick?" I think is what she asks.

I lift her chin so that she has to look at me. Her cheeks are glowing, and I can't not kiss her. My lips just make contact with hers when she pulls away.

"I've probably got morning breath," she says.

"I think you'll find it's afternoon breath."

"That does nothing to reassure me, that it doesn't smell like a fart."

I can't help but smile. "You said fart," I say with a grin.

"And you've got a hard-on," she replies.

"Oh my God, now you're saying hard-on. What happened to that sweet innocent Nina Amoeba I used to know?"

"She was kidnapped and corrupted by some wicked rock star."

I pull her in tighter and grind against her. "I'd like to corrupt you," I tell her while kissing her neck.

"Can't wait," she replies.

I lean back so that I can see her face. I'm not sure if she's joking or being sarcastic.

"What?" she asks

"You can't just joke about things like that, Meebs. Not when you're in my bed all pressed up against me."

She blinks a couple of times and then lets out a long sigh.

"What do you want from me, Con? Where do we go with this now?"

I sit up and lean my back against the headboard. I pull Meebs into my lap, and she straddles me. I pull up my knees, and she leans back against them. I tuck her hair behind her ear and decide to be totally honest with her.

"I want this… I want there to be an *us*, Meebs."

I write this shit all the time in my songs but right here, right now, with her sitting in front of me, all blonde and little and hot as fuck, I can't think straight.

"It just feels right. You being here, in my home, in my bed. It just feels right. Like it's where you and I are meant to be."

She tilts her head and gives me a smile. "That rhymes. You ever think about writing poetry, or maybe even songs?"

"I have, but I'm not sure I'd be any good at it," I tell her.

"I think you'd be good at anything you set your mind to." And that makes my heart stutter and miss a beat.

Pussy.

"You have too much faith in me," I tell her.

"I trust you to do the right thing," she replies.

"I'm not sure you should."

"Should I walk away now then?" her eyes are all over my face as she asks.

"That would probably be the wise thing to do."

"I'm actually not known for my wisdom. My life is full of bad choices." That causes a little stab of pain in my chest.

"I think you're possibly the wisest person I know. It's hard to do the right thing when you're being manipulated by bullshitters that don't have your best interests in mind."

"So, what if I told you that I think you're right. That we are right where we're meant to be. That I want this, whatever it is. I want to give it a go. Do you still think I'm wise?"

Well, she's got me there.

"Is that really what you want?" I ask.

"I think it is," she says quietly.

"You think, or you know?"

"I know."

I reach out and touch her cheek with the back of my knuckles. "I'm so scared I'm gonna fuck this up," I tell her honestly.

"Please try not to. I don't think my heart could stand losing you again."

"Fuck, Meebs." I pull her in. One hand grips her hip, the other in her hair at the back of her head. My mouth melds with hers, but it's not enough. I need to taste. I pull on her hair, a little too hard and when she attempts to protest at the pain, I slide my tongue inside her mouth. It tangles with hers. I drag it over her teeth and around her mouth.

She moans and grinds against me. Her nails claw into my scalp, and I tilt my head back when she pulls her mouth from mine and drags her teeth along my jaw.

"Meebs. Baby, you need to either stop what you're doing or take your clothes the fuck off. Coz I can't hang on much longer. I want you too much."

She pulls back and looks at me. Without saying a word, she lifts my T-shirt over her head and throws it to the floor.

My head spins.

I drag my eyes from her face and down to look at her tits. Her creamy skin is perfect. Her tits are fuller than I remember, but her nipples are that same pale pink, almost the same shade as her lips.

I reach out slowly and drag my three middle fingers down to her cleavage from her throat. She looks down and watches me. I stroke my fingertips up and down a few times, mesmerised by the way goose bumps form across her skin and her nipples darken in colour slightly as they harden.

I stroke across to her right nipple and gently squeeze and pull it with my thumb and index finger. She tilts her head back and lets out a little moan. I lean into her left nipple and gently bite down, before sucking it into my mouth and lapping at it with my tongue.

"Fuck Con," she sighs. Gripping my hair at the back of my head, she forces my mouth down on her harder.

Moving my mouth over her throat, along her jaw, I find my way back to her mouth.

"I need to be inside you," I tell her.

"You have condoms?" she asks.

"Shit!" I do have condoms. Of course, I do. I've never had sex without them, except twice, with Meebs and look what that led to. The problem is, the condoms are in the round room.

"I need to go and get them," I tell her. She frowns in confusion.

"From where? Please tell me you don't have to run to the shop?"

"No." Shit, how do I explain this one?

"They're in... I don't... I don't keep them in here."

She looks even more confused.

"Why? Where do you keep?"

I feel my cheeks burn. I'm blushing. I'm Conner fucking Reed, and she's made me blush.

"In the other room, the other bedroom."

I lift her from where she's still straddling me and stand up. I try and adjust my hard-on, but it's too stiff to do anything with.

"Don't move. I'll be right back," I tell her, before running down the hallway to the big bedroom at the front of the house.

I grab a box of condoms and run back to my room, which is not easy when you're sporting a boner as hard as mine. Something I'd never before been aware of, running with a hard dick is, in fact, painful.

Meebs is sitting cross-legged on the bed when I walk back in the room, and for a moment, I'm terrified that she's changed her mind now that she's had a few seconds to think.

I grab her legs and pull them over the side of the bed. Pushing gently in the middle of her chest, I tell her to lay back. I reach for a pillow, and before placing it underneath her hips, I pull down my boxers that she's wearing. I position the pillow so her hips are tilting up, then lift her left leg and kiss the arch of her foot.

She props herself up on her elbows and watches me kissing along the inside of her leg. I flick my tongue along the crease at the back of her knee and can't help but smile when she lets out a whispered, *"Fuck,"* and arches her neck so she's looking up at the ceiling. Her eyes come back to mine when I start gently biting up the inside of her thigh.

My plan, when I get to the top, was to start at the bottom of her right leg, but now I'm here I need to taste her.

She's neat and trimmed and wet to the point that I can see her juices glistening on her skin. I let out a groan as I push her legs apart and spread her with my thumbs.

"Fuck baby, best view ever," I tell her. Not waiting for a response before I push my tongue inside her. I twirl it clockwise, then anti-clockwise a couple of times, before licking up to her clit and flicking my tongue over her. It's been years since I tasted a woman and I honestly don't remember the last occasion, but this… the sight, the sound, the taste and the smell of her… this I will never forget.

"Best taste ever," I tell her.

"Ahhh," she moans.

"Shit. Fuck. Oh fuck, God, Con." I'd forgotten how vocal and responsive she was during sex. It took me a long time before she let me get in her knickers, but once I'd made her come with my fingers against a wall in a multistorey carpark one night, she couldn't get enough.

"Best sound ever."

I move my mouth away and pick up her right leg, licking at the inside of her foot.

"Awww man. Seriously? You gonna start all the way back there and make me wait?" she whines.

I kiss her ankle and give a little chuckle. "Tell me what you want baby, and I'll give it to you, but you have to tell me."

"Mouth," she says. "Tongue, fingers. All of you. I want you inside me, Con. Fuck me like you used to. Love me like you used to. Fuck me and love me and make me forget the past fifteen years."

Everything I'd planned goes out of the window. The sweet slow torture I had in mind for her body will have to be saved for later. I need to slide inside and fuck her. Right now.

Standing up, I pull down and kick off my boxers. I slide on a condom and lift Meebs to the middle of the bed. I position myself between her legs and look down at her while holding my body weight off of her with my elbows.

"I love you, Nina Amoeba. I've loved you most of my life."

She frowns and shakes her head. "Con?" she says my name questioningly on a sob.

"I don't care that we've spent so long apart, I don't care that we've only just met back up. I don't care whether or not this makes sense, it is what it is. I love you, and you and everyone else will just have to get their fucking heads around it."

She looks at me wide-eyed but doesn't say a word.

"I'm gonna fuck you now. I'll try and take it slow and gentle, but I want you. I want you so fucking much that I don't know if I'm capable of slow and gentle. If I hurt you or if it's just too much, I need you to tell me, okay?"

She licks her lips.

"Fuck Meebs, baby, please. At least give me a chance not to blow in the first five seconds."

She smiles and says, "Fuck me, Con, right now."

I slide inside her, and she whimpers. I roll my hips, and she lets out a moan. I rock my hips forward and she, "Oh God's." She's as tight as I remember and I know that I'm not going to last long.

I press my forehead against hers. "Open your eyes and look at me, baby. I need to see you."

She bites down on her bottom lip and shakes her head, no.

"I can't," she whispers.

A little wave of panic ripples through me. "Why not, babe? Tell me what's wrong."

"I'm scared, Con."

"Of what, Meebs?"

"That none of this is real. That you're not really here. That we're not really doing this."

My heart bangs so hard in my chest, I'm sure she must be able to feel it in hers.

"This is real baby, don't you worry about that. This is you and me, and it's definitely real. Now open your eyes and look at me."

I kiss each of her eyelids before she looks up at me.

"I love you," I tell her, before again rocking my hips into hers. "You feel so fucking good. I thought about this so many times, but this is better. You feel, taste and smell so much better than you ever did in my head."

"Con?"

"Meebs?"

"Stop talking and fuck me."

So I do. I aim for long, slow and sensual, but when she crosses her ankles around my back and squeezes my arse cheeks in an attempt to pull me deeper inside her, I lose all control and fuck her like I've never fucked before. The second she calls out my name and I feel her tight little pussy pulse and clench around my cock, I shoot off like a rocket. I seriously hope these condoms are reinforced. Otherwise, she'll be feeling my load hit her tonsils.

When I look down at her face, her head's thrown back, and she has tears running from the corners of each eye. I feel myself start to shake. I know that I'm losing it. For a few seconds, I try to regain control, but looking down at her gorgeous face makes me want to just let go. I want her to see *me*. The *real* me. The Conner Reed that only my dad, my brothers and my bandmates know. The pure emotion of not just this moment, but a lifetime of hurt, pain, loss and loneliness, overcome me. I let out a sob it feels I've been holding on to for a lifetime.

Being with her. Having my Meebs in my bed, in my arms, has both freed and consumed me. And now that they've started, fifteen years of tears don't seem to want to stop.

"Con? Baby, you okay?"

I try to keep my weight off of her, but my shoulders are shaking so bad that I'm scared I'm going to collapse. She slides out from underneath me, causing me to slide out of her. I pull off the condom, tie it in a knot and throw it down on the floor, not really caring where it lands.

I push myself to sit back against the headboard, and when she climbs into my lap and wraps her arms around me, the feel of her skin against mine, her fingers combing gently through my hair, I come completely undone. I gasp for air as the sobs come thick and fast, the tears stream down my face and all the while she just holds me tight and strokes her fingers over my arms, my back and my head.

She takes my face in her hands and makes me look up her. "They tried to break us, Conner Reed. They tried, and they failed. What we have is stronger than they could ever have imagined. We fought a war we had no idea we were a part of, and we've found our way back. We don't need anyone else. We might be broken and damaged, but we'll fix ourselves. As long as we have each other, we'll be stronger than ever." She leans in and kisses my face, my eyes and my nose.

She kisses away my tears and my fears, and I feel each and every one of them in my heart, my soul, in my DNA.

She holds me tight while I cry and then, later on, she holds me tight while I make love to her in the shower. This time I do take it slow and gentle. I lick and suck her from head to toe, until she's once again, calling out my name.

She's got me… hook, line and sinker. I'm one hundred percent in love with this girl, and I can't wait to tell the world. Yep, I'll also gladly admit to anyone that wants to listen, that where she's concerned, I'm a complete and utter pussy.

CHAPTER TWENTY-FOUR

NINA

I WALK INTO THE BIG kitchen, dining and living area that Conner calls the 'family room' to the sound of Sigma singing about having nobody to love and I stop dead in my tracks as I take him in.

"You fancy Chinese?" Conner looks up from the menu in his hand and asks.

He's leaning against the kitchen worktop, wearing a pair of football shorts and nothing else. His dark blond hair looks almost brown where it's damp. He's pushed it back from his face, which is covered in a few days stubble. He's still lean but not skinny. In fact, he's ripped. He has a well-defined six pack, that V thing which girls want to kiss, lick and suck, and well-defined muscles in his arms and legs. And ink. Ink on his arms, around his neck, his hands, and it's so fucking hot, he's so fucking hot, I could combust just looking at him. Conner Reed was once a beautiful boy, now he's a breathtakingly beautiful man.

"Meebs, stop perving. I'm starved. You want Chinese or d'ya wanna pop out and get something?"

I keep staring. Pop out? Be seen out, in public, with Conner Reed?

The reality of the last few hours hits me like an avalanche, and I can barely draw breath.

He's the boy I fell in love with when I was fifteen, but then at the hands of lies, deceit and spitefulness, we've spent years apart only to meet back up and fall straight into bed.

What on earth was I thinking?

Our lives have gone in entirely different directions. Conner's a world famous rock star, I'm a soon to be divorced hairdresser from Surrey. I live in the real world of bills, work and a dog to walk, while Conner poses on the front of magazines with six foot tall, stick thin, fake titted models. I don't know what's been going through my head, but this can never work. I'm not some fictional character from one of the many contemporary romance novels I have on my Kindle. I'm me, a real, living breathing person with a life I need to get back to. While Conner, Conner is just the fantasy I've held on to for far too long.

"Meebs?" I look up as he puts the menu down and starts to walk toward me.

"What's wrong?" he asks while wrapping his arms around my waist.

"I need to go home, Con. I've got work tomorrow. I need to do some washing and walk the dog. I… this, this won't work, Con. I have this life, and it's not going to work." My brain is thinking clear and cohesive thoughts, but for some reason when I try to say them out loud, they come out as a jumbled mess.

He leans back and bends his knees so he can look at me. I've never seen a look like it on Conner's face before, not aimed at me anyway. He's angry.

"I'm not letting you go, Meebs. Don't fight me on this. You don't get to walk in here and give me hope and then just walk away again." He breathes heavily, his hands gripping my shoulders. "We can, and we *will* make this work. What are you scared of? Why the fuck are you suddenly trying to run?" His eyes are looking more blue than green as they look into mine right now.

"I'm a hairdresser, Con. A five foot nothing, UK size twelve hair-dresser. My arse is too fat for my height, my tits are too small for my arse, my legs too short and my muffin top hangs over my skinny jeans. I don't fit into your world. I don't look like the women I've seen you on the telly and in the magazines with," my voice is getting higher as I try not to cry.

"I'm just me, Con, I'm just plain old me," I whisper.

His mouth unexpectedly comes crashing down on mine. He kisses me fiercely, intensely. He takes and leaves me with no option but to give back. With one arm snaked around my waist and his hand gripping my hair, he pulls away and looks at me.

"There's nothing plain about you, Nina Amoeba. I love your arse, and your tits and your legs are fucking perfect. You have more beauty and sex appeal in your little fucking finger than any of the anorexic, bubbleheads you've ever seen me photographed with." He holds each side of my face in his hands so that I have no choice but to look at him.

"This is our time, Meebs, our chance. We've both been fucked over and had shit to deal with in the past, but this, us…" he gestures between our bodies, "This our fairy tale. This our chance at a happy ever after and I'm not letting your misplaced insecurities deny us this chance." He leans his forehead against mine.

"I love you. I love you, and I'm not letting you go."

We stand in the middle of the kitchen, our heads pressed together. Both of us breathing heavily. Ed Sheeran starts to sing.

"This song," Conner whispers, "I'm so jealous that I didn't write this song and dedicate it to you. This whole album, Meebs, nearly every song reminds me of us. There's even one called Nina."

Us. He's listened to this album, which I know has only just been released, and it makes him think about *us*. As recently as this month, he's thought about *us*.

I let that fact wash over me for a few seconds. I like the way it makes me feel. Warm, loved, content and safe. Feelings that I've ached for lately.

Conner starts to sway to the music. He wraps one arm around my waist and laces his fingers through mine and pulls it up to settle between our chests.

"Dance with me?" he asks softly, already moving gently to the music.

"Listen to the words and dance with me, Meebs."

And there, in the middle of the kitchen, dancing to Ed Sheeran's 'Thinking out loud,' while Conner sings into my ear, words about falling in love with me, every single day, I give up the fight. I'm his. I have no idea where this will go, but I'm going to give my very own fairy tale a chance. If all goes well, then the rock star and the hairdresser will get to live out their happily ever after.

CONNER

I WAKE TO THE SOUND of my phone. I've ignored the calls and text messages all weekend, but I know I need to answer it now.

I went back to bed after Matty dropped Meebs back at home this morning. We spent the rest of Sunday afternoon and night reacquainting ourselves with each other, but she needed to go into work today and so, reluctantly, I let her go, but only after she promised to come back tonight.

My house is only about five miles from hers, and she's agreed to drive herself over here once she's finished work. I've told her to bring an overnight bag and stay. Actually, I told her to pack up her life and move it in with mine, but she just stood looking at me with her hands on her hips and her eyebrows raised as if I was some kind of nutter. Maybe I am, but now that I've got her back, I don't want to let her go, and I don't see why I should.

"It's nine-thirty on a Monday morning, this better be good Lawson," I mumble into the phone to my manager. My face is buried in my pillow. It smells of Meebs. Me, Meebs and sex.

"What the fuck are you doing, Reed? You sound like you've got a pillow over your face."

I roll over onto my back.

"What d'ya want?" I ask.

"And good morning to you, too. I take it things didn't go too well with bacteria?"

He's such a funny fucker... not.

"Her name's, Nina. The only bacteria around here is what you have around your dick after you've been shoving it inside Amanda," I tell him.

"Wow, you really are pissed off this morning. What's up? Little miss muse not let you into her knickers?"

"Fuck you, Knight. You have five seconds to tell me what you want before I hang up this call and sever all ties," I tell him.

"I've spoken to the label. If we can agree on a percentage of royalties from Shift's back catalogue, you're free to sign elsewhere. I've spoken to Layton's people, SNL wants you on the show. There are a few other interview requests as well. Lots of enquiries about whether you and Marley will be working together in the future, and yeah, that's about it."

I stare up at the ceiling, digesting all of that information.

"Can we not pre-record SNL and just send the tape?" I ask.

"No, you know that's not how they do things. There's a reason the last word in the show title is 'live' Reed."

I let out a long sigh. I wonder if Meebs can get time off to come out to the US with me. I don't want to go if she can't.

"Okay, find out when they want us on, and I'll see what I can do. The only other interviews I'm interested in are the ones that Marley agrees to. I'm happy to discuss the charity event, but nothing else."

"SNL wants you to perform too," he states.

"If Layton's up for it, then that's fine with me. Anything else?"

"Like you said Reed, it's only nine-thirty on Monday morning. Give them a chance. I'm sure after your surprise appearance Saturday there'll be more. I've already had over a dozen enquiries about who the girl is you dedicated the song to, and who it was you left with Saturday night."

My stomach drops at this news. I've never bothered hiding too much of my life from the press before, but I want to keep Meebs out of the spotlight for as long as possible. She's already nervous about my career impacting on hers, and we agreed last night to lay low for a while, at least until her divorce is finalised.

"Don't tell them a thing. I don't want them getting a hold of her name or any details about her," I tell him.

"Gotchya."

We're both silent for a few seconds. He knows this is different for me. Usually the women I'm seen with want it known who they are. They want their name bandied about as Reed's latest lover, and I have no problem with that. I'm happy to help anyone's career, but sometimes, sometimes it would've been nice if just one of those women had been interested in me and not just in where being seen with me could get them.

"So, you sorted your shit out with the muse then?" Lawson asks.

I let out a long sigh before answering him, "We talked, but we still have a lot more talking to do. It's early days Laws, but we're gonna give it a go." A vein in my neck throbs as my blood rushes through it. Lawson Knight has seen me at my most vile and destructive. He's seen me at my most perverse. He's only too aware of how adverse I've been to intimacy over the years, so admitting my feelings for Meebs to him now is a bit of a big deal for me. Not because I'm ashamed of what I feel for her. *Fuck no!* I want the whole world to know. I'm just ashamed that he knows about my past behaviour.

"Give it a go? As in… what?" he asks.

"I love her, Laws. I've never stopped loving her. Seeing her again, it just all clicked back into place." I rake my free hand through my hair. "I know it sounds like bullshit, but it's like we've never been apart," I admit.

"Fuck," he says quietly into the phone. "Well, I s'pose when you know, you know, mate."

"And I sure as fuck know," I tell him.

"And she feels the same?" he asks.

"She does. She's terrified, but she wants this as much as me. I just need to keep this out of the press for as long as possible, Laws. I don't want those fuckers scaring her away. We need a bit of time to sort through this before we go public," I can hear an almost pleading tone to my voice.

"Of course, man. Whatever it takes." There's a moment's silence. "I'm really pleased for you, Reed, you know. After everything else that's gone on in the past, I really hope you can make a go of things with this girl."

"Thanks Laws. I'll talk to ya later."

I end the call when I feel a lump forming in my throat. Nina Matthews has been back in my life for less than forty-eight hours, and I'm a bigger emotional mess than your average fourteen-year-old girl getting her first period.

I HEAD DOWNSTAIRS WHEN I hear my dad and Sandra talking and moving about in my kitchen. They must've known that I had company yesterday because they didn't come over, didn't even let the dogs run loose.

"Morning sunshine," Sandra greets me with a cheery smile.

"Morning," I greet back.

"Dad." I give him a smile and a nod.

"You want a coffee, boy?" he asks, and I shake my head no.

"I had one earlier, thanks." I grab a carton of orange juice from the fridge and pour myself a glassful, only too aware of the two pairs of eyes on me. I put the juice back in the fridge and turn back around to face my audience.

"What?" I ask, looking between both of them.

"Have a good weekend, son? We watched the show on the telly.

The crowd seemed more than pleased with you and that Carnage bloke."

"Yeah, it went well thanks. I haven't had a chance to watch it back yet."

"No, well, we saw you had company yesterday. That's why we stayed out of the way," my dad says. Sandra wipes at non-existent crumbs on the worktop.

"You spoke to Ty, didn't you?"

Sandra turns around with a massive grin on her face. "How'd it go, Con? Can you believe it, after all these years? I noticed she didn't leave until this morning."

"So it's true?" my dad joins in.

I'm staring between him and Sandra. Glass in one hand, the other on my hip. My mouth probably hanging open.

"I don't believe this. Don't take long for news to travel around here, does it?"

"Oh, come on, Con. Over ten years I've been with your dad, and I've never known you to have a proper girlfriend. I'm just pleased for you."

"Who says she's my girlfriend?" I ask.

Sandra and my dad look at each other. "No need to get on your high horse son. Tyler said that you bumped into that Nina girl that you went out with years ago, at the show Saturday," my dad says.

"Yeah, and that you left with her," Sandra adds.

"Well, Tyler's got a big fucking mouth," I reply.

Sandra's face falls, and I feel bad. I love Sandra, she's been a mum to me longer than my own mum was. A better one too.

"Sorry," I tell them both. "We're just trying to keep things quiet for now. We need some time to get to know each other again before the press are all over us. I'm just worried about them finding out and ruining things."

"Well, they won't hear anything from us. You should know we'd never say anything. This is your home, we're your family. What goes on here and between us, stays here and between us. I thought that went without saying," my dad gives me daggers as he speaks. Shit, now I feel really bad. I walk over to the dining table and sit down. My dad and Sandra join me.

"I know that Dad, and I'm sorry. That didn't come out like it was meant to."

I look at them both. "I like her. I mean, *really* like her. She's concerned about how we're gonna make this work. What with me doing what I do and her having a business to run." I take a swig of my juice. "I don't want to scare her away before we even get a chance to work things out. I don't wanna lose her Dad. I can't lose her, not again."

Just saying those words out loud stirs all kinds of emotions in me I never thought I'd feel again.

I know I sound like a whiny little bitch, but I need my family on board with this. I need them to be aware of exactly how important Meebs is to me.

"All right son, we understand." He seems to study me for a minute.

"So, did you find out what happened, all them years ago? Did she tell you why she didn't show up?"

My dad knows the entire story of Meebs and me. When he went through rehab, we also had family group therapy, along with my brothers and we talked about a lot of things, including Meebs. We have very few secrets between us now. I might have money in the bank, have met the Queen more than once, and have a Grammy or three sitting on shelves around the place, but I have very few secrets that I keep from my family.

I spend the next half hour telling them about what happened that fateful New Year's Eve. They're as shocked as I was when they hear the story and can't believe the lengths her brother went to, to keep us apart, and the more I think about it, the more I wonder to what extent her husband was involved.

I'm going to make some calls later and give someone the job of digging up every piece of dirt that can be found on those two. I'll do it quietly and discreetly, but one way or another, they are going to pay for what they put her through.

"You know her mum's an MP now? You're gonna cop it from all angles when the press gets a hold of this. Especially with your past."

My mouth goes dry when I think about this. Heat rises, along with a sense of panic. Up from my toes to my chest and suddenly I'm struggling to get a breath.

Fuck!

My dad reaches out his hand and covers mine.

"Slowly boy, slowly."

When my breathing is more under control, I speak, "I can't lose her Dad, I can't. I'll give it all up. I'll walk away."

I stand up from the table, walk outside and pull my T-shirt over my head. It's a beautiful summer's day, so I head down the steps from the deck and jump into the pool.

After a few lengths, I feel calmer, but I keep swimming until my lungs burn. Once I'm out of the pool, I collect my dogs from my dad's back garden and take them for a run with me around the grounds of my house. I'm just trying to kill time until Meebs gets back. I'm embarrassed to think about the number of times I've checked my phone since I've been out of the pool, but I've not heard from her by twelve, and I've got to admit, yeah, I'm a little disappointed.

I shower, then head to my office. I call Marley Layton, and he informs me that SNL wants us on the show this coming Saturday. Luckily it's filmed in New York so the flight won't be too long. If Meebs can get away from work on Saturday, we could fly out Friday night and be home by Monday morning.

Marley also informs me that the EP containing the recording from Saturday of our versions of 'With You' and 'Where I Are' have gone straight to the top of the download chart. It's been a while since I had a number one and it feels good. I can't help but think as Marley talks though, that for Meebs, I would still give it all up. I've had ten years in the spotlight. Ten years of touring, cameras going off in my face, interviews and intrusion. It's made me a shit load of money, and I've experienced things that would blow your mind, but right now, I feel the time is right. I'm thirty-four-years-old and ready for the next stage of my life, and I want Meebs to be a part of that. I'll find another way to be involved with music. I'll write, produce, whatever, but I'm more than happy to step out of the glare of the public eye now.

I reply to a couple of emails. I talk briefly to Jordan and Ty on the phone as well as make some calls to a couple of people that can hopefully dig some dirt on the arsehole brother and soon to be ex-husband of Meebs. Then, I finally give in and text her.

Me: *Hey x*

I must check my phone at least twelve times a minute for the fifteen minutes it takes for her to reply.

Meebs: *Hey baby. Watchya doin'? x*

Me: *Missin u. x*

Meebs: *Baby, you have no idea. x*

Me: *I think I do. x*

Meebs: *I've been to four different salons today. Carried out 2 disciplinary actions and sacked one apprentice. :(x*

Me: *That's harsh. x*

Meebs: *That's business. x*

Me: *So, you haven't actually cut anyone's hair today? x*

Meebs: *Sadly no. it's not often I get to cut or colour hair these days. Maybe one day a week. x*

Me: *Does that mean you'll have no problem getting Saturday off and coming to NY with me? x*

Meebs: *WHAT????*

Me: *NY, you fancy it?*

Meebs: *Shit!*

Me: *Is that a yes? x*

Meebs: *No.*

Me: *What???? x*

Meebs: *I mean, yes. x*

Meebs: *I mean shit. Let me see what I can sort out. x*

Me: *OK. What time will you be here? x*

Meebs: *Not sure, why? x*

Me: *You remember the gate code? x*

Meebs: *Of course. Might not get there till late tho. :(x*

Me: *How late. :(*

Meebs: *Real late. x*

I HEAR DUKE AND KAIZER going mad at something at the front of the house. Paranoid that it's the press I head out the front door, only to find Meebs stepping out of a little black mini, fully sprayed up with black and white Union Jacks on the wing mirrors and roof.

My dogs are jumping around her like a pair of psychos.

"Shit, I didn't realise you had dogs. Oh my God, Con. You got a Pointer."

She totally ignores me as she bends down and rubs the dogs around their necks and ears.

Many years ago, Meebs and I'd been lying under a tree in our local park when a dog that we later discovered was a German Pointer came over and sat with us. His name was Trevor, and for some reason, he took a shine to Meebs and had to be dragged away with great force by his owner. We'd decided there and then, that one day, we would own a pair of Pointers. A boy and a girl, and we would call them Duke and Duchess.

I'd never forgotten that day, and when this house was finished, I went in search of a Duke, a year later I rescued Kaizer from the dog's home.

Meebs leans back against her car and looks across to where I'm standing on the steps that lead up to my front door. She smiles at me, her eyes shining with tears and I know she remembers that day in the park too.

"You got our Duke," she says quietly.

"I got our Duke, then I rescued Kaizer," I tell her. Both of my dogs now laying at her feet. She steps over them, and I think she's about to walk toward me when instead she goes around to the passenger side and undoes the door. My mouth drops open as another Pointer comes bounding toward me.

"I got our Duchess," I watch her jaw tremble as she speaks.

I take the steps two at a time down to her and pull her into my arms.

"This is surreal," I say into her hair.

"It's not fair," she answers with a sob.

"Baby don't cry, please don't cry."

"But it's so unfair," she says into my chest.

"I know, I know it is but we won, we're here. We found our way back Meebs, and we're here." I look over the top of her head as the three dogs chase each other around on the front lawn. I turn her around so that she can see them.

"They were meant to be together, Meebs. I think Duchess and her owner need to move in."

She turns back around to face me. I pull her arms up and wrap them around my neck.

"It's been forty-eight hours, Con. Can we just ease ourselves into this gently?"

"It's been about seventeen years since we planned all of this actually, Meebs. I think we've done plenty of easing in gently."

We stand still, just looking into each other's eyes for a few long moments.

"I've missed you," I tell her.

"Ditto," she replies.

I kiss her gently on the mouth and love when she responds by wrapping her legs around me, hanging onto my neck as she lifts herself off the floor.

"Fuck, I love you," she says against my mouth.

I carry her inside, kissing her all the way, only sliding her down my body when I see my dad and Sandra standing in my kitchen.

"Hmm kitchen? We didn't get to christen the worktop yesterday did we? That granite might be a bit cold on… Fuck, I'm… I mean, shit. I'm so sorry."

She looks up at me, eyes wide with mortification.

"Don't be deceived," I tell my dad and Sandra. "She may look like an Angel, but I can… Ugh" I don't get the rest of my words out because Meebs elbows me in the ribs.

"Nina Matthews. I'm so sorry about that. I didn't realise Conner had company."

She puts her hand out to shake theirs, but Sandra pulls her in for a cuddle. My dad, not known for his affectionate traits, holds her by the shoulders and kisses her cheek.

"Good to see you, Nina, it's been far too long coming."

I don't know what makes me laugh, but as soon as my dad says the word coming, it bursts out of me. Nina glares. It's her fault for getting busted talking about christening the granite.

"Just popped over to see if you fancied barbequing some steaks and chops for dinner? It's such a nice afternoon, seems a shame to waste the weather," my dad says.

What I really want to do is drag Meebs to bed and eat *her* for dinner, but I can hardly tell them that.

"That sounds good, Dad. D'ya want us to make anything?" I ask Sandra.

"You knock up a salad for us Conner, and I'll marinate the meat and put some nice big potatoes in the oven to bake."

"Sounds perfect, I'm starving," Meebs replies.

"Say about… four-thirty-ish?" Sandra asks.

"Cool, we'll see you then."

My dad and Sandra head out the back doors, when I turn back inside Meebs is standing with her hands covering her face.

"Please tell me that didn't just happen?" she groans.

"Oh, it happened baby. Now my dad's gonna tell the whole world what a foul-mouthed little harlot his sweet, innocent, son is in love with and that he has to do everything in his power to save his honour."

She looks at me for a moment, mischief written all over her face. She's wearing the old Shift T-shirt of mine she went home in this morning. It's tied in a knot at the waist of her skinny jeans. A pair of black and red Converse on her feet. Her hair is piled on top of her head, and she looks about fifteen again.

My heart rate accelerates, and I can feel myself getting hard as I look her over. She knows I'm turned on and I love the fact that she knows me so well.

She moves and starts toeing off her Chucks, eyes still on me. Once her shoes are off and kicked aside, she pulls off her jeans, wiggling from side to side as she eases them over her hips.

My mouth goes dry.

Fuck. Me. She's gorgeous, so soft and curvy.

"What… What, ya doing? I ask her.

"What does it matter to you, oh sweet and innocent one?"

I smile, shaking my head at her, watching as she unties the knot in the T-shirt and pulls it over her head, throwing it on the floor to land on top of her jeans.

"I reckon we have about an hour or so before your dad comes back to save your honour. D'ya reckon that gives me enough time to corrupt you?"

She's standing in the middle of my kitchen, wearing a red bra and a black thong and I can't think of a single word to say to her. I open my mouth at least twice, but nope, I got nothing.

She puts her hands on her hips, her fingertips digging into the soft flesh just below her waist. The rush of blood to my dick makes my head spin. Without a word, I move forward, pick her up under her arms and lift her onto the granite worktop.

I kiss her like a man possessed at the same time as I pull my T-shirt over my head and undo my jeans. I didn't put any boxers on when I got out of the shower earlier, expecting to be taking Meebs straight back to bed as soon as she got here. Bed, not the kitchen, but I'll be fucked if I'm gonna stop now.

I pull the lacy fabric of her black thong to one side and slide inside her. She's wet and warm and tight.

She's my home.

My sanity and salvation.

She's the love of my life, and I never want to be anywhere but at her side.

"Fuck," I groan through gritted teeth.

I keep a tight hold of her hips, her ankles lock together behind me, forcing her heels to dig into my bare arse. My hips move, driving my cock deep inside of her, but it's not enough, I want more, need more.

"Harder, Con, harder," she orders, before biting down on my shoulder.

"I want you. I want you so fucking much," I growl out.

Her nails scrape and claw at the skin on my back, my hips and my arse as she drags me closer, tighter.

"You've got me, Con. I've always been yours. Always have, always will."

I slow things down and grab at the handful of hair that's fallen from the bird's nest thing she has happening on the top of her head. I pull it, hard so that she looks up at me.

I feel like I'm seriously going insane. I want to kiss her, fuck, suck and lick her. I want to love her, stroke, bite and slap her, all at the same time. I don't know what I fucking want except her. Any way I can get her.

"Stay Meebs. Love me like you used to. Stay with me. Live with me. Marry me. Don't ever fucking leave. Be mine, just be mine," the words just keep coming, as fast as they rush into my head, they rush out of my mouth. "I wanna give you everything. The fucking world. I want you to have every part of me. Every fucking part."

My legs start to turn to jelly. My balls tighten, and an icy tingle travels up my spine.

Meebs face actually looks like she's in pain as she cries out, "Yes Con.

Yes. Everything, all of it. All of me. Take everything," she starts to sob as she tells me that she's coming, that she loves me, wants me. Her internal muscles squeeze my dick so tight it's almost painful. Her little body shudders in my arms. She throws her head back, and I witness the most beautiful sight I've ever seen. Nina, my Amoeba, coming, crying, sobbing out my name as she falls apart from the pleasure that I'm giving her.

I struggle to stay upright and have to lock my knees in place as I come, shooting hard, deep and hot inside her.

I hold onto her tightly, our foreheads pressed together as we breathe in each other's air.

"Con," she pants, and I assume she's saying my name.

"Condom. We didn't use a condom," she finally manages to get out.

Shit, no, we didn't. I kiss her temple.

"It's okay. I'm clean." I kiss her temple again.

"You safe?" She looks up at me, eyes wide and shakes her head.

"What?"

"No, I'm not." What the fuck does that mean?

"You're on the pill or whatever right?" She frowns and shakes her head again.

"No, no, I'm not." We're both silent as I digest this news. I actually don't care. In fact, I hope my spunky little swimmers are torpedoing their way up inside her to make us a baby right now.

I run my fingertips up and down the tattoo at the back of her neck.

"I would've loved this baby, ya know, Meebs."

"I know, I know you would've, Con."

"There'll be more. Four maybe or five." She shakes her head, and my heart feels like it's just dropped to the deepest depths of my belly.

"No?" I ask her. Confused at her response.

"I don't know if I can, Con. We... I was trying, but it never happened."

Shit! She was trying to get pregnant with that slippery little toad. Yuk!

I push down the feelings of jealousy that start to rise up and tell her, "Well, you and him just weren't meant to be, but you and me, we already know that we have what it takes. We did it once, we'll do it again. We'll find a way," I reassure her. Absolutely confident in that moment that I want a baby. Our baby. I want to see Meebs' belly round and full with a combination of our genes. Filled with a little person made from our love.

I want that.

I want her.

I want it all.

CHAPTER
TWENTY-
SIX

NINA

I STEP OUT OF THE shower to Conner standing waiting for me, wearing nothing but a smile and a hard-on.

"You have got to be kidding me," I comment with raised eyebrows. He holds out a big fluffy towel and wraps me in it, grinding his hips into me as he rubs me dry.

"What?" he asks, feigning innocence.

"I thought we just took care of that." I gesture toward his dick.

"We did, but then you climbed out of bed, and I watched your tits bounce and your hips and arse sway as you walked toward the bathroom." He shrugs as if that explains everything.

"And?" I shrug back.

"And now I need to be taken care of again," he replies, giving me his best puppy dog eyes and pouting those deliciously full, plump, kissable lips of his.

"Tough titty, Everhard. I have to go to work," I tell him. I wriggle out of his arms and head toward the apartment sized wardrobe, where a few of my clothes now hang.

Conner and I have spent the past three weeks, hidden away in absolute domestic bliss. Apart from his weekend in New York, which

I couldn't attend because I'd stupidly forgotten that my passport was still at my old house, leaving it too late to apply for a new one, we've hardly been apart or left his home. Obviously, I've been going to work every weekday, but our together time has all been spent at Conner's.

In the three weeks that we've been together, I've only spent two nights at Sophie's, and this weekend I've finally conceded and will be bringing all of my stuff here and moving in.

Life is good! I'm head over heels in love with the man I was destined to be with. I'm moving in with him, and I couldn't be happier. Yes, everything has happened at lightning speed, but like Conner keeps telling me, *'When you know, you know, right?'*

The only thorn in my side right now is Marcus. He's refusing to sign any of the divorce papers and has contacted my solicitors, telling Nate that he's still prepared to go for counselling to try and save our marriage. He has no idea about Conner. No one outside of Conner's trusted circle of friends, family and bandmates knows, except for Soph, of course.

I've agreed to meet Marcus at lunchtime today. He wanted to meet in a restaurant, but I refused and told him the park across the road from the salon and Sophie's flat would suffice. He wasn't happy but eventually agreed. The only problem is, I've yet to tell Conner, and I just know he's going to flip when I do.

I throw some underwear on the bed and go back to pull a dress off the hanger. When I come back out of the wardrobe and remove the towel from around me, I realise my bra and knickers are missing. Conner is standing with his back to me at the bathroom sink, cleaning his teeth.

"What the fuck have I done with them?" I mumble to myself.

"What?" Conner asks through a mouthful of toothpaste.

"Nothing," I call back while lifting the duvet and then bending to look under the bed.

"What you lost?" Conner asks from beside me.

"My bra and knickers. I swear I just put them on the bed. I'm seriously going nuts. All this sex is messing with my brain."

When I stand back up, he's leaning against the wall. Face serious, his dick still hard, my bra and knickers hanging from it.

"You fucker, Reed. That's so not funny. I'm gonna be late, my first client is in at nine, who, it just happens, is my mother, and she's *not* someone you wanna keep waiting, believe me." I stand naked, arms folded across my chest, trying to look as serious and as pissed off as possible.

"Well, there's a way to sort out my hard-on, just mention your mother. I usually use your brother as a cure."

What?

"You think about my brother when you get a hard-on? I find that seriously disturbing Con, like wrong, really, really wrong." I shudder at the thought.

I hold my hand out, hoping he's going to pass me my undies. He wiggles his eyebrows and gives me his favourite smile, the one that takes me back to when we were kids, and he used to flirt and make me blush. The memories of what we've been through to get to this point cause a lump to form in my throat, tears to sting my eyes and my heart to squeeze.

"I'm meeting Marcus today," I can't help blurting it out. When he smiles at me like that, it just does something to me, and there's no way I could leave this morning without being honest with him. The smile instantly falls from his face.

"What?" he frowns as he asks.

"Marcus. I've agreed to meet him at lunchtime, today."

He pulls my underwear from his dick and slings them down on the bed. I grab them and step into my knickers.

"No way, Meebs! No way are you meeting with that fucker," he paces as he talks.

"Con, I want a divorce. I need to keep him sweet so that he'll sign the papers. He wanted to go out for dinner to discuss our issues," I use air quotes on the 'discuss our issues' part.

"But I refused. Then he suggested lunch and I said no, telling him the park opposite the salon, or nowhere. He eventually agreed."

He walks past me into the wardrobe and emerges as I'm trying to reach my zip, wearing a pair of sweat shorts. Without me even asking, he zips up the back of my dress, and that one small act sends a rush of emotions through me and again causes tears to sting my eyes. I turn and wrap my arms around him.

"I'm going to be in the park, across the road from the salon. It'll be broad daylight, in the middle of summer. The schools have broken up for the holidays, there'll be people everywhere. I'll be fine."

He pulls me in close and kisses my neck.

"He's a slippery, slimy little fucker. I don't trust him, Meebs. What's he trying to achieve by seeing you anyway?"

I return his kisses, running mine up his throat and along his jaw. His erection is back, and he grinds into me, probably without even thinking about it.

"I don't know, Con. Apparently, he wants to discuss the house and some joint shares we have."

I'm not going to tell him that he wants us to try again, that will just raise Conner's paranoia levels to DEFCON 12 or whatever level that shit goes to.

"I want you to keep your phone in your hand, and I want you to stay in view of the shop."

He rakes his hand through his hair while still grinding his dick into my belly.

"And don't let him walk you away from the crowds. You stay where the people are, you understand?" He lifts my chin up so that I'm looking at him. "You listening to what I'm saying, Meebs?"

My eyes meet his, and I nod. "I'll be fine. I have to go else I'm gonna be late."

I kiss him long and hard on the mouth and turn to leave. He grabs me by the waist and pulls me back into him.

"I love you. Ring me as soon as you're done with dickwad." He kisses my nose.

"I will. I love you too."

THE REST OF MY MORNING is horrible. I spend three hours listening to my mother telling me what a royal disappointment I am to her and my father. That she's embarrassed by my divorce. That I'm making a huge mistake, I'll never find another husband like Marcus and why can't I be more like my brother's wife Tierney and be happy staying home and running the odd charity.

I don't bother trying to explain any of my actions. I remain silent and instead take my mind to the two toe-curling orgasms Conner gave me this morning. I actually blush as I think about the way I went off like a rocket when he lapped at my clit with his tongue, slid and curled two fingers inside my pussy at the same time as he slid two inside my arse.

I've never been touched there, like that, but my orgasm was instant and intense. Conner is now adamant that we need to seriously consider me giving up my anal virginity to him sometime in the very near future.

My blush deepens when I realise I'm entirely on board with that idea.

I feel the heat rise to my cheeks as my mother drones on and on while I almost come on the spot thinking about Conner Reed and his amazing tongue, mouth, lips, fingers and dick.

Despite her immense disappointment in me as a daughter, and a human being in general, my mother is apparently impressed with my hairdressing skills and leaves the salon, reasonably happy and without offering to pay a penny. She doesn't even leave a tip for the poor apprentice.

I have thirty minutes until I have to meet Marcus and as I step into mine and Sophie's office, she passes me a glass of wine.

"Your mother's a cunt. Sorry, but I just needed to put that out there." I chuckle at the truth of Sophie's words.

"Na," I tell her, "cunts are useful. Whereas my mother, well, she's just—"

"A cunt," Sophie and I say together, bursting into a fit of laughter.

By the time I walk over to the park to meet Marcus, I've had three glasses of wine and nothing to eat. I feel more than a little intoxicated, which I think was Sophie's ultimate aim when she offered/shoved the first glass of wine into my hand. She knows I'm less likely to hold back with a drink inside me. I sit on the bench facing the gate so I can see when he enters. Despite it being late July, the day is grey, overcast and a bit chilly. The instant Marcus appears, I shiver.

Marcus isn't ugly, not by any means and if I didn't know his personality or lack of, I would definitely look twice and think *phwoar*. Especially right now, dressed in a light grey suit and pale blue shirt and tie that match his eyes perfectly. His blond hair is over-styled though. It's in need of a cut, and he's put too much product in to try and hold it in place.

My wine-addled thoughts wander, and before I've noticed, he's standing in front of me.

"Nina. I've missed you, baby. How are you?" He reaches for my hand, which I refuse to give him and instead, give him a look like I think he's insane. I watch as a nerve twitches in his jaw. Something that I know happens when he's pissed off.

"What's so important that we had to meet in person, Marcus? I've really got nothing to say to you."

I'm suddenly feeling angry. Pissed off with the way the path of my life has been twisted and turned to suit other people. Pissed off with myself for being so weak and staying in a loveless, sexless marriage for so long.

Now I'm with Conner, it's opened my eyes up to how it should be. We talk. Conner and I, we talk and talk for hours on end, about everything and nothing. We make love on a whim. He makes me feel desired, wanted, needed. He makes me feel valued, that what I have to say and my opinions are important. I know it's still early days, but I never experienced any of these things with Marcus. Not even in the beginning, and even though I didn't have Conner back then, I still should've ended my sham of a marriage sooner, for both our sakes.

"I wanted to see you, Nina. I'm really missing you," he says, sitting down on the bench next to me.

"Why Marcus? What exactly is it you're missing about me?" I stare straight ahead as I speak. Despite the grey skies, I've kept my sunglasses covering my eyes. They're probably a little glassy looking, and I don't want him to know that I've had a drink this early in the day. I want him to think that my new found confidence and bravery is my own doing and not alcohol induced.

"What do you mean, what do I miss? I miss everything. I miss you being a part of my life, Nina. You're my wife, your place is with me."

I finally turn and look at him.

"I'm soon to be your ex-wife, and I really don't see what difference not having me around has made to your life. You were hardly ever home anyway, and when you were, you barely acknowledged my existence. My thoughts and opinions were never sought, my attendance in your life rarely required. We didn't even have a sex life to fall back on. So tell me, what is it exactly that you miss? Someone to belittle, someone to judge, or just someone to ignore?"

What the fucking fuck? I have no idea where all of that just came from, but yeah, go me!

"I gave you everything, Nina, fucking everything. We have a beautiful home together, holidays to the best places. You didn't even have to work if you didn't want to." He pushes his own glasses to the top of his head and looks down at me with his cold, unfeeling eyes. "I picked you up from the gutter. You were the slutty little hairdresser that got knocked up and abandoned by a junky convict when she was just sixteen. I fucking made you what you are today."

I can barely contain my anger. I want to kick, punch and scream at him, but despite the wine in my bloodstream I remain calm on the outside and think very carefully about what I'm going to say next. Marcus has always thought he was better than me, his university education making him assume he was intellectually and articulately superior.

"You know what Marcus? You should've left me in that gutter… because I was far happier there than I ever was being married to you… and FYI, I was never abandoned by anyone. My brother's lies and deceit kept Conner and me apart, and it was *his* tenacious black-mailing skills which forced me into marrying you in the first place."

The twitch in his jaw goes into overdrive. He looks me over like I'm shit on his shoe.

"You think you've got it all worked out, don't you Nina?" he sneers. Giving me his most insincere smile yet.

I hate him.

I fucking hate him.

"You really think Pearce could've come up with that little black-mailing scheme on his own? The timing and convenience never seemed coincidental to you, Nina? Are you that stupid and naïve that it never occurred to you that it was straight after you turned down my proposal that your brother came to you with an offer that you had no choice but to accept?"

My scalp tingles and I fight the urge to throw up all over his feet. I'm grateful to be sitting down and wearing sunglasses as I feel my eyes close and my body sway.

I feel like I'm drowning.

Choking.

Suffocating.

They were in it together.

My brother and Marcus.

My mouth waters as I swallow down the bile that keeps rising in my throat.

"Something you'd be wise to learn, Nina, I always get what I want."

I snap out of my haze at his words. He links his fingers together, places them behind his head and leans back on the bench, crossing his legs in front of him.

He's just left me devastated with his words and now he's sitting here so smug and casual, almost like he's sunbathing.

I've never considered myself capable of an act of violence, but right now, if I had a knife in my hand, I would stab him in the heart without a second thought.

Actually, I would slice his throat because it would be pointless stabbing him in the heart when he so obviously doesn't have one. I'd slice his throat and walk away leaving him to bleed out. Hopefully, his brain would register the fact that he was beyond help and was going to die before he passed out from blood loss.

Apparently, when pissed off, and with wine inside me, I do have a violent streak.

"The thing is though Marcus, you didn't win. You may have lied, blackmailed and manipulated, along with whatever else it took to make me your wife, but I never loved you, never really even cared for you and now, well now you've lost me completely."

I watch as he uncrosses and crosses his legs again, but I don't give him a chance to speak.

"You see Marcus, I'm now with someone else. I'm the happiest I've ever been in my life. I'm loved, cherished, worshipped and desired, and it's by someone with more honesty, humility and integrity than you could ever wish for in a thousand lifetimes. He owns me Marcus, heart and soul. I'll be his till the day I die, in fact, I've *always* been his. Even throughout our marriage, it was ultimately *him* I wished, dreamed and imagined I was with instead of you."

His arms are now folded across his chest, and I know my words are cutting him as deep as any knife ever could.

I mirror his pose from earlier and sit casually back on the park bench, not quite believing the sight that is headed toward me along the pathway is real. He's wearing tan coloured cargo pants, a loose, light grey jumper and has a grey beanie on his head. He's on a long-board, confidently zigzagging his way through the lunchtime park walkers. He looks nothing like Reed the rock star. He just looks like Conner, the man I love.

"In fact, here he comes now."

I stand up and finally lift my glasses from eyes and push them to the top of my head. I can't help but smile as I watch the joggers, walkers, office workers and even the mums pushing prams take a second look as his sexy self passes them on his board.

"Are you serious, Nina? He's on a skateboard. A grown man, on a fucking skateboard. Obviously another loser who can't even afford a car."

Conner's eyes meet mine, and my heart honestly skips several beats when I watch them light up, and that smile I love takes shape on those lips that make me squirm inside. He stops right in front of where I'm standing, flips his board up pressing his right foot on the end and tucks it under his left arm. His eyes don't leave mine during the whole process, and he totally ignores Marcus.

I want to fist pump the air and shout out 'he's mine. All fucking mine,' to everyone in the park. Instead, I stand and grin.

"Meebs, I missed you, baby," he greets me almost word for word the same way that Marcus did. The difference in my reaction is visceral. It's welcome, and it warms me. He reaches out and strokes the back of his knuckles over my cheek.

"Marcus Newman… and you need to take your hands off my fucking wife," I hear from beside me.

Conner takes my hand and moves me away from Marcus. He puts his board down on the path and pulls off his beanie. Standing up straight, he looks Marcus in the eye.

"Conner Reed… it's been a while. What? Must be fifteen, sixteen years or so?"

Marcus's mouth actually drops open.

Wide.

Open.

His eyes flick from Conner to me, and I take absolute pleasure in his discomfort as realisation dawns on him.

"Back with the junkie-ex-con, Nina?" He shakes his head. "You'll end up back in the gutter, but then that's where all sluts belong."

I grab Conner's arm, knowing instinctively that Con will want to punch him.

"Go on, I dare you," Marcus almost spits the words. "Just try it, and I'll sue you for…" He stops talking when he notices Conner shake his head and laugh.

"I wouldn't waste my time on a little toad like you, Newman. You're nobody! Just another jumped up lawyer on the corporate ladder, trying to make it big in this world. I really couldn't be fucked to raise an eyebrow in your direction, let alone my fist. You know why? Coz, I'm Conner *fucking* Reed, that's why. I'm already at the top of my world. I got the fame, the fortune, the house and the cars, but best of all… best of all, Marcus Newman… I got your wife." He turns his gaze to me and smiles. "She'll be your ex-wife very soon and then she'll be *my* wife, but in between now and then, I'll be keeping not only my hands but my mouth, lips, dick and tongue, all over your wife. I'll be keeping them on her in my bed, in my bath, shower, over my office desk, anywhere I fucking like in fact, and no doubt, your wife will enjoy every last lick, fuck and suck I give her." He turns to me again. "Won't you baby?"

I look up at him, giving him the best star-struck, dreamy-eyed look I can muster without falling on the floor laughing. I shrug my shoulders and look back at Marcus.

"What can I say Conner Reed rock star? Hell yeah."

I raise my palm in the air and Conner gives me a high-five, I keep grinning like the drunk girl I am.

Marcus points his finger at me. "Expect a call from my lawyer." He turns and starts walking away.

"Look forward to it Newman. *We,* look forward to it," Conner calls after him.

He turns to me, eyebrows raised in concern.

"You all right?" he asks.

He wraps his arms around me, pulling me in close. It's then that I realise, how badly I'm shaking.

"That was intense," I tell him, noticing people looking our way as I speak.

"He was behind Pearce's blackmailing that forced me into marrying him."

"No shit, Sherlock? I'd already worked that one out. I wouldn't be surprised if he was also behind my calls not getting through while you were in the hospital. He probably put Pearce up to it."

I stare at him for a moment, mulling that one over. He's probably right. I suddenly feel drained. Overwhelmed by all of today's revelations, and possibly the day drinking.

"I just can't believe this. You couldn't make this shit up," I shake my head as I speak.

"It's fucked, that's what it is. The situation, your brother and him, all fucked."

I notice two boys, aged about sixteen looking at Conner as we speak.

"You better get your beanie back on your head, Conner Reed rock star," I tell him with a smile. "The public are starting to stare. Someone is gonna recognise you in a minute."

He kisses my nose. "I love you, do you need to go back to work?"

"Not really, my mother was my only client today."

"Well, can I make some calls and get someone with a van over so we can get the last of your stuff moved to my place?" he asks.

"It doesn't need a van, Con. I only have some clothes and a few personal bits."

"You don't have any furniture or anything at Sophie's?"

"No, I left with nothing. I went back and grabbed a few clothes and bits, but other than that, nothing."

We start walking back to the salon, hand in hand. It feels so good being out in public with Conner, just walking through a park, holding hands. A nice, normal, everyday act and yet one that probably neither of us have done with anyone for years, but for entirely different reasons.

He kisses the back of my hand.

"Good, I'm glad you're starting fresh with me. I'm glad there's nothing from your marriage that you want. I don't want any reminders of him in our home."

I smile at my rock star's jealousy and the fact that he just called his house, *our home*. I'm cool with that. Our home works for me.

WE HEAD STRAIGHT UP TO Sophie's flat, and I pack my last few bits and pieces I have here into plastic carrier bags. Very classy I know, but that's all I have to hand.

Conner calls Matt and asks if he can come and collect us. We take all of the bags downstairs, and Conner waits with them while I go into the salon and tell Sophie that I've taken the last of my stuff.

She's standing with Maria and Donna, watching a rep from a permanent hair straightening supplier work their magic on a volunteer model. I watched a demo at a hair and fashion show, so I don't need to see it.

I haven't told any of our staff about Conner yet, so I try to speak quietly to Soph.

"I've taken the last of my stuff. I'll give you a call a bit later. Thanks so much for everything."

She gives me a smile. "You're more than welcome, baby chick. How'd it go with the fucker?'

"It was fucked." I shrug. "I have so much to tell you. I could really do with a wine and a chat. I'll give you a call a bit later."

She nods. "Coolios."

Before I get a chance to move, Maria says from beside her, "Oh my God, my ovaries just exploded."

"Holy shitballs," Donna responds from the other side of the rep and her volunteer.

"Jesus wept, that's hot," the rep adds. I follow their gaze. Conner is leaning against the archway that leads into our treatment room. He's lifted his jumper, and his fingertips are stroking his bare belly. He winks at me, knowing full well the reaction he's getting from my girls.

"Matty's here Meebs. You ready?" He nods his head at the hormonal puddle of women surrounding the sink.

"Ladies."

"Hey."

"Wow."

Oh my fucking God."

"Fuck. Me."

Are the collective responses. I roll my eyes, first at them, then at him.

"If we don't catch up tonight, I'll see you next week," I tell Sophie, not missing the look she shoots Conner.

"What?" I ask. Looking between them.

"Erm," is all Sophie says.

"You're not here next week, Meebs. I've sorted it with Sophie, you've got a couple of weeks off."

"What?" I ask, having no idea what's going on.

"We're going away. It was gonna be a surprise, but you might as well know, I'm taking you away. I've sorted it all with Soph, your clients are all organised and rescheduled."

There're a few loud sighs and 'awws' from Conner's fan club.

"Fine," is the only thing I can think of saying. I say goodbye to everyone and head out to the waiting Land Cruiser with Conner.

I DON'T END UP MEETING up with Sophie Friday night. The combination of the wine I drank earlier in the day and my run in with Marcus has left me feeling a little bit shaken and a whole lot stupid.

I've always considered myself a reasonably intelligent person. I did well at school and was expected to get great exam results and go on to university. Dropping out when I had my little meltdown over what happened with Conner and the baby, probably wasn't one of my wisest decisions but look how that turned out. I'm now the joint owner of a chain of hair and beauty salons, and they're all doing very well, thank you very much.

So, I can't help but wonder, how did I not see what my brother and Marcus were doing? I feel like an idiot.

I have a long swim when we get home, which calms me considerably, on the outside at least. On the inside, I still feel queasy and unsettled. We end up walking with the dogs around the grounds, and then I lay sprawled out on top of Conner and force him to watch 'When a Man Loves a Woman,' with me. It's one of my all-time favourite films, Andy Garcia being one of my first ever crushes.

"Would you still love me if I became an alcoholic?" I ask him, still watching the film.

He runs his fingers up and down my spine, and I can feel that he's already more than at half-mast, as his dick is pressing into my belly button.

"What d'ya mean if? You stunk of wine when I met you in the park earlier."

"Yeah, well, you'd stink of wine too if you'd had the morning I'd had."

"How was your mother?"

"A cunt," I tell him.

"Nothing new there then."

"Na. Soph and I tried to come up with something more… well, just something less offensive but failed. That word fits, so that's what I'm going with."

He pulls at my hair so I have to move from where my cheek is resting on his chest and look up at him.

"I love how your mind works. I love your 'it is what it is', attitude."

My heart rate accelerates at his words. They're just what I need to hear tonight. With him is just where I need to be. My throat constricts, and my nose tingles.

"Thank you, I needed that."

"Why. What's wrong?" He frowns and tilts his head while asking.

I shrug and swallow a couple of times, really not wanting to cry again.

"I just feel like such an idiot. Not seeing what Pearce and Marcus were up to. It all just makes me feel… I don't know. Dumb? Naïve? All the things that Marcus said I was earlier."

He wraps his arms around me and moves us so that we're lying on our sides facing each other.

"Your brother and Marcus are lawyers, they're experts in manipulation and making people believe whatever it is they're saying." He brushes my hair from my face. "You had no reason whatsoever to suspect Marcus of any wrongdoing, so why would you think that they were in it together?"

"You did."

"But I'm an outsider looking in. It's always easier to see the bigger picture from that vantage point." He leans in and kisses me, very gently, very softly. "Don't beat yourself up over this. What's done is done. We're here now, together. Right where we're supposed to be, and there's no reason why we need have any contact with Marcus again. Or your brother for that matter."

I know he's probably right, but I go to sleep with a feeling of unease settling over me. I have horrible dreams of me searching for something. I keep being given directions by faceless people, but when I follow them, I just end up back where I started. It never becomes clear to me in the dream what it is exactly I'm looking for.

I wake twice in the night, shouting and crying. Conner doing his best to calm me down. After my broken sleep, I eventually wake up to an empty bed and realise why, when I pick up my phone and note that it's almost eleven o'clock.

We have Conner's entire family coming over for a barbeque later today, and I've told Sandra that she's not to lift a finger.

My mum had a housekeeper when we were growing up, but I just find it a bit awkward now. Somebody vacuuming and washing my floors is great and always having a nice clean bathroom works for me too, but it's the washing and the cooking I find a bit hard to deal with. Having somebody I don't know that well fold up my thongs and changing the sheets that Conner and I get up to all sorts of intimate things between, just bothers me.

I also don't mind my dinner waiting for me when I get home, but when I'm here doing nothing and Sandra comes over and asks what I fancy eating, I just feel like I should get up off my lazy arse and cook for me and Conner myself.

When I finally make it downstairs, I find Conner in his office. He looks up when he sees me, but I don't get his usual smile as a greeting. He's wearing a frown, and I can't help but notice that he looks tired. He holds his hand out for me to come over to him. I sit on his lap and curl into him.

"You all right?" he asks.

"Yeah, I'm all right."

"What the fuck was going on last night, Meebs? You didn't stop shouting and crying," he runs his fingertips up and down my bare arm as he speaks, causing goose bumps to spread out across my body from his point of contact.

"Yeah, sorry about that. It was the same dream every time I went back to sleep."

"You wanna tell me about it?"

"Nothing to tell, really. I was looking for something that I couldn't find. I don't know what it was and I never did find it."

"Strange," he says.

"Yeah, strange."

The intercom for the front gates buzzes, and we go to the front door to greet the local butcher who's dropping off steak, chicken, chops, burgers and sausages. Conner tells me that the supermarket shop we did online Thursday night was delivered earlier.

We spend the next few hours marinating meat, making potato salad and coleslaw, all while dancing around the kitchen to Conner's playlist. My mood lifting exponentially as I realise how many of the same songs we've downloaded over the years.

By three o'clock his family are all here. His nieces and nephews are all in the pool apart from Evie, Beth and Jordan's six-year-old daughter, who hasn't left my side.

"So, do you have any little girls?" she asks from her spot on my lap. She has dark hair like her dad, but as the sun shines through it, I can see the auburn highlights she's inherited from her mum. Like Conner's dad and his brothers, she has the brightest of blue eyes.

"I don't have any little girls, no," I tell her.

"Do you have any babies?" she asks. Conner is sitting next to me, his arm's resting across my shoulders, but his fingers instantly head under my hair, and he runs them up and down my tattoo as soon as Evie asks her question. I don't know exactly what he's told his family about our history and in the moment it takes me to answer, Conner jumps in.

"A very long time ago, Nina and I had a baby that went to heaven."

The entire conversation around the table stops. Conner keeps stroking my tattoo.

"That's sad," Evie states.

Jordan and Tyler are staring at him wide-eyed. Jenna is sitting next to me and reaches out her hand to mine.

"Oh Nina, I had no idea." She gives my hand a squeeze, and an unexpected tear escapes my eye and rolls down my cheek.

"Evie, why don't you go and play in the pool before we have something to eat because you won't be able to go in there for a while after," Beth suggests.

"Oookaaay." Evie slides off my lap and heads down the deck steps to where the rest of the kids are. I turn to Conner. I can't tell this story, I have a lump in my throat that I know I will choke on if I attempt to speak.

Conner continues stroking beneath my hair while explaining to his brothers and their wives what happened on the night, that for them, they lost two members of their family.

By late evening, the adults have plenty of food and drink inside them, and the boys and Conner's dad are telling tales of the awful dinners that they endured growing up. The children are all inside, Ethan playing FIFA on the PlayStation against an online opponent while the girls all watch Frozen.

Eventually, Sandra and Conner's dad take all the kids, except for Ethan, over to their place to sleep. The rest of us head inside and sit on the sofas, the boys carrying on with their tales of growing up.

I just get comfortable when I hear my phone ringing from where it's on charge in the kitchen. Picking it up, I see that I have missed calls from Sophie and a couple of other friends. I call Sophie back first.

"You watching the news, Neen?" is her greeting. Last time I had a call like this from her, Jet died.

"No, why? What's wrong?"

"The press have found out that you're seeing Reed, they've just broken it to your mother as she was leaving some charity function."

"Shit, how'd she take it?"

"Put it this way, it's the first time I've ever seen Veronica without a comeback. In fact, she looked stunned. Put Sky News on, they've been all over it."

"Yeah, I bet they have. Thanks for the heads up."

"No worries, baby chick. Love ya."

Conner turns and looks over the top of the sofa at me. He's had a fair bit to drink, and his eyes are bright, their unusual bluey-green colour shining. I've loved seeing him so chilled and relaxed, enjoying time with his family today. It warms my heart that we're the privileged few who get to know and love the real Conner Reed, not the public perception of him.

"Who's that?" he asks as I walk toward him.

"Soph. The press know about you and me and have just broken it to my mother, in front of the cameras as she was leaving some charity function. It's been on Sky News."

"Why the fuck are Sky interested in me and you? The gossip shows yeah, but why Sky?"

My stomach feels like it's twisting itself into knots. I have a really horrible feeling about this, and I know that my husband and brother are behind it. Everybody starts reaching for their phones as I speak, all too aware that whatever's going on, social media will have the most up-to-date, but probably less than accurate information.

"Oh shit!" Beth is the first to speak.

Ethan comes walking into the room, he looks at his mum and dad before looking at Con and me.

"They're saying on Twitter that you got Nina pregnant when she was underage, then left her in the hospital on her own when she had a miscarriage."

He looks back at his parents. "What's a miscarriage? Is that when the baby's born dead? Is that what Evie was on about in the pool earlier?"

Everybody else seems stunned into silence. I like Ethan, he's a nice kid. We went to watch him play in a football tournament the Saturday before, and because everyone is so used to seeing Conner at his games, nobody bothered him, he just got to enjoy the matches like everyone else.

"Come here," I tell him. He walks over and sits on the coffee table in front of me.

"Conner and I, we've known each other most of our lives. We went to primary school together, but then on to different secondary schools. We still used to see each other out and about, and when I was fifteen, we started going out with each other, like boyfriend and girlfriend." I look at Tyler and Jenna, unsure of how much I should tell him. He idolises Conner, and I'd hate for him to judge his uncle on a fabricated story.

"Tell him what happened, Neen. The truth," Tyler tells me.

Conner sits silently, gripping my hand and stroking my tattoo as I tell his biggest fan the truth about that night. Making a point of letting him know I was sixteen, not breaking any laws, and were very much in love.

"Next time one of my mate's tweets that you're a dirty perv who shagged a fifteen-year-old-girl, I'm gonna tell them to shut the fuck up," he says, marching out of the room before anyone can pull him up on his language. -

We don't put the news on. I've no desire to listen to the horrible things that are being made up about Conner right now. The happy glow he had going on earlier is gone. His mood seems to be somewhere between anger and sadness, and I'm not really sure how to handle him, especially as he seems more determined to drink than to talk.

Deciding that leaving him to get drunk with his family, might be what he needs, I eventually head off up to bed at the same time as Beth and Jenna, leaving Conner sitting around the dining table with his brothers and his dad, who had come back over when he heard the story on the news.

After my fitful sleep of the night before, I fall instantly into the deep, dreamless land of nod.

IT TAKES ME A FEW moments to get my bearings when I wake up to the sound of a woman laughing. Reaching for my phone, I check the time. It's three in the morning, and I've been sleeping for about three and a half hours.

I get up and make my way downstairs, assuming that Beth or Jenna have gotten back up and are talking with Conner, but instead I find Lawson Knight and a dark-haired woman sitting on the sofa. Conner has his back to me, and the woman looks over his shoulder and straight at me as I enter the open space of the family room.

I feel extremely uncomfortable, dressed just in sleep shorts and another old Shift T-shirt of Conner's. Her eyes give me a cold stare as she looks me up and down. Conner turns to see what she's looking at and my eyes meet his. He smiles, and my legs move instinctively to where he is.

Holding out his hand, he pulls me into his lap when I attempt to sit next to him. He nuzzles his nose into my neck and says loud enough for everyone to hear, "You smell like sleep and our bed."

"You smell like your mate Jack, the one you've spent most of the night with."

He smiles lazily, or drunkenly, or maybe it's a bit of both.

"Sorry Nina, did we wake you?" Lawson asks, "I'd completely forgotten you'd moved in and came over to check Reed was doing okay after the shit that's been on the news tonight."

I look up at Conner. "You doing okay?" I ask him. He shrugs, and I know instantly that he's not, that knowledge makes my heart hurt for him.

"We'll get our legal team onto it in the morning and make sure the press report the truth. I just suggested to Reed that perhaps an interview with the pair of you wouldn't be a bad idea. If the public hears your side of the story, Nina, it'll put all of this underage sex bullshit to rest," Lawson says.

"Were you though, having underage sex I mean?" the woman sitting next to Lawson asks.

"I'm Amanda, by the way. I'm Lawson's PA and sometimes fuck-buddy of his and Reed's."

My head jerks back at her words and I feel a nerve twitch at the corner of my eye. Conner's arm snakes around my waist and pulls me tighter into him.

"Get out," he says, his words moving my hair. "Get the fuck out of our house and don't you ever come back here again."

I watch as her eyes move between his and mine. She's a beautiful woman, probably around forty, slim, with dark hair and brown eyes. She pulls her shoulders back and looks to Lawson.

"Let's go."

He shakes his head at her. "Why'd you do it? Every time I give you the benefit of the doubt, and every time you have to open your fucking mouth and cause trouble?" Lawson tells her.

"That's the last time, Laws. I don't know how many times I've said it now, but that's my final warning. You keep her away from my house, and you keep her away from Nina and me. Now fuck off, both of you." They get up and leave in silence. Conner tilts his head back and looks up at the ceiling.

"So," I eventually say, "You've fucked her?"

"I've fucked a lot of women, Meebs."

I know this is true and yet my nose still stings, my eyes fill with tears, and my heart feels a sharp stabbing pain at his words. "Wow, just what every girl wants to hear from the man she's just moved in with." I try to push up from his lap, but he tightens his grip. He turns his head to look at me. His eyes are glassy and a little bloodshot, which isn't surprising considering the amount of Jack Daniels he's consumed.

"You knew what you were getting yourself into Meebs. You've heard the stories, seen the pictures and read the newspaper reports. What? You didn't think for a minute the press made that shit up did you?" He gives a little laugh. His eyes are narrowed, and they don't break their hold on mine. He's breathing heavy, and I can feel his chest move up and down.

"Why are you angry with me, Con?" I ask, feeling my lip tremble as I talk. *Fuck him.* What an arsehole.

"Why not?" He asks.

"Fuck you," I tell him. This time I twist and buck until I break free of his hold and make my way back up to bed. I don't remember Conner being an angry drunk. I remember his dad was, but the few times I ever remember Conner being drunk, he was always happy.

I take a quick shower and try and calm myself down. That woman has a fucking cheek coming in here and telling me that she's fucked Conner. Why would she do that? A million images a minute rush through my mind as I imagine Conner and her together. Conner, her and Lawson together. I don't want to feel jealous, like he said, I knew what I was getting myself into. I know he has a past and a reputation as a womaniser, and if we're ever going to work, then I need to just accept that. He loves *me*, I *know* he loves me but, it all still hurts just the same.

I get out of the shower and head into the bedroom feeling a little calmer. Conner's sitting on the edge of the bed, drinking JD straight from the bottle.

"Don't you think you've had enough? You're gonna make your-self sick."

"What d'you care?"

"Now you sound like a child."

His eyes meet mine, and we stare quietly at each other for a while.

"I've only fucked her, as in actually fucked her a couple of times and then I fucked her face a couple of times more." He pats the side of the bed, and I go and sit down next to him with the towel still wrapped around me.

"There's something you need to know, Meebs. I need you to know the things that I've done. I'm not a good person, there's some-thing wrong with me."

I take the bottle out of his hand and put it on the bedside table. Unsure of what he's trying to say.

"Talk to me," I tell him. My heart's pounding hard against my ribs, my palms are sweating, and my mouth is dry, but I need to hear this. I'd much rather hear the worst from him than pick up a newspaper or magazine one day and find out.

"After you, there was no one. I avoided sex, relationships. I avoided women as much as I could, but once the band started to make it big, they were everywhere." He rakes his hands through his hair and lays back on the bed, his legs still hanging over the side, feet on the floor.

"I found this way to get off, without getting close to anyone."

He turns and looks at me. "I got other people to have sex, and I'd watch, telling them what to do."

What?

I don't even know what that means.

What to think?

What to feel?

"I don't understand," I tell him.

He closes his eyes for a long moment, and I wonder for a second if he's fallen asleep.

"Jet and I would pick up girls or couples, take them to a hotel room and get them to have sex. Jet would usually join in, I might get a blowjob, occasionally I'd fuck somebody up the arse, but mostly, mostly I'd just wank myself off as I watched them all do things to each other."

He opens his eyes and turns to look at me, waiting for a reaction, I give none and hopefully hide the fact that my thoughts are scattered in every direction, and my stomach is twisting and tying itself into knots.

He lets out a long so slow sigh or breath as he stares at me.

"I was scared, Meebs. It's a piss poor excuse, but I was scared. Scared of intimacy, of being touched. I didn't want to look into anyone's eyes. I didn't want to feel their skin on mine." He sits back up, still watching me.

"We'd take people back to our hotel, and I'd tell them what to do.

Take off your clothes, suck him, lick her, fuck each other. I got off on giving out orders and seeing how far I could push people. That's how I've conducted my sex life for pretty much the past ten years."

My head swims. I don't know where to even begin processing this. *A slow sense of panic builds in my chest, as I wonder if I will I ever be enough for him?*

"Is that what you want? You want me to do that, with other people?"

"What? No! Fuck no! I was doing all of those things because I didn't have *you*, because I was trying to forget *you*." He shakes his head. "It was horrible, Meebs. Horrible, empty, meaningless fucking. It was everything that we're not."

I shiver. I'm still sitting on the edge of the bed with just a towel wrapped around me. He tilts his head to the side while looking at me. "Do I disgust you?" he asks very quietly.

I shake my head no, without a second's hesitation. "You don't disgust me, Con. You were broken and lost your way. What you were doing then, has nothing to do with what we have now. I just hate that she brought part of that world into our home. I don't like her, Con. I get that you have to work with her, but I don't want her here again."

He shakes his head. Reaching out to run his fingertips over my cheek.

"You heard what I said to her, to both of them. I was just coming to bed when they turned up. Lawson said that Amanda was worried and insisted they come and check on me."

I bet she fucking did.

"Wouldn't a phone call have been enough?" I ask.

"It would. I know it was just an excuse. She's always wanted more, I told her from the very beginning that it was just sex, but she calls and texts continuously. Just about every time I see her I make it clear that she needs to stop, that she'll never mean anything to me," he's getting angry again as he speaks. "I'm sorry Meebs. I'm sorry for having such a fucked up past, and I'm sorry for all the shit that's going on in the news about us right now. It pisses me off that they never give me a chance. That they never just come and ask me outright for the truth. They'll print and report their made up stories, and it won't matter what I say or do afterwards, the public will only remember the shitty parts." He stands up and starts to pace.

"Con, it's okay. We'll deal with it. *We* know the truth," I try to reassure him.

"That's not the point though, Meebs. You don't know what they're like. They won't see us as people. They'll just see us as a story. Their next headline. It scares me. I've dealt with their bullshit before, they know all of my secrets, but they'll dig up everything they can on you, Meebs. Everything." I watch the column of his throat move as he swallows hard. "I'm scared you'll run. I'm scared you won't be able to handle it. Just for once, I wish they'd see me as a person. One that's capable of feelings, of loving and hurting. Then perhaps they'd see us as a couple in love, not a fucking commodity. Just for once, I wish they'd see me for more than this, Meebs." I recoil as he slaps himself, hard around the face. "And this." He grabs at his crotch. "They think that that's what I'm all about, that there's nothing but my face and my reputation as someone who fucks a lot of women. Someone who's been to prison, who was in a car crash, trapped, upside down, watching as his brother took his last breath. That I'm someone that hid in the corner and watched as his mother's pimp, dealer or whatever the fuck he was squeezed her throat until the light went out of her eyes, which just happened to be looking at me at that moment." I watch as he stands in front of me and wipes his nose across the back of his hand. My heart is breaking into so many tiny pieces as I witness his anguish, that I doubt that it'll ever be whole again. "It's always the shit, Meebs. They never see the good in me, only the shit and I'm so scared, so fucking scared that eventually, one day, that's all you'll see too."

My entire being hurts for him, my heart, lungs and bones, my hair and my skin. Everything that I am is in pain as the man I love bares his soul to me.

"I love you, Con. I love you so much, and I'll never leave. We'll get through this. I swear I won't run. We'll stand and fight the fuckers together. As long as I have you, Con, I can do that."

He drops to his knees in front of me and puts his head in my lap. I rake my fingers through the hair of my poor broken rock star and try my hardest to make his world just a little bit better as he cries and I cry.

The birds start to sing, the sun eventually begins to rise, a new day dawns, and we eventually climb under the duvet still clinging to each other, cocooned from the outside world. Just me and him hanging on tight until sleep finally claims us.

CHAPTER TWENTY-SEVEN

CONNER

I'VE GIVEN MATT TWO WEEKS off and drive Meebs and myself down to Cornwall, after causing a diversion to avoid the press hanging about outside the gates of our home, we escaped unnoticed. I bought the house here last year, but I haven't visited it since and I want to give Meebs the opportunity to decorate it to her taste. I want her to feel like this is hers as much as mine.

Cornwall is the place we were going to hide out when we ran away. We never made it, but it's always held a special place in my heart. It's the place that I spent the only holiday of my life with all of my family. I was around four, and it was straight after that my mum left my dad and moved myself and my brothers back to London. None of us then realising that within less than a year, our beautiful, funny, vibrant Mum would be dead.

The house overlooks the water in Truro and is relatively isolated, and apart from the odd meal out, I plan on keeping the pair of us locked away from the rest of the world.

Sunday was horrible. The papers running with stories ranging from me being some kind of pedo, to Meebs being a dirty little harlot.

We put out a joint statement saying the reports of an underage sexual relationship were pure fabrication. We admitted that yes, Nina had lost a baby, but that she was almost seventeen at the time. Other than that, we were giving them nothing.

Meebs' parents and her brother had called to add their opinions, but my girl had done me proud when she told them to fuck off and mind their business. She'd told her brother that she knew exactly what he'd done to get her to marry Newman and that he'd better stay out of her life from here on out. I had a strong suspicion that her brother and/or husband were behind the press finding out about our relationship. They were always going to find out at some stage, but I'd just wanted more time to make sure we were solid before it all blew up.

I felt ashamed of my little breakdown in front of Meebs, but it also made me feel good... cleansed. She knew the truth. She knew about my fucked up sexual encounters, and she knew about my insecurities regarding the press and the public's perception of me. She was also now aware of the fact that I was terrified she'd leave me. She's promised that will never happen and I'm going to make sure of that by asking her to be my wife sometime during this break. I know she's not divorced yet, but as of today, I've got a little team on board finding out everything they can about Marcus Newman and Pearce Matthews. Hopefully, by the end of this holiday, I'll have something on Newman, which will convince him that he needs to sign those divorce papers, sharpish.

"There's no furniture," is the first thing Meebs says as she walks through the house.

"No shit Sherlock," I mock.

"How can we stay here if there's no furniture?" I pull her into my arms as she asks.

"You like the house?"

"I love the house."

"Good, well I want you to pick the furniture, new carpets and tiles too. I've arranged for a team of interior decorators to come in over the next few days. They'll bring samples, and we can make this place, a home, together," I tell her. She looks up at me with those big blue eyes of hers, and I have to start undressing her. I need her naked and underneath me, like right now.

We don't even make it up to the bedroom and simply fuck on the floor of what will be the family room, in front of the vast open fire.

THE NEXT WEEK GOES BY in a blur. Meebs consults with furniture makers, kitchen fitters and the interiors people. She's got a firm opinion of how she wants the place to look, so I just nod and agree.

By the time Friday arrives, we have everything organised with all of the trades to come in and start work the Monday after we leave. We've interviewed a local bloke from the village to come in, and project manage for us. He'll liaise with all of the contractors on our behalf and contact us if there are any problems. His name is Mick, and we liked him as soon we start talking to him. He's retired but ran his own construction firm for over forty years, eventually handing it down to his three sons. We're happy and confident that he'll keep everything in order until we can next get back.

The following week we have days out, exploring the beaches and countryside nearby. I keep my cap and glasses on, and the only time I'm recognised is when we surf on the day before we're due to leave, but after smiling for a couple of pictures, we jump into the car and head back home. I'm happy to sign autographs and pose with my fans all day long. What I'm not prepared for though, is the press finding out where I am, or about this house.

I still haven't gotten around to popping the question to Meebs.

Last week was just so busy, and this week, something just seems off. Don't ask me to put my finger on it because I've tried and can't. Meebs has been unusually quiet, she's slept in most days, hasn't wanted to go out for dinner in the evenings and just generally doesn't seem herself. She's assured me she's fine and just chilling, enjoying our time away. But I'm not stupid, I know something's up. I had to beg her to come and surf with me today and even then, she only stayed in the water for ten minutes, choosing to watch me from the beach instead.

When I ask her Friday evening where she'd like to go for dinner, she tells me nowhere, that she has a headache and is gonna have an early night.

She went out for a walk on her own earlier, and I thought she might come back happier, but that didn't happen. I stand out on the balcony, looking over the water for a few minutes after she leaves, and think and over think every conversation we've had these last few days. She was fine up until about Monday, since then, she's just withdrawn more and more, and I'm crapping myself that all of this turn out with the press has made her change her mind about us. I can't stand it anymore and decide to head up and ask her outright what the fuck's going on. I can't lose her. I won't lose her. I'll walk away from it all if that's what she wants. We can move here, just her, me and the three hundred and seventy-one children I plan on us having, or maybe five. We can get married on the beach and live here. It's actually a great place to raise a family, and the house is plenty big enough for our five kids and us.

I walk up to our bedroom, she has her music playing and Paloma Faith is singing about the fact that only love can hurt like this. Ain't that the truth.

I catch her walking out of the bathroom. Her eyes are shining like she's about to or has just finished crying and her face is devoid of colour. She looks terrible.

"Baby, you okay?"

Tears roll down her cheeks as she shakes her head, no. "We need to talk. I have something to tell you."

My heart shatters, and it takes everything in me not to throw it up out of my mouth as I feel myself sway where I stand.

CHAPTER TWENTY-EIGHT

NINA

I'M PREGNANT. THE ONE THING that I've hoped and dreamed of has finally happened. It's both the happiest and saddest day of my life. I'm about to break the heart of the man I love.

He'll leave.

He won't want me now.

I don't think we're strong enough to survive this.

I grip the pregnancy test stick in my sweaty hand and go and sit on the edge of the bed, but I can't breathe. Panic is starting to set in, so I stand up, and Conner follows me outside to the balcony. I look out over the calm, serene water below us. The waves are lapping gently, the yachts barely bobbing with the motion. Conner leans on the railing next to me.

"You promised Meebs. Don't do this, please don't do this." I can't look at him. I don't know how he knows. I'm assuming he's guessed from my crazy arsed behaviour this week, or maybe he's heard me being sick the last three mornings.

"You said as long as you had me you'd fight. Well, you've got me, all of me. Every fibre of my fucking being is yours, you own it, so please, just love me enough to want to stay and fight."

My head's pounding and spinning. I can't think straight and don't quite understand what he means. "Of course I'll fight, I'll never stop fighting for us," I tell him.

He's silent for a few seconds. "You're not leaving me then?" His frown matches mine as I finally turn to look at him.

"No, of course I'm not. Why ever would you think that?"

He thought I was leaving him, he was that panicked because he thought *I* was leaving *him*.

I burst into tears. He reaches for me, but I step away before his skin makes contact with mine. I have to be able to see his face clearly when I give him this news. I need to know that whatever the outcome, he's one hundred percent on board with this. It doesn't matter what he wants or needs, and it most certainly doesn't matter what I want or need, my only concern right now is the baby that I'm carrying inside me.

"I'm pregnant." His eyes spark to life in an instant.

"What?" he laughs as he speaks.

And now I have to deliver the killer blow. "I'm pregnant, and it's not your baby."

I watch as his whole body moves, it's almost identical to the movement of the waves below as he seems to roll on the spot.

"Wha… I don't understand. What d'ya mean, it's not my baby? What the fuck, Meebs? What does that even mean?" his eyes are all over my face as he speaks.

"I've been trying for a baby with Marcus for months now. We… I haven't been using any kind of protection with him for well over a year. I told you this already."

I hate myself for telling him. It hurts my heart so bad, and by the expression on his face, I'm hurting him too.

"But when… I thought you hadn't slept with him in a while?"

And this is the worst part. Much worse than admitting to him that I'm pregnant, is going to be admitting to him *how* I got pregnant.

"I hadn't. We hadn't in a while and then we did. The night I left him, we did."

His head flies up from where he was looking down at the water. Eyes wide. His mouth hangs open for a few seconds.

"The night you left him? You mean the night he attacked you..." his words trail off, and I can see his thought process registering in his eyes and facial expressions. His frown deepens, and he actually backs away from me a couple of steps.

"No. Meebs. Baby, did he..?" he trails off shaking his head no, as I nod mine yes. He moves at speed toward me, pulling my body to his. Wrapping me in his protective arms.

"Fuck, baby. Why? Why didn't you tell me?"

I try to speak, to explain, but I can't talk around the ball of emotion that's well and truly lodged in my throat. Ella Henderson is singing about a ghost, and I listen to the soothing tone of her voice to calm me down.

Eventually, I manage to form words. "I love you. I love... I'm so sorry, Con. I wish it was yours. I'll love the baby regardless, but I wish it was yours."

He kisses my head, my hair, my face and nose. He kisses away my tears.

"He will be mine, Meebs, he'll be mine and yours. The genes don't matter. He'll still be ours. Anyway, you don't know that he's not yet."

I look up at him, confused. "How can he... it, be yours?"

He shrugs and smiles. Through all this shit, he finds me a smile.

"Well, think about it. You've been trying all this time with Marcus and nothing. A coupla months with me and bang, you're pregnant."

"But we've been careful."

"No we haven't, not every time."

He leads me inside by the hand and pulls me into him as we lay down on the bed.

"That first week, remember? Once on the kitchen worktop and

twice in the pool. That's three times, Meebs. That makes the odds more likely to be in my favour."

We're both very quiet as we consider this. I listen to the strong, steady rhythm of his heartbeat and despite the turmoil churning inside me, that combined with the way Conner strokes his fingers up and down my spine, I'm soon drifting off to sleep. As I do, I have one continuous thought running on a loop through my head... *I'm pregnant, and I don't know who the father is.*

WHEN I WAKE LATER, I'M lying in the middle of the bed with the duvet folded over me. I'm alone, but I can hear Conner's voice from somewhere. After listening for a few seconds, I realise he's out on the balcony.

"So, who would you recommend?"

"Well, could you find out?"

"Could you do that for me? Get me a name and a number, and I'll get it sorted so that we can be seen Monday."

He laughs. "Too fucking right Jen, not always, but sometimes it *is* good to be me."

He's talking to Jenna, but I'm not sure what about.

"Love you too, Jen, thanks for this and don't forget, for now, it's just between us."

He walks back into the bedroom, just as I'm pushing myself up to a sitting position in the bed. I feel like shit. My face feels dry, and it stings from the salty tears I've cried. My eyes feel puffy, and I don't even want to consider what my hair might be doing.

Conner, on the other hand, wow. He's showered, his hair's still damp and pushed back from his face, which is tanned from all the sun we've been getting the last couple of weeks. Those bluey-green eyes look amazing against his darker skin, and I love the way they're all over me right now. He gives me a smile, a different smile. It's a combination of the boy I used to love smile, his sexy, I'm Conner fucking Reed smile and something else.

"Let's get married," he suggests as he walks toward the bed. My belly does a few backflips, followed by a forward roll.

"I'm still married to Marcus."

"Fuck, yeah. How could I forget about the orange?" he crawls across the bed as he speaks, pulls the duvet back and settles on his knees between my legs.

"What orange?"

"Marcus, that orange."

"Why's he an orange?"

"He's a Jaffa."

"What are you talking about, Con?" He sighs and rolls his eyes like a thirteen-year-old girl.

"Jaffa, they grow seedless oranges. Marcus is seedless, so I call him the orange."

"That's wicked, and you don't know that for sure."

He looks up at me through raised eyebrows and shrugs. "It is what it is babe? I know what I know and when I'm right I'm right."

He winks.

I melt.

He picks up my right leg and starts kissing up the inside of it. When he gets to the top and lifts the T-shirt of his I'm wearing, his eyes look up to meet mine, and I could dissolve into a puddle of lust from what they're expressing to me.

He wants this.

He wants us.

We're gonna be okay.

"You've got no knickers on," he says quietly.

"No, I don't got no knickers on."

"Fuck Meebs, take off that T-shirt."

I do as he says, keeping my eyes on his. As soon as I'm naked, he grabs my hips and pulls me further down the bed.

"Touch yourself," he orders. I bite down on my bottom lip and slide one finger between my legs. He watches intently, his lips slightly parted.

I watch in turn as he pulls down his boxer trunks, freeing his cock and his balls. He strokes himself, up and down, up and down at a slow, measured pace. The tip instantly begins to glisten.

I know it's wrong to think of Marcus at that moment, but I can't help it. His family are Jewish, and as with tradition, he's cut, his cock always looked ugly to me, like it was angry, but Con's is the opposite. Long, hard, sleek and smooth. Like a sports car.

"What are ya smiling at, Nina Amoeba, you like what ya see?"

I realise that I've been staring at his dick for a while now and blush when I look up to meet his sexy stare.

"You have the most beautiful dick," I blurt out.

"Baby, shit! Fuck, I'm gonna come in my hand if you say things like that," he continues to stroke himself with one hand, then reaches between his legs and starts to cup and squeeze his own balls with the other.

"Open your legs wider for me. I wanna see how wet you are," he orders.

I do as I'm told, sliding my middle two fingers down from my clit and dip them inside myself. He gives out a little groan, so I pull them out and offer them up to him. He rubs his middle fingers over the head of his glistening cock and brings them up to meet mine. He puts his other hand around the back of my neck and pulls me up to straddle him, then brings his mouth to mine. We kiss our wet fingers between us.

"That's us, Meebs," he says into my ear. His breath hot on my skin.

I'm not sure if I'm too hot but melting or freezing while I'm on fire.

"That taste is us. Me and you. That taste is what we do to each other. That taste is want, need, lust and a love like no fucking other," he leans back so that he can look at me as he talks. "I need you to know. Whoever that is, growing in your belly, whatever combination of genes, I'm gonna love them like my own. I don't ever want you to be scared, worried or doubt that for a moment."

He blows me away.

This man that has been through so much in his life.

This man that could choose any woman that's walked this planet.

He wants me.

He wants me and everything that's a part of me.

We make love.

Slowly.

Tenderly.

Reverently.

We make love in the bed, then we make love in the shower.

We lay talking long into the night, planning our future. A future that we will spend together, raising the child that's now growing inside of me, and the many more we hope to create in the future.

We make love again in the morning, before packing up the few belongings we brought with us and head back to Surrey.

THANKFULLY THERE ARE NO PRESS at the gate when we arrive home. The interest in us has gradually died down once we agreed to both appear on a prime-time chat show and tell all about our relationship. The interview will be recorded on Friday and aired Sunday night and will be carried out by one of the best in the business. They're flying in from the US on Wednesday and spending the following few days living with and getting to know about our lives.

I'm nervous as shit, but I want to do this for Conner. I want the world to see him for who he really is and not just the serial shagging rock star they think they all know.

I'm meeting Sophie at the wine bar later for belated birthday drinks. It was her birthday last weekend, and I missed it, so we're catching up tonight instead. Conner's not happy and insisting that Matty drives me, which I have no problem with whatsoever. Shame that now I can't drink, I get my very own driver.

I spot Sophie straight away when I arrive at Plonk, the wine bar across the road from our salon. I wave at the bar staff as I walk in and immediately notice the tall, skinny blonde woman that my brother and Marcus were talking to on the one and only occasion I've seen them in here.

I actually do a double take when I realise that she's with Tierney, my bitch of a sister in law. We've never really hit it off. She's the kind of woman my mother so desperately wishes for me to be. She doesn't work. She spends her days lunching, beautifying, playing tennis and riding her horses. She looks down her nose at everyone, including my parents if only they could see it. She's as dull as fuck. Her expression doesn't change when she spots me. Well actually, it can't. She has so much Botox and filler pumped into her face that it's probably caused a shortage in Hollywood more than once. I nod my head in her direction but carry on walking. I don't like her, and I most certainly don't want to have a conversation with her.

"I was just texting to warn you the ugly sisters were here. How are you, baby chick?" Sophie asks as she stands and gives me a cuddle.

I make sure that my back is turned on the audience that I have at the bar when I sit down and tell Soph, "Pregnant, that's how I am. Pregnant and there's every possibility that the baby belongs to Marcus," I watch Sophie's shoulders physically slump as I tell her.

She nods her head but remains silent for a few seconds. She goes to pour me a wine from the bottle in the cooler which is sitting on the table, but stops before I get a chance to protest and pours water from the jug sat next to it instead.

There's an antipasto platter staring up at me, and I help myself to an olive. I've no idea how pregnant I am, but today, I've constantly been starving. We had a full English breakfast in a little café before leaving Cornwall this morning. Then we stopped and grabbed fish and chips halfway home, sitting and eating them out of the paper in the car. Then Sandra made us a steak, bacon and cheese, with rocket and caramelised onion baguette before I came out tonight. That's how obsessed I've suddenly become with food in the space of one day. I actually remember where, when and what I've eaten over the last twenty-four hours and every memory makes my mouth water.

"Does Reed know?" I nod as I dunk a cracker into a beetroot and parmesan dip. "Everything?" I nod again my mouth full of cracker, dip and a chilli stuffed olive.

"What makes you think this baby isn't his? I didn't think that you and… Oh no, Neen." Her hand covers her mouth, her eyes wide as she looks at me.

"Not that night?"

I gulp down some water and nod. "I must've been an evil person in a past life for the way I've been fucked over in this one."

She ignores that comment, something that she does whenever I'm down on myself.

"Have you always been careful with Reed?" she asks.

"EeeUms," I tell her through a mouthful of sourdough bread, dipped in warm olive oil and dukkha.

"What?" She screws up her face in disgust as she looks at me. "Will you stop fucking troughing and talk to me. This is life-altering news that's going on here. These are important facts that we need to clarify before we jump to any conclusions."

"Three times and food's important too."

She sips at her wine, still giving me a look of disgust.

"So, you shagged Reed bareback, three times?"

I nod my head, not wanting to revolt her any more by talking through the breadstick and prosciutto I now have in my mouth.

"Was it good?" she wiggles her eyebrows as she asks. I take another sip of water before answering.

"Bareback or condom, its mind blowing either way," I divulge. She knows this anyway, we're girls, we talk. I take another sip from my glass, giving my belly a chance to digest some of what I've just shoved down it and now hoping that it actually stays there.

"Have you tried anal yet?"

I spit my water.

"Soph," I say a little too loudly

"Oh, come on. You're shagging Conner Reed, I'd be up for anything," I notice people's heads turn in our direction at her words and look down at the table.

"For fuck's sake, Soph. Sure you don't wanna say it louder?"

"Oh, hush woman, everyone knows anyway. Your pictures have been in the papers and all the gossip mags. It's been great for business. I think some people have come in expecting him to be there, washing hair, making tea or some shit."

I keep watching the pair of trolls at the bar while listening to Sophie. They're both currently on their phones.

"So did you have to fight off the press?" I ask her.

"Not really. The security team Reed sent kept them at bay."

"Conner sent a security team?"

Why did I not know this?

"Yeah," she says waving a piece of bread in the air.

"We had two assigned outside every shop, but four here so that they could watch the shop and my flat too." She pulls her duck face and tilts her head from side to side like she's debating telling me something.

"What?" I ask her.

"One of them was so good at his job, that I assigned him a special detail." I can't help but smile.

"Dare I ask?"

"I put him in sole charge of my orgasms," she tells me, totally unashamed.

"And how's that working out?"

She shrugs. "Meeeh, was all right for a week's play, but something better came up." Now my interest is piqued.

"Well, come on, don't leave me hanging."

She takes a long slow sip of wine, draining her glass. Then just as slowly, she tops it up again.

"Will you fucking tell me before I pour that bottle over your head," I order.

"Lawson Knight took me out for my birthday last weekend." My eyebrows hit my hairline. I've only ever tried Botox once, so my forehead muscles are still somewhat active.

"How? When? How did this come about?" I ask. I'm not sure how I feel about this. Lawson seems an okay sort of bloke to me, it's just that horrible woman that he chooses to spend time with I don't like, and I also don't like the fact that he's been involved in some of Conner's past group sexcapades.

"That first night you got back with Reed, after the charity show. I spent a lot of time chatting with him, and he took my number."

I nod my head. "Hmmm, soooo, tell me. How'd it go?"

She gives me her best attempt at a coy smile. "Good actually. We went to dinner and then to some bar in Knightsbridge."

"And?"

"And then we went back to his place, and I ended up staying there till Monday, before doing the walk of shame." She's actually grinning from ear to ear. I just know that there's more.

"And?" I encourage her to go on.

"And, he stayed at mine Tuesday night." I give her my 'really?' expression.

"And Thursday night." My mouth actually opens in surprise.

"We came over here for a drink last night and spent all day together today. He wanted me to go to the boxing tonight, but I wanted to catch up with you."

Conner has gone to some boxing thing tonight with Gunner from the band and Lawson. I was worried earlier that Amanda might be there. Conner assured me she wouldn't be and now hearing that Lawson invited Sophie along, I feel better. I know I should trust him, but I'm pregnant, hormonal and female, give me a break.

Sophie and I spend the rest of the night chatting about anything and everything, catching up on how things are going with the business and any other work-related issues. I feel like I've abandoned ship since I've been with Conner, but everything seems to be running smoothly.

I give in to temptation at around nine and order up a bowl of wedges, but end up disappointed in the sweet chilli dip I have to settle on when Soph tells me I can't have the aioli because it contains raw egg, which apparently is dangerous when pregnant. *How does 'Mrs Not A Maternal Bone In Her Body, know this and yet Mrs I've Been Broody Since I Was Fifteen', doesn't, I wonder?*

By eleven, I'm yawning and ready for my bed. I leave Sophie chatting on her phone to Lawson while I run outside to see if Matty's about before calling him to come pick me up.

"Stay away from Reed you slut, he's ours." I swing around to see where the voice is coming from when I feel the first blow. A fist, I assume, connects with my jaw and I feel my legs go from under me. Instead of putting my arms out to try and break my fall, I instinctively wrap them around my belly instead. The crack as my head hits the pavement echoes throughout my entire body as I whisper to myself, to someone, anyone… "Please, my baby."

CHAPTER TWENTY-NINE

CONNER

I RUN... I RUN LIKE I'VE never run before. I need to get to her. I need to be with her.

I.

Need.

Her.

There was already a small army of press at the hospital doors when we got here. Lawson, my brothers and the hospital security holding them back as I fought my way through.

Being me comes in handy sometimes, and there was someone on the other side of the doors waiting to take me to her, or at least to where she was.

As soon as the young woman tells me which floor, I rush off to find the lift, and now I'm running down the corridor, on the ninth floor of the hospital trying to find her room.

I stop

Why?

Why is he here?

Marcus fucking Newman is standing outside of a room, talking to the police.

"Mr Reed, if you would just slow down." I turn and see the woman that met me at the door emerge from another lift, followed by my brothers and Lawson.

My brothers had met us outside. Lawson and I had driven from the boxing event in central London at law-breaking speeds. Laws had jumped red lights and gone the wrong way around a roundabout to get me here.

But he's here. Why?

"Shit," I hear Tyler say from beside me.

"Why's he here?" he asks.

"No fucking idea, but I'm about to find out."

We walk down the hospital corridor like a single unit. Ty at my side, Lawson and Jordy behind. The police turn around and watch our approach. I don't even acknowledge the orange before I speak.

"Why is this man here? He needs to be kept away from Miss Matthews."

The copper frowns and looks at his colleague.

"Sir, we were led to believe that the young lady in question is Mrs Newman, Mr Newman's wife?"

I haven't got time for this bullshit. I just need to see Meebs.

"Where is she? I need to see her. Lawson, get me a doctor or someone that can tell me what's going on," I shout at anyone that's listening.

"Calm down, Con." Tyler walks around to face me. "We're in a hospital. I know you're scared and worried, but you can't be shouting. They'll throw you out."

I nod. There's no fucking way that's happening. I swallow and take a couple of breaths.

"I'm Conner Reed," I speak to both of the policemen, unsure of who is the superior.

"I'm Nina Matthews's partner, we live together. Nina and Mr Newman here, are legally separated, and Nina is seeking a divorce from him. I can give you the number of her lawyer if you need to check any of that out."

Before I can add another word, orange boy interrupts, "I'm still her husband. Still her next of kin. I have more right to be here than any of you."

I'm about to tell the police exactly why Nina left him when Sophie steps out of the room.

She looks at me, then at Marcus.

"Why the fuck's he here?" she asks the policeman.

"I'm her fucking husband," he says through gritted teeth to Soph.

"Will you please get him out of here, he is the last person she'll want to see."

Marcus stares at her for a few seconds and then turns and starts off down the corridor. I turn back to Soph. Her face is tear-stained, and she has blood on her clothes.

Meebs' blood.

I can't talk.

I can't make a sound.

I can't even breathe.

We've drunk beer and bourbon and champagne. It was supposed to be a happy night.

Without warning, I heave and throw up all over the floor.

I still can't breathe, and I can't stop shaking.

Meebs' blood. Sophie's covered in Meebs' blood.

Someone sits me in a chair.

Someone passes me water.

"Reed, listen. She's in theatre. Her head hit the pavement hard, and the X-rays and MRI showed that there's some swelling and she was bleeding on the brain. They don't think it's life-threatening, but they wanted to do something to relieve the pressure.

I drop my head in my hands. This can't be happening, it can't be happening.

I can't do it. I need to go. I've got to get out of here.

And then I see him, he hasn't left. He's just sitting on a chair a bit further down the hallway. I can't leave her. She's hurt and pregnant and probably so fucking scared. Someone hurt her. Why?

"The baby Soph, what about the baby?"

She shakes her head, and my heart can't decide if it wants to slide into the pit of my stomach or explode in my chest cavity.

"They can't tell yet, Reed. She wasn't bleeding or anything. I told them that she's pregnant and they took all the necessary precautions when they were doing the X-rays and what have you."

Lawson appears and puts his arms around Sophie, and she starts to cry. The police ask if they can get a statement from her and I sit back down in the chair. Surely there must be somewhere better to wait than this?

As if reading my mind the woman who introduced herself to me earlier as Angie, the patient/family liaison officer steps forward.

"Mr Reed, why don't you go into the family room? It'll be much more comfortable than waiting out in this corridor. I'll go and get an update and let you know what's going on."

I stand up, but before I can move, that fucker Newman is in my face.

"She's pregnant?" he asks, actually looking concerned.

"Mr Reed." One of the policemen steps forward.

"Mr Reed. The information we're gathering so far seems to suggest that Mrs... Miss Matthews was attacked by some fans of yours. Has she been receiving hate mail or anything of that nature?"

All of the air leaves my lungs. I look to Tyler because I know, that he'll know what's happening.

All I can hear is Marcus fucking Newman. "This is your fault, Reed, this is all your fault rock star." I try to step forward, try to swing a punch, but I've got hands on me, arms around me. I try to lock my knees, but they won't keep me up.

This is all my fault.

Someone did this to her because of me.

Jordan's on one side of me, Tyler on the other. They walk me into the waiting room and sit me on a chair.

I need to get a grip, and I need someone to get that fucker Newman out of here before I do him some damage.

I PACE. I SIT. I walk. I stand. I sit.

And then finally Angie comes back. I watch as she looks around the room for me. It's packed. Every member of my family, except Sandra who stayed home with the kids, is here. The only one sleeping is Sophie, she's curled on a chair with her head in Lawson's lap. She's put me to shame tonight. She held it together while I lost the plot.

Angie beckons me outside, and I follow.

"Everything went well." For about the twelfth time tonight, everything spins.

"It was a very small bleed, and the surgeons have managed to control it. They'll be along later to give you all of the details, I just thought you'd want to know specifics." I nod my head. I just want to hear that she's okay.

"The baby's fine, no problems at all there and the obstetrician will be along at some stage to talk to both of you."

I continue to nod. Too scared to attempt speech, in case I embarrass myself in front of this woman, who has somehow managed to not lose her patience with me tonight.

"Now, the surgeons aren't exactly sure how long Nina was unconscious for before she was found, but they're hoping it wasn't long and that she's going to make a full and fast recovery. Would you like to see her?"

Again, I go for the nod.

She leads me along the corridor and swipes a card through a set of doors, which takes us into a small space with just a pump bottle of hand sanitiser hanging from a stainless steel basket on the wall. We both coat our hands in the stuff.

"Now I don't want you to panic when you see her Mr Reed."

"Please call me, Conner," I croak, my voice sounding nothing like my own.

She nods and rubs my arm in a manner that Sandra would use.

"She took a bit of a beating tonight, Conner. She's been punched and kicked in the face, head and back. Whoever did this, meant to get a message across."

The strangest sensation passes over me. Like pins and needles, it's instant and spreads rapidly from my head to my toes. My scalp prickles and the hairs all over my body stand on end. This doesn't sit right with me. My fans would never do something like this… never.

Angie presses the button that opens the next set of doors.

"Don't be concerned with the machinery, it's just to monitor that she's doing okay. She's breathing by herself, so not on a ventilator or anything."

The area is big. There's a nurses station in the middle, with four beds around it, further down are four rooms. We keep moving until we reach the furthest room. This is good, I remember reading or seeing on one of those reality hospital shows that the sicker you are, the closer they keep you to the nurse's station, so the furthest room is good.

We enter. I make a noise. I don't know what it is.

If complete and total desolation, heartbreak, guilt and sorrow had a sound, that might be it.

Angie takes my hand and moves me toward the bed. I sob. Angie squeezes my hand tighter.

She looks like a child. A bruised, broken and battered child.

The left side of her head's been shaved, and she has a row of staples running through the middle of the shaved area. Twelve, there are twelve staples. Meebs was born on the twelfth.

I don't know why I think of that, it's just the first thing that enters my head.

Her right eye is purple and so swollen that even if she opened it, she wouldn't be able to see out of it. Pretty much the whole right side of her face is bruised.

She has a blood pressure cuff around her right arm, one of those peg things on her finger and a drip, feeding liquid into the back of her left hand.

Two little tubes are blowing oxygen up her nose.

This is so unfair. *Why do this to her?*

She's the girl that catches spiders and sets them free. She'd rather swerve into oncoming traffic than hit a bird, rabbit or fox on the road. She goes out of her way to never hurt anyone.

I sit down in the chair at the side of her bed. Leaning forward I kiss her forehead as there doesn't appear to be any bruises there. I take her right hand in mine, lay my head on her belly, and I cry. Angie remains silent while she rubs and pats my back, just letting me cry.

When my tears slow down, she says very quietly, "I'm going to leave you alone for a bit. I'll go and explain to your family and friends what's going on. Sit yourself in that big chair and try and get some sleep."

"Thanks Angie, thanks for everything."

"You're very welcome, Conner. I'll come back and see you both later."

I hold Meebs right hand in both of mine, rest my head down next to hers and close my eyes.

I need to make a call to Tom Bradley, the private investigator my dad put me on to. I'm not leaving a stone unturned. I'm gonna find the fuckers that did this, and I'm gonna make them pay.

CHAPTER THIRTY

NINA

"YES PLEASE, AND ONION, LOADS of onion," I tell Conner.

He finally went home last night after sleeping at the hospital for four nights.

He had me moved up to a private room, but it's still a hospital, not the bloody Ritz. So why he wants to stay here when there's a perfectly good bed at home is beyond me, although it has been nice having him around. I'm hoping that I can leave before the weekend. The doctors are happy with the way my head injury is healing, and we're just waiting to speak to a consultant about the baby. The baby's safe, we've been assured of that, and at the end of the day, that's all that really matters.

I don't remember the attack. I remember being in the wine bar with Soph and then that's about it until I started to wake up after my surgery.

I somehow knew I was in a hospital and I knew Conner was there, so I just focused on breathing in and out and tried to remain calm when I first started to regain consciousnes. I could hear the machines and various voices so allowed my body to recover from the effects of the anaesthetics and brain surgery. By Monday morning, I was back with it. In fact, I was probably more with it than Conner.

He was sleeping when I first woke up fully, his head resting on my shoulder, curled on his side beside me on the bed. I worked out straight away that I wasn't in your average hospital room because the bed was huge, almost a double. Next time I opened my eyes, he was awake and looking at me.

"You look like shit," I whispered.

"While you are the most beautiful thing I have ever laid eyes on." It hurt to smile, but I gave it my best shot regardless. I also had tears, I didn't cry as such, but both Conner and I had tears that rolled down our cheeks. We sat silently for a few minutes, smile crying at each other.

"Meebs?" Conner's voice sounds over my phone, which I have on speaker.

"Sorry, what?"

"What else did you say you wanted? I've packed joggers, a hoodie, some T's and your flip-flops, anything else?"

I thought about it for a second.

"Just your sexy self, babe."

"No problem. I can deliver that. Fuck, I need to be inside you. I'll be about half hour."

"Till you're back inside me?" I ask with a smile. Despite the fact I *feel* like I've been hit by a bus, I'm horny, and despite the fact my face *looks exactly like* I've been hit by a bus, Conner still wants me. We sort of got it on a little bit last night, but my ribs hurt and the nurse came in and told him she'd send him home if he kept making my blood pressure go up.

"I wish, baby, I wish. Half hour till I get there."

"Okies. I'll see you then. Love you."

"Love you too, Metal Head."

"Not funny, Conner."

"Come on, babe, you know I'm hilarious."

"Goodbye Conner."

"Bye Meebs. Love You."

I end the call with a smile and throw my phone down, so it's out of reach. As tempting as it is in my boredom, I'm avoiding social media. Reports on my attack are everywhere, and the speculation about what had happened is varied, but most going with what the police suspect, that some crazy, stalker fan girls of Conner's took things just a little too far.

The door to my room opens ten minutes later and the last person in the world I want to see walks in. Not my mother, she was here all of ten minutes yesterday, delivering her 'if you live by the sword then you'll die by the sword' speech, before thankfully fucking off. My dad and my brother haven't been near or by. Not that I want to see either of them… ever, if I'm honest about it.

Marcus walks toward my bed.

"Why are you here?" I ask.

"You're my wife, I wanted to see you."

"Well, if you were to just sign the divorce papers I wouldn't be. Then you could save your concerns for someone that wants them and yourself a trip."

He tucks his sunglasses into the front of his Ralph Lauren Polo. As usual, he's wearing it the way I hate, tucked in, collar up.

"I want a paternity test carried out on the baby, and if it's mine, I'll be fighting for full custody." The room spins.

I laugh. I don't know what else to do so I laugh at him.

"Conner Reed will not be going anywhere near my child, he will not be a part of his life. If you leave him, I'll agree to joint custody, or you could just do the sensible thing and come back home with me." I can't believe what I'm hearing. It actually takes me a few seconds to stop just sitting and staring at him with my mouth hanging open.

"I'll drag your name and his through the courts, Nina. I'll do everything I can to prove that you're an unfit mother. I'll use every piece of evidence I can find. I don't have to do a thing to prove that he shouldn't be around children, just look at his track record. He can't even keep the adults around him safe. Come back to me Nina, and I'll give you the life you've always wanted."

"Are you out of your fucking mind?"

"No Nina, I've never been more serious."

"What on earth makes you think that this baby's yours? We tried remember and thankfully failed. This baby's Conner's, so sign those papers and let us get on with being a family. He's the life I've always wanted, being with him is what I want. I married you because I had no choice, but my heart always belonged to him, always has, always will. When will you get your head around that?"

I watch as his fists clench and unclench. His jaw twitching at a rapid rate.

"I want the paternity test carried out while the baby's still in the womb. I've looked into it, it can be done. When it's proved to be mine, I'll go to court and get an injunction, so that he has to stay away from my child and, therefore, you will have to stay away from him."

He's insane, he's actually certifiably insane.

The thing is though, I've got a whole stack of diaries at the house I used to share with him, and if he were ever to read some of the entries I made after I miscarried, he would have all the evidence he needs to prove that I'm insane, or at least was.

My increased heart rate is making my headache, and I start to feel panicky.

"Get out. Get the fuck out of my room and don't come back here again."

I press the call button for the nurse, who appears instantly.

"Can you please show this man out Lisa and let everyone know that he's not allowed in here again, under any circumstances."

I try to appear as calm as possible. If he ever finds those diaries, we'll be fucked. If he ever showed them to a court, I'd probably never be allowed within a ten-mile radius of a child. I was lost, lonely and a whole lot depressed. They were just ramblings, but I made the mistake of writing them down.

Lisa nods and turns toward Marcus. "If you wouldn't mind following me, sir." He turns and looks at me and nods.

"You'll be hearing from me, Nina… me *and* my legal team."

I don't reply. I can't.

What if the baby is his?

What a fucking mess!

If I'd have just gone to the police when he first attacked me, none of this would matter. There's no way he would get custody if they knew how this baby was conceived.

Conner comes through the door about five minutes later, carrying an overnight bag and another stuffed toy. The hospital doesn't allow flowers so instead of a florist, my room looks like the Disney store.

The instant his eyes meet mine, he knows. "Meebs?"

I cry.

"Marcus was here. He knows I'm pregnant. He wants full custody unless I leave you," at least, that's what I attempt to say.

"He was here? What the fuck. Why? Why was he here?"

He climbs onto the bed next to me, gently lifting me onto his lap. I've cut right back on the painkillers as they made me too sleepy, but now I can feel the pain in my back where I was kicked. He kisses the top of my head.

"Right, start from the beginning and tell me everything the fucker said."

Before I've even finished, Conner is on the phone. "Get in touch with the legal team. I need the best divorce and child custody lawyers there are out there. Call me back when you've got someone lined up." He ends the call.

"I need you to leave this to me, Meebs. I don't want you stressing yourself out. I've got people on this." He looks down at me. He has dark circles under his eyes, and I can see that he's lost weight just in a few short days. Now I'm going to give him even more to worry about when I tell him about the diaries and what they contain.

"Just concentrate on getting better. I've spoken to the doctor, you can come home tomorrow."

I know what I need to do. As soon as we leave here, I need to go to my old house and get my diaries. I can't give Marcus any more ammunition than he's got to prove we'd make unfit parents.

"Con, there's something I need to do tomorrow." I shift on the bed so that I can see him.

"You know how I always used to keep a diary?"

He smiles, I used to let him read them when we were younger. He'd make me read out the bits where I'd written about him, the bits where I described how he made me feel.

"Of course, I remember. '*He has the most amazing eyes. They see me, they really see me'.*" He recalls something I'd written many years ago, and I'm momentarily blown away that he's remembered it word for word

We sit and smile stupidly at each other for a few seconds.

"I'm amazed that you remember that. Blown away, in fact," I admit.

"Of course, I remember. We may not have been together Meebs, but you were always up here." He taps at his temple. "You were in my thoughts and my heart. Don't ever doubt that."

I let out a long sigh, debating whether to just say nothing about the diaries and going to collect them on my own in a few weeks, once I'm feeling better, and don't look like I've been in the ring with Anderson Silva.

"What's going on Meebs, what's going through that beautiful brain of yours, apart from a dozen staples?"

"That's evil. Talk about ruining the moment."

"Well, talk to me. I know something's bothering you."

I both love and hate the fact that he knows me so well.

"After we weren't together anymore, I still kept a diary, but my thoughts and feelings were a lot darker for a few years."

He says nothing and I can't get a read on what he's thinking.

"I've still got all of those diaries. The ones from when we were together and the later ones. They're at my old house. They're hidden, but with all the threats that he's made today, I'm worried."

I need to confess my mental state after our separation.

"I was a mess, Con. Some of the things that were going through my head back then. They were seriously fucked up."

"Like what?" he asks quietly.

I let out a long sigh.

"Like suicide. A lot of mentions of suicide." I look down at my hands until I feel his fingers under my chin, lifting it till my eyes meet his.

"I thought about it too, for a few years. Even recently, before you I mean. Not now."

We stare at each other in silence. We don't need words. He gets what I was feeling, and I have a pretty good idea what would've been going on in his head back then too.

"We need to get those diaries away from that vindictive bastard," he says before kissing the top of my head.

"D'ya have keys?" I nod my head.

"Yeah, but they're at Sophie's."

He rakes his fingers through his hair.

"I'll go over there later and get them. Meanwhile, you need to eat the lunch Sandra made ya."

By the time I'm seen by the doctors, discharged, and we get to my old house, it's after eleven.

Despite knowing that Marcus will be at work, I'm still nervous. I unlock the front door, but Conner steps in first, telling me to stay behind him. I'm not sure what he thinks will be lying in wait. The scary monster is at his office right now, but I let him get on with his protective mode, secretly enjoying it.

I give him directions up to my old bedroom, and he stands and watches as I walk into my wardrobe. There are drawers fitted along one wall, I lift the bottom one out and find my diaries still safely hidden. It's not the best spot, but it's done its job for the last eight years. Conner passes me an old suitcase of mine, and I throw my diaries in.

"Anything else you wanna grab while you're here?" Conner whispers.

"Why you whispering?" I whisper back, initiating the best smile from Conner, which makes me smile and wince at the same time.

"I don't know, I was…"

His phone rings.

"Shit," he says, still whispering.

I watch as he answers. I feel nothing being back here. I've no attachment to this place whatsoever, but at the same time, it still seems surreal that Conner's here.

For years, I used to have sex with my husband in this bed and pretend I was with Conner. I'd think of him before I went to sleep at night, dream about him as I slept and think about him as soon as I woke in the morning. And now, here he is, in all his glorious perfection and best of all, I get to go home with him. I get to leave this house behind and go home with Conner.

He ends his call and looks at me, looking at him for a few seconds.

"Well?" he asks.

"Well what?"

"You've got the incriminating stuff, is there anything else you wanna grab?"

"Ah, yeah. Passport."

"Where is it?' he asks.

Hmmm. See, there's the thing.

"I don't know, Marcus always used to keep it. In the safe I assume."

I wait for the comment.

"Marcus used to keep your passport? And you let him?"

"No, it wasn't like that. He just always looked after it."

Another one of those things I never really thought odd until I left him. Marcus was always actually a little bit obsessive about knowing where my passport was, saying it was because it was a pain in the arse to get it replaced if I lost it and because I was forgetful and always losing things, it was better if he kept a hold of it. The thing was though, I've never been forgetful, or careless. I've never been one to lose stuff, but I never questioned his motives or reasoning. I just rolled over and let him take control.

I go back into the wardrobe and end up where Marcus has all of his clothes. The safe is hidden behind his suits. I just hope he hasn't changed the combination.

It opens at my first attempt… two, four, zero, seven. Twenty-fourth of July, the date we got married.

I pull out everything inside. My wedding and engagement rings that I sent back to him via our solicitors, as well as some other jewellery and a whole stack of paperwork.

I carry everything out to the bed and sit and go through it. There are share certificates, insurance and mortgage paperwork and all sorts of other boring stuff. I pull out my passport and pick up the paperwork when a letter catches my eye. The sender's address is printed across the top of the envelope, it's from a Harley Street day surgery unit. I pull out the letter and start to read.

As what I'm reading starts to sink in, the words begin to move around the page. My hand covers my mouth as I'm actually afraid I'm going to vomit. I look from the page to Conner, who's talking on the phone, he looks thoroughly pissed off and is only just not shouting.

I'm not sure how I feel at this moment. Totally and utterly betrayed or completely overjoyed. As I wait for Conner to finish his call, I go through a range of emotions, causing my body to feel hot, cold and tingly. I feel angry, sad, happy, disappointed and elated all at once.

Conner ends his call.

"We need to go to the police. Right now, Meebs. We need to go to the police and get this fucker arrested."

"He had a vasectomy."

Conner steps toward me, looking as confused at my words, as I do at his.

"What? Who?" he asks.

"Marcus, over a year ago, he had a vasectomy. All this time, Con, he made me feel bad. He made me believe that it was all my fault that I didn't fall pregnant. All those threats he made at the hospital, knowing the whole time the baby wasn't his. The baby's not his Con."

"The baby's ours," he almost sighs the words, before wrapping his arms around me. "We're having a baby, Meebs. We're having a fucking baby."

And there, in the most unlikely of places, our happily ever after starts to come together.

"Shall we shag on his bed?" he whispers in my ear.

"You're twisted, Conner Reed."

"Tell me something I don't know, Nina Amoeba."

As tempted as I am, I just want to get out of here now.

And then my heart skips a beat as I hear a car pull up on the drive. Looking out of the window, I can see that it's Marcus and he's already getting out of the car.

"I'm calling the police," Conner says. I don't argue. My days of worrying about Marcus are over. Our entire marriage and life together has been a complete façade. I've been lied to and manipulated, and I could no longer care less about the consequences he may be about to face.

Conner puts a call through to the emergency services, passing the phone to me to give the address. I end the call as Marcus comes through the bedroom door. Conner moves me behind him. He watches us for a few seconds, swinging his car keys around his fingers.

"So, what have we here? Con the Con, living up to his name. Adding, breaking and entering to your charge sheet now are you?"

Conner squeezes my hand a little tighter for a second, then lets it go. I watch the smirk leave Marcus's face and fear take over as Conner takes two steps toward him. Without a word, Conner lands a punch that lifts Marcus off his feet. He doesn't get up, and I move closer to make sure that Conner hasn't killed him.

Conner leans down and pulls Marcus up by his tie, pressing their foreheads together.

"Games up you slippery little cunt. We know what you've done. We know everything. Now you're going to prison while I skip off into the sunset with *your* wife to raise *our* baby. Together." He turns and looks at me, his eyes a steely grey despite the smile on his face.

"And you know why I'm gonna do that?" Marcus blinks but doesn't answer. "Because I'm Conner fucking Reed and I can."

He then headbutts Marcus, right between the eyes. I don't even wince when I hear bones crunch and watch blood spray everywhere. Conner stands and holds his hand out to me.

"Meebs."

I step toward him and take his hand, but as I step over my husband, who's still lying in the bedroom doorway, I can't resist affording Marcus the same favour he bestowed upon Sophie and I a couple of months ago, and I spit, right beside his head.

I hear Conner chuckle from beside me.

"Is that it, Meebs? After everything he's done to you, to us, that all you got?"

Knowing what will hurt Marcus more than anything else, I turn to Conner, wrap my arms around his neck and say, "I love you, baby, let's go home and fuck." Just as the sirens sound outside.

THE NEXT FEW HOURS ARE a blur. Despite his injuries, Marcus is arrested, and we're also escorted by the police to the station for questioning. We take the paperwork regarding Marcus's vasectomy with us. On the way, Conner explains that he's had a private detective watching both Marcus and my brother for the past couple of weeks.

It's taken a bit longer than expected to gather the evidence that Conner was after. Initially, he just wanted something to bargain with, to force Marcus into signing the divorce papers, but with what's been uncovered, we want charges pressed.

After giving our statements regarding how I went to my old home to collect my passport when Marcus attempted to attack me, Conner then had to step in to save me, causing Marcus to break his nose in the process, we're released.

IIt's not entirely the truth, but with everything else that's been uncovered, my soon to be ex-husband isn't contradicting our statements, he's got bigger things to worry about.

It turns out that Marcus paid someone to attack me outside the wine bar and over the next few days, we discover that he was convinced that if I thought it was fans of Conner's, I wouldn't feel safe and would go running back to him. Me being pregnant, he thought would help his plans by convincing me that I needed to be with someone who could keep me safe.

He thought that by threatening me with a custody battle, I would easily fold and merely move back with him. He never planned on telling me about the vasectomy. If Conner ever asked for a paternity test in the future, he assumed that I would've fallen back in love with him and Conner would be out of my system.

And why the vasectomy? Because he could. The one thing he

knew I wanted was a family, but he wanted ultimate control over that decision, and ultimately over me and my life.

I'd married a sociopath. Marcus showed no remorse for his actions and considered it his right to make that choice for me.

But the 'holy fuck' moments just kept coming.

It was Marcus that had leaked the fabricated underage sex story to the press, along with the news that Conner and I were together.

It had taken Tom a while to put everything together as Marcus was using two phones. Tom was only tracking his smartphone, unaware that he also had a cheap pre-pay from which he'd arranged the assault on me.

But it gets better. Turns out that the reason that Marcus had two phones in the first place was to hide his affair. The affair he was having with my brother's wife.

My. Brothers. Wife.

They have a child together. My brother's only child isn't his, he belongs to Marcus.

Marcus has not only confessed all of this to the police, but he's also sent me a long and detailed letter explaining everything, assuming that by coming clean, I would forgive and go back to him. The letter contained not one word of apology, not a single sorry. Just the facts about what he'd done, and how he'd only ever had my best interest at heart.

I'm not sure if he's suffering from some type of mental break-down, but he is most definitely delusional, and I can't help but feel just a little bit guilty. His life and his business are in pieces, along with my brother's and my parents. But it's the little boy involved that I feel the sorriest for. Henry's not an attractive or likeable child, there's nothing warm or loving about him, and I know that in the past, he's been bullied at school. He's just a kid, and little arsehole or not, I hope all of this doesn't affect him long term, turning him into a replica of his father.

The scandal has been all over the newspapers, and my mother has resigned from her ministerial post. If it wasn't for the impact this is having on Henry's life, I'd be happy because all of it has nothing to do with me. Not that that'll stop her from blaming me. My family wanted nothing more than for me to marry Marcus and just look at what it's achieved. My brother and mother have lost their jobs, and Marcus is facing a conviction and will most likely be struck off.

Who would've thought that my boring husband could be leading such a double life? Not me. Not anyone.

I COME INTO THE KITCHEN wearing Conner's Shift T-shirt, the one I wore the first night I stayed here.

I've been out of the hospital for just over two weeks, and in that time we've only left the house once. We made a trip to Harley Street to meet the obstetrician Conner had arranged for me, and then to the solicitors to sign the final paperwork for the divorce that Marcus has finally agreed to.

I'm approximately nine weeks pregnant. Our baby was very probably conceived right here on this kitchen worktop, the first weekend we got together, which makes me feel kinda slutty but happy.

Conner has Ed Sheeran on shuffle over the loudspeakers, he sings along to 'Photograph' while boiling milk on the stove for me. I would normally just throw it in the microwave, but he's banned me from using it. In fact, he's gone as far as having it removed from the house.

He pours my milk into my favourite china mug and turns around, finally noticing me right at the moment 'Thinking Out Loud' starts to play.

He smiles his eighteen-year-old Conner smile and, as usual, I melt a little bit.

"You look beautiful," he holds his hand out as he speaks.

"I look horrific, like someone threw up rhubarb and custard on my face and I had an allergic reaction that made my hair fall out." My bruises have faded to pale yellow and a pinkish-purple in colour and are barely noticeable now, but my hair, my poor hair is growing back in tufts.

He spins me around, before tilting me backwards over his knee, then pulls me upright to start dancing around the kitchen with him.

"Well, I love the rhubarb and custard look. I might even taste it later too. Especially if you put your green shoes on for me."

"You're obsessed with those shoes." He licks up my neck to my ear. "I'm obsessed with you," he says right in it.

Eargasm?

Whispergasm?

I don't know, but it feels good. So good.

We dance around the kitchen in silence for a bit, until he says in my ear, "Meebs?"

"What?"

"Marry me?"

"Of course."

He pulls back and looks at me. "Are you serious?"

"As a brain bleed."

"That's not funny."

"Well, neither is calling me a metal head."

"Yea, now that's funny." He bends his knees, so we're eye to eye. I'm not laughing.

"Oh, come on, metal head's funny?"

"You called me bruised brain the other night too. I didn't laugh then either."

He throws his head back and gives a big belly laugh. "Bruised brain, now that one was hilarious."

"D'ya wanna marry me or what?"

His face straightens. "Yeah, sorry. So is it still a yes?"

"Yeah, it's still a yes."

"Thank you. Let's make a baby."

"We did, it's still cooking inside me."

"Well, let's practise so we know what we're doing when we make the next one."

So, right there, right then. With Ed serenading us, we practice.

EPILOGUE

"**I** swear to God if you rub my back one more time I will chop off your fucking hands and beat you with them," she growls at me through gritted teeth.

"No you won't."

"Yes. I. Will."

"I love you."

"I don't care."

"Yes, you do."

"No. I. Don't. This is all your fault. I didn't sign up for this."

I reach out to rub her shoulders but move my hand back to hold hers when she gives me *the look*.

I hate seeing her in pain like this. I'm torn between being pissed off and admiring her stubbornness and determination.

"How we doing?" the midwife Sian asks, as she breezes back in.

Meebs gives her *the look* too.

"Like I'm trying to pull my top lip over my head, but apart from that, fine. Thank you for asking."

"Meebs," I warn her.

"What?" She glares at me.

"My vag is going to be ruined after this. Three kids, Con. Three. It's just never going to be the same." She grips my hand as another contraction takes hold.

She's silent and focused all the way through it. Just panting and blowing and I love her so fucking much.

"Your vag is perfect. You've had two caesareans, Meebs, so stop being a drama queen. Your vag is fine."

Sian pops her head up from between Meebs' legs. I have to look away when they examine her. I know it's medical and has to be done, but I get this angry knot in my chest and belly when someone touches what's mine. Irrational I know, but it is what it is.

Sian pulls off her gloves, disposes of them, then turns and faces us.

"Okay Nina, here's the thing. You've been here for five hours now."

"Not through choice," Meebs interrupts her.

Sian lets out a long sigh, her patience wearing thin. Meebs wanted a home birth, the doctors said no because our boys had to be delivered by emergency C-section. Once they explained the complications that could arise, I said no. Hence the anger, and the look that I'm continually getting from my wife.

"We've let you go an hour longer than we normally would, but you've made no progress. You're still only around three centimetres dilated, and the baby is starting to show signs of distress. I'm gonna call the doctor down and let them discuss your options with you."

She turns and leaves. Meebs looks up at me, and I know what's coming.

She bursts into tears.

"I'm so sorry. I'm so crap at this."

I climb up on the bed with her, kissing first her belly, then her mouth.

"You're not crap at this. You're just too little."

"It's your fault. Our kids all have big fat heads like you." I chuckle at her instant mood change. Meebs is the happiest pregnant woman I know. She loves being pregnant, and I fucking love her being pregnant. That's why she's about to give birth to our third child, in less than five years. There's just something that brings out the caveman in me when I watch her belly growing. Not that she ever gets very big. She moans that she's huge, but she just looks like she has a basketball shoved up her T-shirt.

She tried for a natural delivery with both boys, but that didn't work out. She was hoping that because we're having a girl this time, she might be smaller and she'd be able to do it, but that's now being ruled out. I hate that she's disappointed but at the end of the day, why would any woman choose to put themselves through that, seriously?

"Our kids don't have fat heads, they have perfect heads, they're perfect in every way. Just like their mum."

Shit, more tears.

I CARRY BUZZ ON MY hip, while Jett walks beside me proudly carrying the pink teddy bear that we went and bought for their new baby sister this morning. Mia Grace Amoeba Reed was born safely at seven-eighteen last night. She's tiny, pink, pale and perfect. She looks just like her mum, which I'm more than pleased about. Poor Meebs didn't get a look in with the boys, the pair of them are clones of each other, and of me. Brownish blond hair and blue-green eyes. Jett's the eldest and is about to start school in September. He's loud and noisy, can't sit still for more than five minutes and is always asking questions. He started playing football last season and is already the captain of his team.

Buzz… Yeah, we let Jett choose his name, Buzz being the better option over Nemo or Lightning McQueen. He's another little livewire. Loves music. I'm already teaching him the guitar and drums. Jett loves music too but can't sit still long enough for me to teach him anything.

We get buzzed into the ward, and I smile and nod at the

midwives at their station. They all swoon, what can I say? I'm still Conner fucking Reed at the end of the day.

I'm not out front and centre of the music world so much these days. I write, I produce, and I manage.

Mitchell White is the young kid that handed me some songs he wrote, the night before Jet died. I'd completely forgotten about them, but Meebs found them about six months later. We read them, and both knew instantly they were something special.

I used him to buy myself into CC music and promotions and now work alongside Marley and Lennon Layton, with Mitchell as my little protégé. He's been living with us this last summer while he worked on his new album. Myself and Marley both appearing on tracks with him. The first was a multi-award winner, and I'm sure this new one will do the same. He's a talented boy.

We round the corner to Meebs' room. She's sitting cross-legged, Indian style on the bed. She's wearing a pair of hammer pants and an old Shift T-shirt of mine. She's always wearing an old Shift T-shirt of mine, and I fucking love it. Seeing her in my clothes never gets old, and right at this moment, I'm swallowing back tears. My T-shirt is hoisted up while Meebs feeds our daughter at her boob. She looks up, and when her eyes meet mine, I want to drop to the floor, crawl to where she sits and worship at her feet. She's my princess, my love and watching my boys climb up on the bed and meet their sister for the first time, I know I've achieved what I thought for so long was out of reach... My very own fairy tale.

The hairdresser and the Rock Star got their happily ever after.

THE END

PLAYLIST

Alex Gaudino's—Destination Calabria

Pharrell and Daft Punk—Get Lucky

Red Hot Chili Peppers—Scar Tissue

Clean Bandits—Rather Be

Sigma—Nobody To Love

Ella Henderson—Ghost

Paloma Faith—Only Love Can Hurt Like This

Ed Sheeran—Thinking Out Loud

Ed Sheeran—Photograph

Ed Sheeran—Nina

ACKNOWLEDGMENTS

So, where to start with the love for this one? This past year has been incredible, exciting, daunting and at times overwhelming. I've attended my first Australian and overseas signings, where I got to meet some of you crazy lot. This year I'm attending a total of seven signings, three here in Aus, two in the UK and one in both the US and Canada, where I look forward to meeting more of you.

So, let's get on with the shout outs. I've got to start with my husband, my rock, who is at this very moment vacuuming the floors so I can get this written. You get the finished product while he deals with the tears, tantrums, insecurities and meltdowns required to bring you that bright and polished book. When my characters hurt, I hurt, when they're miserable, I am too. Meaning my husband has no idea what he'll be walking into on any given night. Regardless of which characters head I've been in all day, he's there for me throughout it all, putting up with my shit, an untidy house and unwashed clothes.

To my boys, who now basically ignore the crazy lady that appears unwashed in their home occasionally and have pretty much learned to fend for themselves.

To Vix, my sister from another vagina. You've gone over and above anything I could ever ask from a friend I met online, over a love of books. It was an absolute pleasure to not only meet you in person last year in Edinburgh, but to share a room, a drink and the entire experience with you. Thank you for putting up with me.

To Jen Lynn my PA, our conversations make me realise that there is someone else in this world who shares a similar thought process as me… random and rarely professional, in fact, if it's possible for a conversation to be illegal, then yeah, guilty as charged. On the rare occasions we are behaving, we make a great team and I wouldn't have survived the last ten or so months without you, and I'm looking forward to enjoying a wine or three when I get out to Cali later this year.

To my admin team, Marian, Lynsey, Vix, Karen, Jen, Angie, Lisa, Sharee, Sian and Sam, I thank you. Your patience, wisdom and humour have kept me sane and grounded. It's a pleasure to have you in my life and to call each and every one of you a friend. You run my groups with true professionalism and do it all because of your love of the words I write and, of course, because I'm your queen :)

To my Beta's, Vix, Kaz, Lynsey, Bianca and Jeanette, thank you for your valuable time, input and all of your feedback.

I would like to give a special shout out to Kimmy and all of the admin and members of the Fictional Men's Room For Book Ho's page. You ladies have overwhelmed me with your support, and both enthralled and terrified me with your posts and comments.

Thank you, thank you, thank you… Mr. Ed Sheeran whose words and music inspired the words written in this book. You sir are a truly talented man.

Special thanks to my muse for Conner Reed, Jacey Elthalion. Staring at his face over the last six months for inspiration, has been an absolute pleasure. Added thanks to Sam Shemeld for introducing me to his gorgeousness. Luv ya guts girly.

That leaves me just to mention all of you, my readers. Your messages, passion and love for my words floors and leaves me humble. I started this journey writing to mentally escape a shitty time in my life, never did I imagine it would lead me to all of you. Saying thank you will never be enough of a way to express my gratitude.

ABOUT THE AUTHOR

Lesley Jones was born and raised in Essex, England but moved to Australia ten years ago. She now lives by the beach on the Mornington Peninsula, just outside of Melbourne.

When she's not writing, she loves to read, listen to music, watch football, sing badly and drink good wine.

FOR MORE INFORMATION:

http://lesleyjonesauthor.com/

f facebook.com/LesleyJonesAuthor

instagram.com/lesleyjonesauthor

CPSIA information can be obtained
at www.ICGtesting.com
Printed in the USA
LVHW051608260420
654441LV00015B/2336